A Christmas Gift

KATIE FLYNN

A Christmas Gift

C

CENTURY

1 3 5 7 9 10 8 6 4 2

Century
20 Vauxhall Bridge Road
London SW1V 2SA

Century is part of the Penguin Random House group of companies
whose addresses can be found at global.penguinrandomhouse.com.

Penguin
Random House
UK

First published in Great Britain by Century in 2019

www.penguin.co.uk

A CIP catalogue record for this book is available from the British Library

ISBN 9781529123869

Typeset in 13/16.5 pt Palatino LT Pro
by Integra Software Services Pvt. Ltd, Pondicherry

Printed and bound in Great Britain by Clays Ltd, Elcograf S.p.A.

Penguin Random House is committed to a sustainable future for
our business, our readers and our planet. This book is made
from Forest Stewardship Council® certified paper.

MIX
Paper from
responsible sources
FSC® C018179

Acknowledgements

With thanks to all the staff at Western Approaches.

To the unsung heroes.

Prologue

June, 1939

Lizzy Atherton sat on the small wooden seat in the Brougham Terrace register office. Looking at the wilting bouquet of chrysanthemums and Michaelmas daisies in her hands, she supposed that her mother's new husband, Albert, must have either picked the flowers from someone else's garden or gathered them from the floor of one of the flower stalls in Paddy's Market.

As the registrar droned on Lizzy glanced at her mother, who was wearing the two-piece suit that Lizzy's father had bought for her as a surprise birthday present when Lizzy had still been in primary school.

Absentmindedly picking the leaves off the stem of one of the daisies, Lizzy turned her thoughts back to the day when her mother had first seen the suit in Blacklers window. She had been taking Lizzy to buy some fish from the market on Great Charlotte Street when she had come to an abrupt stop outside the window, pointed to the suit, and asked Lizzy for her thoughts.

Lizzy popped the lolly she had been sucking out of her mouth and tilted her head to one side. 'Ooo, it's

1

very pretty, Mam, but we can't afford stuff from 'ere,' had been her brief but honest reply.

'I know we can't, but it's nice to dream, and you never know your luck: one of these days your dad might win the pools.'

Lizzy hesitated, the lollipop hovering in front of her lips. 'If he did, d'you reckon he could afford a pony too?'

Mary had shaken her head with a chuckle. 'Pony indeed! Where on earth would you keep it?'

'In the back yard like Cathy Wainwright's dad. He's one of them carters what you see down the docks,' Lizzy said in a matter-of-fact fashion.

Mary squeezed Lizzy's hand. 'It's a bit different for Cathy Wainwright's dad; that's how he makes his livin'. It wouldn't be fair to keep a pony in our tiny yard, and I dread to think what the landlord would say.'

Now, sitting in the register office, Lizzy smiled as she remembered the day her father had presented her mother with the large brown paper package at the breakfast table.

'Happy birthday, Mary luv. I hope you like it—'

He had been interrupted by a squeal of delight.

'Eric! It can't be ... you must take it back. We can't afford ...' Mary had stammered as she held the suit up against herself.

'We've won the pools!' Lizzy had shrieked.

Ruffling the top of her head with one hand, her father had chuckled. 'Not quite, half-pint. Sylvie made it for me. I showed her the one in Blacklers, and ...' he gestured towards the suit with both hands, 'ta-dah!'

Mary clutched the jacket to her chest. 'Eric Atherton, you spoil me rotten.'

'Not worth doin' all them hours if I can't spoil my girls every now and then, now is it?' Placing his arm round her shoulders, he kissed his wife. 'Happy birthday, luv.'

Lizzy jutted out her bottom lip. 'I thought we'd won the pools,' she said miserably. 'I thought I was goin' to get a pony.'

Eyeing her with sympathy, her father had chuckled softly. 'Sorry to disappoint you, Lizzy luv, and who knows? Mebbe one day I really will win the pools.'

'And I can have a pony?' said Lizzy hopefully.

Taking a seat by the table, Eric fished out his tobacco tin. 'We'll see. It'd have to be a bloomin' big win to afford the likes of a pony, but mebbe summat like that rockin' 'orse, the one in Blacklers winder, 'cos that don't want feedin' or a special place to live.' Licking the length of a cigarette paper, he glanced at Lizzy in feigned contemplation. 'Lemme see. What was his name again?'

'Blackie,' Lizzy squealed in delight. 'That's his name, and you're right, he's better'n a real horse 'cos he can't chuck you off.'

Now, Lizzy dusted the fallen petals from her knees as she considered the unfairness of it all. Her little family might not have had much money, but Lizzy, Mary and Eric Atherton had been very happy with their lot. Even though they couldn't afford to go on holidays, Eric had always ensured they had enough money put by for a day trip to Seaforth Sands, or New Brighton. Lizzy liked going to the fair in New Brighton best

3

because her father always took her for a ride on the carousel. Lizzy would choose which horse she wanted to ride and her father would sit behind her to make sure she didn't fall off, whilst shouting at their steed to 'Gee up, Neddy!'

Lost in her thoughts, Lizzy chuckled out loud, causing Albert, who had been promising to love and to cherish, to glare at her over his shoulder. She mouthed the word 'Sorry' before turning her attention back to the petals, which now lay about her feet like confetti. They reminded her of the day her father had come home from work carrying a rather dishevelled Christmas tree in his arms. He had appeared in the kitchen doorway looking pleased as Punch with his efforts. 'I said I'd get us a tree and I did.' He pulled gently at the branches. 'It might be a bit wonky, 'cos it had a bit of an accident on its way to market. That's why the feller said I could have it for half price, but if it's good enough for Father Christmas it's good enough for us, what d'you reckon?'

Lizzy had nodded eagerly. 'It'll look grand with a few decorations. We're mekkin' paper chains in school tomorrer, and I'll ask Miss Gregory if I can make a star to replace our old 'un as well. She's got all sorts of stuff I can use, and I'm sure she'll say yes, 'specially when I tell her we've gorra tree what looks stronger than the one we 'ad last year.'

Her mother coughed on a chuckle. 'You mean the one that fell over as soon as you looked at it?'

'Aye, it was a bit flimsy,' agreed Eric. 'Still, a tree's a tree, you ask any dog.'

'Eric!' protested Mary, before casting her daughter a reassuring glance. 'I'm sure no dog's been near this 'un, luv. Just you ignore your father.'

Eric had winked at Lizzy who was giggling behind her hand. 'Your mam's right, half-pint. I were only pullin' your leg. You mek sure you get them paper chains done quickly so as you can do us a special star tomorrer!'

Early next morning, as Lizzy walked past the tree they had decorated the previous evening with baubles and tinsel, her tummy fluttered with anticipation. She loved making things in school, and could not wait to ask Miss Gregory if she could use some gold glitter to make her star look extra special. As she entered the kitchen she smiled broadly at her mother, who was standing next to the small stove, but when she saw the worried frown etched on her mother's brow her cheery demeanour faded.

'Mornin', luv. I've done you some toast. You're goin' to have to see yerself to school this mornin', 'cos your dad's got the bellyache.' Mary handed Lizzy a slice of thickly buttered toast. 'Knowin' him he's ate summat he shouldn't've, although he insists he 'asn't, and even though he can 'ardly stand on his own two feet he's still insistin' on goin' to work.' Shaking her head, she tutted to herself. 'I've told him he's to stay home till it passes, but will he listen? Will he 'eck as like, so if I don't stay 'ere to keep an eye on him he'll be sneakin' off as soon as me back's turned.' She started to wrap Lizzy's sandwiches in greaseproof paper. 'Be a good girl and go straight to school. I'll be there to pick you up at home time.'

Lizzy nodded. Her mouth full of toast, she managed a muffled ''es' before swallowing hard and adding, 'I'm goin' to mek me special star in school today. I bet that'll mek Daddy feel better.'

Mary handed her the neat greaseproof packet. 'I'm sure it will. You know how excited your father gets at Christmas – he's worse than most kids! Now be a good girl and kiss your father goodbye before you leave.'

Lizzy jogged up the stairs and knocked briefly on the door to her parents' bedroom. Hearing a distant 'Come in', she crossed the room to where her father lay huddled beneath his bed sheets and leaned forward to kiss his forehead. She recoiled with a look of distaste. 'You're all sweaty! Does me mam know?'

He nodded briefly as he wiped his forehead on the top blanket. 'It's just a bit of gut ache. I'll soon be right.' He opened an eye and focused on her. 'You on your way to school to make that special star of yours?'

Lizzy nodded. 'Is Mam goin' to call the quacks?'

He chuckled, then winced in pain. 'Cheeky mare. It's the doctor to you, not the quacks.' Gazing into her eyes, he stroked her cheek with the back of his fingers. 'I can't wait to see your star. I bet it'll be brighter than the real ones. Probably do me more good than any silly old medicine ever could.'

Lizzy beamed proudly. 'I'm goin' to ask Miss Gregory if I can use gold glitter!'

'A gold star,' he said, looking impressed. 'That really will be extra special.'

Mary called up from the bottom of the stairs. 'That'll do, Lizzy. Your father needs all the rest he can get no matter what he may think, so best you get yerself off to school, else you'll be late.'

Lizzy kissed her father's forehead. 'See you later hot potater!'

Her father smiled wearily at her. 'Ta-ra, half-pint.' Seeing his daughter's disapproving look, he corrected himself. 'Have fun, hunny bun.'

'That's more like it,' said Lizzy with a satisfied smile.

She approached Miss Gregory straight after morning break. 'Can I make me dad a star to go on top of our Christmas tree? Only he's got really bad bellyache and he says a nice glittery gold star will make him better, and I've finished me paper chains.'

Miss Gregory nodded. 'I'm sure it will, and of course you may. You know where everything is, so help yourself.'

Lizzy painstakingly cut out a star from an old shoe-box and covered the surface with glue, only to find that the gold glitter and tinsel that she had laid out in readiness had vanished. Looking round the room, she soon spied the culprit.

'Charlie Jackson! I knew it'd be you! Give it back. Miss Gregory give me special permission.'

Charlie grinned, revealing a deep-set dimple in each cheek. 'Dunno what you're on about, pipsqueak.'

She scowled at him. 'Don't call me pipsqueak. I'm nearly as tall as you and youse older'n me. Now give me back my stuff.'

Holding his hands behind his back, Charlie stuck out his tongue in a rude fashion. 'Not got your name on it, 'as it ... pipsqueak?'

Lizzy folded her arms firmly across her chest. Charlie Jackson was the class clown, who seemed to spend most of his time devising tricks and practical jokes to torment his fellow classmates. He loved nothing better than a good game of cat and mouse, but after the pigtails incident she knew there was only one way to deal with someone like Charlie. With a half-smile she screwed up her eyes and opened her mouth wide. 'MISS GREG—'

Charlie ran across the room and plonked the glitter and tinsel down on the table beside her. 'Blimey, you've gorra pair of lungs on you. I were only 'avin' a bit of fun!'

'Well you mustn't. I need this star to make me dad better.'

Sitting on the chair next to Lizzy's, Charlie leaned his elbows on the table. 'Why, what's the matter with him?'

Lizzy carefully pulled the stopper off the tube of glitter and began to sprinkle the contents on to the glue. 'He's got the bellyache. Mam reckons he's ate summat what didn't agree with him.' She raised her brow in contemplation. 'My dad eats a lot, so it could've been anythin'.'

Charlie grinned. 'Nowt wrong wi' a healthy appetite.'

Lizzy glanced sidelong at him. 'What's one of them?'

He chuckled. 'Put it this way, you ain't got one, that's why youse like a scraggy kitten wi' no meat on yer bones. People what have healthy appetites are big and strong, like me.' Sitting up straight, he flexed his non-existent muscles.

Lizzy shook her head. 'I ain't like a scraggy kitten, and you ain't big and strong. I've seen bigger knots in cotton.'

Frowning, Charlie looked at the muscles in his arms. 'You just can't see 'em 'cos I got me jumper on. Hold on a mo ...'

As he started to pull his school jumper over his head Miss Gregory's voice rang out across the classroom. 'We don't need to see your muscles thank you, Charlie.'

Lizzy giggled. 'Don't worry, Miss, 'e ain't got any.'

Charlie opened his mouth to respond but Miss Gregory cut him short. 'If you're keen to show how strong you are you can always help me carry these books over to Miss McCarthy's class.'

Charlie hastily pulled his jumper back over his head. 'Can't I stay here and help Lizzy do her star?'

Miss Gregory raised her eyebrows. 'Only if Lizzy doesn't mind?'

Charlie looked imploringly at Lizzy and hissed from the corner of his mouth, 'Please say I can. Miss McCarthy's not best pleased with me 'cos I accidentally threw a snowball at her this mornin'. I promise not to take the mick.'

Looking into his brown eyes, Lizzy nodded reluctantly. 'You'd better not.'

'She said I can help, Miss!'

'Very well, but I don't want to hear any tales of you misbehaving.'

When he turned back Lizzy was frowning. 'How can you accidentally throw a snowball at someone?'

He grinned. 'Well, maybe it wasn't so much that I hit her by accident, but I didn't mean for her to see it were

9

me who threw it!' Lizzy felt her own lips twitch with amusement. That was the trouble with Charlie, she thought to herself. He might be irritating and always up to no good, but there was something about him which she found quite endearing. He was what her father often referred to as a loveable rogue.

She indicated the piece of tinsel which she was starting to wind around the edges of the star. 'Put your finger there.'

Charlie's eyes twinkled as he did as she asked. 'I must say it really is a very good star. Have you gorra big tree?'

Lizzy shook her head. 'Doesn't matter though, does it?'

Charlie pulled a face. 'Shouldn't think so.' The impish grin returned, ''Specially not if you're a dog.'

Lizzy stifled a giggle. 'That's what my dad said.' She held the star up for examination. 'More glitter, or do you reckon it looks good as it is?'

Charlie nodded approvingly. 'Looks grand to me. Besides, I don't think we could fit any more glitter on if we tried.'

When the school day came to an end Lizzy waited patiently for Mary's arrival, the star clutched between her fingers as she jiggled with the anticipation of showing her mother the result of her morning's work. One by one she watched the other children leave until she stood alone, and as a few flakes of snow drifted lazily to the ground she decided it would be sensible if she set off to meet her. Placing the star in her satchel, she hopscotched her way along the pavement, wondering what could have happened to prevent Mary from meeting her on time. Soon the snow began to fall more thickly, and she abandoned her slow progress and broke into a trot.

Entering the small terraced house on Sun Street she ascended the stairs two at a time, calling out as she went, 'I'm home! Don't worry, I've got the star. I told Miss Gregory how ill you were ...' the door to her parents' room was ajar, and she knocked briefly before entering, 'and she let me make it.' As she spoke she pulled the star from her satchel. She had half expected to find her father still in pain as he had been when she had left him earlier that morning, and was pleased to see that instead he lay peacefully in his bed, his face calm and relaxed, her mother holding his hand.

Mary looked up, then crossed the room and enveloped her daughter in a tight embrace. 'I'm so, so sorry ...' was all she could manage before bursting into tears.

Confused, Lizzy peered at her father through the crook of her mother's shoulder, but his face remained impassive. Her eyes travelled to his motionless chest, and as realisation dawned the star she had been so proud of fell from her fingertips and drifted to the ground. Burying her face in her mother's chest, tears coursing down her cheeks, she spoke through stifled sobs. 'You ... you said he had bellyache ...'

Cradling her daughter, Mary rested her cheek on top of Lizzy's head. 'I thought that was all it was, but he took a turn for the worse, so I sent for the doctor, only your dad passed before he could get here.'

'Off bellyache?' said Lizzy, her words coming out thick and slow as she tried to come to terms with the dreadful news.

Leaning back, Mary smoothed Lizzy's hair back behind her ears and looked into her eyes. 'Sort of. The doctor said it were a burst appendix. Probably been nigglin' 'im for days, but you know what he's like, never one to complain ...'

Risking a glance at her father, Lizzy tried to gulp back the sobs which were rising in her throat, but it was no use. Wailing with the pain of her loss, she buried her face against her mother, pointing at the star which lay below them. 'It's my fault. I should've got here sooner ...'

Mary kissed the top of her daughter's head. 'Oh, Lizzy luv, you mustn't blame yourself. All the stars in the sky couldn't've saved your father.'

Lizzy had nodded, but she hadn't been able to help wondering whether things might have turned out differently had she got home sooner. Either that, or she had made the unluckiest star in the world.

Now, with the memory of her father clear in her mind, she eyed the man who stood next to her mother, and cast her mind back to the day when Mary had told her she intended to marry him.

Lizzy had gaped at her mother in disbelief. 'Why him, Mam? You could do so much better. You're still young, you're attractive, you've got all your own teeth ...' she had giggled as her mother took a playful swipe at her.

'Cheeky mare!' Mary said as she smiled lovingly at her daughter. 'We're broke, Lizzy, and there's not a lot of men who'd tek on a widow wi' no money. Besides, Albert's not a bad man, he's just not very good at showin' his feelin's.' She sighed. 'I know you say I could do better, but they ain't exactly queuein' up, are they? In fact Albert's the only feller that's shown any interest since your dad's passin'. Quite frankly, beggars can't be choosers.'

'I know it's been a long time since we lost Dad, but I reckon you'd be better off on your own than wi' a miserable bugger like 'im. You're not askin' a lot, but someone who cracked a smile every now an' then would be nice.' Lizzy shook her head as her mother opened her mouth to interrupt her. 'I ain't comparin' 'im to Dad, before you start, 'cos we both know no one could step into 'is shoes, but you ain't known Albert that long, so why the big rush?'

''Cos he asked an' I said yes before he changed his mind.' Mary poured the boiling water out of the kettle into the teapot. 'I know you see it as rushin', but I've been on me own for nine years and you're sixteen now, so I dare say it won't be long before you start courting. Then one day you'll get married and start a family of yer own, and where will that leave me?'

Lizzy shrugged. 'You could move in with us.'

Mary shook her head. 'Even the most reasonable of men don't want their mother-in-laws livin' with 'em.'

Lizzy shrugged. 'I still reckon you should wait. That Albert's miserable. Whenever he comes round it's as if he can't wait to leave, and he's right twitchy, like he's got fleas or summat.'

Mary wagged a reproving finger. 'That'll do, my girl. Has it ever occurred to you that he might be a bit wary about coming down the courts after dark? It's all right for us what live round here—'

'So he's a coward to boot!'

Mary heaved a sigh. 'I know you don't like Albert, and I'm not suggestin' he should take the place of your father – no man could ever do that – but I do ask that you at least try to get along with him, if only for my sake?'

Lizzy had nodded reluctantly. 'I'll try, but he don't like me – it's as plain as the nose on your face. He allus rolls his eyes whenever I enter the room.'

Mary's voice cut through Lizzy's thoughts. 'Dolly Daydream, are you ready?' She looked up at her mother and Albert, who was looking impatient.

'As I'll ever be.' Standing up, she smiled reassuringly at her mother as she kissed her cheek. 'I'm happy for you, Mam, really I am.' Then, albeit reluctantly, she turned to do the same to Albert, but whether he guessed her intention or not he had turned away and was walking towards the table to sign the papers.

Mary squeezed Lizzy's fingers in her own. 'He's just a bit shy, chuck. He'll soon warm to you, just you see. In the meantime let's get these papers signed and witnessed so we can go and have us a celebratory lunch at Lyons. You've never really spent any time together, the two of you. I'm sure you'll like him once you get to know him.'

Linking arms with her mother, Lizzy settled with the thought that her mother's judgement could not be too far off kilter, as she had made a good choice when she married Eric, who had been the most kind, caring, loving man Lizzy had ever known. She was right about me dad, so mebbe I've got Albert all wrong, thought Lizzy. Perhaps we just need to get to know each other properly.

Chapter One

September, 1939

Hiding beneath the bench, Lizzy placed a hand across her mouth in an effort to calm her breathing as she heard the sound of her pursuer's heavy footsteps thundering towards her along the deserted platform. As Albert's feet skidded into view she screwed her eyes shut in case her very gaze drew his attention to her hiding place. In her mind she hurriedly repeated the same sentence: *Please keep moving, don't look down. Please keep moving, don't look down.*

'I know you're in here, so there's no sense in hiding,' Albert barked, his voice resonating round the empty station.

An unfamiliar voice broke the silence. ''Oo you talkin' to?'

Lizzy's eyes snapped open. A new set of feet had appeared just in front of Albert's. Carefully tilting her head to one side, she thought she recognised the uniform to be that of a railway guard. For a moment Lizzy's heart raced with the thought that Albert might try to coerce the guard into searching for her.

Albert folded his arms across his chest. 'I'm lookin' for a young woman.'

The guard laughed throatily. 'Then you've come to the wrong place, pal. This is a train station, not a whorehouse.'

Albert stiffened. 'Not that kind of woman. It's my wife's daughter; she's … run off. You know what kids are like.'

The guard eyed Albert suspiciously; there was something about his demeanour which he found unsettling. 'When did you lose her?'

Albert glared angrily at the guard. 'I didn't lose her. I told you, she ran away from me, and I think she came in 'ere.'

The guard tilted his head to one side. 'She in trouble?'

Albert gave a short, false laugh. 'Nah, it were just a bit of a misunderstandin' – she got hold of the wrong end of the stick – but it's dangerous for a young girl to be out at night on her own, and I know her mam'd never forgive me if owt 'appened to her. I don't suppose you could give me a hand to find her? She might come to you.'

It was all Lizzy could do to stop herself from shouting 'Liar' at the top of her lungs.

'She's not in any trouble, you say?' said the guard, and to Lizzy's dismay she saw his eyes swivel to something on the floor, before flicking towards her hiding place.

Lizzy peered sidelong at the small piece of card on the floor, which she realised was the family photograph that must have fallen out of her pocket as she dived beneath the bench. Holding her breath, she prayed the guard would not betray her, then breathed an inward sigh of relief as she watched him surreptitiously place one foot over the telltale card. She glanced at Albert to see if he had noticed, but he had not taken his eyes off the other man and was clenching and unclenching his fists behind his back, although you would never have known by the calm manner in which he replied. 'Not at all,' he said.

Lizzy rolled her eyes in disbelief at such a wild untruth. As she awaited the guard's response she replayed the evening's events in her mind. Everything had been relatively quiet up until an hour ago, when Albert had decided to have one of his tantrums. Lizzy, who had been in her bedroom, could hear the argument as clearly as if Mary and Albert were in the same room. Crossing her fingers that it would not escalate into violence, she had swung her legs over the edge of her bed and listened hard.

'I want you to get that bastard child of yours out of my 'ouse before the week's out,' yelled Albert. 'I married you – although God only knows why – not 'er, an' I've been patient up till now, but enough is enough.'

'But where's she meant to go?' said Mary in reasonable tones. 'She can't afford to rent a place of 'er own, and I ain't 'avin' 'er livin' on the streets.'

Albert gave a short bark of laughter. 'That ain't my problem, you can go with her for all I care. Worst thing I ever did was marry you.'

Lizzy cocked her ear as Mary's voice quietened. 'How can I go anywhere when you've taken all me money and papers?'

There was a loud thud as Albert's fist connected with their bedroom door. 'Why, you ungrateful bitch! After all I've done for you.' Lizzy heard the door open. 'If that's what you want you can go with 'er, but you ain't tekkin' me money, nor anythin' else in this 'ouse save the clothes on yer back. Let's see 'ow far you get wi'out me.'

The door slammed shut, followed by the sound of Albert thundering down the stairs. There was another loud bang as the front door closed violently behind him.

Lizzy knocked tentatively on the door to her mother's bedroom. 'Come in, love,' called Mary. 'I 'spect you 'eard all that?'

Lizzy nodded. 'You'd think 'e'd get fed up of 'earin' 'imself dronin' on and on about the same old thing. I know I do.'

Mary heaved a sigh. ''E's never 'ad any kids of his own, so he don't understand what it means to be a family.'

'Bloomin' good job an' all if you ask me,' said Lizzy. 'He'd mek a rotten dad.'

Mary nodded. 'Look, love, I'm the one who got us into this mess by marryin' 'im, but that don't mean you've gorra suffer an' all. You allus used to say you quite fancied the idea of joinin' the Wrens.'

'And leave you 'ere on yer own with 'im?' said Lizzy. 'Not on your nellie! God only knows what 'e'd be like if it were just the two of you.'

Mary placed a loving arm around her daughter's shoulders. 'I appreciate your concern, but like I said, this is my problem not yours.'

Lizzy shook her head. 'I'll leave all right, but only if you promise to come with me.' She pulled a photograph of herself and her parents on New Brighton beach out of her skirt pocket and handed it to her mother. 'That's the sort of man you deserve, one like me dad, not that beast you're with now.'

A tear trickled down Mary's cheek as she gently stroked the image of Eric with the tip of her forefinger. 'You're right, but like I told Albert, I've got no money, no papers, nothin'.'

'You've got me,' said Lizzy. 'There's gorra be somewhere we can go.' She cast her mother a sidelong glance. 'What about Great-aunt Cissy's in Speke? We've not been there for years, but she allus used to say we was welcome any time, or at least I think that's what she said. It's been a long time since we saw her last.'

Mary chuckled as she handed the photograph back to her daughter. 'Fancy you rememberin' Great-aunt Cissy. But she's awfully old; she may not appreciate us landin' ourselves on her doorstep.'

Placing the photograph back in her skirt pocket Lizzy pulled out an old sock and shook it up and down. She smiled as the coins chinked together. 'I've been holdin' a bit back off of me laundry, and I reckon I've got enough to get us both to Speke, and pay Great-aunt Cissy summat for our keep whilst we find us a couple of jobs.' She clicked her fingers. 'I reckon we could easily get work in Bryant and May. I seem to remember someone sayin' they're allus lookin' for women there, so that's our jobs sorted.' She glanced at her mother from the corner of her eye. 'Albert doesn't know we gorra Great-aunt Cissy, does he?'

Mary shook her head. 'I've never said owt.' A frown creased her brow. 'But what about our papers? We'll need 'em if they start issuin' ration books and the like.'

Lizzy grinned. 'Easy. We can say we lost 'em in a fire—' She gave a small gasp as the door to the bedroom burst open and Albert, his face purple with rage, came in.

He pointed a shaking finger at Lizzy. 'You sneaky, connivin', thievin' little bitch! I said from the start you shouldn't be livin' with us, and I were right, weren't I, 'cos 'ere you are, tryin' to persuade your mam to steal all me money and run off wi' you.' He clapped both hands on Lizzy's shoulders and lifted her off the bed. 'Gerrout of my 'ouse before I ruddy well kill yer.'

Leaping to her feet, Mary grabbed hold of his arm. 'Let go of her! Albert, you're drunk. You don't know what you're—' She yelped as he cracked her across the face with the back of his free hand.

'Drunk my arse! I've hardly touched a drop. I knew that little bitch were plannin' summat so I thought I'd catch her out, and I did, didn't I?' His fingers dug into Lizzy's shoulder blades, causing her to cry out. 'If I find you 'ere again, I swear to God, I'll choke the life out of you.' As he dragged her towards the bedroom door Lizzy swung the sock full of money, catching him across his temple. Roaring with pain, he instinctively released his grip on Lizzy to clutch his face.

Lizzy held out her hand to her mother, who was lying on the floor. 'C'mon, Mam ...'

Still clutching his forehead, Albert ploughed into Lizzy, knocking her through the bedroom door and down the stairs. Scrambling to her feet, Mary screamed, 'Lizzy! Are you all right?' She tried to push past Albert.

'You've done it this time, Albert Tanner. You can rot in hell for all I care.'

'You ain't goin' nowhere,' snarled Albert, and with one hefty shove he sent her sprawling across the bed. Before she had a chance to get back on her feet he slammed the door on her. At the bottom of the stairs Lizzy was wondering what to do, but she had no time to think. Albert was clattering down towards her, his eyes filled with murderous intent, and Lizzy turned and fled. Shouting threats as he went, Albert gave chase. As Lizzy ran blindly down the deserted jiggers, a thought occurred to her: the further she led Albert away from her mother the more chance Mary had of escape. He'll be buggered then, Lizzy thought with satisfaction, and serve him right too; he don't deserve a woman like me mam. As she heard the echo of Albert's feet dying, she slowed her pace, and turning to look over her shoulder she stuck her tongue out at him. 'Fat old bugger,' she taunted.

'Cheeky bitch!' he roared. Lizzy smiled, content in the knowledge that she had bought her mother some extra time.

The guard's voice cut through her thoughts. 'I don't think so.'

Lizzy could hear the disbelief in Albert's tone. 'What do you mean, you don't think so?'

The guard rocked from his heels to the balls of his feet and back again. 'I mean, I don't think I'll help you find her.'

Shaking his head in annoyance Albert grabbed the guard's shoulder in one hand. 'I've got no time for this. Get out of my way.'

The guard shrugged Albert off. 'You ain't goin' nowhere.'

Albert laughed scornfully. 'Who's goin' to stop me?'

'You havin' a bit o' bother, George?' came a voice from behind him. Turning to address the third party, Albert let out a groan of dismay.

'A bloody scuffer? Ain't you got anythin' better to do?'

The policeman glanced at the watch on his wrist. 'I've got a half hour to kill before the end of my shift, so no, I haven't got anythin' better to do, and if I'm honest I'd far rather have a cup of cocoa with George, but I suppose that depends on how things pan out, as it were.'

The guard leaned round the back of Albert and nodded to the policeman. 'This feller's lookin' for a woman.'

The constable raised a surprised brow. 'Bit of a rum place to go lookin' for women.'

Clearly outnumbered, Albert stepped back. 'It's just been a bit of a misunderstandin'. I can allus come back later ...' As he spoke, he turned towards the exit, only to find the policeman barring his path.

'That misunderstandin', as you call it, seems to've ended you up with what looks like a right nasty bruise on the side of your head.' He peered at the area where Lizzy had hit Albert with the sock full of coins. 'In fact, it looks like you've been in a bit of a fight.'

George nodded. 'He's had a fallin' out with his stepdaughter. It's her he's chasin' after.'

Albert went pale. 'I weren't chasin' after anyone. I were just tryin' to mek sure she's all right.'

The policeman's gaze reverted to Albert's temple. 'If someone clouted me round the noggin I dare say I wouldn't be best pleased either. I'd be mad as fire.' He stared Albert straight in the eye. 'She must've been really keen to get away from you.'

Albert's throat had gone dry, and his voice when he spoke came out in a croak as he indicated the injured temple with his forefinger. 'You talkin' about this? I did this earlier on; it's nowt to do with Lizzy.'

The policeman arched his brow. 'Lizzy? Is that the girl you're chasin' after?'

It was all getting too much for Albert and he shook his head. 'I'm sorry if I've caused any trouble. It's been rather a long night, so if you don't mind I'll be on me way.'

The policeman shrugged his indifference. 'You're free to go any time you please ...' Albert found his way being barred by the policeman's outstretched arm, 'but whilst you're free to leave, you aren't welcome back any time soon. Do I make myself clear?'

Albert nodded.

'And if I hear of any young girl getting a hidin' tonight from a feller matching your description I shall be straight round to your house ... where did you say you lived?'

Albert jutted out his bottom jaw as he tried to think of an excuse to not give the policeman his address. Finding none, he muttered it under his breath.

'Snowdrop Street? But that's miles away from here.' The policeman tried to catch Albert's eye. 'You must've been pretty desperate to chase her all this way.'

Albert gave a weary sigh. 'Just tryin' to look out for the girl.'

The policeman slowly withdrew his arm. 'Glad to hear it.'

Grunting some kind of acknowledgement, Albert made his way towards the arches of the station. Behind him, George bent down and retrieved the photograph from under his boot and handed it wordlessly to the policeman, who studied it intently.

As the echoes of Albert's footsteps died, George said something that Lizzy couldn't catch, and she saw the policeman's boots turn in the direction of her bench. 'You can come out now.' Dropping to his haunches, he peered under the seat and held out a hand. 'Or do you intend to spend the entire night under there?'

Taking his hand, she became aware of the familiar scent of Vinolia shaving foam: the same brand her father always used. She wriggled out from underneath the bench and dusted off her skirt. 'Thanks for that. I'm Lizzy Atherton, by the way.' Her voice faded as she looked into the policeman's handsome face. He had deep-set brown eyes, which sparkled as he smiled at her. Lizzy stared at him, and her brow furrowed as she tried to work out who he reminded her of. She could swear she had seen him somewhere before, but as she didn't know any scuffers she felt she must be mistaken. Then an impish grin formed on the constable's lips and a large dimple appeared in each cheek. Lizzy pointed an accusing finger. 'Charlie bloomin' Jackson!'

He nodded. 'Wondered when the penny 'ud drop, only that ain't my middle name.'

24

The guard looked from one to the other. 'You two know each other then?'

'A long time ago!' said Charlie, staring into Lizzy's eyes. 'Where did you and your mam go?'

'Hopwood Street,' said Lizzy. 'We couldn't afford the rent in Sun Street after Dad died.'

'Blimey, no wonder I ain't seen you. That's miles away from where you used to live,' said Charlie.

'Was you in school together?' George asked.

Nodding, Lizzy turned reproving eyes on Charlie. 'He used to sit behind me in school, an' a right little bugger he was. I'll never forget the day he thought it'd be funny to dip me pigtails in the glue pot and leave 'em there.' She shook her head at the recollection. 'By the time I realised, it was too late. Me mam went 'nanas when she seen me, marched me straight 'ome and scrubbed an' scrubbed, but it were no use. She had to cut them off in the end.'

George chuckled. 'Bit of a rascal, was you, lad?'

Charlie had gone crimson. 'I was eight!'

'And that made a difference how?' sniffed Lizzy. 'Me mam were furious when she seen me 'air. She give me a right shoutin' at and it weren't even my fault.'

George's brow furrowed in thought. 'How long were they in the glue for?'

Lizzy folded her arms across her chest. 'Ages, or at least I think they were.'

Charlie cocked an eyebrow. 'If you'd've been awake instead of snatchin' forty winks, it wouldn't have been so bad.'

Lizzy scowled defensively at him. 'You're sayin' it was my fault?'

25

Charlie shrugged. 'Kind of.'

George held up a hand. 'How's about you two let bygones be bygones over a nice cup of cocoa?'

Lizzy nodded but never took her eyes off Charlie. 'So how come they let you in the force? I'd've thought they had more sense.'

He rolled his eyes. 'It was ten years ago. I've grown up a lot since then.' His eyes travelled up and down her form and he nodded approvingly. 'You're lookin' well.'

Lizzy blushed, but she was determined to keep the high ground. 'You must have is all I can say, although I don't feel safer knowin' you're patrollin' the streets of Liverpool.'

Charlie held out a hand. 'Can't we call it pax? I think it's safe to say a lot of water has passed under the bridge since then, and we've both changed quite a bit.'

'I haven't,' Lizzy sniffed.

He grinned mischievously. 'Oh, I don't know. I reckon you must be all of five foot ...'

Taking hold of his hand, Lizzy chuckled despite herself. 'I'm happy to call it pax if you are.'

'I'm glad you got that sorted out,' said George, 'but what about that other business?'

Turning to face him, Lizzy frowned. 'What other business?'

He jerked his head in the direction of the arches. 'Ten minutes ago you was hidin' under that bench like a frightened kitten, or have you forgotten?'

'Albert,' Lizzy groaned. She looked hopefully at George. 'I daren't go home tonight. Would it be possible for me to kip down on the bench? I promise I'll be out from under your feet first thing in the morning.'

Charlie glanced around the deserted platform. 'I don't think it's a good idea for you to spend the night out here.' He glanced in the direction of George's office. 'What d'you reckon, George? You got room for a little 'un in that office of yours?'

Nodding, George turned to Lizzy. 'But if anyone asks you'll 'ave to say you snuck in there whilst me back was turned, 'cos if me boss finds out he'll have me guts for garters.'

Lizzy smiled gratefully. 'Thank you. I promise I won't be a nuisance.'

Charlie held the photograph of Lizzy and her parents towards her. 'I recognised you as soon as I saw the photo. I take it that was your mam's new husband?'

Lizzy took the photograph and nodded miserably. ''Fraid so, only not for too much longer. With a bit of luck she'll be long gone by the time he gets back. I made sure I gave her plenty of time to escape, so I expect she's lyin' low somewhere like me.'

Charlie withdrew a large notepad from his pocket and wrote something down before tearing out the page and handing it to Lizzy. 'Promise me you'll come to this address should that blighter cause you any more trouble?'

'Of course I will, and thanks for all your help. I dread to think what would've happened had Albert found me first.'

Removing his helmet, Charlie ran his fingers through his hair. 'Just part of me job.'

An image formed in her mind of Charlie as she had once known him. Short and chubby, with thick brown hair, his knees were always covered in bruises and his socks were permanently at half mast. No matter how many times Miss Gregory told him to pull them up, they'd be back around his ankles within a matter of minutes. As the image faded, Lizzy stared at the man before her, smartly dressed in his police uniform. He was a good deal taller than she, and his chubby cheeks had disappeared to reveal smiling cheekbones. She was glad to see he still had those delightful dimples which formed whenever he smiled, and his brown eyes still danced with mischief. Hearing a chuckle escape George's lips, Lizzy averted her gaze.

'Come along then, miss ... Lizzy, was it?'

She nodded.

'Well, Lizzy, let's get you into my office. I'm sure I've got a blanket in there somewhere.'

Before Charlie said goodbye he nodded towards the arches. 'I take it that was your handiwork on the side of his head?'

Lizzy nodded with a grin. 'He grabbed hold of me so hard I couldn't move, so I clacked him me purse.' Digging her hand in her pocket, she pulled out her money sock.

Charlie chuckled. 'Blimey, I'm surprised he could move after bein' clouted wi' that.' His eyes twinkled as he gazed into hers. 'I can see you're still a force to be reckoned with.'

George glanced at his watch. 'I'd best gerra move on. I've got the one-thirty comin' from Stoke in a bit, so if you'd like to foller me ...' His voice trailed off as he turned and headed off down the platform.

Nodding, Lizzy eyed Charlie shyly from under her lashes. 'Ta-ra, Charlie, and thanks again.'

Tilting his head down to one side he managed to catch her eye. 'Ta-ra, queen. Don't forget, you can call in any time even if it's just for a chat.'

Turning on her heel, she smiled as she trotted after George. Charlie was flirting with her, she was sure of it.

Charlie watched as Lizzy headed after George, hoping that she might cast him a backward glance, and sighed with disappointment as she disappeared into the office without turning. With nothing left to do, he broke into the slow methodical plod of policemen the world over, and headed for the arches. Behind him, Lizzy poked her head round the door to the office and watched until he disappeared from view.

'Forgotten summat?' George chuckled.

'No. I ... I ...' stammered Lizzy, as she tried to find a reason for watching Charlie.

'Tek no notice of me; I'm only teasin'.' George held out a rather dog-eared patchwork blanket. 'Tek this an' you can snuggle up on them chairs for the night.' He pointed to a couple of chairs next to the filing cabinet.

As she turned back, Lizzy's eyes met his. 'Thanks, George. It is all right if I call you George, isn't it?'

He nodded. 'I've been called a lot worse, queen.'

Lizzy giggled. 'I'm sorry to be such a nuisance.'

He held up a hand. 'Don't be silly. I dare say it weren't your intention to be spendin' the night sleepin' rough, now was it?' Lizzy shook her head. 'So let's hear no more about it.' He glanced towards a tea tray which stood on top of a filing cabinet. 'You any good at mekkin' cocoa?'

When Albert had slammed the door to their bedroom Mary had raced across the room, but even as she turned the handle she heard the key click in the lock. Hammering her fists against the door, she had begged him to leave Lizzy alone, but when she fell silent she heard the sound of the front door slamming. She strained her ears for any sound that would indicate that Albert was still in the house, but everything remained quiet. She ran to the window and peered through the glass, her shoulders sagging as she watched Lizzy tearing along the jigger with Albert in hot pursuit. Desperate to escape, she looked around the room to see if there was anything she could use to break the door open, but there was nothing. Frantic, she spun away from the window and her feet caught the block of wood they used to prop the sash window open. Without hesitation she pushed the window as far up as it would go and wedged the block of wood firmly in place. Then, gathering all her courage, she straddled the windowsill so that half of her body was outside the room, her heart thumping in her chest. The drainpipe was a few feet away, out of her reach, so she would have to try to swing herself from the window ledge to the pipe, which meant letting go of the windowsill – an idea she did not relish. Looking down at the cobbled yard below, Mary felt her stomach lurch unpleasantly. As a young girl she had gone with her friends to the Scaldy to try to learn to swim, and she had been standing on the long pipe, trying to build up the courage to gently slide her way into the water, when one of the bigger boys had pushed her off with a scornful laugh. The feeling of helplessness as she descended under the surface, water pouring into her open mouth, had left her with a deep-rooted fear of both water and heights.

Casting her eye around the room for an alternative solution, Mary saw the alarm clock on top of the chest of drawers next to Albert's side of the bed, and was vividly aware of the second hand making its way around the face. She was wasting time. If she was going to rescue Lizzy from Albert she would have to move quickly. Taking a deep breath, she swung both legs outside the window and began to shuffle along the ledge towards the drainpipe. When she had gone as far as she could, she turned on to her stomach, holding on to the sill with a steely grip. She tried stretching one hand towards the drainpipe, but as she had feared it was just beyond her reach. Summoning all her courage, she geared herself up for the leap of faith as she began to swing herself back and forth. She was about to let go of the ledge when her fingertips caught the wooden block securing the sash, and before she knew what was happening the window descended with an almighty crash. Without thinking Mary instinctively pulled her hands from harm's way, and, arms and legs flailing, she fell to the cobbled yard below.

By the time Albert returned home, the effects of chasing Lizzy round the streets of Liverpool had caused his bad mood to subside. Tired from his encounter with the policeman and the rail guard, he decided the last thing he needed right now was Mary screaming at him.

Entering the kitchen, he broke the top off a bottle of Cains and took a large swig, sinking down into one of the seats by the kitchen table. He rested his head on its surface and reflected on the evening's activities, none of which, he concluded, were his fault. He had asked Mary to get rid of her daughter time and time again, but would she listen? He shook his head ruefully. Would she heck as like, even though it was obvious to all that keeping Lizzy in the house just caused more arguments. Now, to top it off, he'd nearly been arrested by a scuffer, and all because the stupid woman treated her daughter like a spoiled brat. He cast his eyes to the ceiling above him and frowned. Mary must have heard him come home; he'd slammed the front door hard enough, which in hindsight hadn't been good for his headache, so why wasn't she screeching like a banshee for him to come and let her out so that she could go to look for her precious daughter?

Taking another swig, he glanced back at the ceiling. Surely she couldn't be asleep, not after the way she had been carrying on; she'd be far too concerned about Lizzy just to nod off. He shook his head. Something wasn't right. He gulped down the contents of the beer bottle then hefted it in one hand; one quick blow with this would stop her in her tracks if she made to lunge at him. He eyed the thick glass and placed it down on the dresser. A blow to the head with a bottle like that could kill someone, and tonight had been bad enough as it was without being done for murder. He ascended the stairs as quietly as he could. He had no doubt that Mary was probably on the other side of the bedroom door waiting for him to enter so that she could dart out behind him, and quite frankly, after the night he'd had, she was welcome to leave. He'd miss the extra money but that would be about all. Reaching the top of the stairs, he paused for a moment. What if Mary planned on hitting him with something in order to make her escape? He unbuckled his belt and slowly slid it from his trousers. All I did, he reasoned with himself as he stepped to the door and slid the key into the lock, was come home from a hard day's work to find them scheming behind me back. I'd not done nothin' wrong, not harmed a hair on their heads – if anythin' I were the one who got cracked over the 'ead – and yet there they were, thick as thieves plottin' to leave me, and take me money to boot. He eyed the thick metal buckle. A few lashes with that would teach her, he thought, and then let's see how eager she is to leave me. He turned the key and flung the door open with such force it ricocheted off the wall. Holding the belt up high, he waited for Mary to try to dart past him, but when he looked into the room he could see no sign of her. He slung the belt over one shoulder and went in, his eyes flickering around. He looked under the bed, behind the door, inside the wardrobe, but Mary was nowhere to be found. Scratching his head, he looked around once more. Where on earth was the dratted woman? He looked at the window but it was still closed, so she couldn't possibly have got out that way; besides, he knew she was terrified of heights. His eyes fell to the floor and he saw the wooden block, which lay halfway between the bed and the window. 'Why, you little bitch,' he hissed through gritted teeth. 'Serve you right if you fell and broke your ruddy neck.' Lifting the sash, he leaned out and saw Mary lying in a twisted heap on the cobbles.

Despite his words, the blood drained from his face. If anyone had heard the argument and seen him chasing Lizzy whilst shouting blue murder, they might think he'd pushed Mary out of the window and that's why Lizzy had run off in the first place. He remembered the guard and the policeman at the station. He'd told them he was after his wife's daughter, and that there'd been a bit of an argument … He lifted his fingers to his temple. He glanced around the small dark yard; the gate was still shut so no one had seen her … but what about young Leigh from next door? His bedroom over-looked their yard. He ran nervous fingers through his hair as he tried to figure out what to do. She couldn't stay there, that was certain, but where could he put her? Come to that, was she even still alive? He ran down the stairs and into the yard, approaching the recumbent body with care so as not to attract any unwanted atten-tion from curious neighbours. 'Mary? Are you all right?' he whispered, nudging her with the toe of his boot, but there was no response. Crouching down on his haunches, he rolled her on to her back. Her face was bloodied and bruised and there was a line of blood running from the corner of her mouth to the cobbles.

Falling back, Albert covered his face with his hands as fear gripped him. She was dead, and he would get the blame. He would be accused of murder, especially if that brat of a child had anything to do with it; she'd make sure he hanged for summat he hadn't done. He held the back of his neck as he wrestled with his thoughts. What if there was no body? He could say

34

that she had run away, just like Lizzy. They'd never be able to prove he was lying. He could go down to the docks and chuck her into the sea. If they ever found her they would assume that she had tripped over one of the mooring posts, fallen in and drowned. But what if someone saw him on his way to the docks, what would he say then? He shook his head. He wouldn't give them time to ask questions, just hurry past. It wasn't as if Mary would be struggling; people would assume she was unconscious or asleep. Hefting her on to his shoulder, he carried her to the gate and cast a searching eye along the length of the jigger. No one was in sight as he closed the gate behind him.

His heart pounded in his chest as paranoia took over. Bumping into someone in the street was one thing, but what about all those people who would be popping to the privy in the back yard or having a crafty fag out of the bedroom window? They'd be sure to see him. By the time he reached Princes Dock, Albert was a mass of twitching nerves. Hesitating momentarily, he looked around, searching for any sign of life, but much to his relief the dock was deserted. Trembling with a mixture of fear and relief, he walked towards the edge of the quay. He was standing on the edge, holding Mary over the inky black water, when he heard the sound of approaching voices. He looked around wildly. If he dropped her into the water, the splash would certainly draw attention and people might come running, and if they caught him … Stepping back from the edge, he looked around for a good hiding place, but apart from a few crates that stood in the middle of the quay there was nothing. Glancing back at the crates he noticed

35

that the one farthest away was open. His mind made up, he hastened towards it and placed Mary's body inside before pulling the lid across the top.

'Oi!' The booming voice made Albert jump. 'What's your game? Clear off before I give you a good hidin'.' A large bearded man was walking towards him, hefting a hammer in one hand. 'Go on, sod off before I give you a clout, you thievin' git.'

Albert felt sick to his stomach. A dockworker himself, he recognised the man to be Gerry Davies, one of his fellow regulars down the docks. Desperate not to be discovered, Albert fled.

As Gerry swiftly began to nail the lid to Mary's crate shut, another man sidled out from behind a stack of barrels. 'Bleedin' 'ell, that were a bit close for comfort, weren't it? D'you reckon he seen us mekkin' the switch?'

Gerry continued to hammer nails into the lid. 'Not a chance. The way he took off I reckon he were on the rob himself. You get a lot of 'em down 'ere at night, havin' a snout about to see if there's owt worth tekkin'.'

The man from behind the barrels removed the dog end of a cigarette from his lips and screwed it into the ground with the toe of his boot. 'I'm sure I recognised 'im, not that it matters, of course. But I don't fancy hangin' around 'ere any longer than we have to. If we put our backs into it we shouldn't take too long, and they're a lot lighter now than when they were full of whisky.'

The bearded man nodded. 'Quicker, too. C'mon, give us a hand with this one.'

36

The other man grunted noisily. 'Are you sure you took all the bottles out? It feels a bit heavy to me.'

Gerry stopped trying to lift his end of the crate and glared at his associate. 'You accusin' me of nickin' off of me mates?' Without waiting for an answer he continued, 'I ain't like you; you won't find me crappin' on me own doorstep.'

The other man held up his hands. 'Blimey, I only said the crate felt heavy. I didn't mean nothin' by it.'

Gerry grunted his displeasure but continued to grip the crate in two beefy hands. 'You'd best not, neither. I ain't gerrin' accused of stuff I ain't done, especially not by the likes of you. Now get hold of your end and let's get this back on board before anyone else comes snoopin' round.'

Chapter Two

Clara Granger stood outside the door to her father's study, her ear pressed to the wood. She did not make it a habit to eavesdrop, but when it came to her father's housekeeper, Gertrude Hackney, and her daughter Ivy, Clara made an exception.

Gertrude had arrived at Bellevue after replying to an advertisement for a housekeeper which Clara's father, Arthur Granger, had placed in the *Liverpool Echo*. Clara had opened the front door expecting to find a woman wearing clothes suitable for a housekeeper, and was surprised when she was confronted with a very slender, smart-looking woman with bright ginger hair pulled back into a tight bun and wearing a tweed suit.

'Can I help you?' Clara had asked, slightly put out by this unexpected visitor.

Gertrude had extended a thin white hand, which Clara shook, noticing as she did so how cold the woman was. 'Gertrude Hackney. I've come to see Mr Granger about the vacancy.' She unclipped her patent leather handbag and held out a piece of paper. 'I've brought my references with me, so if you would announce me ...'

Clara took the piece of paper. 'I don't work here. I'm Clara Granger, Mr Granger's daughter.'

Gertrude's eyes had travelled from the top of Clara's head to her shoes. 'Then I've come just in time,' she said, and strolled past Clara into the hallway.

Closing the door behind her, Clara glared at the other woman, who was now admiring the paintings hanging on the walls of the vestibule. 'I'm sorry, but are you sure you've come about the right job? Your suit – it's hardly working dress, is it?' She was half expecting the other woman to clasp a hand to her mouth and say she had made a dreadful mistake, but the woman did no such thing. Instead she cast Clara a look of distaste.

'I should hope not; that's what maids are for. A housekeeper gives the orders; it's the maids what do all the work.'

Clara cocked an eyebrow. Her father didn't approve of people who weren't prepared to get their hands dirty. This woman would not last more than five minutes in his presence before being politely dismissed. Clara extended a hand towards the study. 'If you'd like to follow me, my father's expecting you.'

She knocked perfunctorily on the door before introducing the Hackney woman, as she already thought of her, then headed towards the staircase where she sat on the bottom step to wait for her father to ask her to see the unsuccessful applicant off the premises.

After twenty minutes or so, Clara decided that the dreadful woman must be digging her heels in and refusing to take no for an answer. When the door to the study finally opened, her father appeared. 'Clara! Just the person I'm looking for. I'd like to introduce you to our new live-in housekeeper, Gertrude Hackney.'

Clara stared at him in astonishment. 'Live-in? But I thought you said ...' she began, before being rudely interrupted by Gertrude.

'I told your father that I could not take the job unless he allowed me to live in, and he was kind enough to agree.' She smiled brightly at Clara. 'Besides, your father told me how your mother's death has come as a dreadful blow to the whole family, yourself in particular, so when we move in ...'

'We?' said Clara, folding her arms across her chest.

'I couldn't possibly leave my daughter behind. She's all I have since I buried my husband.'

Clara glared at her father. 'We don't need two people. We barely need one, especially not one like her. She's already said she doesn't intend to do any of the work herself, and we both know that's not the sort of person Mother would have wanted running Bellevue.'

'Clara! What on earth's got into you?' He turned apologetically to Gertrude. 'I'm dreadfully sorry. She's still grieving – she didn't mean it ...'

'Oh yes I did! Mother would turn in her grave if she knew you were hiring such a ... a ...'

Extending an arm, Arthur Granger pointed to the ceiling. 'Go to your room!'

She opened her mouth to object but her father had turned his attention back to Gertrude as he escorted her towards the front door. 'I can only apologise for my daughter's outburst – she's not usually so outspoken. I'll make sure she has a civil tongue in her head when you come back ...'

Unable to believe her ears, Clara ascended the stairs two at a time. At the top, she burst through her bedroom door and flung herself face down on her bed. How could he? Her mother would never have employed such a dreadful woman. Jessica Granger had been a kind, loving woman who wouldn't ask anyone to do a job she wasn't prepared to do herself. She had always been uncomfortable with the idea of having maids, and only did so because Bellevue was too big for her to run on her own.

Getting up, Clara went over to the window and stood gazing down at the gardens as she pondered how her father could hire such a work-shy individual. She shook her head. He wouldn't, so there was only one other answer: the dreadful woman must have lied. Clara nodded to herself: that must be it. Gertrude must have told him that she would pitch in with the maids. He would never have taken her on otherwise.

She heard the door to her room open and looked over her shoulder to see her father walking towards her, his arm outstretched in readiness to place round her shoulders. 'I know it's hard, love, and no one's trying to replace your mother, but I think Mrs Hackney's going to be really good for Bellevue.'

Clara fished a tissue from the pocket of her frock and blew her nose. 'I know we need help, but she said she'd get the maids to do the work for her. I bet she didn't tell you that, did she?'

Her father gave a low chuckle. 'I think there's been a bit of a misunderstanding. She probably meant she would tell the maids what to do, which is very right and proper, but it doesn't mean to say she won't help them.'

He kissed Clara's cheek. 'Are you sure you're not upset because she mistook you for one of the maids?'

Annoyed, Clara furrowed her brow. 'I'd rather be mistaken for a maid than some snooty tart!'

Heaving a sigh, her father shook his head. 'If you're referring to her makeup, I'm sure she was only trying to look her best for the interview, and you needn't worry that I might have hired the wrong person, because she's only here for a trial run. If she doesn't prove to be suitable, she'll have to go.'

Clara brightened. 'Really?'

He had nodded reassuringly. 'Really.'

All this had taken place some months before and Gertrude had turned out to be every bit as dreadful as Clara had suspected, and her daughter Ivy wasn't much better. When Ivy had first turned up at Bellevue, Clara had no need to ask who she was. She was the very spit of her mother, from her bright poker-straight ginger hair to her skinny pale physique. In all the time the pair had been at the house Clara had never seen either of them so much as lift a dishcloth. Indeed, they had proved to be every bit as lazy as Clara expected, so much so that when Arthur Granger called Gertrude into the office Clara felt sure he would be handing the woman her notice, and had sneaked down the stairs so that she might eavesdrop. Now, standing with her ear pressed against the wood, she waited with bated breath.

'War is coming, Mr Granger,' she heard, 'and we all saw what that dreadful man did to those poor Spaniards. I urge you to send Clara into the country. I know she's too old to be evacuated, but I'd hate to think of anything happening to her if she stays here. She's still very fragile after the death of her mother.'

'But we have one of the best shelters, and she's happy here. I don't think she'd be happy—' Arthur began, only to be cut off by Gertrude, who sounded as though her patience was wearing thin.

'It's too dangerous here. Who knows what might happen if they start bombing? You've already lost your wife – do you really want to lose Clara as well?' There was a slight pause before she added, 'Think about what your wife would have wanted.'

It was too much. Furious, Clara entered the room without knocking and pointed an accusing finger at Gertrude. 'You haven't got a clue what my mother would want, because if you did you wouldn't be here! And if you think you can send me off into the country like some silly little girl you've got another thing coming, because I'd rather stay here and do my bit than run away like some coward.'

Arthur clasped a hand to his forehead. 'You say you don't want to be treated like a child, so I suggest you stop acting like one by earwigging on people's private conversations and knock before you enter a room!'

Clara placed her hands on her hips. 'Private conversations about me, you mean? Well I will not apologise for listening to a conversation about my future.' She glared at Gertrude, who was trying to keep the smirk from her lips. 'As you're so concerned, I expect you'll be sending Ivy away also?'

Gertrude pushed her horn-rimmed spectacles up the bridge of her nose. 'You know full well that Ivy can't go into the country because of her hay fever. She has no choice but to stay here and risk the bombs; you don't know how lucky you are ...'

'Since when has being bombed been preferable to sneezing?' Clara said, her tone incredulous. 'You're seriously trying to tell me she'd be safer here than having a runny nose and watery eyes in the country?'

Gertrude threw her hands up in feigned despair. 'I was only trying to help, but have it your way. If you'd rather stay here and face oblivion ...'

Arthur gave the older woman a reproving look. 'That will do, Mrs Hackney.' Clara felt a smile beginning but it soon faded as her father continued, 'I'm afraid when all's said and done Mrs Hackney's right. Your mother wouldn't want you to stay in Liverpool, and I think it best all round if you go to stay with your Aunt Beryl on her farm in Upton, and the sooner the better, as I dare say she'll be allocated more than her fair share of evacuees.'

Clara stared at her father in disbelief. From the corner of her eye she could see the look of glee on Gertrude's face. Well, she would soon change that. 'I won't go, and what's more, you can't make me.' She turned to face Gertrude. 'I don't know what your game is or why you're so desperate to get rid of me, but I promise you this: I will find out, and when I do ...'

Arthur shook his head. 'Clara, that's enough. You're so intent on hating Mrs Hackney and her daughter you can't see past your own nose. I'm not sending you into the country because she wants me to, but because I want you to go.' He held up a hand as Clara began to protest. 'I didn't at first, but the more I think about it the more I believe it to be in your best interest. You've proved today that you are still very young for your age. I'm sorry, darling, but I've made up my mind. I shall ring your aunt this evening and tell her that you will be arriving tomorrow on the midday train.'

With tears brimming in her eyes, Clara turned to leave the study. 'It's not me who can't see past my nose, it's you who've been blinded by her.'

As the door closed, Gertrude laid a reassuring hand on his arm. 'She doesn't mean it; she's just lashing out. She'll soon see it makes sense, especially if they do start bombing.'

He nodded. 'I think a break is just what's needed. She's had a hard time getting over Jessica's death.'

Gertrude smiled. 'Perfectly understandable. You wait and see. She'll be a different child when she comes back from the country.'

He laid his hand over the top of Gertrude's on his arm. 'Thanks for being so understanding. I think most people would've run for the hills.'

'Don't worry. It's why I'm here – to get Bellevue back to the way it was before your wife passed and keep it that way.'

He cast an eye around the drab interior of his study. 'I hope so, because at the moment it feels like I'm a stranger living in a ghost of a home.'

Gertrude nodded. 'Once Clara's in the country, we can concentrate on what's really important.'

Arthur hesitated. 'Clara's important ...'

'Of course she is, but at the moment she's standing in the way of her own happiness. You mark my words, with Clara gone, Bellevue will return to the happy home it once was.'

Lizzy stared blearily around the guard's room as the memories of the previous evening washed over her. She frowned. There seemed to be an awful lot of noise coming from the platform. Swinging her legs off the makeshift bed of chairs, she glanced out of the window. The platform was full of children milling around. They all had suitcases so they were obviously off on some kind of trip, but where were all their parents? True, there were some adults with the children, but not nearly as many as she would have expected.

She opened the door and stepped into the throng, fielding a small boy who was trotting towards a large group of children who looked about his own age. 'What's going on?'

The boy shook Lizzy's hand away. 'You fick or summink? Everyone knows 'bout the 'vacooation ...'

Lizzy's lips parted as realisation dawned. The Prime Minister had handed Germany an ultimatum, the outcome of which they would be told tomorrow, and in the meantime the children were being sent to the safety of the countryside. She watched the boy as he headed towards the other children, presumably his classmates. She glanced at the huge clock that hung above the platform. If her mother were heading for Great-aunt Cissy's, she would either have caught an earlier train or wait until things quietened down a little. By the looks of the crowded platform that would not be for some time yet.

Further down the platform someone was waving their arms in order to get her attention. She looked up

46

in the hope that it was her mother and was disappointed when she realised it was only George.

He grinned. 'You slept well! This lot've been makin' a right din, not that you noticed.' He chuckled. 'Where you off to then? You know you've missed the train to Speke? I 'ad a bit of a gander to see if I could spot your mam, but there was only kids and their chaperones what got on it.'

Lizzy smiled. 'Well at least I know I've not missed her. How long till the next one?'

George looked up at the clock. 'You've got an hour. You can go back to my office and sit in there, if you like. At least that way you'll be able to hear yourself think.'

Lizzy's tummy rumbled. 'That'd be grand, but I 'aven't 'ad anythin' to eat since last night, so I think I might go and get summat.'

He plunged his hand into his pocket and drew out a handful of coins which he started to sort through with his index finger. 'I reckon I've got enough for you to buy yerself—'

Lizzy interrupted him. 'Thanks, George, but I've got me own money.'

George laughed. 'Of course. I'd forgotten about your sock purse.' He craned his neck to see over the top of the crowd and sighed impatiently. 'Sorry, luv, but this lot 'aven't got a clue what they're up to.' He cupped his hands round his mouth and shouted, 'Oi!' Two children who were walking in the wrong direction turned to face him, the taller one pointing a finger at himself. George nodded. 'Yes, you.' As he made his way towards the confused-looking pair he called back to Lizzy over his shoulder, 'Don't forget, you've only got an hour, so keep an eye on the time.'

As Lizzy made her way towards the huge arches she found herself being overtaken by a rather rotund young girl, whose curly blonde bob bounced as she marched away from the crowded platform. Another woman apologised to Lizzy as she tried to keep up.

'Please don't do this, Clara. Your father will be ever so upset.'

The girl cast a backward glance at her chaperone. 'No, he won't. It wasn't his idea for me to come here in the first place, it was that wicked witch who works for him. She's the one who insisted I be "sent away". Evil cow's only got one thing on her agenda – getting into my father's—'

Her chaperone gave a small yelp. 'Clara!'

Clara stopped in her tracks and waited for her to catch up. 'For goodness' sake, Sally, I was going to say my father's bank accounts. And you needn't worry about getting into trouble. I'll make sure they know that none of this is your fault.'

Sally looked pleadingly into Clara's eyes. 'But your father asked me to make sure you got on to the train safely. I know things are tough at home, but—'

Clara shook her head. 'But nothing. I will not let that woman weasel her way into my father's life, and I will not be packed off into the countryside so that she might have free rein.' She threw the small suitcase she was carrying on to the ground and kicked it sharply back in the direction from where she had just come before trotting down the steps, calling over her shoulder as she went, 'I'm nearly sixteen! I'm too old to be evacuated with a lot of silly little children!'

Bending down to pick up the case, which had slid to a halt in front of her, Lizzy trotted after them. 'Hang on a mo,' she called, but with so many people moving in the opposite direction she found it impossible to get through, and it was only a matter of moments before she had lost sight of them.

'Oh no you don't,' came a voice from beside her. A sharp-looking woman dressed in a dark grey suit caught hold of Lizzy's shoulder. 'I know you don't want to leave your mam ...' She hesitated, eyeing Lizzy uncertainly. The girl she had collared was around the same height as the bigger children on the platform, but there was something about her face which made her appear older than a schoolgirl. She glanced at the labelled suitcase in Lizzy's hand, and released her grip on Lizzy's shoulder to catch hold of the tag. 'Clara Granger. Let me see ...' She consulted her clipboard.

'It's not mine,' Lizzy protested, only to be ignored by the billeting officer. Lizzy frowned her annoyance. 'Look, you've got it wrong ...'

The woman stared at Lizzy over the top of her spectacles. 'That's what they all say.' She gave Lizzy a reassuring smile. 'You'll be fine once you get there. I know it's hard to say goodbye ...' She began to steer Lizzy in the direction of the train which was drawing in to the platform.

Lizzy stared at her in astonishment. 'But I'm not Clara Granger. I'm Lizzy Atherton.' She waved the case at the other woman. 'This isn't my suitcase.'

49

The billeting officer, who had dealt with more than her fair share of difficult children that morning, decided she had had enough of this girl's shenanigans. Stopping in her tracks, she arched a single brow. 'So you've stolen it?'

Lizzy dug her heels in and pulled her arm from the woman's grasp. 'No. I picked it up off the floor because this girl—'

A young woman waved at Lizzy. 'Cooee! Not to worry, I'm here now.' She trotted over to Lizzy's side and placed an arm round her shoulders. 'I only popped to the lavvy for a quick one, and by the time I came back you'd vanished.'

Lizzy and the billeting officer both stared openmouthed at the newcomer. The billeting officer was the first to find her tongue. 'Who are you?'

The young woman squinted through thick-rimmed glasses before clasping the surprised billeting officer's hand in her own and shaking it briskly. 'This is my sister. She's a shilling short of a pound if you get my meaning, so I told Mam I'd stay with her until she gets settled in her new billet.'

Lizzy was about to voice her displeasure when the billeting officer, who was staring from one to the other, appeared to reach a decision. 'Now you mention it, she does look a bit vacant.' She glanced at the other woman over the top of her glasses. 'But be more careful next time. She could've wandered on to the tracks or anything.'

Smiling, the woman claiming to be Lizzy's sister linked her arm through Lizzy's and turned towards the arches. 'Don't you worry. I promise not to leave her again, Guides' honour an' all that.'

The billeting officer nodded vaguely as she began to consult the clipboard in her hands again. 'Glad to hear it.'

Lizzy found herself being marched through the arches and down the steps, her companion hissing out of the corner of her mouth, 'Just keep walking. If she thinks we're lyin' she'll have you on that train before you can say knife.' Once clear of the station, she turned to face Lizzy and, grinning, removed her headscarf and glasses. 'Long time no see!'

Lizzy looked in astonishment at the tall, brown-eyed blonde who stood before her. 'Dolly!' she squeaked. 'How on earth did you find me?'

Dolly chuckled. 'I didn't find you, silly, I was passin' by when I seen the ruckus, so I thought I'd lend a hand.' She cast an eye over her childhood friend. 'Where'd you sleep last night? The station?'

Lizzy groaned inwardly. 'Is it that obvious?'

'Crikey, I were only jokin', but you do look a little worse for wear. How come you spent the night at the station?'

Taking a deep breath, Lizzy looked back towards the steps to the station. 'It's a long story. Have you got time for a cuppa and a slice of toast?'

Rooting around in her handbag, Dolly nodded. 'Gotcha!' Looking up she passed Lizzy a comb. 'Here, you can use this to sort that mop out. We can go to the Continental Café on Lime Street – there's a washroom in the back so you can 'ave a cat's lick and a promise in there.'

As they walked toward the café Lizzy ducked into a telephone box and surveyed her reflection in the small mirror. 'No wonder that billetin' officer believed I was a bit daft in the head.' She chuckled. 'Whatever made you say that to her?'

Dolly shrugged. 'She didn't seem keen on lettin' you go otherwise. I thought if I made you more trouble than you were worth she'd give up a bit easier, and I was right.'

Lizzy giggled. 'The look on her face! Mind you, the stuff we used to get up to, me mam allus said we was a shillin' short of a pound.'

Dolly beamed at Lizzy. 'Blimey, how long has it been?'

Lizzy looked up at the bright blue, cloud-studded sky. 'I was six when me dad died, and we moved to Hopwood Street not long after that, so ten years.'

Dolly shook her head. 'As long as that! How's your mam?'

A small bell rang out announcing their arrival as Lizzy opened the door to the café. 'First things first: I'm goin' to nip to the lavvy whilst you order us some tea and toast. It's my treat – call it a thank you for gerrin' me out of the mire.'

Dolly nodded. 'Fair do's, although I don't mind payin' me way, and ...' She hesitated.

'And what?'

'Well, I don't want to leave you short. You did sleep rough last night, so I'm guessin' things can't be goin' too well?'

Lizzy nodded. 'I'll explain everythin' when I come back.'

When she returned to the table, her shoulder-length raven curls had been carefully pinned back from her face. The waitress brought over a pot of tea for two and four rounds of thickly buttered toast, and as they ate Lizzy told Dolly all about Albert and his foul temper.

Dolly grimaced. 'I allus did wonder what become of you and your mam, but I never thought it'd be summat this bad.' Pushing the cups to one side, she leaned her elbows on the table. 'So what're you goin' to do now?'

'Catch the next train to Speke.'

'And what if your mam's not there?'

Lizzy shrugged. 'Dunno. Go back to Snowdrop Street, I s'pose, and see what's what.'

'Not on yer own you're not. Thank goodness it's my day off.'

Lizzy shook her head. 'I can't ask you to waste your day off traipsin' round on what could turn out to be a wild goose chase.'

Dolly snorted her disapproval. 'If you think I'm goin' to let you wander round on yer own knowin' that maniac's out there, then you're wrong.' She nodded towards the suitcase that sat on the floor between them. 'And what are we going to do with that?'

Lizzy took a deep breath then blew her cheeks out. 'Darned if I know. I can't see an address, so ...'

Dolly placed the suitcase on the table and pushed the buttons. There was a clicking noise and the lid of the suitcase flipped open. To Lizzy's surprise, Dolly fished out a piece of paper and turned it round to show Lizzy. 'Me mam allus used to put a piece of paper with our names and addresses inside ours, in case we lost 'em. Looks like her mam had the same idea.'

Lizzy pointed at the address. 'Ullet Road. It's posh round there, so no wonder she didn't want to be

53

evacuated. I wouldn't either; the houses are beautiful. I bet her family are worth a bob or two.'

Dolly placed the paper back in the suitcase. 'Tell you what, how about we go and see your auntie Cissy in Speke? If your mam's there, I'll get the train back and drop this off at this ...' she looked at the name written on the tag, 'Clara's. Whereabouts does your great-aunt live? My nana used to live in a flat above a hair-dresser's in Church Road.'

Lizzy opened her mouth to reply, then shut it again. She looked at Dolly through rounding eyes. 'I don't know! I was only a kid the last time I went there.'

'You must have some idea, surely?'

Lizzy shrugged. 'I think it was close to a bridge, but I wouldn't like to say for certain.' She nodded her head in a positive fashion. 'I'm sure I'll remember the way once I get there.'

Standing up, Dolly smoothed down her skirt before picking up the suitcase. 'Come on then, chuck. Looks like we've gorra long day ahead of us.'

Outside the café, Lizzy linked her arm through Dolly's. 'Aren't I just glad you recognised me, Dolly Clifton.'

Hearing the taxi sound its horn, Albert hurried to the front door. He checked his reflection in the mirror and wiped a smut of soot from his cheek before picking up his small suitcase. Closing the front door firmly behind him, he posted the key back through the letterbox and took a seat in the back of the cab.

As the taxi began to draw away from the kerb, he saw Martha Williams peering at him from across the street. Holding up his suitcase to obscure her view, he tutted under his breath. Trust that old bat to come nosing, he thought bitterly. The last thing he needed was her blabbing to all and sundry.

He cast his mind back over everything that had happened since he returned to Snowdrop Street in the small hours of the morning.

After remembering he had given his address to the nosy scuffer, Albert decided it would be better all round if he left Snowdrop Street and headed for pastures new. In the meantime he would gather all of Mary's and Lizzy's belongings, including any documents they might have, and burn them in the kitchen stove, along with his own marriage certificate. When he had watched the first lot take light, he put a pan of water on the stove to boil and ran upstairs to pack his own possessions. That done, he returned to the stove, removed the pan and headed into the back yard where he scrubbed the blood off the cobbles – fortunately there was not a lot of it. Once satisfied that every trace had been removed, he headed back into the house and pulled up a chair in front of the stove, where he added the rest of his wife and stepdaughter's belongings piece by piece. He waited until the whole lot had burnt to naught but remains before emptying the ashes into the dustbin.

Now, as he sat in the back of the cab, he ran through his plan once more. If anyone asked where Lizzy and her mother were, he would say they had robbed him blind before doing a moonlight flit, taking all their possessions, as well as his, with them.

He shuddered as a picture of Mary's body curled up in the crate entered his mind. Wiping the sweat off his palms on to his trousers, he reassured himself with the facts. By the time anyone found Mary they would assume she had suffocated trying to stow away, and any bruising could be explained by the movement of the ship and the carrying of the crate to its destination.

He glanced back in the direction of Mrs Williams. Perhaps her seeing his departure wouldn't be a bad thing. She would undoubtedly tell people that she had seen him going off in a cab on his own, but where was the harm in that? Especially if he was going to tell folk that Mary and her brat of a child had left him high and dry. If anything it would confirm his story. Safe in the thought that he was in the clear, Albert relaxed as the cab trundled its way towards the docks.

Chapter Three

'Clara! What on earth are you doing back here?' With no answer coming from his daughter, Arthur Granger looked past her to where Sally – the maid who had accompanied Clara to Lime Street Station – leaned against the door as she tried to catch her breath. 'Sally? What happened?'

Sally rolled her eyes. 'She said she didn't want to go and by God she meant it. Who knew she could run so fast?'

Arthur's face was a mixture of amusement and disappointment. He held out a hand to his daughter. 'Your mother was always good at running. Got a few trophies for it in school, as I recall.' He led Clara into the study, calling over his shoulder as he did so, 'I think you've earned yourself a bit of a break, Sally. You can tell Mrs Hackney that I've given you the rest of the morning off ... oh, and I think it's probably best if you tell her why.'

Sally's knees attempted a bob, but finding that her legs had no wish to support her body weight, she quit whilst she was still upright.

In the study, Arthur sat Clara down in the Chesterfield chair in front of his desk and pushed the green reading lamp to one side so that he could sit down on the corner. Leaning forward, he wagged a reproving finger. 'You're a bit old to be running away, Clara.'

'That's my point entirely,' she said, folding her arms across her chest. 'I'm too old to be sent away. I'll be sixteen soon and that means I can join up if I want, with your permission, of course.' She raised her brows fleetingly. 'Although I'm certain there're plenty of girls out there who lie about their age.'

He raised a warning finger. 'Let's not be making threats. You're in enough trouble as it is.' Looking into his daughter's large blue eyes – identical to her mother's – as they began to well up, he mellowed. 'On the other hand, if you're only going to keep running away, maybe it would be best if you did stay here.' He glanced at the grandfather clock which stood against the wall by the door. 'I've got to go and see a couple of clients, but I'll be back in an hour or so. Try not to cause any trouble whilst I'm gone.'

Clara grinned. 'Don't worry, I'll keep well out of their way.'

There was a brief knock on the study door, and before Arthur could bid the newcomer to enter the door opened and Gertrude stood before them. Her eyes narrowed as they met Clara's. 'I've spoken to Sally.'

Arthur nodded. 'There's been a change of plan. It looks as if Clara will be seeing the war out – if there is a war – at Bellevue. Now if you'll excuse me, I'm already late.' Taking his coat and hat from the clothes stand beside the door, he left the room.

Gertrude's eyes flickered in the direction of the stairs. 'I'd better tell Ivy.' She had started to leave the study when Clara called her back.

'Why? What's it got to do with her?'

Gertrude glanced nervously at the ceiling. There was a distinct noise coming from the room above, as though someone was walking across the floor, dragging something heavy behind them.

Clara leapt to her feet. 'Who's in my room?' she demanded, although she was pretty sure she knew the answer.

Gertrude closed the study door and leaned against it, attempting an innocent smile. 'I told her to make sure it was tidy for when you came home.'

Clara strode towards her. 'Excuse me,' she said, her voice steady but her eyes flashing with anger.

'Why? What are you going to do? You can't blame Ivy: she didn't know you would be coming back before she had a chance to—'

'Move!'

Gertrude tried to think of something to say, but it was too late. Clara had reached behind her and heaved the door open, forcing the startled housekeeper to shuffle quickly forward, gabbling excuses as she came. 'Where's your manners? You only had to ask. You could've said excuse me ...'

'I did,' said Clara levelly, pushing past her and heading for the stairs. Behind her she could hear Gertrude shouting, in a voice that could only be intended as a warning to her daughter, 'Clara dear, Ivy's only tidying your room.'

Whilst not obese, Clara was certainly larger than she should have been, yet she ascended the stairs like a panther. As she crept noiselessly towards her bedroom, the door of which was ajar, Clara could see that Ivy was standing in front of her chest of drawers. The drawers were open and the other girl, who had obviously not heard her mother's warning, was emptying them on to the bed. Clara's suspicions were confirmed when she saw that Ivy had pulled her own trunk up next to the chest of drawers. She was so engrossed in her work that she hadn't noticed Clara enter the room.

Folding her arms across her chest, Clara said icily, 'What the hell are you doing in my room? And what is that doing in here?' She pointed toward Ivy's trunk.

Ivy jumped. Spinning round, she stared at Clara, her cheeks flushing red and her small brown eyes growing wider than Clara would have thought possible. 'I – I ...'

As she floundered for a suitable answer Gertrude entered the room, holding on to the door for support. Her face, which was normally white, was flushed from racing up the stairs. 'Ivy, what a good girl you are. I see you've already started tidying Clara's drawers for her,' she panted.

Clara pointed angrily at the trunk. 'If you're tidying my drawers why do you need that?'

Ivy looked towards her mother for help. 'Because ... because ...' she began before Gertrude came to her rescue again.

'Because I told her she needed something to stand on so that she could see the very top of your wardrobe.

We wanted to make sure Sally had been dusting properly.'

Clara glanced wordlessly at the chair which stood beside her dressing table.

Gertrude followed her gaze, and Clara noticed the colour begin to fade from her cheeks. 'Oh … silly me. I didn't think. Although it doesn't look very stable …'

'Get out!' said Clara, her tone firm.

'I'll just put these clothes …' Ivy began, but seeing the expression on Clara's face she changed her mind. 'If you don't mind putting them back in yourself …' Clutching the handle of her trunk she began to drag it out of the room.

Clara watched her accusingly. 'Bit heavy for an empty trunk, isn't it? After all, you must have unpacked all your things a long time ago.'

Gertrude trotted across the floor and grasped the handle on the other side of the trunk. 'It's our Ivy's chest. She's very frail, you know; gets a lot of asthma.'

'First I've heard,' said Clara, adding, 'Mind your nails, Gertrude. You wouldn't want one of them to break.' As the two women carried the trunk past her she said casually, 'I've always found it amazing the way your nails are always in such pristine condition. My mother never had long nails like yours.'

Gertrude stopped just short of the door, causing Ivy to protest. Ignoring her daughter, the housekeeper spoke to Clara over her shoulder. 'That's because your mother didn't know her place.'

Clara's hands balled into fists. 'Oh yes she did. It was by my father's side, somewhere you'll never be, not if I have my way.' She began to follow them out of the room. 'What were you plannin' to tell my father? Did you not think he'd notice that Ivy had moved into my room, or did you think he'd not care?'

She saw Gertrude's back tense as the words left her mouth, but the older woman continued to walk away, saying loudly as she did so, 'Your father trusts me. He knows I have the family's best interest at heart, and if I told him it makes more sense for Ivy to be in another room I doubt he'd even question me. Come along, Ivy. We'd best get this back into your old room.'

Clara shook her head. So it was true: Gertrude had intended to move her daughter into Clara's room. She closed the door firmly behind them and turned the key in the lock. Crossing the room, she began to fold her clothes neatly before placing them back in the drawers. 'Gertrude really is trying to take the place of my mother,' Clara muttered to herself. 'And that dreadful Ivy is trying to take mine. I knew that was why they wanted me to be evacuated; they couldn't give two hoots about my safety.' She looked out of her bedroom window on to the neatly mown lawn below, to the spot near the sundial where she and her mother had spent many a happy hour putting the world to rights whilst having a picnic lunch.

As she put away the last of her clothes she decided it might be a good idea to go and sit in the garden for a bit whilst she tried to come up with a plan to get rid of the dreadful Hackneys. It was unfortunate that her father had been out of the house when Clara had uncovered their conniving ways. If he had been at home he would have witnessed for himself that the two were up to no good, but as things stood it would be Clara's word against theirs, and whilst they might not be very good at cleaning, they were both dab hands when it came to manipulating the truth to suit themselves. Clara sighed. It was going to be tough fighting the two of them on her own, but she had no choice. If she wanted Bellevue to return to the happy home it once was she would have to get rid of the pair of them, one way or another.

Lizzy stood at the top of Byron Street, her face a picture of uncertainty as Dolly encouraged her to 'take a good look'.

'I'm sorry, Dolly, but none of this looks familiar.'

Dolly gave her a determined smile of encouragement. 'Tell you what, let's ask in the corner shop. It's quite a close-knit community round here; I'm sure someone will know your great-aunt.'

Lizzy shrugged. 'Anything's worth a shot.'

When the pair entered the shop a small, squat man appeared behind the counter. He had a chequered tea towel tucked into the collar of his shirt and he was wiping the crumbs from his moustache as he smiled warmly at the two women.

'Afternoon, ladies. How can I help?'

Lizzy smiled hopefully at him. 'We're looking for my great-aunt Cissy – Cecilia Wardell – but I can't remember her address. Do you know her?'

The man's smile faded from his lips. 'If you don't mind my askin', who are you, and what do you want her for?'

Lizzy and Dolly exchanged glances. 'I'm her great-niece, but I've not seen her since I was a kid.'

The man took the tea towel from around his neck and slung it over his shoulder. 'Hang on a mo, I'll just fetch the wife. She's better at these things than me.' He disappeared from view and they could hear a whispered but heated discussion taking place in the room behind the counter.

After a moment or two a woman appeared. Placing her hands palm side down on the counter and leaning her body weight on to them, she glanced shyly at the two girls. 'Which one of you is Mrs Wardell's great-niece?'

Lizzy held up a hand.

The woman smiled awkwardly. 'Sorry, luv, but your great-aunt passed away at least two years back, if not more. It's been a while at any rate.'

Lizzy's shoulders sagged. 'Oh, heck. Mam did say it'd been a long time and anything could've happened, but I never really thought ... I'm sorry to've bothered you.'

The woman wiped her hands on her apron. 'No bother, chuck. And I'm sorry about your great-aunt – she were quite a character.'

As they left, Dolly smiled sympathetically at Lizzy. 'Best we get back to Liverpool. You can come back to my flat – it's above the hardware shop in Pickwick Street. We can have a cuppa and a bite to eat whilst we work out what to do next.'

'I am sorry, Doll, but I did warn you it might turn out to be a wild goose chase.'

Dolly shrugged. 'I had nothin' better to do. Besides, if I can't help an old friend in hard times I ain't much of a pal, am I?'

A short time later outside the hardware shop in Pickwick Street, Dolly pointed to a small alley which ran down the side of the shop. 'The entrance is down 'ere.'

Lizzy peered down the dark alley. She hadn't really stopped to imagine where Dolly might live, but she supposed she had thought it would be somewhere a little bigger than this. Not wishing to appear rude, she smiled at Dolly, who chuckled at her expression.

'Don't worry. I know it doesn't look much from the outside, but it's cheap, dry and the landlord owns the shop below so I never get any bother.' She stopped outside a narrow door and fumbled in her bag for the key. 'Gotcha!' Turning the key in the lock, she ushered Lizzy up a steep flight of steps, at the top of which was another door that led into a large sunlit room. Dolly hung her coat and bag up on a hook behind the door and turned to Lizzy. 'Ready for the grand tour?' Lizzy nodded.

Without moving, Dolly pointed to the far side of the room where a table and four chairs stood beside a small stove next to a Belfast sink and a compact set of cupboards. 'Kitchen, dining room.' She indicated a small sofa by the window: 'Living room.' Finally, she led the way through a half-opened doorway. 'My bedroom, and if you want the lavvy it's back down the stairs and into the yard. I share with the fellers from the shop.'

Lizzy cast an eye around the bedroom, which was bigger than the kitchen, dining room and living area put together. In one corner sat a small metal-framed bed much like the one Lizzy had slept in at Sun Street. Opposite was a large chest of drawers and a wardrobe with a half-length mirror in one of the panels. She

65

followed Dolly back into the living room. 'Where does your mam sleep?'

Dolly shook her head darkly. 'Not here, that's for sure. This place is all mine.'

'Gosh! I thought you still lived with your mam. Doesn't she mind you livin' on your own? Mine'd have a pink fit!'

Dolly gave a short, mirthless chuckle. 'I'll tell you about that another time.' She gestured for Lizzy to take a seat by the table. 'Right now we've got to work out how we're going to get your mam away from Albert, assuming she hasn't left already.' She filled the kettle and placed it on the stove before turning back to face Lizzy and eyeing her shrewdly. 'You said she left the 'ouse not long after you, but 'ow can you be certain? Surely she would've run after you and that Albert?'

Lizzy thought about this for a moment. 'But she must have left because Albert come after me, so there was nothin' to stop her ... oh.'

Dolly took two cups from the Welsh dresser. 'Uh-oh. That "oh" didn't sound good.'

Lizzy grimaced. 'I assumed he'd come straight after me, but their bedroom door has a lock, so I suppose he could have locked her in.'

'Oh, heck ... d'you reckon she might still be there?'

Lizzy shrugged. 'God knows. Nothin' would surprise me, not after seein' the way he was last night.'

Dolly scooped some tea into a dark brown earthenware teapot with three large yellowing lilies painted on the side of it. 'Some men think the only way they can keep a woman is with threats and violence.' She

66

shook her head disapprovingly. 'Lockin' her up indeed. How's that meant to make someone want to stay with you?' The kettle began to whistle as the steam escaped the spout. 'One thing's for sure,' she went on, as she grasped the handle of the kettle in a folded tea towel, 'you can't go back there, else 'e'll 'ave you too.' Carefully, she poured the boiling water into the teapot and put the kettle back on the stove before stirring the tea and replacing the lid. 'I, on the other hand, can.'

Lizzy opened her mouth to object, but Dolly continued before she could speak. 'Don't go sayin' as 'ow I've done enough already, or it's too dangerous, because I shan't be listenin'.' She produced a small tea strainer and placed it over the top of one of the cups. 'Albert don't know me from Adam so he won't get suspicious. I'll call in on our way to Ullet Road and see how the land lies whilst you wait nearby.'

Lizzy held her hands out to receive the cup of tea. 'As long as you're sure … I can wait at the end of the road, but if he suspects anythin's up, promise me you'll leave.'

Dolly held up her right hand. 'Guides' honour.'

Lizzy broke into giggles. 'Don't tell me you were a Guide 'cos I shan't believe you. I seem to remember you kickin' up a fuss when your mam tried to mek you go to Brownies.'

'You're right there! Now how about a nice bit of cheese on toast?'

Mary tried to open her eyes but all she could see was darkness. She could hear the sound of male voices close by, each man shouting as he tried to make himself heard over the one next to him. She tried to make sense of the conversation but it was impossible with them all talking over one another. She wondered where she was and why no one seemed to be able to see her. After all, she could hear some of the men as clearly as though they were standing right next to her, but for some reason they all seemed to ignore the fact that she was there. Perhaps if I move they'll notice me, she thought. She concentrated all her might on trying to raise her head, but it was impossible. Pain shot through her back at the slightest attempt at movement, and her body seemed to have been stripped of any strength. As she lay in the dark she could hear two men talking as they drew nearer and nearer. She was beginning to fear they would stand on her by accident when their voices suddenly switched from approaching to above her, as though they were standing on something tall. She listened to their conversation.

'They reckon war's a certainty and I reckon they're right, but what will it mean for us, that's what I'd like to know,' said one of the men.

'Floatin' mines, U-boats, planes droppin' bombs … I'm guessin' we won't be able to follow the normal routes an' they'll want us to go round, but like I said, I'm only guessin',' replied the other.

Desperate to gain their attention, Mary opened her mouth to scream, to shout, to whisper, anything, as long as they noticed her, but her mouth was so dry that she found herself unable to make even the smallest sound.

'Captain's watchin'. Best gerra move on, 'cos war or no war he'll still want everythin' shipshape.' The speaker grunted loudly as he jumped down off the ledge above Mary.

'Come back!' shouted the voice inside her head. To her it was loud, but of course no one else could hear her thoughts. She opened her mouth once more but it was no use, she couldn't make a sound. Closing her eyes, she drifted into a world where only dreams existed.

As the girls turned into Snowdrop Street Lizzy pointed to the far end. 'Number 35,' she said.

Dolly nodded. 'I'll give 'em a knock, an' if no one comes I'll give you the thumbs up.'

Lizzy watched the other girl walk to the front door and rap her knuckles against the wood. The wait seemed endless, but at last Dolly turned and beckoned and Lizzy trotted up the road to join her, hissing, 'Shove your hand through the letterbox and see if there's a key on a piece of string.'

Dolly grinned as she pulled out a length of string complete with key. 'I feel like one of them spies out of the movies, creepin' around and rescuin' the damsel in distress,' she hissed to Lizzy, who was looking nervously up and down the street. 'Where'd you want to start?'

Placing a finger to her lips, Lizzy walked through the door Dolly was holding open and trod silently up the stairs. Once at the top, she gave the handle to her mother's bedroom door an experimental twist and to her relief it opened easily. Standing back, she gently pushed the wood with her fingertips.

Dolly peered into the empty room. 'They don't have much stuff, do they?' Crossing the floor in a couple of strides, she opened the wardrobe door. 'Don't your mam have no clothes?'

'Course she does, but they've all gone. She must've taken them with her when she went,' said Lizzy, pulling open the drawers in her mother's chest and seeing they were also empty. 'Looks like Albert's done a moonlight flit an' all.'

'Where's all your stuff?'

Lizzy walked across the hall to her bedroom and looked in the small tallboy she used as her wardrobe. 'My stuff's gone too. That's odd.'

Dolly shrugged. 'Mebbe your mam took it with her, either that or I 'spect Albert's takken it outta spite, just to mek life a bit 'arder for you.' She pointed to something peeping out from behind the tallboy. 'What's that?'

Lizzy looked down to where Dolly was pointing. 'I dunno, hang on a mo ...' She carefully slid her forefinger over the top of the object and pulled it into view. 'Good God, it's an old Christmas decoration I made when I were a kid. I didn't know we still had it.' Sitting down beside Dolly, she un-creased the points of the glittery star. 'I made this in school the day me dad died. It was meant to go on top of the tree ...'

'I remember the day your dad died,' said Dolly. 'Me mam picked me up from school and said I wasn't to go round to yours 'cos summat awful 'ad 'appened. I kept askin' her what but she wouldn't say.' She curled her fingers round Lizzy's. 'I liked your dad. He were allus smilin' and he made me feel grown-up 'cos he called me pint-sized.'

Lizzy smoothed the star out with her fingers. 'I'd for-gotten that.' She smiled up at Dolly. 'He called you pint-sized 'cos you were taller than me.'

'And a whole year older.' Dolly chuckled. 'You must miss 'im a lot.' She glanced at the star. 'Lucky I saw it.'

Lizzy shook her head. 'I dunno about that. As far as I'm concerned Christmas brings nowt but bad luck, especially stars.'

A voice called up from the hallway below. 'Coo-ee!'

'Mam?' shouted Lizzy, jumping to her feet and run-ning to the top of the stairs. 'Oh, it's you, Mrs Williams. Have you seen me mam?'

Mrs Williams smiled a toothy greeting. ''Allo, Lizzy. Ain't you gone with 'em, then?'

Lizzy shook her head. 'Do you know where they've gone?'

Mrs Williams stared at her incredulously. 'You mean you don't know either?'

Blushing, Lizzy shook her head once more.

Mrs Williams tutted her disapproval. 'Fancy goin' off and not even tellin' your kid where you're at. Bloomin' disgustin', that is.' She smiled kindly at Lizzy. 'I'm afraid I don't know where they've gone, but I did see 'em gettin' in a taxi.' She nodded at the object Lizzy had left on the hall floor. 'I see you've got your suitcase. Have you got somewhere to stay? Only I dare say you couldn't afford an 'ouse this big on yer own.'

'It's not my suitcase.' She looked earnestly into the older woman's deeply wrinkled face. 'How did me mam look? Was she upset, you know, cryin' an' that?'

Mrs Williams shrugged. 'I must admit I didn't really see yer mam. That bugger 'eld up 'is suitcase so I couldn't have a proper nosy.'

Lizzy smiled weakly at Dolly. 'What do I do now? No forwarding address and not a clue as to where they went.'

Dolly placed a comforting arm round Lizzy's shoulders. 'There's gorra be some way we can find 'em. Did your mam have a job? We could call in there, see if they know anything.'

'Dolly, you're an absolute gem! Why didn't I think of that? She works at Beaslers Bakers on the Scottie Road. I'll go there and see if they've heard owt.' Descending the stairs, she smiled at her neighbour. 'If you should see me mam, can you tell her I came lookin'?'

''Course I will, chuck, although I still think it's a disgrace she went off wi'out tellin' her own flesh and blood where she were goin'.'

Lizzy smiled wryly. 'I think she probably had no choice. Albert chucked me out last night and said I weren't to come back. He's obviously taken me mam off so I can't gerrin touch with 'er.'

'Ah.' The old woman nodded wisely, 'Two's company an' all that.' She squeezed Lizzy's hand. 'Try not to take it personal; I don't reckon he were cut out to be a family man.'

Lizzy gave a mirthless chuckle. 'You're right there!' She turned to Dolly. 'You know you said I could stay ...?'

Dolly raised her eyebrows. 'And I meant it. You're welcome to come for as long as you like. It'll be grand to have a bit o' company.' She turned to Mrs Williams.

'If you see Mary, tell her Lizzy's stayin' wi' me at 52a Pickwick Street.' She held out a hand. 'I'm Dolly, by the way, an old friend of the family.'

Mrs Williams shook Dolly's hand. 'Nice to meet you, Dolly. Lizzy's lucky 'avin' a pal like you lookin' out for her.'

Lizzy nodded. 'I am that. I just hope I can find me mam.'

Mrs Williams nodded. 'You will. She's bound to've gone to work.' Turning to go back to her own house, she added over her shoulder, 'It'll all come out in the wash, just you wait and see. It allus does.'

As soon as the girls reached the bakery where Mary worked, Lizzy was hailed by one of the women who worked with Mary. 'Lizzy! Where's your mam? Mr Escott's not a happy man!'

Lizzy's shoulders sagged. 'Oh, heck. Don't tell me she ain't showed up for work, Mabel.'

Mabel shook her head. ''As summat 'appened?'

Lizzy nodded. 'That bloody Albert's gone an' taken me mam off somewhere so I can't live with 'em no more.'

Mabel pulled a face. 'Doesn't surprise me. Mary said he were bein' a right pain in the neck, allus bangin' on about two's company an' all that.' She eyed Lizzy shyly. 'Reckon that's where a couple of her shiners come from too, not that I ever liked to ask, of course.'

Lizzy nodded grimly. 'Can you do me a favour?'

Mabel smiled. 'Course I can.'

'If she turns up can you tell her I'm stayin' at 52a Pickwick Street with Dolly Clifton?'

Mabel's brow creased. 'You said "if" she turns up ... does that mean you think she might've quit? Only Mr Escott won't be pleased if he thinks one of his best workers has upped and left without so much as a by your leave.'

Lizzy sighed. 'Your guess is as good as mine, but I reckon Albert might even've left the city. He's a docker so he can go anywhere, and 'e was as mad as fire last night. If I'm honest I wouldn't put anythin' past him.'

Mabel wagged a reproving finger. 'I told Mary he was a wrong 'un, but would she listen?'

'Well she knows now. He got into a real rage wi' me last night, 'cos he found me and Mam plottin' to leave him.'

Mabel's brow shot towards her hairline. 'From what I 'ear you're lucky you got away from 'im in one piece.'

'I'm faster than him, but he must've locked me mam in the bedroom 'cos she never got away. We've been back there today and all their stuff's gone, and mine too.'

Mabel shook her head. 'Crafty git.' Casting an eye round, she slipped Lizzy a couple of iced buns with a wink. 'Get these down yer, and if your mam does come in I'll be sure to tell her where you're at, then you'll both be free of the bugger.'

Lizzy fumbled in her pocket, but Mabel shook her head. 'They're on the 'ouse. If anyone asks I'll say I dropped 'em on the floor.'

Lizzy smiled gratefully. 'Thanks, Mabel. It's good to know me mam's got friends like you.'

Sitting on the lawn beside the sundial, Clara twiddled the key to her bedroom between her fingers, muttering beneath her breath as she did so. 'What's Dad doing? He can't seriously think that dreadful woman could take the place of my mother—' She stopped short as she heard the squeak of the iron gate which separated the garden path from the pavement. Clara craned her neck to see who was coming to Bellevue. She knew it couldn't be the postman, because he'd already been. She shuffled round to watch as two young women came through the gate and one of them, a tall girl with blonde hair, closed it behind them. Clara eyed them suspiciously when she noticed that the one with the raven hair was holding her suitcase.

Wiping her eyes on the backs of her hands she stood up and pointed an accusing finger at the suitcase. 'That's mine!' she said, her voice nasal from crying. 'If you've come to try and make me leave you can forget it. My father says I can stay no matter what that dreadful woman says.'

Lizzy looked from the suitcase to the house then back to Clara. 'I think you've got the wrong end of the stick. You see, I was on the platform when you …' she hesitated, 'dropped this.' She held the suitcase towards Clara. 'Have we come at a bad time?'

Clara looked back at the house and fresh tears formed in her eyes. 'There's never a good time, not any more, but if I have my way that'll soon be a thing of the past.' She took the suitcase from Lizzy. 'Thanks for this. I must have looked like a right spoiled brat, but I'm not, you know.'

Lizzy glanced towards Bellevue. 'I gather you weren't keen on being evacuated, and I must say I can see why.'

Clara shook her head. 'I don't mind leaving the house, I just don't want to leave it in the wrong hands.'

Dolly frowned. 'Whatever do you mean?'

'It doesn't matter. The last thing you need is me lumbering you with my problems.'

Dolly glanced at Lizzy. 'A problem shared, an' all that. Besides, we're not in any rush.' She held out a hand to Clara. 'I'm Dolly and this is Lizzy. We know you're Clara, of course, because of the suitcase.'

Smiling, Clara shook both girls by the hand before leading them to a wooden bench, talking as she went. 'To cut a long story short, my mother died unexpectedly from a brain aneurysm in June ...' Clara went on to explain the arrival of the Hackneys, finishing with: 'I'm the only one standing in the way of her plan to trap my father, so she won't stop trying till she's got rid of me, but there's no way I'm just going to roll over. Would you?'

Lizzy shook her head. 'No fear. I think she sounds perfectly horrid. I'm surprised your father can't see through her, 'cos he sounds like an intelligent man.'

'He is, but not when it comes to her. For some reason he just can't see how manipulating and calculating she really is. Take the time I pointed out that if I were being evacuated so should her daughter.' Clara shook her head in disbelief. 'She turns round and says Ivy can't go because of her hay fever! How ridiculous is that? Anyone could see it didn't make sense, but not my dad, he agreed with her.'

Dolly nodded. 'I'm afraid that's men for you. Quite often they don't see past the paint and perfume.'

'So what do I do?'

Lizzy pulled a face. 'I don't see that there's anything you can do, except hope your father comes to his senses.'

'You mentioned you had a brother. Can't he help?' said Dolly.

Clara shook her head. 'He's in Plymouth with the Navy.'

'Is there no one else you can talk to?'

'No, and I daren't involve the staff because they could lose their jobs.'

Dolly pulled a piece of paper from her coat pocket and scribbled something on the back of it before handing it to Clara. 'This is our address. If you ever need a shoulder to cry on, you're allus welcome.'

Taking the piece of paper, Clara said gratefully, 'That's awfully kind of you, but I wouldn't want to be a burden.'

Dolly snorted. 'Don't be daft! Besides, you've already said you've no one to talk to.' She nodded towards Lizzy. 'Between the three of us we've more than our fair share of woes, and it's good to talk things through.'

Lizzy smiled. 'I must admit I don't know where I'd be if it weren't for Dolly, and I'd hate to think of anyone else going through hard times on their own.'

Tucking the piece of paper into her pocket, Clara smiled. 'Thanks for this. It's nice to know I've got someone on my side.'

As they made their way back to the flat on Pickwick Street, Lizzy turned to Dolly. 'D'you remember Charlie Jackson?' she asked.

Dolly giggled. 'Cheeky Charlie? Course I do. Why?'

'Believe it or not, he's a scuffer, and it was him what chased Albert off last night.' She paused outside a large building. 'An' this is where he works.'

Dolly blinked. '*Our* Charlie? The same one what done your pigtails, and stuck pins in your chair?'

Lizzy nodded. 'I know, you'd never believe such a little terror could become a scuffer, would you?'

Dolly frowned. 'Blimey, I allus thought he'd be the sort who'd end up gerrin' nicked. It never entered me 'ead he might become one of the nickers.'

Lizzy giggled. 'I was as surprised as you are, but he had the uniform an' everythin'.'

'Do you reckon he's on duty? It'd be good to catch up wi' him again, and you never know your luck, he might know summat about your mam.'

Lizzy nodded. 'Good idea. He did say I could call in any time.'

Entering the small, musty-smelling station, the two women approached the desk where a large sergeant with a walrus moustache leaned against the other side of a tall counter. Nodding to the girls, he stood up straight. 'Afternoon, ladies, what can I do for you?'

Lizzy smiled. 'I'm Lizzy Atherton, and this is Dolly Clifton. We're looking for PC Charlie Jackson. Is he here?'

The sergeant turned his head from side to side before glancing under the counter. 'Can't see him. Will I do?'

'I'm lookin' for my mother,' Lizzy began.

'You'll not find her here, unless she's been nicked, of course,' he said with a chuckle.

Lizzy giggled. 'No, she's not been "nicked". Kidnapped yes, nicked no.'

He raised a questioning brow. ''Oo kidnapped her?'
'Her new husband.'

His brow rose further still. 'Her 'usband, you say ...
is that even possible, to kidnap your own wife, I mean?'

'When she's trying to run away from you because
you've a nasty temper then yes, I would say it is possible to kidnap your own wife.'

The sergeant eyed Lizzy with uncertainty. 'And 'ow
d'you know she's been kidnapped and not stepped out
to do some shoppin'?'

This, Lizzy thought, was where she would be able to
prove her mother had been kidnapped. 'Last night she
was making plans with me to run away from him, 'cos
he'd threatened to chuck me out, an' this mornin' when
I come back the 'ouse was empty, save for this.' She
pulled the star from her pocket and laid it on the
counter.

He rubbed his chin thoughtfully. 'Let me get this
right. Your stepfather gave your mam an ultimatum?
You or him?'

Lizzy nodded eagerly.

'So she chose him?'

'What? No! I told you, we were makin' plans to run
away when he come in. He was furious and chased me
as far as Lime Street Station, where I met Charlie – I
mean PC Jackson.' She peered through the open door
of the office behind the counter. 'If you could just ask
PC Jackson, he'd vouch for me. He even said I should
come and see him if I needed help.'

The sergeant nodded knowingly. 'So you've really
come to see Charlie ...' he gave a small sarcastic cough,
'I mean PC Jackson.'

Lizzy scowled. 'It's not like that. I've come to see if anyone can help me find me mam. Are you sure he isn't here?'

The sergeant looked up sharply. His temper was beginning to wane; he hated working the front counter, but they were short-staffed so he had no choice. 'Course I'm sure. Unless you think I'm lyin', that is?'

'No, it's just—' Lizzy began, only to be interrupted once more.

'I take it you've proof she was taken against her will?' he said, folding his arms across his chest. He'd decided to put an end to the silly girl's antics. 'After all, if she were that scared I dare say she'd've put up a fair old fight. Someone must've seen or heard summat, and I bet the house looks a shambles, what with all the broken windows and smashed crockery.'

Lizzy stamped her foot impatiently. 'Of course it doesn't! But only 'cos she'd've been too scared to struggle!'

The sergeant pulled a disbelieving face. 'Don't sound like a kidnappin' from what you've told me. More like they've buggered off without tellin' you first.'

Lizzy gaped at him. 'You 'aven't listened to a word I've said, 'ave you? I told you, he was angry because he heard me tryin' to persuade Mam to leave him. There's no way ...'

He placed his hands palm side down on the counter. 'So your mam didn't want to leave? You were havin' to persuade her?'

Lizzy's mouth opened and closed but no words came out. She knew how ridiculous it all sounded, knew too that she was beginning to sound like a petulant child.

Heaving a sigh, the sergeant pointed to the queue that was forming behind her. 'As you can see, miss, I'm a very busy man. If you ask me, your mam and 'er new 'ubby've done one in order to be on their own, and there's folks here what want to report a real crime, so if you don't mind ...'

Lizzy slapped her hand on the counter. 'But mine's a real crime, you're just too thick to see it.' She knew as soon as the words left her mouth that she had said too much, especially when she heard the sharp intake of breath from the woman in the queue behind her.

Pointing towards the door, the sergeant spoke through pursed lips. 'I have your details; if anything comes up I shall be sure to let you know.' He averted his gaze to the woman who had gasped. 'Next!'

Dolly laid a hand on Lizzy's elbow and led her out of the police station. 'Come on, chuck. I think we've out-stayed our welcome.'

'He didn't take me seriously,' said Lizzy miserably as they stepped on to the pavement, 'and what's more I don't blame him. I know the truth and even I didn't think it sounded plausible.'

Dolly gave a reassuring smile. 'I'm sure summat you said will've sunk in, and if anythin' gets reported you'll be the first to know. It's been ever such a long day, and I think it's best all round if we go home. I've got plenty of bread and a couple of tins of beans, so we can have beans on toast for us teas.'

'Thanks, Doll. You've put up with an awful lot from me today. You're a real pal,' said Lizzy, who felt as though Dolly were the only friend she had in the world. 'How long have you been livin' on your own?

I bet it's a lot more expensive than payin' keep to your mam.'

Dolly pulled a face. 'It is, but me mam's new 'usband's a real letch, and quite frankly I'd rather be on me own with bills to pay than live with them.'

'What's a letch?'

Dolly thought about this for a moment before answering. 'You know when you walk past a group of dockers and they start shoutin' and whistlin', and starin' at you in a way that makes you want to slap them?'

Nodding, Lizzy giggled.

'That's a letch. Seein' 'im fawn over other women was bad enough, but when he started turnin' his sleazy eyes on me ...' She shuddered. 'He was allus puttin' his 'and on me shoulder or round me waist, and when I told him to sod off he'd just laugh an' say I were over-reactin' or bein' silly and that he was just tryin' to be friendly.' Dolly tutted under her breath. 'We were sittin' in the parlour one evenin' when he tried to slide 'is 'and up my skirt.'

'Did you scream?' said Lizzy, looking horrified.

'No, I give him a good hard slap across the chops.' She shook her head. 'Me mam burst into the room and demanded to know what was goin' on, an' before I could utter a word he jumped in, spoutin' a pile of rubbish an' sayin' as 'ow I wanted to split 'em up 'cos I was jealous and wanted 'im meself.'

Lizzy gaped. 'What did your mam say? Surely she didn't believe 'im?'

Dolly gave a mirthless laugh. 'Hook, line and sinker. She told me she'd allus known I were a troublemaker, and I were either to apologise or get me things and go. Well, there weren't no way I were apologisin' for summat I 'adn't done, so I took me stuff and went, and I've not been back since. I don't know which is worse, 'im for tellin' such whoppers or 'er for believin' 'im.'

Lizzy shook her head. 'I'd never've thought she'd tek the side of a man over her own daughter.'

Dolly smiled. 'You 'n' me both, but she did, and 'ere I am. At least your mam saw sense in the end.'

Lizzy nodded. 'Let's 'ope it's not too little too late, an' that she manages to gerraway from 'im same as me.'

Charlie half carried, half dragged the recumbent figure into the station. 'Someone's in for a rollickin' when his missus sees 'im like this.'

The desk sergeant looked up from his paperwork and shook his head. 'I know 'im, that's Barry Clifton from down Tynwald Street. 'Is missus'll bring 'er rollin' pin when she comes lookin', so I reckon it's best if we put 'im in the cell, if only for 'is own safety.'

As the sergeant lifted the counter lid to come through to the reception area, something drifted gently towards the floor. Bending down to pick it up, Charlie peered at it. 'You been makin' Christmas decorations, Fred?'

Rolling his eyes, the sergeant held open the cell door so that Charlie could manoeuvre the unwieldy Barry into the room. 'Some young lass brought it in. She was lookin' for you. 'Ere, lemme give you a hand with 'im.'

When they had laid Barry on the bench in the corner of the cell, Charlie raised a questioning brow. 'Some young girl brought me a star?'

Fred shook his head as he returned to the front desk. 'She reckoned her mam'd been kidnapped. Said you knew all about it.'

Charlie picked up the star again and read the writing on the back. *Lizzy Atherton, December 1929.'*

'Lizzy Atherton,' he exclaimed.

The sergeant nodded. 'So you know about her mam, then?'

Charlie shook his head. 'I don't know anything about her mam bein' kidnapped, but I met Lizzy last night at Lime Street Station, hidin' from her mam's husband. He was a right nasty piece of work, even tried to start a fight with George, and we all know George wouldn't harm a fly.'

'I've been around a lot longer'n you, Charlie boy, and if you want my opinion that Lizzy were tryin' to split her mam 'n' stepdad up, an' when it didn't work she caused a ruckus before runnin' off. He probably had good reason to be angry wi' her.'

Charlie shrugged doubtfully. 'Mebbe so, but she seemed pretty scared to me, and he had a right bruise comin' on his 'ead where she'd given 'im a good clack.'

'She can't be that scared of 'im, otherwise she'd not've dared to 'it 'im. If you ask me, the only thing she were scared of was not gerrin' 'er own way.' Seeing the doubtful expression on Charlie's face, he clapped a reassuring hand on the young policeman's shoulder. 'We gerrem in 'ere all the time, Charlie, bleatin' a load of crap about their stepdads. Comes with the territory of takin' on someone else's kids ... I should know,' he added bitterly.

Charlie turned the star over in his hands. 'I'm surprised she left this behind. I remember 'er makin' it for 'er dad. He'd been took ill that mornin' and she reckoned it was goin' to make 'im better, but from what me mam said he died that very day, an' I never saw her again, until last night.' He glanced at the open doorway before drumming a tattoo on the counter with his fingers. 'She must've forgotten it. I can't imagine she'd've left it behind on purpose.'

The sergeant eyed the star. 'Can't be that important else she'd've been back for it.' He held out a hand. 'Pass it 'ere, I'll chuck it in the bin.'

Charlie looked up. 'I'll keep it if it's all the same to you, Fred. She still might come lookin' for it.'

The sergeant rolled his eyes. 'That's sarge to you, you cheeky blighter, and as for that piece of crap, suit yourself. I've got more important things to worry about than some spoiled brat who's thrown 'er toys out of the pram 'cos she can't get her own way.'

'It's a woman, captain.'

The captain scowled at the deckhand. 'I can see that. What I want to know is, what is she doing aboard my ship?'

The sailor who had found Mary frowned at the captain. 'Ain't she one of yours?'

The captain blinked under the hot sun. 'One of mine? I'm running a ship, not a bloody harem.' He turned to the men who had gathered on deck. 'Do any of you know how this woman came to be aboard my ship?' His eyes searched the crowd, but no one spoke up. 'Fantastic! Not only have we got ourselves a stowaway, but we'll probably be at war in a few hours.' He scanned the crowd with a cautious eye. 'Is there anything else I should know about, or is that it for today? Although I can't imagine how much worse things could get.'

'I don't think she's very well, captain,' said the sailor who had found Mary. 'She were groanin' summat awful when we found her, weren't she, Cyril?'

Cyril nodded. 'Al thought she were a ghost, didn't you, Al?'

A growing chuckle swept through the gathered men.

'No I never, I said it *sounded* like a ghost, all that groanin' and moanin'.' He scowled at his shipmates. 'Never mind laughin', we all know 'avin' a woman aboard is bad luck, and I reckon it's right, 'cos unless that Hitler's left Poland we're goin' to be at war.' He eyed his audience with satisfaction. 'Not laughin' now, are ya?'

Captain Forbes rolled his eyes. 'Do you honestly believe that Hitler only invaded Poland because we've a woman on board?'

A ripple of laughter swept the crew.

'Mebbe ...' Al began, but Captain Forbes had had enough.

'Some of you get this crate on to its side, and be careful about it. From what I can see, she already looks as though she's been put through the wringer, and I very much doubt that was caused by her stowin' away in a crate. As for the rest of you, stop your lollygaggin' and get back to work.'

A short while and several splinters later, the captain laid Mary gently on his bed and turned to the sailor named Cyril. 'Get me some water and a clean cloth.' As Cyril left the cabin the captain laid a hand on Mary's forehead. 'By God, you're burnin' up.'

When Cyril returned the captain gently laid a cold flannel over Mary's brow before attempting to clean up the blood-matted hair which was stuck to the side of her face. Cyril turned to leave, and the captain addressed him from over his shoulder. 'Tell the men to hold their tongues. If anyone finds out we've a woman aboard all hell'll break loose, and there'll be a lot of questions they'll want answerin'.'

'Right you are, captain,' said Cyril. He looked at Mary. 'What d'you think 'appened?'

The captain shrugged. 'God knows, but she's obviously got on the wrong side of someone, 'cos she never got into that state by herself.'

'What'll you do with her if she dies?'

The captain shook his head. 'Dying's not an option, because then we would have to tell the authorities. They'd want to know why we didn't tell anyone we had a stowaway on board in the first place, and since I don't particularly want to answer that question she has to pull through, for all our sakes.'

'Wouldn't it be best to tell someone now? That way ...'

The captain stopped mopping Mary's cheek. 'If we go to war with Germany, they'll change our course and there'll be all sorts of new rules and regulations. The bosses will be comin' down hard on anyone who looks suspicious, includin' those who found her, and I'd call havin' a woman who looks like she's been beaten half to death hidin' in a crate on a ship bound for Africa pretty suspicious, wouldn't you?'

Cyril ran the back of his hand over his face. 'I'll tell 'em to keep shtum or get thrown overboard.'

The captain rolled his eyes. 'I'm not Blackbeard and this isn't the *Queen Anne's Revenge*. Just tell them to keep their mouths shut if they know what's good for them.'

Cyril nodded. 'Righto, captain.'

With Cyril gone, Captain Forbes turned his attention back to Mary's bloodied and bruised face. 'What could such a small woman do to cause so much trouble?'

It was just before 11 a.m. on 3 September and everyone in Bellevue had gathered around the wireless in Mr Granger's study. Clara was standing amongst the maids whilst Arthur, Gertrude and Ivy stood behind his desk. Arthur twiddled the knobs on the set until a man's voice broke the silence.

'I am speaking to you from the Cabinet Room at 10 Downing Street. This morning the British Ambassador in Berlin handed the German government a final note, stating that unless we heard from them by 11 o'clock, that they were prepared at once to withdraw their troops from Poland, a state of war would exist between us. I have to tell you now that no such undertaking has been received and that consequently, this country is at war with Germany.'

Sighing, Arthur switched the wireless off. 'We all thought as much, but it doesn't make the news any easier to take.'

Gertrude stared fixedly at Clara. 'They're going to attack us. We seen what they did to the Spaniards, that'll be us, you mark my—'

'That's enough,' said Clara, who could see the fear in Sally's eyes. 'You seem to forget I've a brother in the Navy, so unless you've got something useful to say ...'

Gertrude glanced at Clara's father. 'Sorry, I didn't mean to cause upset. I'm just frightened, especially when it comes to the safety of our children.' She looked pointedly at Clara again. 'I think the Prime Minister was right in evacuating the cities.'

Clara shook her head. 'If I go anywhere it'll be to do war work, not to hide in the country, so you can get that idea out of your head for a start. Although you might want to consider sending Ivy; she'll not suffer from hay fever at this time of year, and as you say it is dangerous ...'

Gertrude's cheeks turned pink. 'I expect a lot of the staff will want to do their bit for the war effort, so I'll need Ivy here to help me.'

Clara smiled. 'You mean with the cooking and the cleaning?' She was watching Ivy from the corner of her eye and could see the warning look the girl was giving her mother.

'If need be,' Gertrude said firmly.

Clara snorted on a chuckle. 'If there's a chance I'll see Ivy with a dishcloth in her hand, a herd of wild horses couldn't drag me away.'

Arthur rubbed his forehead between his finger and thumb. 'That's enough, Clara! It's bad enough our country's at war without you adding to it.'

Clara's cheeks grew crimson as she saw a smirk spread across Ivy's lips. Dratted girl, why did she always have to have the last laugh? She turned her attention back to her father. 'Sorry. I ...'

Arthur waved her into silence. 'Don't worry, darling. I expect we're all a bit fraught at the minute, and whilst I hope we don't get attacked the way Spain did ...'

Clara nodded. 'If Mum was here you can bet your life she'd be organising everyone as we speak.'

Her father's mouth twitched into a smile. 'Very true, and it doesn't surprise me to hear you say you're keen to join the war effort – your mother was a Wren in the last lot, but there's no sense rushing into these things.'

As Sally and the others filed out of the room, Clara noticed that Gertrude and Ivy remained, as though they did not include themselves among the members of staff. Clara looked at them enquiringly. 'Is there some reason why you're still here? Only the rest of the maids have left already.' She noticed with some satisfaction that Gertrude's face flushed pink, whilst Ivy glared icily at her. Enjoying their discomfort, Clara raised her eyebrows. 'Well?'

Gertrude ignored her and looked towards Arthur for support, but he was busy with one of the drawers in his desk and did not appear to be listening to the conversation. Pursing her lips, Gertrude strutted slowly towards the door, and was halfway there when she appeared to notice she was on her own and looked over her shoulder. 'Ivy!' she snapped. Ivy, who had still been glaring at Clara, followed her mother reluctantly from the room.

Clara closed the door, making sure that Gertrude and her daughter weren't lingering close by, and turned to her father. 'You're not going to send me off to the country, are you?'

The drawer he was fiddling with came free. 'Voilà!' he said triumphantly and looked up at his daughter. 'What was that, darling?'

Clara sighed. 'I said, you're not going to try and send me off to the country?' He shook his head absentmindedly as he rooted through the contents of the drawer, and leaning over the table she kissed the top of his balding head. 'Thanks, Dad.'

'There's no sense in sending you off to the country if you're just going to turn up on my doorstep two or three days later. Now be a good girl and help me find my cheque book. I'm sure it was here yesterday.'

She wagged a reproving finger. 'You've got to start keeping things in better order, Dad.'

He chuckled. 'I had thought about asking Gertrude to help.'

Clara stared disbelievingly at him. 'You can't be serious? Please don't tell me you're going to let her loose on the accounts?'

He frowned disapprovingly at her. 'I know you don't like her, but she's been very helpful these past couple of months. She's even helped me prepare one of the auctions, and I must say her work was most satisfactory. Besides, it's only the household accounts. It's not as though I was going to give her the keys to the safe.'

'I wouldn't trust that woman as far as I could throw her, nor her daughter.'

Placing his elbows on the desk, he looked at her from over the top of his steepled fingertips. 'I know you wouldn't, but would you mind telling me why?'

Clara blinked. 'Because I don't. There's something about her ...'

'So you've nothing to go by, just a feeling in your water, as your mother used to say?'

Clara nodded. 'Precisely.'

He shook his head. 'You're just like your mother. She always used to let her heart rule her head.' Clara opened her mouth to speak, but her father continued, 'Trust me, darling, I know what I'm doing, so show a little faith. After all, I didn't hire the Hackneys to be your new best friends, I brought them here to work.'

He continued to rummage through the desk. 'I must've turned this room upside down and I still can't ...' He glanced up at Clara to see her holding a cheque book out to him. 'Where on earth did you find that?'

Clara picked up the waste-paper bin from beside her father's knee. 'It must've fallen from that stack of bills and landed in the bin by accident. You're lucky I found it before the bin got emptied.'

He shook his head. 'Gertrude will have to take over. I can't afford to be making mistakes like that. That cheque book could easily have fallen into the wrong hands.'

'You give it to that woman and it will be in the wrong hands.'

Arthur sagged back in his chair. 'I can't do everything, Clara. Things are getting on top of me and that's why accidents like this are happening.' He rubbed his hand across his forehead. 'This isn't the first time I've mislaid something important, and if I start mislaying clients' information they'll lose their trust in me and I shan't have a business. I'm sorry if you don't like it, but Gertrude will have to take charge of the household accounts.'

'Couldn't one of the others do it?' said Clara hopefully.

Arthur arched a brow. 'Who do you have in mind? None of them were chosen for their literacy, or arithmetic skills, whereas Gertrude has shown herself to be quite proficient.'

'I bet she has! It's probably the whole reason why she came here. She's had this planned from the very beginning.'

Arthur rested his head in his hands. 'Clara, stop it. I've been running my business for the past forty years, and I do not appreciate you implying that I'm some kind of imbecile who can't see what's what!'

Clara felt her cheeks grow crimson. 'Oh, Dad, I'm sorry. I didn't mean to, and that's not what I think at all, but things have changed a lot since Mum died, and you've been under such a lot of stress.'

Arthur shook a weary head. 'Precisely, which is why I could really do without your constant accusations against the Hackneys, especially when they've not done anything wrong.'

Shamefaced, Clara nodded. 'I'm sorry, Dad. I suppose I was letting my feelings get in the way. I promise that from now on I'll leave you to deal with the Hackneys and everything else in your own way.'

'Good girl. Now if you'll excuse me I'd better put this,' he waved the cheque book, 'in its rightful place.'

As Clara left the room she thought about what her father had said. Maybe he was right. Just because Clara didn't approve of the way the Hackneys seemed to think they were above the rest of the staff, did that matter as long as they were getting the job done? As for Gertrude trying to wheedle her way into her father's affections, it would only work if her father reciprocated her advances. Clara conjured a picture of her mother and Gertrude standing side by side in her mind. She smiled. There was no comparison. Her mother's cheeks were always lifted in a smile and her wide blue eyes shone with love and happiness, whereas Gertrude's face was pale and pinched and she had beady little eyes. Clara heaved a sigh of relief. You've been worrying over nothing, you silly girl, she told herself. Even if Dad did find her attractive he also said he'd been drawn to the way Mum wore her heart on her sleeve, whereas Gertrude likes to play her cards close to her chest. For the first time in a long while, Clara smiled with real happiness.

Chapter Four

December, 1939

Mary opened her eyes and peered into the gloom. Slowly, she sat up on one elbow and gazed around the room ... if you could call it that. It was so small it was more like a cupboard. Hearing the approach of two male voices, she lay back down and closed her eyes.

The door to the cabin opened. 'She's still asleep, captain.'

Mary heard footsteps cross the small room and stop next to her. A warm hand touched her brow. 'The fever's not returned, so that's good. If only we could get her to wake up.' The voice paused. 'Pass me the water; I'll see if I can get some more into her.'

As he spoke, the man lifted her shoulders and slid an arm behind her back, and a moment or so later Mary felt a cup or a glass being gently pressed to her lips. 'C'mon, Lizzy, let's see if we can get some of this inside you.' A little water entered her mouth and she swallowed gratefully before realising he had called her Lizzy. Opening her eyes a fraction, she found herself looking straight into the face of the most handsome

95

man she had ever seen. He had thick black curly hair and eyes of ice blue, and when he smiled he revealed a set of strong white teeth. 'Welcome aboard, Lizzy. I realise you must be frightened and confused, but there's no need to be. You're perfectly safe.'

Mary frowned. 'Why do you keep calling me Lizzy? I'm Mary. Lizzy's my daughter's name.'

'Your daughter? You just kept saying Lizzy – we thought you were trying to tell us your name.'

Her shoulders sank. 'So she isn't here? Do you know where she is?'

The man shook his head. 'Sorry.'

Glancing around the cabin, Mary frowned once more. 'I heard someone call you captain – are we down the docks?'

He smiled. 'I'm Captain James Forbes, and you're on my ship, the *Kilmallock*.'

Mary's eyes grew wide. 'Don't be silly. I can't be on a ship – I can't swim.'

He laid a reassuring hand on her arm. 'Don't worry, you're not going to need to swim. We're in port.'

Mary's shoulders sagged with relief. 'Thank goodness for that. You had me worried for a moment there. But what I don't understand is how I got here.'

'We were rather hoping you could tell us that.' He handed Mary the cup of water.

Mary drained it and wiped her mouth on the back of her hand. 'Thanks,' she said, giving the cup back to the captain and sliding her legs over the side of the bed. 'I'm afraid my memory of last night's a bit fuzzy, so you know as much as me. The only person who may be able to shed some light on this is our Lizzy, and I bet she's worried sick.' She smiled up at the captain. 'I'm ever so grateful for your help, but I really should be gerrin' back.' She paused momentarily. 'Golly, I feel ever so funny, like I've got no strength. Could you give me a hand?'

Captain Forbes eyed her carefully before looking at his shoes. 'I, er, I don't quite know how to say this, but you're ... we're ... in South Africa.'

There was a moment of complete silence, and then Mary's eyes darted wildly around the room. 'Don't be daft. I was only in Liverpool yesterday. How can I possibly ...' Her voice trailed off as the captain shook his head.

'We were already at sea when we found you. You looked like you'd done ten rounds with Len Harvey, and you had a really bad fever ...'

'Just how long have I been here?' said Mary.

The captain hesitated. 'About seven weeks, give a day or two.

'Seven weeks!' squeaked Mary. 'That can't be right, surely I'd be dead by now?'

The captain appeared affronted. 'We've been lookin' after you, givin' you soup and water ...'

'How come I can't remember?' said Mary.

'Like I said, you had a fever for a few weeks and you were swimming out of consciousness for the rest. You weren't really aware of your surroundings or what was going on.'

Mary gazed at him in horror. 'Lizzy must be goin' frantic ...' Suddenly, her eyes widened, and she cupped a hand over her mouth. 'I've just remembered Albert ran after her. He was mad as fire. He threatened to ...' Her eyes brimmed with tears. 'He said he'd kill her.'

97

Lizzy looked out of the window. It had been snowing heavily all night and the back yard now lay under a thick blanket of snow. Dropping the curtain back into place, she skipped lightly across the cold linoleum floor and jumped back into the warm bed she had left to check on the weather. Snuggling down, she cast her mind back over the past few months.

When nothing more had been heard of Mary, Lizzy had wondered again about joining the Wrens, but she had quickly decided it would be best all round if she stayed in Liverpool.

'If I'm in the city I've got more chance of bumping into her, but if I join the Wrens I could be sent any-where and I may never see her again,' she told Dolly.

Dolly had nodded. 'You can come and work with me mekkin' parachutes in Langdon's. They're allus tek-kin' on at the minute 'cos of the war, so at least you won't have to worry about money.'

Lizzy enjoyed working at Langdon's and had said as much to Dolly as they admired the Christmas decora-tions in Lewis's windows.

'I wish I'd've gorra job like this years ago. The girls are so friendly, and yer 'ands don't go like prunes like they do with the laundry.' She had sighed wistfully. 'If I could just find me mam it'd be the icin' on the cake.' She pointed to a huge Christmas tree full of tinsel, deli-cate coloured glass baubles and fairy lights. 'Bet there's not many in the city that've got fancy stuff like that in their 'ouses.'

'It's all very well if you've got kids,' mused Dolly, 'but I've not bothered decoratin' the flat since I've lived there. It's allus seemed a bit silly when there's just me, and besides, some of that stuff costs a fortune!'

Lizzy nodded. 'Me and me mam've never really bothered pushin' the boat out since Dad died. It brings back too many bad memories, not to mention bad luck, so we hang up the old paper chains and that's about it.'

As they spoke the air raid siren filled the air. 'Oh blimey,' said Dolly. 'Here we go again.'

Even though everyone was calling it the phoney war, people still crammed into the shelters every time the siren wailed its warning. They grumbled and moaned that it was probably a waste of time, but Lizzy was always hopeful that she might bump into her mother.

'You never know your luck,' she had said to Dolly once as the two raced towards the shelter. 'If Mam's in the area she'll have to use the same shelter as us.'

Now, as she lay in her cosy little bed, Lizzy fumbled under her pillow for the bar of scented soap she had bought for Dolly as a Christmas present, and sniffed its delicate fragrance before pushing it back into its hiding place. Swinging her legs out of bed, she padded into the other room to add a few pieces of coal to the stove before giving it a good prod with the poker. In the street below she could hear some children squealing with delight. Pulling the cord of her dressing gown tight, she peered out of the window, and smiled. Four small children, beaming with delight, sat one behind the other on a wooden sledge whilst their father towed them along the pavement.

Lizzy sighed wistfully. When she was a child her father used to take her sledging in one of the city parks. They couldn't afford a real sledge like the one she had just seen; instead they made do with an old potato sack or a bin lid. She remembered the time her father had tried taking one of her mother's tea trays to use.

'Eric Atherton! Stop where you are!' Mary had said before snatching the tray from his guilty hands. 'Last time you did that it weren't fit for anythin' by the time you came back. I've an old sack in the kitchen; you can use that if you want.'

'Oh, come on, luv, it is Christmas, and me an' half-pint are only goin' out so's we're not gerrin' under your feet. Sacks don't slide the same way as a tray. We'll be the slowest ones there!'

Mary waved a tea towel at him. 'You shouldn't be on a sledge, you're too old.' She looked at Lizzy, whose large brown eyes were shining hopefully, and heaved a sigh. 'Oh, for goodness' sake take it, but it'd best not come back covered in lumps and bumps like the last one.'

Closing her eyes, Lizzy let the memory wash over her. They had walked to the top of the rise, but instead of standing to one side like the other fathers Eric had sat down on the tray and placed Lizzy between his knees. 'Hold on tight, half-pint, and don't forget to yell if someone gets in the way!'

They had shot down the slope, her father holding her tightly in his arms and whooping for joy as they hurtled past the others.

Now, with the memory clear in her mind, a tear trickled down Lizzy's cheek at the unfairness of having lost both her parents.

'Merry Christmas, chuck.' Dolly joined Lizzy by the window.

Looking at her through eyes filled with tears, Lizzy managed to smile back. 'Merry Christmas, Doll.'

Without need of explanation, Dolly encompassed Lizzy in a warm embrace. 'Cheer up, chuck. I know it's not the Christmas you hoped for, but look on the bright side: things could be a whole lot worse.'

Lizzy nodded. 'I know, and I'm grateful to you for gerrin' me into Langdon's and lerrin' me stay here with you. It's just ...'

Dolly shook her head. 'I know, but even though you don't know where your mam is, no news is good news.'

Lizzy nodded. 'You're right. And who knows what the day may bring?'

'That's the spirit! I'll tell you summat else you can be grateful for ... a bacon sarnie for your brekker. 'Ow does that sound?'

'Delicious! They were me dad's favourite, along wi' a good dollop of Daddie's.'

Dolly glanced at the scene below. 'Oh, Lizzy, look at all that snow!'

'That's what started me off. I was thinkin' about 'ow me dad used to take me sledgin'.'

Dolly's eyes shone with excitement. 'What a brilliant idea!' she said over her shoulder as she disappeared into the bedroom again, heading for the washstand. 'I 'aven't been sledgin' for years. We'll have to have a bit of a think as to what we can use as a sledge, though.' She inhaled sharply as the cold water from the ewer hit her face. 'Don't have a wash just yet. That stuff'd give a brass monkey nightmares.'

Lizzy blinked. She hadn't meant that they should go sledging, but Dolly seemed so excited by the idea she hadn't the heart to say so. 'What time d'you want to go?'

Dolly, who was enthusiastically rubbing the circulation back into her face with a hand towel, stood in the doorway to their bedroom. 'After lunch?'

Standing at the stove, Lizzy nodded her approval. 'Sounds good to me,' she said as she dropped a knob of lard into the pan. 'Gosh, I nearly forgot. We haven't opened our pressies.'

Dolly pulled her vest over the top of her head. 'You know what our problem is, don't you?'

Lizzy shook her head.

'We 'aven't planned anythin'. 'Ow about we come up with a tradition of our own, then next Christmas we'll know what we're about.'

'I think that's a grand idea,' Lizzy approved. 'I vote we put bacon sarnies for brekker at the top of the list.'

Dolly giggled. 'Agreed. What about pressie openin'? Should we do it before or after lunch? I reckon we open them—'

'Before breakfast!' said Lizzy as she put two rashers of bacon into the hot fat, which was beginning to spit. 'Mam allus used to make us wait until after, so me and Dad 'ud be chuckin' our brekker down us necks as quick as we could so that we could open our pressies as soon as possible.'

Dolly chuckled. 'C'mon then, only don't get too excited: we've only got one each.'

Lizzy handed Dolly her small gift, which Dolly carefully unwrapped so as not to tear the tissue paper. Holding the soap to her nose, she sighed beatifically. 'Lily of the Valley, my favourite! Thanks, Lizzy. It's lovely.' She handed Lizzy a thin parcel and smiled shyly at her. 'I hope you like it.'

Lizzy held up a small square of pink linen. 'It's a hanky ...'

'Look in the corner.'

Holding the handkerchief up, Lizzy read aloud the carefully embroidered letters. 'E, M, E?'

Dolly nodded. 'It's all your initials: Eric, Mary and Elizabeth. I know we all call you Lizzy, but ...' She finished the sentence with a shrug.

Lizzy stroked the letters with her thumb. 'I love it, and it's so thoughtful of you. How on earth did you ever come up with such a clever idea?'

Dolly beamed with pride. 'Remember the other week when you were hunting for your hanky and you kept picking mine up by accident?' Lizzy nodded. 'I thought it would be easier if we had a way of telling one from the other, and ... ta-dah!'

Lizzy fingered the beautifully stitched embroidery. 'Did you do this?'

Dolly smiled. 'Yup. That's why I've been goin' to bed early an' closin' the door.'

Lizzy chuckled. 'I was worried you might be gerrin' fed up with me.'

'Not a chance. I love 'avin' you 'ere ...' her nostrils flared, 'the bacon!' Hastily, she reached past Lizzy and transferred the bacon from the pan to a plate. 'Phew, that were close. Perhaps it would be better to open our pressies after brekker next year.'

Lizzy giggled. 'Mebbe that's why me mam allus made us wait.'

Clara winced as Gertrude gazed adoringly at her employer. 'Thank you so much,' the housekeeper cooed, 'it's beautiful.' Holding the necklace across the palm of her hand, she showed it to Ivy. 'What do you think, darling? Isn't Mr Granger the most generous man you've ever worked for?'

Clara glared at her father. 'Did you give jewellery to all the staff?'

Arthur Granger's cheeks began to redden. 'Well no, but it's not as if I bought this. It's just a bit of old costume jewellery ...' He faltered.

Seeing the look on her father's face, Clara turned to Gertrude. 'Can I look?'

Gertrude looked to her employer for his approval, but Clara, who had a bad feeling, wasn't waiting for permission. Standing in front of Gertrude, she held out her hand imperiously, but Gertrude held the necklace defensively behind her back whilst she waited for Mr Granger to speak.

He nodded. 'You may as well.'

Gertrude tried to hide her smirk as she handed the necklace to Clara. 'Please don't be angry with your father; it's not his fault. I saw it one day whilst I was dusting, and ...'

Clara folded her fingers around the necklace and turned to face her father. 'I gave this to Mum for her fiftieth birthday.'

Realising what he had done, Arthur began to apologise. 'I'm so sorry. It was a mistake ... she had so much jewellery ...'

'It wasn't yours to give away,' Lizzy snapped. 'It belonged to my mother, and she would've given it to Sally before she gave it to the likes of *her*.'

'Clara, I realise you're upset—'

'*Upset*? What else have you given her?' Her eyes flickered across Gertrude's fingers. 'Good job Mum took her wedding ring to the grave, that's all I can say.'

Her father's stance went from ashamed to defensive. 'That's enough! How dare you suggest I would give your mother's wedding ring away? This was an honest mistake for which I'm very sorry, but if you can't keep a civil tongue in your head you can go to your room immediately!'

Clara knew she had gone too far, but the words had left her lips and there was no taking them back. Instead, she continued on her downward spiral. 'Don't you worry, I'd rather be in my room on my own than watch these two smarming their way into your wallet.'

'Out!' bellowed her father.

Tears coursing down her cheeks, Clara began to ascend the stairs, and stopped beside the portrait of her mother. 'I miss you so much. I wish you were here.'

'Wishes are for babies.' Turning, Clara stared into Ivy's sneering face. 'Boo hoo, boo hoo. Stop snivellin', you spoiled brat.' The girl's eyes flickered towards the portrait of Clara's mother. 'If you ask me your mam should've given you a good slap years ago, taught you some manners.' She glanced from the painting to Clara and back again, ''Ow come your mam ain't a big fatty like you? Or did you tell the artist to paint her thin?'

Hot, furious tears rushed down Clara's cheeks and before Ivy knew what was happening Clara had leaned over the banister and slapped her across the side of her face as hard as she could. 'You evil little bitch!'

Ivy let out a scream of fury and she reached to grab the vase that stood on a pedestal beside the banister, but changed her mind when she heard the door behind her click open.

'What on earth is going on?' said Gertrude.

Turning to face her mother, Ivy pointed a trembling finger towards Clara, but Gertrude was looking at the side of Ivy's face.

'What happened to your face? Is that ...' she peered closely at her daughter's cheek, then raised her hand to cover her open mouth, 'a hand mark?'

Ivy nodded before burying her face against her mother's shoulder. 'I came out to make sure she was all right, and she hit me for no reason.'

'You lying little ...' Clara began, but as the words left her mouth she caught sight of her father's expression as he stood in the doorway. 'It wasn't like that. She said horrid things about Mum.'

Her father looked at her through disappointed eyes. 'I don't care what the reason is, you don't have the right to strike anyone.' He shook his head. 'You talk of your mother's good nature and how much you admired her, but this is not how she would have behaved.'

'But ...' She looked at him, then across at Gertrude, who was comforting her daughter.

Arthur sighed. 'Go to your room and don't come down until you are ready to apologise. Gertrude and Ivy have done their best to fit in, to befriend you, to help you, but all you've ever done is make false accusations and throw their kindness back in their faces. Gertrude was right, you should have gone away the first time around so that you could heal after the shock of your mother's death. As soon as Christmas is over I shall make the necessary arrangements.'

Clara turned away and continued to ascend the stairs, tears falling silently down her cheeks. Once in her room she picked up a suitcase far bigger than the one she had been given before and began to pack her clothes.

They've won, she thought miserably, and what's more I helped them over the finishing line.

A short while later the luncheon bell rang. Clara went downstairs and placed her suitcase by the front door, then walked calmly towards the dining room. Inside, she saw that her father was sitting at the head of the table and Gertrude, who normally sat further down the table with Ivy, was sitting in the chair which used to be Clara's mother's. She was holding Arthur's wrist and talking quietly to him. As Clara entered the room they both turned to face her.

'I shan't be staying for lunch,' she said.

Arthur smiled. 'Don't be silly, Clara. We all say things we don't mean in the heat of the moment. Just apologise and all this can be forgotten. I've had a word with Ivy and she has been most generous.'

Clara shook her head. 'It's not just about the argument, it's me. I don't feel I belong here any more.'

Turning on her heel, she heard the sound of her father's chair scraping across the wooden floor. 'Clara! Please have your lunch. We can talk about this later. I'm sure you're sorry for slapping Ivy. I'm sure—'

Turning back, Clara looked at him levelly. 'But I'm not – sorry, that is. I shouldn't have interfered in your affairs, I should have relied on you to see things for yourself, so that's why I'm not asking you to choose. I would never do that to you.' Her eyes darted towards

Gertrude and Ivy, who both sat with gaping mouths. 'I want to be like my mother, a strong woman who can make her own way in life independent of others.' Leaning forward, she kissed her father's cheek. 'I love you, Papa.'

As her fingers slipped through his, Arthur tightened his grip. 'It's Christmas Day. Where will you go?'

'Don't worry about me. I have friends who will take me in.'

As she left the room, she half expected Gertrude or Ivy to say something, to try to talk her out of leaving so that they would win favour with her father, but they remained silent.

Picking up her suitcase, she had opened the front door when a voice hailed her from behind. It was Sally. 'Clara, take this with you.' She handed Clara a large chunk of silver foil. 'It's a chicken and stuffin' sandwich, and if you'll wait a mo Bert's bringing you a flask of tea.'

Clara stared at the maid. 'But how did you ...'

'Know you were leavin'?' said Sally, and Clara nodded. ''Cos you're yer mam through 'n' through. She wouldn't have stood for all these shenanigans no more'n you, only o' course she were in a better position to kick 'em out.' She took Clara's hand in her own. 'You mustn't blame your father. He's still smartin' from her death.'

'So am I,' sniffed Clara, 'but I can still see them for what they are, so why can't he?'

Sally smiled sympathetically. 'You've lost your mam and your best friend, but your father's lost a lot more than that. He's lost his first sweetheart, his wife, his best friend, and the woman who bore his children.' She sniffed. 'She were the one who made his heart beat, the glue what held the family and this house together. The day she died, his whole world fell apart.' She eyed Clara thoughtfully. 'You must've noticed the fire what sparkled in your father's eyes has all but gone?'

Nodding mutely, Clara gripped Sally's hand just as Sally shook her head sadly. 'Your father ain't thinkin' straight 'cos grief's cloudin' his judgement.'

Bert appeared by the other woman's side holding a flask of tea. 'Here you go, Clara.'

Clara took the flask. 'Thank you.' She turned her attention back to Sally. 'I'll come back and see Dad after I've settled in.'

Sally wiped the tears from her eyes. 'It shouldn't be like this, not after you losin' your mam an' all. It's wrong, that's what it is.'

Afraid that her emotions would get the better of her, Clara blinked back the tears and smiled brightly. 'Merry Christmas, Sally, and you, Bert.' Turning on her heel, she acknowledged their returned Christmas wishes with a wave of her hand before setting off down the path. Glancing at the spot where the family would take picnics on hot summer days, a clear image formed in her mind of her father, his arm round her mother's waist as they sat on the tartan rug, whilst she and her brother made light work of a bowl full of ripe straw-berries smothered in cream. The tears came slowly at first, but by the time she had reached the gate she could barely see the snow-covered path.

There had been a time when she would try to make up her mind what she wanted for Christmas. She had no such difficulty now: all she wanted for Christmas was to have things back the way they were before the dreadful Gertrude and Ivy turned up. I should've slammed the door in her face, Clara thought bitterly, and waited for someone else to come, someone nice and kind like my mother. She removed a handkerchief from her pocket and blew her nose, but it was no use dwelling on what might have been. She should concentrate on the future. Pushing the handkerchief back into her pocket, she made her way toward Pickwick Street.

Charlie stamped his feet in a bid to get rid of some of the hard lumps of snow that had accumulated in the tread of his boots. He didn't mind working on Christmas Day when it was wet and windy, but this morning he had opened his bedroom curtains to find that a thick blanket of snow had fallen during the night, and by the time he and his beat partner, PC Jimmy Briscoe, left the police station the pavements were covered in sledge tracks.

As he bade yet another family a merry Christmas he turned to Jimmy. 'Bet Princes Park'll be chocka. Fancy takin' a look?'

Jimmy chuckled. 'Aye, go on then. There's not much goin' on otherwise.'

Charlie clapped a hand on the other man's shoulder. 'That's the spirit!'

'Great to be young, ain't it?' said Jimmy as they passed a group of children rolling a ball of snow larger than themselves towards the base of an old oak tree. 'Playin' in the snow till you're frozen to the bone, then goin' 'ome to a nice hot Christmas dinner.' He looked at Charlie. 'D'you know what you're 'avin' for your Christmas supper?'

Charlie rolled his eyes. 'Scouse at me mam's.'

'Real not blind?' said Jimmy with a look of envy. 'Blimey, I wouldn't be pullin' a face if I were havin' real scouse for me tea.'

Charlie shook his head grimly. 'Not when you got our Phoebe wailin' fit to bust down your ear 'ole.'

'Don't she like scouse?'

'Not this one; it's got rabbit in it.'

'Ahh. Likes rabbits, does she?'

Charlie grimaced. 'She called him Peter. Mam told her he wasn't a pet, but would she listen?' He kicked the toe of his boot through the snow. 'What with 'avin' to work on the first white Christmas we've had in years, then eatin' me supper with her wailin' like a banshee – I don't see how this Christmas could get any worse.'

Jimmy pointed to a slope filled with children. 'See them rough-lookin' buggers at the top of that slope, the ones usin' an old car bonnet as a sledge?' Charlie nodded.

'They're me brother's kids. Do you fancy goin' over to wish 'em a merry Christmas?'

Charlie shrugged his indifference. 'Don't see why not.'

Jimmy glanced at the watch on his wrist. 'Once the slopes go a bit quieter I reckon you'd be all right to have a turn, providin' you want to, o' course.'

Charlie looked uncertain. 'What if someone sees us?'

'Firstly there's no "us" to see 'cos there's no way I'm getting on that death trap, and secondly, take your hat and coat off and what is there to see? Just some feller a bit underdressed for the weather havin' a ride on a sledge.'

Charlie grinned. 'You sure the kids won't mind me havin' a go?'

Jimmy shook his head. 'Nah, they're a good bunch. C'mon, I'll introduce you.'

Dolly and Lizzy lay in a giggling heap at the bottom of the slope. 'Oh, oh, my sides, I've gorra stitch,' gasped Lizzy as she attempted to get up without falling. The slope they had come down had been used so much the surface was more like ice than snow. Pulling themselves to their feet, the two women surveyed each other's unkempt appearance before breaking into another bout of giggles.

'We're like a couple of drowned rats in hats,' chuckled Dolly. 'How about one more race before we leave?'

'You're on,' said Lizzy.

Back at the top of the slope the girls placed their tea trays side by side. As Dolly sat on hers she dug the heels of her wellingtons into the snow. 'How's about this time we race for a bet?'

Lizzy nodded. 'I'm game. What d'you have in mind?'

'First one to the bottom gets first go in the tub.'

Taking her place on her tea tray, Lizzy nodded again. 'Deal! On the word go?'

Dolly nodded. 'Ready, steady ... go!'

Charlie glanced around as he handed his heavy woollen coat and policeman's helmet to Jimmy. Satisfied that no one was watching, he took his seat on the upturned bonnet.

Chuckling, Jimmy shook his head. 'You ready?'

'Not yet. Let those two girls go, then you can give us a push.'

Jimmy watched the two women, using their hands to gather speed, set off down the slope before he and his nephews gave Charlie a hefty shove.

Gripping on to the rim of the bonnet, Charlie whooped for joy as the sledge began to pick up speed. Jimmy's nephews had had lots of races on it against all manner of contraptions, and they had beaten everyone, but whilst it was the fastest Charlie had to admit it was probably the most dangerous, as there was no real way of stopping should things go wrong. With the thought came the proof: as he gained on the two women on the parallel track one of them skewed off course, lost her balance, and fell on to the path that he was heading down. Waving his arms and shouting at the top of his voice, he saw the woman turn to face him, her eyes rounding as she watched him hurtling toward her. She tried to scramble to her feet, but her wellingtons slipped precariously on the smooth surface of the snow. Fearing the worst, Charlie crawled to the front of the bonnet, then at the last moment leapt ahead of it and knocked her out of its path.

The woman cried out as Charlie landed heavily on top of her. As quickly as he could, he pushed himself off and turned her on to her back. 'You all right, miss?'

Lizzy, who was winded from hitting the ground so hard, grimaced. 'No, I'm bloody well not.'

'Pipsqueak!'

She opened one eye and glared at him. 'Charlie ruddy Jackson. Why am I not surprised?'

Dolly and Jimmy appeared by Charlie's side. 'That was quick thinkin', jumpin' off the bonnet like that. God only knows what would have happened if you'd hit her on that thing,' Dolly said breathlessly.

'That's another thing,' snapped Lizzy, who, if she had wanted to see the handsome officer again, would not have chosen to do so whilst looking like a drowned rat. 'What on earth were you doing on a car bonnet instead of using a proper sledge like normal people?' She followed his gaze to the tea tray which Dolly was holding in her arms. 'A tea tray isn't likely to kill someone if it gets out of control, is it?'

Charlie's cheeks grew crimson. 'I suppose not.'

Dolly held out her hands. 'Come on, Lizzy, you can't stay there. Your bum'll freeze to the floor.'

Scrambling hastily to his feet, Charlie tried to put an arm round Lizzy's waist. 'Here, let me help you.'

'No thanks, I'm sure I can cope,' Lizzy began, only to cry out sharply as she tried to stand up.

'What's up? Is it your leg? Don't say the bonnet caught you,' Dolly said.

Lizzy shook her head. 'I think I twisted my ankle when I was' – she glared at Charlie – 'knocked over.' She tried to place her weight on her ankle, which was beginning to ache.

Sinking down on one knee, Charlie tentatively took her booted ankle into his hands and gently rotated her foot. 'I think you're right; nothin' broken, just a nasty twist.' He stood up, took his heavy police coat from Jimmy and placed it round Lizzy's shoulders. 'Here you go, Lizzy, this should keep you warm. Now let's get you home.' Effortlessly, he scooped her up in his arms.

'What the ...'

'You can't walk in the snow on a twisted ankle, so I shall carry you home.'

'But you don't know where I live.'

Tilting his head so that he could look directly into her eyes, Charlie smiled. 'Then you shall have to tell me.'

Lizzy smiled back. After all, she could think of worse ways to spend an afternoon than being carried home by Charlie Jackson. Nestling into his arms, which engulfed her, she glanced up at his firm jaw, noting as she did so that he had a slightly protruding Adam's apple, which bobbed up and down whenever he laughed.

The walk home was a long one, but Charlie carried her with ease, and even though the pain in her ankle had subsided well before they reached the flat she decided that it wasn't necessary to tell him, since it would mean she would no longer be held tightly to his chest.

Bringing up the rear with Jimmy, Dolly hurried ahead to open the door to the bottom of the stairwell and glanced doubtfully up the narrow passage. 'D'you think you'll be able to carry her up the stairs? It's awfully narrow.'

Charlie shook his head. 'Don't you worry about the stairs, I can manage.' He drew his arms close together so that Lizzy's knees were by his chest and her cheek brushed against his, and as he did so she noticed the scent of Vinolia shaving foam.

Inside the small flat, Jimmy stood by awkwardly while Dolly trotted over to the sofa and pulled the cushions to one side. 'By there'll do.'

Lizzy felt a twinge of disappointment as he laid her gently on the sofa. 'I'm going to take your boot off. It might hurt a bit, especially if the ankle's swollen, so if it gets too much let me know and I'll stop.' Kneeling down beside her, he slowly and carefully removed the wellington boot. 'Does that feel better?'

Lizzy's reply came out in a squeak. 'Yes.'

Charlie smiled. 'Good! Is there anything else we can do before we go?'

Lizzy found herself searching for an excuse to make him stay, but Dolly, who was spreading a blanket over her legs, shook her head. 'Thanks, but I think I can take it from here.'

Standing up, Charlie clapped a hand to his forehead. 'I almost forgot. Fred said you'd been into the station to report your mam missing. Did she turn up?'

She shook her head.

'Well, maybe he was right.' Seeing the angry frown that instantly formed on Lizzy's forehead, he knew he had said the wrong thing.

'You agree with that great lump of lard? You actually think me mam abandoned me to be with my beast of a stepdad?'

Confused, Charlie desperately tried to back-pedal. 'What? No! That's not what I meant at all.'

'Well that's what he said to me, so I assume it's what he said to you too.' Lizzy flung the blanket off her legs and leapt to her feet. 'If that's what you think, that I'm still some silly little girl ...' She strode across the room and opened the door to the stairwell. 'If you'll excuse me, I'd like to get out of these wet things.' She glared at Charlie as he approached the door, closely followed by Jimmy. 'Thanks for nearly killing me, and thanks for nigh on breakin' me ankle. I suppose I should say thank you for carryin' me home, but considering ...'

'I'm glad your ankle's better,' he said.

Lizzy's flush of anger turned into one of embarrassment. 'No thanks to you,' she muttered beneath her breath, feeling extremely foolish, and when Charlie opened his mouth to speak again she cut him short. 'I think you've said enough, don't you?'

He smiled awkwardly. 'Could I have my coat back?'

She stood blinking for a moment or two before shrugging the coat off her shoulders and handing it wordlessly to him.

'Thanks.'

She mumbled an indistinct 'Thank you'.

As he turned to face the stairs he glanced at her over his shoulder. 'Merry Christmas, Lizzy.'

Her eyes flickered up to meet his. 'Merry Christmas.' She saw a small smile cross his lips as he turned to follow Jimmy down the stairs.

Closing the door firmly behind them, Lizzy rested her back against it. 'What?' she said to Dolly, who was grinning from ear to ear.

'When you told me 'ow you'd bumped into Charlie Jackson, you failed to mention 'ow he'd turned from a chubby frog into a handsome prince. He could plough me down and carry me home any day of the week!'

Lizzy sniffed. 'I suppose if he's your type ...'

'Tall, dark and handsome? Isn't that every woman's type?'

There was a sharp knocking on the door, which caused both girls to jump. Dolly's eyes rounded. 'He's come back,' she grinned.

Lizzy gaped at her. 'Tell him I'm not here.'

Dolly giggled. 'He may have fallen for the bad ankle but I don't think he'll fall for that one.'

Lizzy sniffed. 'I did have a bad ankle … in the beginning.'

Laughing, Dolly ushered her to one side. 'I'll see what he wants.'

A voice spoke from the other side of the door. 'If you're referring to that handsome policeman I just passed in the street then I'm afraid you're in for a disappointment.'

Dolly and Lizzy exchanged puzzled glances. Dolly opened the door a crack then swung it wide open.

'Clara!'

Back at the station Charlie warmed his hands on a large mug of hot tea. Blowing the steam from the top, he took a tentative sip then glanced at Jimmy. 'Am I missing something?'

Jimmy's eyes scanned Charlie from head to toe. 'Not that I can see.'

'I mean when it came to Pipsqueak.'

Jimmy chortled. 'I wouldn't let her hear you say that, else she'll give you another ear bashin'.'

Charlie frowned at him over the top of his mug. 'She was the one who fell off her tea tray and landed in my path. If anything I saved her from getting mowed down, yet she seemed to think I was the one in the wrong.'

Jimmy drew out a rather grubby-looking handkerchief from his trouser pocket and wiped his nose. 'It would appear so.'

'Then I carry her all the way home from Princes Park because she had a sprained ankle, yet when I said I was glad it was better she looked at me as though I'd grown horns.'

Jimmy chuckled. 'Again, it would appear so.'

'And how was I to know what Fred'd said to her? I only meant we thought her mam was safe, but she didn't even give me a chance to explain, just gets up and orders me to leave!'

Jimmy sipped his tea. 'That's about the long and short of it.'

Charlie placed his mug down on the table. 'It is. So where did I go wrong? Because I'll be blowed if I can see it.'

'Ah, that's an easy one,' Jimmy said confidently. 'You're a feller.'

Charlie scratched his head. 'I don't understand.'

Jimmy shrugged. 'In the eyes of a woman, if you so much as think the wrong thing, you're guilty.'

'I never thought nothin', and she didn't give me a chance to explain—'

'All she needed to know was that you'd sided with Fred.' He chuckled as he recalled Lizzy's description. 'Don't matter what over, point is you agreed with him.' He pointed at his wedding ring. 'And when you get one of them on your finger, you'll've as good as admitted you're wrong for the rest of your life.'

'But I was being nice!' Charlie protested. 'She was the one who got in my path; I saved her from being run down and then carried her home, so why can't she see—'

Leaning forward Jimmy began ticking the points off on his fingers. 'Number one, whether you hit her with the car bonnet or not, you'd have been in the wrong; number two, you agreed with someone who didn't agree with her so you were wrong again; three, you pointed out that she were fibbin' about her ankle, which you should've kept shtum about, but you'll learn that with time.'

Charlie scratched the top of his head. 'Blimey! And you reckon it gets worse after you're married?'

Jimmy shrugged. 'That depends if you're a quick learner. I soon realised that if I agreed with my Reenie whether she were right or wrong I could lead a peaceful life with three square meals a day.'

A picture of Lizzy's scowling face appeared in Charlie's mind. He stared Jimmy squarely in the eye. 'So when it comes to Pip— Lizzy?'

Jimmy grinned. 'See? You're learnin' already ... but if you're askin' what I reckon it would be like to be married to a woman who's not afraid to tear a few strips off a copper, I'll tell you this: there's nowt wrong with a woman who's got a bit of spirit.' Nudging Charlie's elbow with his own, he pulled a suggestive face. 'If you foller my meanin'.'

Charlie paused for a moment, and as the penny dropped his cheeks grew crimson. 'Steady on, Jimmy ...'

Jimmy wagged his finger. 'That's what I call a real woman that is, one what's filled with vim and vigour. On the other hand, don't go dismissin' the quiet ones, 'cos some people reckon they're even worse ... or should I say better?'

Charlie shook his head. 'I bet your missus doesn't know you talk about women like this!'

Jimmy choked on his tea. 'Damn right she don't. Blimey, she'd have me nuts for garters.'

Charlie chuckled. 'I think you mean guts.'

Jimmy pulled a grim face. 'I know what I meant.'

Charlie pictured Lizzy as she returned his Christmas wishes. She might have been angry with him, but she had still wished him well. Charlie didn't have many female friends, but he had lots of aunties and cousins and none of them blew hot and cold the way Lizzy did. He searched for the word which made Lizzy different from the other women in his life. An enigma! That was it, or at least something near as damn it. Lizzy was a woman of mystery, he corrected himself, a beautiful woman of mystery. His mouth twitched into a faint smile as an image formed in his mind: Lizzy standing defiant, the wind blowing her ebony locks. He heaved a sigh.

As Jimmy walked past he clapped a hand on Charlie's shoulder, causing him to jump. 'It don't take no Einstein to work out what's goin' on in your head.'

'Can you blame me?'

'I just hope you're up for a challenge, 'cos a woman like your Lizzy ain't goin' to be easily tamed.'

Charlie grinned. 'I wouldn't want to tame her. Besides, there's nowt wrong with a challenge; that's what makes life interestin'.'

Clara sat on the sofa between Lizzy and Dolly. 'So you see, that's about the size of it. I'm so sorry to have landed myself on your doorstep, but I've not got anyone else I can turn to.' She corrected herself. 'I'm not saying I haven't got any friends, but their parents know

121

my father and it wouldn't do his business any good if word got out that we were having problems.'

Lizzy smiled sympathetically. 'Don't worry, we'll not say owt.' She hesitated. 'You said summat about your father's business. What does he do?'

'He's an auctioneer, but he specialises in jewellery. He's very well respected in that community and it wouldn't bode well for him if people thought his judgement couldn't be trusted.' Clara sniffed as a tear rolled down her cheek. 'Trouble is, by walking out I've as good as given Gertrude full rein to get her claws into him.' She glanced at Lizzy. 'What have I done?'

Lizzy clasped Clara's hand in hers. 'You've not done anything. That wicked woman and her awful daughter forced you into this position and what's more they know they did. If anyone had a plan to ruin Christmas it was them, not you. They know your dad's vulnerable at the moment, and they're takin' full advantage of it.'

Clara smiled. 'I'm so glad I came here. It's good to be able to talk to someone about personal matters without worrying what they'll think.'

Dolly stifled a chuckle. 'You needn't fear judgement off me and Lizzy; we know what it's like.'

Lizzy blinked. 'I've just realised summat. When I woke up this mornin' I were dreadin' Christmas wi'out me mam, but what with Charlie knockin' me for six I've hardly thought about her at all.' She nodded approvingly. 'Seems he does have some uses.'

Dolly rolled her eyes. 'Stop pretendin' you don't like him, 'cos it's as plain as the nose on your face that you do.'

'I never said I didn't like him.'

Dolly's brow shot towards her hairline. 'You've a funny way of showin' it!'

Lizzy folded her arms defensively. 'He was the one who ran over me, don't forget, and made a fool out of me when me ankle got better, not to mention …'

Dolly cocked an eyebrow. 'Handsome, strong, kind, caring …'

'That's easy for you to say. He never tried to mow you down.'

Shaking her head, Dolly turned to Clara. 'Wait till you meet him.'

'What on earth makes you think he's comin' back?' said Lizzy.

Dolly grinned. 'Oh, he'll be back all right.' She turned to Clara. 'But enough about handsome scuffers. You're welcome to stay with us for as long as you need.'

Clara smiled gratefully. 'Thank you so much, but I can't stay here for free.' She rooted in her bag for a moment before producing a small beige booklet, which she handed to Dolly. 'I've got my ration book, which will help, but I need to get a job.'

Dolly shrugged. 'I could get you a job at Langdon's no problem. People are leavin' left right and centre in order to sign up, so there's plenty of work about.'

'Gosh, that would be marvellous.' Clara's bottom lip quivered. 'I can't begin to tell you how grateful I am.'

Lizzy waved a vague hand. 'Don't worry about it. We're like birds of a feather in this flat.'

Dolly nodded. 'We're like the three musketeers.'

'One for all …' said Lizzy.

Clara smiled. 'And all for one.'

Chapter Five

February, 1940

Holding out her hand, Mary tried to stop her fingers from trembling. 'I know I've got to do this, but I'm scared.'

Captain James Forbes smiled reassuringly at her. 'Keep your head down and stay in the middle of the men. Once we get to the *Spaniard*, some of her crew will be gathered by the gangplank. As we walk past we'll stop for a chat and you can slip amongst them; then, after we move on, they'll sneak you aboard the *Spaniard*.

'Sounds easy enough, but what if someone tries to stop me?'

He slipped a reassuring hand into hers. 'They won't.'

She clasped his fingers. 'I hope you're right, and thank you. I don't know what I'd've done without you.'

He smiled, and Mary felt a reassuring warmth flow through her. 'I've asked my sister Jean in Liverpool to meet the *Spaniard* when she docks; she'll look after you.'

Mary shook her head. 'You've risked enough for me already. I can't ask your family ...'

He wagged a reproving finger. 'You're not asking anyone to do anything. And the message has already been sent.'

'I'm so sorry to've lumbered you with all this trouble. If there'd been any other way ...'

'Nonsense,' said James, 'it's been a pleasure having you on board. Besides, you didn't do anything wrong; it was that nasty piece of work you were married to. He's the one to blame, not you.'

She glanced shyly up at him from underneath her lashes. 'Will I see you again?'

He squeezed his fingers around hers. 'Of course you will.' He glanced at his wristwatch. 'It's time we were off.'

Wiping the sweat from her palms on to her borrowed trousers, Mary got to her feet. 'How do I look?'

James nodded his approval. 'Best-looking sailor I know.'

She laughed. 'I should jolly well hope so!' Standing on tiptoe she kissed him lightly on his bearded cheek. 'I'll never forget what you've done for me.'

His smiled down at her. 'Come along, First Mate Tanner, let's be getting you back to Blighty.'

Crossing her fingers, Lizzy walked into the bakery where her mother used to work and raised a hopeful brow at Mabel, who shook her head sadly.

'I tek it you've still not found her, then?'

'No, and I'm sorry to keep bothering you, only I keep hopin' you'll have seen her walkin' past the window, or that she may've called in.'

Walking around the counter, Mabel handed Lizzy a pastry tart. 'Here you go, chuck, get on the outside of that, and don't worry about me gerrin' into trouble, 'cos it don't matter after today.'

Lizzy, who had already taken a large bite of the tart, swallowed quickly. 'How come?'

'Escott's sold the place, reckons it's goin' to be too dangerous stayin' in Liverpool, so he's movin' to the country. The new owners are keepin' things in the family, as it were, so I'm chuckin' it in to be a cook in the WAAF.'

Lizzy sagged. 'I'm sorry to hear that. About your job, I mean. I know you loved it here.'

Mabel nodded. 'I never saw it comin', neither.' She eyed Lizzy shyly. 'What'll you do about your mam?'

'Keep lookin'; that's all I can do.' Lizzy brushed the crumbs from her skirt. 'Thanks for the tart. I hope it goes well for you in the WAAF. For all I know Mam could've joined up herself, so if you should see her ...?'

Mabel embraced Lizzy. 'I'll tell her where she can find you.'

As Lizzy left the shop, she eyed the façade of the building and wondered what her mother's response would be to the news of the sale, or whether she already knew. She shook her head. She didn't know where her mother was, but she reckoned it must be a long way from Liverpool, or someone would have seen her. Stuffing her hands into the pockets of her winter coat, Lizzy tried to resign herself to the fact that she might never see her mother again. Not that that'll stop me lookin', she told herself. I won't do that till I've no breath left in me body.

Mary held her breath as the large wooden crate she was hiding in was lifted from the *Spaniard* on to the quayside. Outside, she could hear the sound of men shouting to each other. Pulling the seaman's jacket tightly around her, she peered out of the small spy hole the captain had made for her. A woman stood on the quayside deep in conversation with a couple of dockers. Mary could see from an old photograph James had shown her that it was Jean. The men she had been talking to exchanged glances, then nodded their approval. Jean glanced around before handing them an envelope, and all three turned to face the *Spaniard*. Mary crossed her fingers. So far it seemed as though James's plan to smuggle her back into Britain was going without a hitch.

It was several hours before Mary heard the sound of the nails squeaking as the lid of the crate was prised off.

'Mary?' hissed Jean. 'Time to go, luvvy. Quickly now, before someone comes.'

Mary stood up and the two men with Jean lifted her out with ease. She smiled briefly at them before her face crumpled into tears.

Placing a thick coat around Mary's shoulders and holding her in a warm embrace, Jean spoke softly. 'Come here, chuck. James told me all about it. You've had a terrible time, bless you. Let's go home and have a nice cup of tea and a sarnie, and after that you can get your head down for a bit. I expect you're worn out with all the worry.'

Mary smiled gratefully at her as the two women began to walk away from the quay. 'I'm so sorry. I don't know what came over me,' she said in between gulps. 'I s'pose you're right; it's all what's gone on. You say James told you all about it?'

Jean nodded. 'As best he could, but as you know it's hard to say much any more. I gather you've lost your daughter and you think your husband might've harmed her.'

Mary nodded. 'He were as mad as fire when he chased after her. I tried to go after them, but I fell out of the window, and I don't remember anything after that until I woke up on your brother's ship.'

'You poor love. You must've been petrified.'

Mary nodded miserably. 'I was. Albert was shouting blue murder.'

'Have you decided what to do next?'

Lifting her hand up, Mary crossed her fingers. 'I've an auntie who lives in Speke. That's where I'm hopin' to find our Lizzy.'

'We'll go there first thing tomorrer.'

Mary smiled gratefully. 'I really don't expect you …'

Jean tightened her arm round Mary's shoulders. 'I know you don't, but our James is worried about you.'

Mary looked up guiltily. 'I know he is, and he shouldn't be. I'm not his responsibility, and what with the war an' all he's got enough on his plate as it is.'

'I know, chuck, but that's the way he is. He's gorra heart of gold has our James.'

Mary nodded. 'I know, but he needs to concentrate on crossing the Atlantic safely. The men on the *Spaniard* said they saw floating mines …'

Jean held up a hand. 'Please don't; it's bad enough imaginin' what's out there without hearing about it first hand.' She stopped walking. 'That's why I want to help you find your daughter.'

Mary spoke through gritted teeth. 'I rue the day I laid eyes on that Albert Tanner.'

'Are you goin' to report him to the police?'

Mary shook her head. 'Can't, can I? I've no proof he hid me in that crate, because I've no memory of it, and until I find Lizzy I've no proof he's done anything to her either.'

'But surely you can't mean to let him get away with it? It's obvious it was him what put you in the crate. Why would anyone else do such a thing?'

Mary shrugged. 'Once I find Lizzy I'll have another think, but if I'm honest, I'm just glad he's out of my life.'

'And what if you don't find Lizzy? What then?'

Mary took a deep breath. 'Then I go to the police and tell them everything.' Seeing the look of concern on Jean's face, she added, 'I won't mention your brother. I'll say the fall caused me to lose my memory, and I can't remember anything from that day to this.'

Jean smiled. 'Let's hope you find her.'

'I've told you, the powers that be have said you're to go to Vauxhall 'cos of them new recruits what started 'ere last week. Seein' as 'ow me an' Jimmy've got more experience than you, it's us what's doin' the trainin', just like Jimmy done wi' you, so there's no point in you bein' 'ere as well.' Fred sighed breathily. 'I don't see why you're so bothered, lad. It's only for a few months.'

Charlie had opened his mouth to reply when Jimmy cut across him. ''Cos he's worried a certain young lady may come lookin' for him, and he won't be here when she does.'

Fred shook his head in disbelief. 'Not that one what gives you grief? I'd've thought you'd've welcomed 'er not bein' able to 'ound you.'

Charlie furrowed his brow. 'She doesn't hound me, and she's not the reason why I'm bothered about goin'. It's as rough as a bear's arse round that neck of the woods for one thing, and for another, them two lads you mentioned don't know their arse from their elbow. I reckon it makes more sense for me to stay here whilst you're babysitting them.' Looking at the expression on Jimmy's face, Charlie could see he wasn't fooling anyone, including himself. Not one day had gone by when he hadn't hoped to see Lizzy walking through the door to the station. He knew his workmates thought her to be more trouble than she was worth, but that was their opinion. As far as Charlie was concerned there was something about Lizzy that he found captivating.

'We can allus tell her where you're stationed, should she ever come askin', if that's all that bothers you,' said the sergeant. 'But if I were you, I'd count me blessin's. She's pig-headed and stubborn, that one; I shouldn't fancy gettin' in an argument with her as to why I was late home from work.'

Jimmy grinned. 'I don't reckon our Charlie would want to be late home from work if he had his little Pipsqueak waitin' for him.'

Charlie rolled his eyes. 'Crikey, I only asked why I was bein' moved, and there's you two marryin' me off!' He paused before adding, 'And I wouldn't be lettin' Lizzy hear you callin' her Pipsqueak.'

'Ooo,' chuckled Jimmy. 'Already got you dancin' to her tune.'

The sergeant nodded. 'Jimmy's right – you're not even courtin', so imagine what it'd be like if you were.'

Charlie leaned on the counter top. 'I'm not goin' to get a chance to, am I? She doesn't live anywhere near Vauxhall, so it's not as if there's any likelihood of bumping into her by accident. But if I did, you mark my words, she'd be like putty in my hands.'

The sergeant was wheezing with laughter. 'By 'eck, lad, I admire your courage, but she'll mek mincemeat out of you.'

'Courage my arse!' grinned Jimmy. 'He's got rose-coloured specs when it comes to that Lizzy. Let him learn the 'ard way, Fred; she'll send him off with a flea in 'is ear, that's if he can ever muster the courage to ask her out.'

Chuckling, Charlie shook his head. 'I've changed me mind. I'll be glad to get away from you two for a bit if nowt else!'

'Tell you what,' said Fred. 'If you ain't scared of her, why don't you go round and tell her you're leavin'?'

Seeing the colour begin to drain from Charlie's face, Jimmy roared with laughter. 'Oh aye, and get kicked out like he did last time?'

'I've no need to be tellin' anyone where I'm goin' 'cos I ain't bothered who knows,' Charlie lied. He lifted the lid of the counter and passed through, making sure Fred and Jimmy couldn't see his face. If he was honest, Jimmy had hit the nail on the head. There was no way Charlie would go round to tell Lizzy where he was off to, as he suspected she wouldn't give two hoots, and would not be shy about telling him so. Going into the office behind the counter, he heard Jimmy chuckling to Fred.

'Lamb to the slaughter, Fred; lamb to the slaughter.'

'I went to Snowdrop Street, like you said, but the woman that answered the door said she'd been livin' there since October, and she had no idea where the previous tenants were.'

'Thanks for that. I didn't fancy seein' Albert if he were still livin' there,' said Mary.

Jean stirred the pot of tea. 'If only your great-aunt Cissy were still alive.' Tapping the spoon against the top of the teapot, she glanced nervously at Mary. 'Did you go to the police station?'

Nodding, Mary smiled reassuringly at Jean. 'You needn't worry that I dropped James in it, because I never mentioned his name. The young feller they had on the desk hasn't been there long, so he's still wet behind the ears. Everyone else was out of the station, but he went through the motions, took my name and address and said he'd get back to me if he heard owt, although I'm not holdin' my breath. He reckons they have a lot of folk comin' in lookin' for their kids 'cos half of them have beggared off to join the services and lied to their folks about it. He asked me whether Lizzy might've joined up.' She heaved a sigh. 'I told him it was quite likely and I could tell that he wasn't interested in anything else I had to say after that, so I left.

Then I went to Beaslers – that's where I used to work – but it's changed hands, an' all the old staff have gone. When I asked they said they hadn't heard of anyone comin' in to look for me, so that's that. I don't know what to do next.'

Jean pushed the round spectacles which had made their way slowly down her nose back into place. 'You say you think Lizzy might have joined one of the services?'

Mary nodded. 'It's what our Lizzy were on about doin' before she took off. She were goin' to get me settled somewhere first and then sign up for the Wrens. She's allus loved the water, but I was terrified of it because I never learned to swim until your James said he'd teach me in South Africa, and he did.' She glanced up at Jean. 'I'd be more than happy to join the Wrens now that I know how to swim, and if that's what Lizzy did I reckon I'd stand a good chance of findin' her, don't you think?'

Jean nodded. 'You should try and get into the MT. That way you'd get to go all over the country.'

Mary blinked. 'What's the MT?'

'Mechanical Transport. They train women up to drive all sorts of vehicles.'

Mary nodded slowly, then stopped abruptly. 'But what about my papers? Albert has them all.'

Jean smiled. 'Our James used to be in the Navy, did he tell you?'

Mary nodded. 'He said he was stuck in an office all day, which he hated, so when the time came he took early retirement and applied to be captain of the *Kilmallock*.'

Jean beamed. 'Well, he's been commandeered to go back to the Navy. They reckon they need his experience.'

Mary turned pale. 'But why do you look so pleased? Surely that's far more dangerous ...'

Jean shook her head. 'He'll not be on a ship, but behind a desk in Admiralty House in Plymouth.'

Slowly the colour returned to Mary's cheeks. 'That sounds better, but what has it got to do with me?'

'If anyone can get you in the Wrens then it's our James, and I know he'll want to help, because ...' she raised her brows fleetingly, 'he's obviously taken quite a shine to you.'

Mary chuckled. 'I'd take that as a compliment if I didn't know I was the first woman he'd spent time with in years.'

'That's not strictly true; he's had his fair share of female admirers, but he's never shown an interest in any of them. You, on the other hand ...'

Mary's cheeks flushed. 'I dare say it's 'cos he were forced to spend time wi' me. You can't tell what would've happened if we'd met under different circumstances.'

Jean shook her head. 'He could've handed you over to the authorities at any one of the ports between here and Cape Town, but he didn't.'

Mary looked startled. 'He told me he was worried about the consequences.'

'He took far greater risks keepin' you with him.' She smiled knowingly. 'He risked a lot to be with you, Mary. I've never known him do that for anyone else.'

'I thought he only did it because he didn't want to have to explain what I were doin' on board.'

'Partly true,' Jean conceded, 'but let's face it, he had a whole crew to back him up.'

Mary turned round eyes on Jean. 'But why take such a risk?'

Jean smiled. 'Haven't you been listenin'?'

Mary placed a hand across her chest. 'But I'm just plain old Mary Tanner, nowt special.' She coughed on a chuckle. 'A widow whose new husband couldn't wait to get rid of her: hardly what you'd call a great catch!'

'Well, James seems to think you are, and it's his opinion that counts.'

'But he could have any woman he wanted. Why me?'

'Because you're kind and caring, not to mention beautiful.'

Mary shook her head. 'He'll soon change his mind once he's back on dry land and he's got Wrens throwin' themselves at him left right and centre.'

Jean grinned. 'We'll see.'

Chapter Six

November, 1940

'I hope it's another false alarm,' moaned Clara as the three girls headed for the shelter.

Lizzy nodded. 'Me too. I must admit I think we'd all got rather blasé about the whole phoney war thing.'

'They've only done a couple of raids, so mebbe they think it's not worth comin' all this way,' said Dolly optimistically.

Lizzy heaved a sigh as they entered the crammed shelter. 'Brilliant. Not enough room to swing a cat.'

A man sitting near the door leered at them. ''Allo, me darlin's. Looks like it's your lucky day.' He patted his lap. 'I reckon I got room for at least one of youse on 'ere.'

Clara shot him a withering look. 'Thanks all the same, but I'd rather take my chances out there.'

The grin disappeared. 'Suit yerself, ya snotty cow.' He belched, and the smell of ale filled the air. 'That's the last time I offer a young lady a chance to share my seat.'

'C'mon, girls, there's more room at the back,' said Dolly, jostling her way through their cramped surroundings. 'Fingers crossed we won't be here long.'

A large-bosomed woman shifted to one side in order to make room for the girls. 'Ignore Pete, 'e's 'armless as long as you keep 'im at arm's length.' She placed her darning in a large woven bag. 'You girls got work in the mornin'?' They nodded in unison. 'In that case youse welcome to tek this bench for yer own, ducks.'

Clara smiled gratefully. 'Thanks, but I'm sure we can manage.'

Getting to her feet, the old woman placed her bag on the floor and was about to sit on it when she appeared to remember something. After a moment of rooting around in the bag she produced a large pair of knitting needles. She grinned toothily. 'Imagine if I'd've sat on these buggers.'

Lizzy giggled. 'Good job you remembered, else it'd be a rather painful, not to mention embarrassing, trip to the hospital for you!'

Chuckling, the old woman sat on the squashy-looking bag.

Lizzy turned to Dolly. 'Next time we come down 'ere I'm goin' to bring my knittin'.'

'But you don't knit.'

'I know, but I can always start. It'll give me summat to do in the evenin's.'

Dolly looked surprised. 'I thought you were happy goin' to the dances in the hall.'

'I'm not!' Clara piped up. 'They're always packed to the rafters. I reckon that's why I'm always treading on people's toes.'

Lizzy shrugged. 'I agree with Clara. I'd like to go somewhere a bit bigger, like the Grafton, but I'm not showin' me face in there until I've learned the proper steps. I know you've tried your best to teach me, Doll, but I still ain't gorra clue what foot I'm meant to put where.'

The old woman looked up from her knitting. 'I used to be a dance teacher. I don't mind showin' you the basics.' Heaving herself to her feet, she held out her hands.

Lizzy's eyes rounded. 'You mean here and now?'

'Unless you got somewhere else you need to be?'

'But there's no music and everybody's starin',' said Lizzy as she looked around at their audience.

Placing one arm round Lizzy's waist, the old woman glanced over her shoulder. 'Any of you lot know the waltz?'

There was a mixed murmur of 'yes's' and 'I think so's'.

She cocked an expectant eyebrow. 'Then give us some music to dance to!'

Several voices began to hum the 'Blue Danube' in unison, and by the time the all clear sounded Lizzy, as well as some of the other less capable occupants of the shelter, had mastered the waltz and the rumba.

'A few more of these air raids and I reckon you'll be able to give that Ginger Rogers a run for her money, luvvy,' said the old woman, whose name was Gladys.

Lizzy smiled. 'Thanks for all your help. You're a brilliant teacher.'

Gladys grinned. 'That's kind of you to say. I must admit I did think I might be too old.'

'Tosh!' said Dolly as they emerged into the open air once more. 'I reckon you've more life in you than half that lot in there!'

Gladys chuckled. 'Nice of you to say so, though me arthritis don't allus agree, 'specially in the winter months.' She yawned. 'G'night, girls.'

'Night, Gladys.'

'We used to hold dances at Bellevue,' said Clara wistfully. 'I used to sneak out of bed and watch from the top of the stairs. It was like something out of a fairytale, all the women in the most beautiful dresses ...'

'Missing home?' said Dolly.

Clara nodded. 'I miss what used to be my home. It's how my mother met my father; she came to one of the dances at Bellevue. He reckoned one look at her in her blue taffeta dress was all it took for him to know that she was the woman he intended to marry.'

'How romantic!' said Dolly, whose eyes had glazed over dreamily.

'Is that why you're so worried about Gertrude? Do you think history might repeat itself?' said Lizzy.

Clara shook her head with a mirthless chuckle. 'Hardly. She and my mother are polar opposites.'

'But they both met your father for the first time at Bellevue.'

'Dad doesn't believe in that sort of stuff. Mum, on the other hand, was a huge believer in fate. Her and her pals from the WI often used to go and have their fortunes read.' She chuckled softly. 'Dad could never understand why they were willing to listen to a complete stranger. He used to tell Mum they were nothing but a bunch of charlatans, just out to get their money, although ...'

Lizzy looked sidelong at Clara. 'Although what?'

'Not long after Mum died, this old woman came to the house, saying she had a message from the other side.' She rolled her eyes. 'We all knew it was a load of old tosh, but Dad invited her in.'

Dolly shook her head disapprovingly. 'What on earth did he do that for? From what you've said he knew those people are nowt but a bunch of fraudsters, especially when it comes to preying on folk when they're at their lowest.'

Clara nodded. 'That's what me and Sally thought, so we were flabbergasted when he invited her into his study.'

'What happened next?' said Dolly, intrigued despite herself.

Clara shrugged. 'Dunno, Dad wouldn't say, save that Mum had said she loved us all and wanted the best for us.'

Dolly wrinkled the side of her nose. 'That's it?'

Clara nodded. 'I know, stupid, isn't it? She told us what we already knew. You'd have thought she'd have made up some huge story to swindle him out of a bob or two.'

When they reached the flat in Pickwick Street, Dolly yawned noisily. 'I'm whacked. I hope we manage to get some shuteye before mornin'.'

As Lizzy bade the girls goodnight, she turned her thoughts to how her search for her own mother had drawn a blank. What with the bakery's changing hands and Mrs Williams's disinterest, Lizzy had decided she had nowhere else to turn. Even visiting the house in Snowdrop Street seemed pointless after her last visit to the Williamses.

'She ain't come to no harm, else you'd have heard by now, believe me, chuck. She's fine, ain't she, Kevin?' Mrs Williams had said, turning to her husband, who was scuffing the grit on the paving back and forth with the toe of his boot. She glared expectantly at him as he looked up.

'What? Oh, yes, she's fine,' he said although it was plain for all to see that he had no idea who he was talking about, let alone the state of their health.

Mrs Williams rolled her eyes. 'What we's tryin' to say is that no news is good news.'

Now, sliding her nightie over the top of her head, an image of Charlie appeared in her mind, smiling down at her as he helped her out from under the bench. This image was replaced with another of him rocketing towards her on the car bonnet, then one of him apologising. Lizzy frowned. She hadn't seen Charlie for a long time, not that she particularly wanted to, she told herself, but now she came to think about it she realised he was probably avoiding her. And quite right too, she thought sternly, but even as she did so her brow furrowed further as a nagging doubt entered her mind. Since Mrs Williams was no longer interested in Mary's whereabouts and the bakery was also a dead end, Lizzy had no idea how to continue looking for her mother. Dolly and Clara were more than happy to help, but they were as clueless as she was about what to do, or where to go for help. There's you celebratin' gettin' rid of Charlie, Lizzy thought to herself, and he's the only one who might be able to help. She rolled her eyes. Why had she been so hard on him? She couldn't afford to push people away, especially the ones who believed in her, and she felt sure that he did. Climbing into bed, she pulled the blankets up around her ears. I shall go and see him tomorrow and apologise. Even though it wasn't my fault that he ran me down, I shouldn't have been so rude when he tried to make amends. Closing her eyes, she formed an image of Charlie scooping her up into his arms before he carried her home from the park, and a faint smile appeared on her lips as she slowly drifted off to sleep.

Standing outside the police station where Charlie worked, Lizzy patted her hair and straightened the belt on her coat before stepping through the door. She strode towards the policeman who stood behind the desk and was relieved to see, when he lifted his head, that it was not the same man she had spoken to before. He smiled a greeting. 'May I help you, miss?'

Lizzy nodded. 'I'd like to see PC Charlie Jackson, please. My name's Lizzy Atherton, and he's been dealing with something for me.'

The man frowned. 'PC Charlie ...' The lines on his brow dissipated. 'He's not at this station any longer. Didn't you know?'

Lizzy's heart sank. 'Where is he?'

The policeman leaned his forearms on the counter. 'He got moved to Vauxhall Street station a while back.' Seeing the disappointment on Lizzy's face, he continued, 'Is there anythin' I could help you with? Or would you like me to ring through and tell him ...' he rubbed his chin thoughtfully, 'sorry, what was your name again?'

'Lizzy Atherton, and no, it's a personal matter, thanks all the same.'

'I see. Well, if you're sure—' He got no further before Lizzy, smiling politely, cut him off.

'Yes, thank you,' she said as she hurried out of the station. She had decided before she entered that the only person she would trust with information like this was Charlie. He had seen Albert on the platform that night, so he knew she hadn't exaggerated Albert's temper.

She glanced up and down the street before she realised she hadn't a clue which way she should be heading. She stopped a policeman who was about to enter the station.

'Excuse me, can you tell me the way to Vauxhall Police Station?'

Back in the station Fred entered the area behind the counter. 'Did someone just come in?'

PC Walker nodded. 'A young woman lookin' for Charlie Jackson, so I told her he was up at Vauxhall.'

Fred eyed the young officer curiously. 'Don't suppose she told you her name, did she?'

'Lizzy Atherton.' PC Walker scratched the top of his head. 'Funny, 'cos I've never seen her before, but I'm sure I've heard her name somewhere.'

Fred chuckled. 'She's the one me an' PC Briscoe were talkin' about the other day.' He leaned towards the new recruit in a conspiratorial fashion. 'Our PC Jackson's carryin' a torch for young Miss Atherton, whether he admits it or not!'

'Ah!' said the young constable. 'That must be it.'

* * *

Had any of the staff who worked in Bellevue overheard the Hackneys talking in private, they would have been surprised to hear how the pair appeared to lose their posh accents for a more regional one.

Gertrude frowned her displeasure. 'The trouble with you, Ivy, is you think Arthur's not gorra brain in his 'ead, but you're wrong. You need to 'andle 'im with kid gloves, not boxing ones!'

'If we walked out now 'e'd lose everythin', an what's more 'e knows it. I don't see why we can't—'

''Cos we're in it for the long run, that's why, but if you wanna insist on wadin' in like a bull in a china shop you can go back to your cousins.'

Ivy pouted. 'I'm not goin' back to that dump. It smells, and as for the people who live there ...'

Gertrude rounded on her daughter. 'Don't you start gerrin' above your station or you'll gerra clout. I've told you time and again, there's nowt wrong with 'em, they're the salt of the earth, not like the high and mighty Grangers what look down their noses at people like us.' She wagged a reproving finger. 'I'm tellin' you for the last time, toe the line or sling yer 'ook. I don't care where you go, but I won't 'ave you messin' up all my 'ard work.'

'Some mother you are, sayin' you don't care where I go ... if Arthur could 'ear you talk like that I reckon 'e'd realise wharra mistake 'e'd made. And you've lost your snotty posh accent, by the way.'

'Well if you'd shut your yap and do as you was told I wouldn't 'ave to raise me voice.' She took a deep breath. 'We ain't goin' to be 'ere for ever, but if you keep

144

pushin' your luck then all my 'ard work'll come to naught and we really will 'ave to move back in with your cousins.'

Ivy folded her arms across her chest. 'Fair enough, but you'll have to buy me some new clothes. You've got the cheque book, so he'll never know.' Seeing the look of disapproval in her mother's eyes, she added, 'New from Paddy's Market, not Blacklers.'

Gertrude relented. Her daughter was headstrong, so getting this far without a physical altercation was quite an achievement. 'But nothin' too fancy, else he might get suspicious. As I keep remindin' you, the man ain't stupid.'

Clapping her hands in an excited fashion, Ivy grinned at her mother. 'I don't know why I wanted her old clothes anyway. Clara's much bigger than me; we'd probably've spent as much gerrin' them all taken in. Mind you, she does 'ave some nice stuff.'

Gertrude walked over to where her daughter sat staring at the wardrobe full of Clara's old clothes. 'One day you'll 'ave dresses just as nice as those, but when you do we won't 'ave to worry about gerrin' chucked out on us ears wi' nowt but a bunch of fancy clothes to show for it.' She tucked a lock of hair behind her daughter's ear. 'We've allus lived 'and to mouth, but once I've finished with Arthur Granger and his stuck-up daughter that'll never be the case again. In the meantime you're goin' to 'ave to be patient.'

Ivy smiled brightly at her mother. 'And I will, but I'm sick of seein' 'im mopin' round the 'ouse like a wet weekend. The staff are just as bad, all the ones that 'aven't upped and left.'

Gertrude bit her lip. This was the ideal opportunity to address something she had been dreading. 'About the staff leavin' ... you know 'ow I'm still collectin' their wages?'

Ivy nodded with a grin.

'I've tried sharin' their jobs out amongst the rest of the staff, but there ain't enough of 'em, and I'm worried Arthur'll notice, so I was wonderin' if you ...'

Ivy's eyebrows shot towards her hairline. '*Me?*' she said incredulously. 'You seriously expect me to pick up the slack?'

Taking Ivy's slim hands in her own, Gertrude spoke with haste. 'It's not like I'd be expectin' you to clean out the fireplaces or owt like that. I can switch things about a bit and get that Sally doin' the dirty stuff.'

Ivy snatched her hands back and pointed at Gertrude's long fingernails. 'If you're that bothered, why don't you do it? It was your fault they left in the first place, so I don't see why I should pay for it.'

Gertrude turned pale at the very thought. 'But I couldn't possibly. If someone saw me, they'd lose all respect, and what if Arthur wanted me to 'elp him with one of his clients? I could hardly turn up covered in dirt, could I?'

Ivy shook her head and her ginger curls danced about her shoulders. 'I might've known. Well, you can forget it. I ain't doin' anythin' you won't do yourself. Why should I?'

'Because I'm doin' all this for us. I'm the one takin' the risk; it'll be me what gets banged up if it all goes pear-shaped. Or don't you care what happens to your dear old ma?'

Ivy nodded reluctantly. 'I'll help with the small stuff, makin' beds an things like that, but nowt dirty or heavy, agreed?'

Gertrude grinned. 'Agreed. Now how's about that trip down to Paddy's Market?'

Lizzy had gone over the conversation a million times in her head, but as she stood at the counter her mouth ran dry. It's because I don't know anyone here, except for Charlie, she thought as she tried to calm her nerves. I might not have liked that fat old sergeant, but at least his was a familiar face. Taking a deep breath, she struck the bell. A young man appeared and smiled welcomingly at Lizzy. 'Can I help you, miss?'

'I've come to see PC Charlie Jackson.'

He sagged a little. 'Oh, I'm afraid you've missed him. Only just, mind. I'm surprised you didn't bump into him outside. He'll be in tomorrer if that's any good?'

Lizzy deflated. 'What time?'

The desk sergeant shrugged. 'If you come before five you should catch him before he finishes his shift.'

Lizzy glanced at the clock behind the counter. It was getting on for ten past five. She nodded. 'Thanks, I'll do that.'

The sergeant pointed over her shoulder. 'Now that's what I call a stroke of luck. This young lady wants to see you.'

Turning to face the newcomer, Lizzy's face lit up. Charlie arched his brow in surprise, but seeing the smile slowly spread across his cheeks, Lizzy thought the surprise was a welcome one. 'You after me?' Charlie asked.

Lizzy nodded. 'Only you've finished for the day, so I said I'd come back tomorrer.'

Charlie picked up a pair of gloves from the counter and pushed them into his pocket. 'Why wait until tomorrer when I'm here now?'

'But you're not on duty.'

He gave her the benefit of a large wink and Lizzy felt her tummy flutter. 'I'm a scuffer, Lizzy, so accordin' to the criminals what roam the streets I'm never off duty. Besides, I've allus got time for a pal, and we are pals, aren't we?'

Lizzy nodded. 'Course we are.'

'Good. In that case, why don't we go for a cup of tea and a plate of fish and chips? I've nowt in for dinner, so we could call it my way of apologisin' for mowin' you down last Christmas. Have you seen the news today?' He offered her the crook of his arm.

Blushing Lizzy slipped her arm through his. 'No, why? What's happened?'

He shrugged. 'I dunno, but I thought if you wanted we could make an evenin' of it an' go to the cinema first, see if we can't catch the latest reel, then if there's summat decent on afterwards we could watch that an' then have supper in the caff?'

'Sounds good to me. I've not had a fish supper in a long time.'

He squeezed her arm in his as they left the station. 'That's that settled. Now to the important business of what's brought you halfway across the city to see me?'

Settling into her stride, she glanced sideways at him. 'I wondered if you might have heard owt about me mam. You get around the city a fair bit and you know a lot of people, so I was hopin' someone might've mentioned summat. Only the bakery she used to work in has changed hands, and there's no point in goin' back to Snowdrop Street because the neighbours don't know owt.'

He shook his head. 'Sorry, chuck, but no, I've not heard a dickie bird. What's more I wouldn't know who'd be best to ask. Your mam's been gone an awful long time, and things have moved on.'

Lizzy nodded. 'I suppose I was hopin' you might 'ave some advice on what to do next. No one seems to care any more.'

He looked at her with sincerity. 'I care. We're old pals, you and me, and even though I didn't know your parents very well, I did meet them a few times outside the school gates.'

The corner of Lizzy's mouth turned up. 'And in the headmaster's office ...'

He grinned awkwardly. 'I was a bit of a rascal.' He stopped outside the entrance to the cinema. 'Here we are. Just in time too.' He looked up at the large posters that adorned the entrance to the building. '*The Spy in Black*. Have you seen it yet?'

Lizzy shook her head.

Releasing her arm, he approached the teller. 'Two for the evening performance, please ...'

Lizzy smiled as they sat side by side in the dark of the cinema auditorium. I wonder if I'm on a date, she thought, as she watched the curtains lift towards the ceiling. She looked at Charlie, who was focused on the newsreel. I know he said he was taking me out by way of an apology, but really he hasn't got anything to apologise for. She wondered how you were supposed to know if you were on a date, and thought it was at times like these that she missed having her mother around to give her advice. Leaning to one side, she hissed in his ear. 'How come you moved?'

'Jimmy and Fred've been trainin' up two new constables, so I was sent to Vauxhall. Too many cooks an' all that.'

'I wondered where you'd disappeared to.'

'You've been looking for me, then?'

Lizzy, grateful for the darkness which hid her blushes, shrugged. 'Not as such. I was jolly upset with you for quite some time, only then I realised I was being unfair, and when I realised I hadn't seen you round and about I thought you might have been avoiding me.'

The cinema light glinted off his teeth as he smiled. 'I was going to pop over and tell you where I'd gone in case you needed me, but I thought you might send me off with a flea in me ear again!'

Lizzy pulled an embarrassed face. 'Sorry about that.'

He waved a dismissive hand. 'No harm done, and I'll be back in my old station around Christmas, which is good, 'cos I miss Jimmy ...' he glanced at her, 'amongst other things.'

Lizzy giggled. 'When they told me you'd been moved to Vauxhall I thought you'd put drawing pins on the sergeant's chair or summat daft like that.'

'Shhh!' said a woman behind them. 'If you wanna chat you can go outside, but some of us've paid good money to watch this.'

The usher shone his torch directly into the woman's face. 'Quiet please, madam.'

She gasped indignantly, but rather than start an argument she settled back into her seat.

Chuckling, Charlie patted Lizzy's arm. 'Stop chattin' else you'll get us chucked out.' Smothering a giggle behind her hand, Lizzy settled into her seat.

When the film came to an end Charlie stood up and stretched. 'You ready for your supper, Pipsqueak?'

Lizzy rolled her eyes. 'We're not kids any more.'

He chuckled. 'Says she who got someone else into trouble for talkin'.' He dodged sideways as Lizzy punched him playfully on the arm. 'Only teasin'. Are you ready for your supper, Miss Atherton?'

'Lizzy will do, and yes I am.'

As they entered the cinema café, Charlie pointed to a table near the counter. 'By here do you?'

Lizzy nodded, then eyed him suspiciously as he pulled a chair out for her to sit on. 'You ain't goin' to pull it out from under me, are you?'

Laughing, he shook his head. 'Blimey, you really do think the worst of me, don't you?'

Settling into her seat, she watched him take the one opposite. 'I don't. It's just … well, once bitten twice shy, only with you I got bitten more than once!'

An elderly waitress approached their table. 'You folks ready to order?'

Charlie looked at Lizzy. 'Ladies first.'

'I'll have whatever you're havin'.'

He turned to the waitress. 'In that case, we'll have two fish and chips and a pot of tea for two please.'

As the waitress shuffled off, Lizzy turned to Charlie. 'Not often I get called a lady, nor taken out for a bite to eat come to that, so thanks for tonight, it's been a real treat.'

He smiled. 'I'm glad you're having a nice time. Maybe it'll make up for our last encounter.'

Lizzy gave a small groan of despair. 'Please don't bring last Christmas up again. I feel dreadful about that as it is. I treated you so badly, and you'd not done anything wrong – or at least you'd not done it on purpose. If anyone should be treating someone to an evening out, it should be me taking you.'

He laughed. 'Tell you what, next time you can pay.'

Lizzy chuckled. 'You saying you want to see me again, Charlie Jackson?'

He rubbed his chin thoughtfully. 'It's you who's askin' me out, unless I've got it wrong.'

Lizzy threw the paper napkin she had been twisting between her fingers at him. 'Don't tease. You know full well what I was sayin'.'

He grinned. 'Of course I want to see you again. Besides, we've still got to try and find your mam, and we aren't goin' to do that if we don't talk occasionally, although I must say I'd've thought you'd've heard summat by now.'

Lizzy nodded. 'Me too. I have wondered whether she might have joined one of the services; if so she could be anywhere by now.'

He eyed her thoughtfully from across the table. 'You ever thought of joinin' up?'

'Oh, yes. I wanted to join the Wrens, only I couldn't leave Mam with me stepdad, and when she disappeared I thought I'd be better off stayin' put.'

He nodded. 'Sounds sensible, and if I'm honest I'd've thought she'd've done the same. You say she couldn't go back to her old job, but that wouldn't stop her workin' somewhere else, and there's plenty of work to be had in the factories ... ah. Here's our supper.'

Lizzy waited until the waitress had handed out the plates before she replied. 'That's what I thought,' she said, shaking the salt cellar vigorously over her chips. 'Thanks for listenin' to me. I knew you would; that's why I came lookin' for you and didn't talk to that fat sergeant.'

His mouth full of fish, he coughed on a chuckle. 'Poor old Fred. He's all right once you get to know him, just a bit old-fashioned, that's all.'

She shrugged her indifference. 'Whatever the weather, I'd still rather have seen you. But that aside, what should I do about me mam?'

He paused, a forkful of chips poised before his open mouth. 'I don't see there is a lot you can do bar keep lookin'. Police resources are stretched to the limit with all the extra duties an' that, so unless you've any proof ...'

Lizzy heaved a sigh. 'I haven't though, have I?'

Placing the forkful of food back on his plate he cupped his hand over hers. 'Don't give up hope. We will find her, it's just goin' to take a bit of time.'

Lizzy felt a rush as his hand touched hers, and tried to hide her blushes by dipping her head. 'Thanks for standin' by me. It means a lot.'

Charlie ducked his own head to catch her eye. 'I promise not to give up until we've found her.' He paused. 'Chin up, Pipsqueak.'

She smiled shyly at him. 'You remind me of me dad when you call me that. He used to call me half-pint, and you use the same shaving foam, Vinolia.'

Charlie smiled. 'You always were the apple of that man's eye.'

She nodded, then ducked her head again to hide the tears which formed against her will.

Still holding her hand in his, Charlie moved his chair next to hers and placed an arm around her shoulders. 'You've had a rare old time of it lately, haven't you?' He placed his forefinger under her chin and gently turned her to face him. As soon as their eyes connected a blush bloomed out of nowhere and rose towards her hairline. Instinctively she lowered her gaze to his lips, then focused on her half-empty plate.

Fearing that he might feel the heat coming from her cheeks, she indicated the unfinished food before her. 'Come on, we'd best get stuck in before it goes cold.'

Releasing her chin, he chuckled. 'You sound like a girl after my own heart. No sense in lettin' good food go to waste, eh?' He returned his chair to its original position. 'How's your fish?'

Lizzy nodded with relief. Much as she enjoyed being close to the handsome Charlie, she lost all her defences whenever he gazed into her eyes. 'It's grand, ta. Yours?'

He stowed his mouthful into one cheek. 'That's why I come here: you can't go wrong wi' the grub.' He paused. 'If it's any consolation, I only called you Pip-squeak because you were so short.'

Lizzy stifled a giggle. 'Same reason me dad called me half-pint. I hated being short.'

He smiled endearingly at her. 'But that's one of the things I liked about you – still do. Besides, I wasn't exactly tall myself.'

'You are now though,' she said.

He nodded. 'I used to hang from me bedroom door by me fingertips hopin' it would stretch me out a bit and it must've worked, 'cos I'm six foot one!'

Lizzy giggled at the image that formed in her mind. 'It's all right for us girls, we can wear high heels as we get older.'

Pushing his empty plate forward he sat back and rubbed his stomach. 'That's one option we fellers haven't got!' He pointed to her empty plate. 'If you're ready I'll walk you home.'

'Oh no, there's really no need …' Lizzy began, but Charlie shook his head.

'I know this part of Liverpool better'n you do, young lady, and there's no way I'm lettin' you walk home on your own.'

She shrugged her indifference. 'Suit yourself,' she said, but inside her heart was dancing. He'd called her a lady, *and* he wanted to walk her home: could this evening get any better? If Moaning Minnie goes off we'll have to spend the night in an air raid shelter together, she thought, then chastised herself for wishing such a thing.

A short while later they stood outside the entrance to the shop beneath the flat. Charlie moved a stone around with the toe of his boot. 'I'm glad I got to see you. It would be nice if we could do it again soon?'

Lizzy smiled. 'I'd like that.'

He had lifted his arm as if to reach out to her when a voice called from the window above them. 'Coo-ee,

155

Lizzy!' There was a pause. 'Oh, sorry, I didn't know you 'ad company. Are you comin' up?'

Lizzy looked at Charlie but he shook his head. 'I've got work tomorrer, but thanks for the offer.' He squinted at the woman leaning out of the window. 'Is that you, Dolly?'

Leaning further out, Dolly peered at him. ''Allo 'allo 'allo, if it ain't our Cheeky Charlie. 'Ave you 'ad to arrest our Lizzy?'

He chuckled. 'Nope, she's been as good as gold.'

'Glad to hear it. You sure you don't wanna come in and warm your cockles?'

'Dolly!' Lizzy exclaimed. 'I do wish you'd think before you speak sometimes.' She turned apologetically to Charlie. 'She didn't mean anythin' by it. She wasn't suggestin' anythin', you know, indecent.'

Dolly pouted mischievously. 'I might've been!'

Charlie chuckled. 'Same old Dolly.'

Lizzy rolled her eyes. 'He's goin' 'ome, Dolly. He just walked me back, that's all.'

Dolly shrugged. 'Suit yourselves!'

She was clearly not about to go back inside, so Lizzy smiled at Charlie.

'Thanks again. If you're ever passin' by ...'

'That'd be nice, although I must admit I am rather busy these days, what with the extra work and bein' a voluntary fire watcher in me spare time.'

'Gosh, you have got your hands full. I've often thought about volunteerin' for summat, but I work most days so I'm only free evenin's and nights.'

Charlie grinned in the darkness and Lizzy saw the dimples form in his cheeks. 'You should try fire watchin'; you could even come with me if you fancy it.

I'll show you what to do, and we'll make sure you get the proper trainin'. I could take you when I'm next on duty up this neck of the woods.'

Lizzy nodded. 'I'd like that. Make sure you let me know when you're back, won't you?'

He pushed his hands into the pockets of his thick coat. 'Course I will.' He looked up at Dolly, who gave him a small wave. 'G'night, Doll.'

'Ta-ra, chuck.'

Lizzy ducked into the alley and opened the door to the flat, closing it softly behind her. At the top of the stairs she found Clara and Dolly grinning like a couple of Cheshire cats.

'And to think you said you wasn't keen on him,' beamed Dolly.

Lizzy feigned a yawn. 'I just wanted to ask him about me mam.'

'Did he know anything?'

Lizzy shook her head. 'He was surprised I hadn't found her yet, but he's not heard owt himself.'

'That's a shame. Do you reckon you'll see him again?'

Lizzy shrugged. 'We've not made any plans.'

'Oh,' said Dolly, clearly deflated. 'In that case, it's off to bed I go, unless you've got any juicy details to tell us regarding your evenin' with the handsome officer?'

Lizzy pushed Dolly lightly in the small of her back. 'No I have not. You saw for yourselves he was the perfect gentleman.'

Dolly chuckled. 'Better luck next time!'

Having joined the Wrens, Mary had taken James's advice to appear versatile and adaptable, in the hope

157

that she would be sent all over the country, which would give her a better chance of running into Lizzy. So when she had been approached by the leading Wren and asked whether she could ride a bicycle, she had crossed her fingers behind her back and nodded enthusiastically. 'Course I can,' she said.

The leading Wren smiled broadly. 'Marvellous. We're in desperate need of motorcycle messengers, so—'

Mary held up a finger. 'Sorry, I don't mean to interrupt, but I thought you said bicycle?'

The leading Wren shrugged. 'Bicycle, motorbike, what's the difference? Apart from the engine, of course, and you needn't worry about that: we'll teach you how to change gear, where the brakes are and general maintenance, which is all pretty easy stuff. The hardest part, as I'm sure you're aware, is balance, but if you've ridden a bicycle, and you said you had ...?'

Mary nodded gloomily. 'But it's been a long time since I've been on one, so maybe I'm not the best choice.'

The leading Wren slapped her heartily on the shoulder. 'Nonsense! We all know the saying "it's like riding a bike, you never forget".'

Mary desperately sought another excuse that would enable her to back out without admitting her fib, but none came to mind. 'When do I start?'

'Tuesday week, so it's best all round if you take your leave now ...' She paused. 'What's up? Most girls'd be cockahoop at the thought of a week's leave.'

Mary managed to curve her lips into a smile. 'I was quite happy in the kitchens, but I suppose I must go where I'm needed most.'

'That's the spirit. We've all got to do our bit, and even though feeding our troops is a worthy job, taking messages across the country in the dead of night is a bit more exciting, wouldn't you say?'

Mary saw a glimmer of hope. 'I can't read a map and I've never been any good at geography, so I'm afraid I won't be any use to you after all.'

'Don't worry, it's all part of your training. Dear God, Tanner, most of the signposts have been removed because of Fritz, so we'd be in a right pickle if we sent you off into the wilds of Scotland without teaching you how to read a map first.' Seeing the expression on Mary's face she laid a comforting hand on her shoulder. 'Stop doubting yourself. No one's going to send you off half cocked; you'll be fine. I know the forces have a knack of putting a square peg into a round hole, but not when it comes to something like this. That's why we make sure all our girls can ride bicycles!' She gave a short snort of laughter. 'Could you imagine trying to ride a motorbike if you'd never even ridden a bicycle?'

Mary had spent her week's leave with Jean. 'It's all your brother's fault, tellin' me to be as versatile as possible,' she moaned, rubbing her bruised knee.

Picking the bicycle up from the ground, Jean shook her head. 'You can't blame this on our James. He didn't tell you to lie, he told you to be versatile.'

Getting to her feet, Mary glared at the bicycle. 'I don't understand how kids take to this like a duck to water, when I can't seem to go more than a few feet without losin' control.'

'It's 'cos they've got no fear,' explained Jean. 'Once you get goin' you'll be grand.'

Mary sniffed. 'Got no sense, more like. Oh well, here goes nothin'.'

By the end of the week Mary could stay upright and make hand signals without falling off, although she still found junctions rather tricky.

'I keep thinkin' I'm goin' to hit the kerb on the opposite side of the road. The more I try to avoid it the closer I get!'

James, who had been granted a forty-eight, took a deep breath. 'I keep tellin' you, look to where you want to go and that's where you'll end up. You keep heading for the kerb 'cos you won't take your eyes off it!'

'And you'll be headin' for it a lot faster on a motorcycle, so you've got to get it right before you get on one of those contraptions,' said Jean helpfully.

On her first day at the training camp, Mary was casting an eye over a row of motorcycles when a voice called out from behind her. 'Hello! I see they've sent us another victim!'

Mary turned, alarmed. 'Do you have a lot of accidents here?'

The man who'd spoken, who was polishing a pair of motorcycle goggles with a rag, shrugged. 'Not as many as you'd think, and it's never worse than a few broken bones; most of the time it's just cuts and bruises.' He held out a hand. 'I'm Able Seaman Matthews, although everyone calls me Stanley, after Stanley Woods, and I'll be your instructor.' Seeing the look of incomprehension on Mary's face, he elaborated. 'Stanley Woods is a motorcycle racer. He's won the Grand Prix, and ...' he smiled, 'and I can see from the look on your face that you're not a fan of motorcycle racing.'

Mary shook her head. 'Only of staying alive, so if you can teach me how to ride one of these and still be alive at the end, I'd be most grateful.'

Walking towards one of the motorbikes, he beckoned her to join him. 'It's a bit daunting at first, but don't worry, you'll soon get the hang of it, and when you do …' he smiled again, 'you'll not want to get off.'

All this had taken place back in March, and now, some nine months later, Mary had to agree that her former instructor had spoken the truth. She loved riding motorbikes, and revelled in the excitement of taking top-secret information to all sorts of different naval bases. Every time she went somewhere new she was sure to ask whether anyone had heard of or seen Lizzy, and even though she had always drawn a blank so far, she still hoped that she would find her daughter one day soon and had said as much to Jean on her last visit to Liverpool.

'If it weren't for your brother, I'd still be stuck in one place.' Taking a sip of her tea, she mulled a thought over in her mind before continuing.

'I've not seen him in a long while, which seems silly as I go to Plymouth quite often.' She looked hopefully at Jean. 'Do you have his address to hand?'

Nodding, Jean walked over to the writing desk and sat down, pulling a pencil out of a pot and beginning to write on a slip of paper, which she handed to Mary. Mary silently read the address, then smiled at Jean as she pushed the paper into her pocket. 'Thanks for this.

It's about time I saw your brother and thanked him in person, and it'll be a good excuse for a catch up.' She took a sip of her tea. 'I know you said he wasn't the sort of man to chase after women, but has he started seeing anyone? I wouldn't want to tread on anyone's toes.'

Jean looked intrigued. 'Why might you be treading on someone else's toes?'

Mary half smiled. 'What I mean is, I wouldn't want another woman to get the wrong idea, because James and I are just friends.'

Jean nodded, but Mary could see by her expression that she didn't quite believe her. 'Well, if that's all you're worrying about, you needn't. James is far too busy with work to get involved in relationships.'

Mary took another sip of tea so that she might hide her pleasure. The last time she had seen James she had been a nervous wreck, but all that had changed since passing her motorcycle course. Riding a motorbike in the dead of night to places she'd never heard of before had given her a new-found confidence, and she now felt comfortable in the company of the most high-ranking officers. She visualised the look of approval on his face as she sped toward him on her motorbike. He would undoubtedly be impressed by her improvement from the days when she had been wobbling down the road on Jean's bicycle, one foot outstretched in case she fell, and for once she would feel worthy of his admiration.

Chapter Seven

December, 1940

Lizzy, Dolly and Clara sat huddled underneath the railway arches at the top of Bentinck Street. They had been at a Christmas dance at the Goat Hotel with some of the girls from Langdon's when the air raid sirens wailed their warning.

'Why can't they just bugger off and leave us alone?' cried Clara. 'Don't krauts celebrate Christmas?'

Lizzy, sitting between Dolly and Clara, put her arms round her friends' shoulders and held each of them tightly to her. 'They're probably doin' it *because* it's Christmas in a few days; tryin' to destroy our morale an' all that.'

In the distance they could hear the sound of bombs falling on their beloved city. From their position they saw fires lighting the tops of buildings as well as the trace of the ack ack-bullets as they streaked across the sky.

'Shoot the buggers down!' yelled Dolly. 'I hope you get every last one of 'em.'

'It's bloomin' freezin' under 'ere, ain't it? Tell you what, how's about we 'ave a bit of a singsong? We can clap along and warm ourselves up a bit,' suggested one of the men who had been in the Goat Hotel with the girls just before the siren sounded.

'Good idea,' said Lizzy. 'What's it to be?'

He grinned. 'As it's Christmas, 'ow's about "Jingle Bells"?'

Clara turned frightened eyes to the brick above their heads. 'Are you sure we're going to be safe here? Only I thought they said the Germans would be targeting the docks and the other transport links, and we're hiding under a railway line.'

Getting down on to his haunches, the man looked Clara directly in the eye. 'It's too dark for them to see it's a railway line. Besides, it's the actual docks they're aimin' for, so they can stop the ships comin' in. I know it's frightening, but try not to worry.'

Clara eyed his uniform. 'You're in the army?'

Nodding, he smiled at her. 'I'm one of the lucky ones: I've been given leave for Christmas, which I intend to make the most of. You don't think I'd be hidin' in here if I thought there was a chance it were goin' to get bombed, do you?'

Reassured by his calmness, she smiled back. 'I suppose not.'

He grinned. 'Good!' He held out a hand. 'My name's Josh. What do they call you?'

'Clara. Nice to meet you.' She hesitated. 'Josh?'

'Yes?'

'Will you stay by me?'

He chucked her lightly under the chin. 'Course I will. What kind of feller would I be if I deserted a beautiful damsel in her hour of need?'

Clara smiled her gratitude and a few moments later the railway arches were alive to the sound of 'Jingle Bells'.

Opening her eyes, Lizzy squinted into the darkness. Her head felt as if it was about to burst and she had a horrible taste of soot and brick dust in her mouth. 'Dolly? Clara? Where are you? I can't see a damned thing. What happened? Was it a bomb?'

In the darkness she could hear the occasional cough and the sound of muffled sobs. She tried again, only louder this time. 'Dolly? Clara ...'

"M here, next to you,' mumbled Dolly. It sounded as though she had something against her mouth when she spoke.

'What about Clara?' said Lizzy, who was trying to keep calm despite the panic rising within.

'I dunno.' Lizzy heard Dolly's voice tremble as she went on, 'There's someone next to me, only I don't know who. They ain't movin' ... Lizzy, I'm frightened.' Lizzy felt a touch on her arm.

'Is that you, Doll?'

'Yes.'

Someone close by started to groan.

'Clara? Clara?' Dolly's voice was frantic.

'Nah, it's me, Josh. I think Clara's next to me, but it's too dark to see properly.' They heard the sound of falling masonry as Josh shifted amongst the rubble. 'Clara, luvvy, is that you? C'mon, chuck, say summat.'

'Mmmhmm, 's me.'

Lizzy breathed a sigh of relief. 'Thank God for that. Are you all right?'

There was a moment's silence. 'I dunno. I can't move, 'n' my leg hurts.'

'Try not to move just yet, chuck, not until we know what's what, at any rate,' said Josh.

'D'you think anyone knows we're here?' said Lizzy. 'D'you reckon anyone else is … you know …'

'Alive?' said Dolly, her voice thick with tears.

Lizzy squeezed the other girl's hand. 'You never know, Doll, they might've got out before the bomb or whatever it was hit. I can't remember much. I know we started singin' "Oh Come All Ye Faithful", but that's about it—' A siren cut her off mid-sentence.

Dolly broke in. 'That's the all clear! How long d'you reckon we've been down here?'

Lizzy shrugged. 'Could be hours.'

'What if it's been days?' sniffed Dolly. 'What if this is a different air raid and nobody knows we're here?'

From above their heads came the sound of voices. 'Hello? Can you hear me?'

They shouted back as loud as they could, then listened.

'Stay where you are. They bombed the railway line above you. Any sudden movement on your part could trigger a total collapse.'

'Clara was right,' said Dolly. 'We shouldn't've been hidin' under the arches. Why didn't we go to a proper shelter?'

'There isn't one,' said Josh. 'Not round here, at any rate. It was the arches or nothing.'

There was a whimper in the darkness. 'I know he said not to move, but I couldn't even if I tried.'

166

'Don't worry, chuck, we're all in the same boat. It's all them bricks and whatnot on top of us,' Lizzy said reassuringly.

'No, you don't understand. My leg was really hurting so I thought I'd see if I could move it, just a little bit, to make myself more comfortable, but I can't move it at all.'

'Do you think there's summat on top of it?' Josh began, but Clara continued, her voice beginning to shake as uncertainty filled her mind.

'I don't know. It hurt like billy-o in the beginning, but I can't even feel it any more. It's as if it's not there.'

Josh called up to the rescuers in earnest. 'Listen up, fellers, we've gorra lady down 'ere what's trapped. I know you have to tek your time, but d'you reckon you could do that pretty damn sharpish?'

A shaft of life penetrated the gloom and a voice called down. 'Don't worry. We'll be with you in a minute.'

As daylight flooded the collapsed arch, the girls could see properly for the first time. 'Clara!' squealed Dolly. 'For God's sake someone help me get this thing off of her.'

Scrambling to her feet, Lizzy helped Josh and Dolly heave the lump of masonry off Clara's leg. Josh looked up at the resecuers silhouetted against the light. 'We need a stretcher,' he yelled.

Clara stared at the plaster cast which encased the lower half of her leg. 'Why does it always happen to me?' she said, flourishing a hand at her foot.

'Never mind that. You could've been killed, and if you had, what were me and Dolly supposed to tell your father?' said Lizzy sternly.

Clara rolled her eyes. 'But I wasn't, was I? And even though I know I should go and tell him before something else happens I'm not goin' like this. First thing he'll say is "What the hell were you doing up that end of the city?" And as for sheltering under the railway arches ...' She moved her fingers up and down, mimicking a pair of lips. '"Gertrude was right, Clara, you should've gone into the countryside with all the kiddies; that way you wouldn't have got a broken leg. Look at Ivy, and Gertrude, have they got poorly legs?"'

Lizzy stifled a giggle. 'I expect you're right, but even so.'

Clara shook her head. 'If you want to go and tell him, you can, but you can count me out.'

'Fine by me. You comin', Dolly?'

Clara, who had not expected Lizzy to take her up on her statement, looked pleadingly at Dolly, but the other girl returned her gaze sternly. 'Don't turn them puppy dog eyes on me, Clara Granger, 'cos I agree with Lizzy. I know your dad hurt your feelings when he sided with them awful women, but war is a dangerous business. You got off lightly this time; not everyone in that shelter was as lucky as you.'

Clara nodded her head in shame. 'You're right. I've been acting like a spoiled brat, so if you don't mind going on my behalf, I'd be grateful if you could tell him where I live and that I'd like to see him and that I'm sorry – for everything.'

Lizzy clapped her hands together. 'You won't regret it, honestly you won't, and don't worry, we'll be tactful.' She glanced at Dolly, who had never been tactful about anything her whole life, and added, 'Or at least, Dolly'll keep shtum whilst I do the talkin'.'

Dolly frowned. 'I'm not that bad … am I?'

'I wouldn't call it bad exactly, just that you tend to tell it like it is.'

'I suppose that's true,' Dolly conceded. 'I've never seen the point in dressin' things up, at the end of the day. A spade's a spade, and if you don't like it, tough.'

Lizzy giggled at the anxious expression on Clara's face. 'Like I said, I'll do all the talkin'.'

Clara smiled her gratitude. 'Thanks. The more I think about it the more I realise how selfish I've been. I dread to think what Spencer would say if he knew.'

Lizzy pulled out the chair beside the kitchen table and sat down. 'Didn't you say he was in the Navy?'

Clara nodded. 'We used to fight like cat and dog when we were younger, but when he joined the Navy everything changed. I don't really know why, it just did.'

'But he writes to you, so he knows you've left home—' Dolly began.

'Course he does,' Clara interrupted, 'but he thinks I'm strikin' out on my own, gaining my independence. I couldn't tell him the truth. He's too far away to do anything about it, and anyway he's got enough on his plate without me adding to it.'

Dolly glanced out of the window. 'Looks like the snow's easin' off. Shame you broke your leg at the beginnin' of winter; if you'd done it later on in the year we could've risked takin' you to see your dad for yourself, but not in all this ice. It's downright treacherous.'

Clara pulled a sarcastic face. 'Sorry, Dolly. Next time I decide to get bombed I'll make sure it's at a more appropriate time of year.'

Dolly started to nod absentmindedly, but stopped when she heard her friends' giggles. She threw the tea towel she was holding at Clara. 'I were only sayin' ...'

Clara caught the tea towel in one hand and tossed it back. 'I know you were. Ignore me, I'm just fed up 'cos I can't leave the flat until this bloomin' snow and ice clears off.'

Lizzy patted Clara's shoulder. 'At least the Jerries are leavin' us alone. For now, at any rate.'

Clara looked uneasy. 'You reckon they'll be back?'

Lizzy shrugged. 'I hope not.' She glanced at Dolly. 'But we don't know, do we? And that's why I think we should go and see your father straight away.'

Dolly pulled Lizzy's coat from the hook behind the door and passed it to her. As she pulled her wellington boots on she glanced at Clara. 'Do you need anything before we leave?'

Clara shook her head, then changed her mind and nodded briskly. 'I'll write him a note.'

'Good idea,' said Lizzy. She rummaged in the kitchen drawer for a piece of paper and a pencil and handed them to Clara.

Clara thought for a moment or two before writing quickly and handing the paper back to Lizzy. 'Thanks for this. I must admit my tummy's turning cartwheels; goodness only knows what I'd be like if I was going with you.'

There was a knocking at the door, and Josh's voice came from the other side. 'Hello? Can I come in?'

'Ah! Just in time.' Dolly smiled. 'You can keep an eye on the patient whilst we go off on a mission.'

Josh removed his cap and shook the snow from its peak. 'On a mission? Sounds exciting.'

Lizzy folded the piece of paper and pushed it into the pocket of her woollen coat. 'I don't know about that, but I would be grateful if you could stop this one from tryin' to do the housework whilst we're gone.'

He pulled off a mock salute. 'You can count on me.'

Clara rolled her eyes. 'Once! I tried to do the dishes just once, and I still don't see—'

Lizzy raised her eyebrows sharply. 'I dare say you don't; that's why Josh is goin' to keep an eye on you.'

'Too right,' said Dolly. 'C'mon, Lizzy, let's go mend some bridges.'

Standing on the pavement outside the entrance to Bellevue, Dolly nodded towards the house. 'I've got the collywobbles. What if he blames us for takin' her away from him, or breakin' her leg, or not comin' to see him sooner?'

Lizzy, who had puffed her chest out with an air of determination, deflated a little. 'He wouldn't do that ...' she paused uncertainly, 'would he?'

Dolly shrugged. 'Dunno. He might think we're inter-ferin'. After all, if we hadn't given her a place to stay she would've had to go home.'

Lizzy frowned. 'Bloomin' 'eck, Dolly, couldn't you have said all this before we left the flat?'

'Hadn't occurred to me then, but standin' here lookin' up at that big posh house ... I bet his slaves are classier than us.'

Lizzy burst into giggles. 'Dolly! People don't have slaves any more. They're maids, not slaves.'

'That's what I meant, his maids.'

Lizzy heaved a sigh. 'Well, whatever the weather, we're here now, and I 'aven't come all this way just to go back wi'out so much as a hello.' She pulled Clara's note from her coat pocket. 'And I ain't goin' to take this back to Clara, neither.' Pushing the note back into her pocket, she opened the gate. 'Best foot forward an' all that.' At the front door she took a firm hold of the large brass knocker and rapped it sharply three times. She smiled at Dolly. 'No goin' back now.'

Turning her head, Dolly glanced wistfully down the garden path just as the door opened slightly and a woman's face appeared in the gap. 'Can I help you?'

Dolly nodded. 'Can we speak to the master of the house?'

'D'you mean Mr Granger?'

Dolly and Lizzy exchanged glances. 'Yes.'

The woman eyed them uncertainly. 'May I ask what it's about?'

Lizzy felt her cheeks redden. 'We're friends of Clara's.'

Opening the door wide, the maid ushered them in. 'Is she all right? I've been ever so worried.' Holding a finger to her lips she glanced up the staircase, then indicated to the girls to follow her back across the vestibule, through a small doorway and down a short, steep flight of steps which opened into a large kitchen. She pointed to a couple of chairs. 'Please, take a seat.' She hesitated. 'It's awfully cold outside – would you like some tea? I've not long made a pot.'

Both girls nodded.

The woman took three mugs down from the hooks under one of the cupboards and set them out in a row. 'I'm Sally, by the way,' she said.

Lizzy clapped her hands together. 'I recognise you! You were with Clara when they were evacuating all the kids.'

Sally nodded. 'That's right. I'm afraid I don't remember you.'

Lizzy explained about the suitcase, and how they had returned it to Clara. Lowering her voice, she went on, 'She told us about that awful Gertrude and her daughter Ivy. We told her if things got rough she should come to us, and of course she did, and that's where she's been this past year ...' She told Sally everything that had happened during Clara's absence, finishing with the bombed-out railway arch.

Sally, who was sitting on the edge of her seat, wrung her hands. 'Poor Clara. To think she could've been killed, and all because of those evil ...' She glanced at the ceiling above her.

Lizzy looked up. 'Are they here?'

Sally nodded. 'But don't worry, they're not likely to come into the kitchen.' As tears welled up she wiped the corner of her eye with her pinny. 'Life's been awful since Clara left; it's like someone let go of the reins and nobody's bothered to regain control. Mr Granger doesn't seem to care what happens to this place, not any more. I don't think he's even noticed that half the staff've gone.'

'Have they joined the war effort?' said Dolly.

Sally gave a mirthless laugh. 'No. She kicked them out, but she hasn't told him, and he don't know no better 'cos he put her in charge of the household accounts. She controls the wages, the bills … everything. He hasn't got a clue what's goin' on under his own nose in his own house any more. '

Lizzy frowned. 'But surely he must've noticed the work's not gerrin' done?'

'No, because me and Bert's had to pick up the slack; either that or get the sack.'

Lizzy stared at Sally. 'So that's her game, she sacks the staff but keeps the wages?'

Sally had opened her mouth to speak when they heard footsteps approaching the door to the kitchen. She pointed to the larder door. 'Quickly, get in there and take your tea with you.'

As the girls closed the larder door silently behind them, they heard the kitchen door open and a voice with a nasal twang address Sally. 'Who was that at the front door?'

'They'd got the wrong house,' Sally lied.

There was a pause as the newcomer appeared to mull this over in her mind. 'Who were they after?'

There was a tiny pause before Sally said, 'Can't remember.'

Lizzy peered cautiously through a crack in the larder door, her mouth dropping open as she watched Ivy glance around the room, searching to find something amiss. 'I'd better not find out you're lyin',' the girl said rudely.

'Why would I?'

Ivy, who had turned to leave the kitchen, glanced over her shoulder. 'You said "they". Were there two of them?'

Sally nodded. 'What of it?'

Ivy stared hard at her before coming to a conclusion. 'I reckern you're lyin'; in fact I'd lay money on it. That's the trouble with you and Bert, you're allus up to no good, plottin' against me and me mam. I bet you're runnin' off to that Clara and gossipin' behind our backs.'

Sally swallowed nervously. 'No we're not. We've not seen her since you drove her out.'

Ivy gave a haughty sniff. 'Best thing that 'appened was 'er leavin' this 'ouse. She were runnin' rings round her dad, the spoilt brat.'

Inside the larder, Lizzy and Dolly held their breath as they waited for an outcome. In the kitchen, Ivy glanced at the mug of tea on the kitchen table. Sally followed her gaze and to her horror saw two rings that had been left from the girls' mugs. Ivy pointed at the rings. 'Clean that bloody table. We're not payin' you to sit on yer arse all day.'

Her heart pounding in her chest, Sally grabbed a cloth and started to wipe the table, keeping her fingers crossed that Ivy wouldn't realise the significance of the two extra rings. Ivy wiped a finger across the top of the stove. 'And mek sure you clean this whilst you're at it.' Without waiting for a reply, she left the room. Sally waited until she heard the door at the top of the stairs click shut behind her before opening the larder door.

Lizzy looked as though she had seen a ghost. 'Was that Ivy?'

Sally nodded.

'Are you sure?' said Lizzy, her tone incredulous.

'Course I'm sure.' She stared quizzically at Lizzy. 'D'you *know* her?'

Lizzy grinned. 'Yes I do, and how on earth her and that godawful mother of hers managed to pull this off I've no idea, but I'm goin' to find out. Only not yet; I'll have to speak to Clara first.'

'What shall I tell Mr Granger?'

'Nothin'. You're not to breathe a word to anyone. If they get wind of this they'll be off before you can say knife, and even though that'd be the best thing all round I reckon they deserve to get caught in the act, as it were.'

Dolly frowned. 'Just who are they, and how do you know them?'

Lizzy's grin broadened. 'After me dad died, me an' me mam had to go and live in the courts, and that's where I met 'em, only the folk in the courts don't call her Gertrude, they call her Dirty Gertie.'

Sally clapped a hand over her mouth to smother a shriek of laughter. 'You're seriously tellin' me that Mrs High 'n' Mighty what reckons she's better'n anyone else is known as Dirty Gertie? But she's allus so squeaky clean!'

Lizzy pulled a face. 'Mebbe she is here, but not when I knew her.' She chewed her lip thoughtfully. 'Is she thin as a rake an' sickly pale, and the spit of her daughter?'

Sally nodded. 'Like peas in a pod.' She shook her head. 'So go on, why do they call her Dirty Gertie?'

'She used to rummage through people's bins.'

Sally sank into one of the chairs. 'No! I don't believe it. Why would she want to do that?'

176

'To see if there were owt worth tekkin'; one man's trash an' all that. Her an' that Ivy of hers never tried to gerra proper job; they'd rather beg, borrow or steal than do a decent day's work.'

'They're the same here! They don't actually do anythin'. Well, Ivy does a little bit, but only 'cos so many staff've left and Gert—I mean Dirty Gertie,' she grinned as the words left her lips, 'don't want to replace 'em, but apart from that all they do is give everyone else orders whilst they sit back and watch.'

Lizzy smiled triumphantly. 'That's them all right. How on earth did they manage to smarm their way into this place?'

Sally pulled a face. 'Hanged if I know. I allus thought Mr Granger might've found' – the grin returned – 'Dirty Gertie attractive. She does spruce up pretty well, if you like that kind of thing, but she wears too much makeup for my likin'.'

Dolly looked at Lizzy in confusion. 'I don't get why you don't just show your face an' have done with it.'

'Because I think they've used their brains this time, and I want to make sure they don't tek off with half his money. They might not be the sharpest tools in the box, but when it comes to connivin' an' manipulatin' they're top of their class.'

Dolly nodded. 'So you want to speak to Clara and find out what she thinks before wadin' in, as it were.'

'Precisely. So until then, mum's the word.'

As the door at the side of the house closed, Ivy quickly stepped out of view behind the bedroom curtain. After a moment she slid one finger down the side of the curtain and breathed in sharply. 'I bloody well knew it. Didn't I say she were a lyin' cow?'

Keeping well back from the window, Gertrude craned her neck for a better view. 'Well, well, well, so Sally's sneakin' her pals into the kitchen. Bet you a pound to a penny she's sellin' stock, and there she is actin' like butter wouldn't melt.'

Ivy lifted the curtain as she watched the two women go through the garden gate. 'Are you goin' to tell her we know what she's up to?'

Gertrude screwed her lips up as she mulled the thought over. 'No,' she said eventually, 'not until I've made the most out of the situation.'

Ivy frowned. 'What d'you mean?'

Gertrude tapped her forefinger against the side of her nose. 'You'll find out soon enough.'

Clara's eyes rounded. 'Are you sure, Lizzy? Is it possible you could be mistaken? It's not like you were face to face. Maybe—' Clara got no further.

'As sure as eggs are eggs.' Lizzy grinned.

Clara shook her head. 'My dad's going to blow a fuse when he finds out.'

Lizzy arched a warning brow. 'Not yet. We 'aven't got a clue what they're up to, but you can bet your life it's not good, and I think it'd be a mistake to go bargin' in, all guns blazin'.'

Dolly nodded. 'Softly, softly, catchee monkey!'

'What've you got in mind?' said Clara.

'Not sure yet,' said Lizzy. 'We'll have to put our heads together and have a bit of a think.'

'Whatever you decide to do, you can count me in,' said Josh, who was thoroughly enjoying the idea of solving a crime.

'It's Christmas. You should be spendin' time with your family. I don't think they'd be very happy if you spent the rest of your leave with us,' said Clara.

'Ha! All I'm doin' is gerrin' under their feet. I reckon they've got used to the extra space.'

'Well in that case, the more the merrier.' Clara looked hopefully at Dolly and Lizzy. 'Have you got any ideas?'

Placing her chin on the palm of her hand, Lizzy rested her elbow on the table. 'What we've got to do is get inside their minds and work out what their game is. In the past all they've done is petty theft – nickin' apples, pinchin' bread, not payin' their rent, pickin' people's pockets, that kind of thing. We know they're takin' wages what don't belong to them, but they couldn't have foreseen the war, no matter how likely, so they must've had summat bigger in mind.'

Clara shrugged. 'I always thought Gertrude was trying to get Dad to marry her, so that she could take all his money.'

Lizzy rested her chin in both hands. 'Gertie's not the marryin' kind, whatever she calls herself; from what I remember Ivy ain't gorra clue who her father is. The thing is, Gertie don't like stayin' in one place for too long. She's allus got itchy feet 'cos she's allus up to no good. If I'm honest I'm amazed they've lasted this long.'

Clara frowned. 'You said they weren't the brightest, so I doubt they've got any kind of master plan up their sleeves.'

179

'Don't underestimate 'em. They're sharp as a knife when it comes to thievin', or just about anything that gets them what they want without having to work for it.'

'So they might be capable of fiddling the business accounts, as well as the household ones?'

Lizzy pursed her lips. 'Honest answer? I don't know. If Ivy's uncle was involved it'd be a different matter, but last I heard he'd been locked up.'

'Blimey,' chuckled Josh. 'What did he do?'

'Mugged some old dear, then tried to sell the stuff to some posh feller, only the feller recognised the jewellery and told the scuffers and 'ad him arrested.'

Clara had gone white. 'That was my dad.'

'No it wasn't,' Lizzy giggled, but when she saw the look on Clara's face her chuckles faded into silence. 'You mean your dad was the one who 'ad him arrested?'

Clara nodded slowly. 'I'm beginning to think that Gertrude and Ivy's arrival in Bellevue was not a coincidence.'

Dolly shook her head. 'Revenge! That's why they're hangin' around. I bet they're takin' orders off Gertrude's brother!'

As tears began to well in Clara's eyes, Josh placed a comforting arm around her shoulders. 'From what Lizzy says they're not the violent sort, so you needn't worry about 'em harmin' your dad.' He glanced towards Lizzy. 'That's right, isn't it?'

'No, they're too cowardly for that, but they will be after summat quite big. Didn't you say your dad was an auctioneer?'

'Yes, that's how he knew Mrs Armitage – she was the lady who got robbed – she'd asked him if he could value her jewellery for insurance purposes. That's what Dad does, he goes to people's houses and values their items, then, if they want, he takes them to auction.'

Josh gave Clara's shoulders a reassuring squeeze. 'The way I see it, they don't know that they've been rumbled, and I seem to remember someone sayin' that Lizzy here has a friend who's a scuffer.'

Lizzy brightened. 'Charlie'll know what they're like: the Hackneys are notorious with the scuffers. He'll know what to do, and he should be back in his old station by now. I reckon we go and see him first thing tomorrer, tell him what we know and go from there.'

'Guess who's got visitors?' Jimmy grinned at Charlie.

Charlie screwed up his face. 'In the cells?'

Jimmy shook his head.

'Oh, nice visitors. That's what I like to hear,' said Charlie, rubbing his hands together.

Jimmy nodded. 'Pipsqueak and her pals have come to see you, although how she knew this was your first day back is anybody's guess.'

Grinning, Charlie rubbed his chin. 'She must've smelt the Vinolia.'

'Must've, only I don't see why she'd bring a feller along with her if that were the case.'

The grin disappeared from Charlie's face. 'What feller?'

'Oh-ho, that made you sit up and take notice, didn't it? And as for the feller, you'd best ask 'em yourself; they're in the back room.'

Charlie disappeared.

'Charlie! Are we glad to see you!' said Lizzy, her face positively beaming.

Charlie nodded, but his attention was focused on Josh. 'I don't believe we've met?'

Josh held out a hand. 'I'm Josh, a friend of the girls. I met them when the bomb hit.'

Charlie shook it firmly. 'Bomb? You all look remarkably well.' His gaze fell to Clara's plastered leg. 'Apart from you, that is.'

Clara nodded. 'We were under the arches on Bentinck Street when the bomb hit, but we're all right.'

'How did you get here with your leg like that?'

'Didn't you see the wheelbarrow outside? We borrowed it from the shop below the flat,' said Dolly proudly. 'It was my idea.'

Charlie grinned. 'Now why doesn't that surprise me?' As he spoke, he sat down behind the only table in the room and pulled a piece of paper out from one of the drawers. 'So what brings the four of you here today?'

'D'you know of Gertrude and Ivy Hackney?' said Lizzy.

'Everyone knows the Hackneys. When you say Gertrude, I take it you mean Dirty Gertie?'

Clara emitted a stifled shriek of laughter. 'Sorry, sorry, I still can't get over that.'

'Do you remember Gertie's brother Nathan?'

Charlie nodded. 'Right nasty piece of work, but he can't've done anythin' 'cos he's banged up.'

Lizzy nodded. 'We know, Clara's father was the man who shopped Nathan to the police.' She looked at the others. 'I think it's better if we start from the beginning.'

So Clara, with various interruptions from Dolly and Lizzy, told Charlie all about Gertrude and Ivy's arrival at Bellevue and how they had systematically got rid of nearly all the staff whilst still claiming their wages.

'We've got no proof that they're up to anything other than the wages, but you have to admit this is far too big a coincidence,' Lizzie concluded.

Charlie pulled a face. 'As far as the wages are concerned, you've only got Sally's word for it. I suspect if you asked her whether she knew for a fact that's what they were doin', she'd say no. So as far as the law's concerned, they've not done anything wrong.' Lizzy opened her mouth to protest, but Charlie cut her off. 'I said as far as the law's concerned, but if you want my opinion, I reckon you're right and all three of them are in it – whatever "it" is – up to their necks. Trouble is, we've got no proof.'

Lizzy stared at the unused sheet of paper on the table. 'We can't just stand by and wait for them to run off with all Clara's father's money.'

Charlie looked curiously at Clara. 'Why haven't you gone straight to your father?'

'We were worried that if Gertrude or Ivy saw us they'd take off and we'd never be able to prove they were up to no good.'

'Does that matter, as long as they're gone?'

Lizzy and Clara exchanged glances. 'They've caused a lot of upset and trouble. I think they should be held accountable for what they've done,' Lizzy said.

Charlie took a deep breath. 'But they won't give two hoots, Liz. People like that never do. If you want my opinion, you're better off talking to Clara's father. For all you know he may have suspicions himself.'

'But what if he thinks we're tryin' to cause trouble?'

'Then you'll have done the best you can by him, and even if he doesn't appear to listen he might decide to keep a closer eye on them.'

Dolly frowned. 'What about the people Dirty Gertie's got rid of? If what Sally suspects is true then surely that's illegal?'

'Of course it's illegal, but you don't know for certain that that's what they're doing, you just suspect it is. I know I'm beginnin' to sound like a broken record, but without proof you have nothing!'

'Sally wouldn't lie,' said Clara.

Charlie heaved a sigh. 'Has she got any proof that that's what this Ivy and her mam are up to?'

Clara opened her mouth to respond, but thought better of it. She shook her head, and Charlie turned his attention back to Lizzy. 'I don't know what else to tell you, other than to speak to Clara's father.'

Clara shook her head. 'So that's it? We just have to let them get away with it?'

'I told you: have a word with your father, tell him what you suspect.'

Clara nodded. 'I know, I know.' She looked at Josh. 'Can you help me get outside?'

Nodding, Josh scooped Clara into his arms. 'Thanks anyway, Charlie,' Dolly said as she followed them out. When Lizzy would have gone after her, Charlie held out a detaining hand and closed the door. His cheeks turning pink, he smiled awkwardly. 'Please don't think badly of me, Liz. I'll do everything I can to help you, only my hands are tied until there's been an actual crime.'

'That's what you said about me mam, and I still haven't found her,' Lizzy said quietly.

He hung his head. 'I know. I've made some inquiries, but it's almost as though she vanished off the face of the earth.'

Lizzy placed her hand in his. 'It's good to know you're still tryin'. If I'm honest I didn't think you'd be able to do anything about the Hackneys other than lend an ear and give advice, but I suppose I rather hoped you'd come up with some kind of miracle solution.'

'I wish I could.' He cast an eye to where Josh had been sitting. 'I've never met Josh before. Do you know him well?'

Lizzy shook her head. 'Me and the girls were at a Christmas party in the Goat Hotel when the sirens went off. The landlord told us to shelter under the railway arches and Josh was brilliant; he got everyone singing right up until the ...' Her voice trailed off momentarily. 'Anyway, he helped us get Clara out, and he's called round every day to check on her since.' She grinned. 'We think he's keen on her.'

Charlie's face lit up. 'He's keen on Clara?'

'Of course! Who did you think ...' Her cheeks flushed pink. 'Did you think me and Josh?'

'I—' He was interrupted by a knock on the door. 'Come in.'

Dolly poked her head round the corner. 'You comin' or what? Only Clara's bellyachin' over the ruddy wheelbarrow!'

185

Lizzy nodded. 'Be right with you.'

Charlie walked Lizzy to the door of the station. 'I'm sorry life isn't cutting you a break, but even though it still seems I can't be of any use I hope you'll always come to me if you need help?'

Lizzy nodded. 'I did this time, didn't I?' She glanced to where Dolly and Josh were waiting. 'When did you get back? To this station, I mean?'

'Today. I was thinking of paying you a visit tomor-row, 'cos I did say I'd call by and we could talk about you startin' up as a firewatcher. Do you still want to? Become a firewatcher, I mean.'

She grinned. 'I'd like that.'

'Good!' He saw that Dolly was tapping her toe impa-tiently. 'I've not had much time off recently. How'd you fancy goin' to Seaforth tomorrer and splittin' a bag of chips?'

Lizzy nodded. 'I'm payin', mind you.'

He held up his hands. 'Whatever the lady wants.'

'In that case, I'd love to.'

Josh was trying to lower Clara into the wheelbarrow without falling on top of her. Charlie called over to him. 'Do you want a hand?'

'No thanks,' Josh called back.

Charlie winced as he watched Josh trying to keep his balance. He turned to Lizzy. 'See you tomorrer around ten?'

She nodded. 'Ta-ra, Charlie.'

There was a disgruntled groan from Clara. 'I hate ridin' in this thing. I'm sure Lizzy said Charlie carried her all the way from Princes Park to Pickwick Street when she hurt her ankle.'

'Yeah, well, there's a bit of a weight difference,' said Josh.

Clara glared at him. 'Are you calling me fat?'

Josh grunted as he tried to pull his arms out from underneath her without upsetting the wheelbarrow. 'No! I simply meant ...'

'That the wheelbarrow's heavy,' said Dolly quickly.

He smiled gratefully at Dolly over the top of Clara's head. 'Exactly! The wheelbarrow's 'eavy.'

Clara eyed him suspiciously, 'Good! Although I must admit I was hopin' all this rationing might have slimmed me down a tad.'

Dolly's eyebrows shot up. Whilst she wouldn't call Clara greedy, not within striking distance at any rate, she had never seen the other girl turn down any type of food, and working in the factory's canteen had certainly not helped her waistline.

'This cushion's not very comfy either,' Clara grumbled. 'It was all right at first but all the puffiness has gone. I can feel the bottom of the barrow through it.'

'Don't worry, Clara, we'll soon have you home,' said Lizzy.

With a grunt Josh picked the barrow off its legs and began to push it rather unsteadily down the bumpy pavement. 'Did Charlie say owt else that might help?' Clara asked.

'No, he just apologised for not being of any real use.'

'I know it's not his fault, but if I'd known he wasn't going to be able to help I'd never have agreed to come. I reckon I'll have some fine bruises by the time we get home.'

Dolly linked her arm through Lizzy's. 'You were in there a while. Are you sure he didn't say anything else?'

Lizzy tried to hide her smile. 'Only that he'd pop by tomorrow and pay us a visit.'

Dolly grinned. 'Us, or you?'

'Us!' said Lizzy.

Dolly's grin widened. 'Did you tell him who Josh was?'

Lizzy chuckled. 'There's no pullin' the wool over your eyes, is there, Dolly Clifton!'

'Nope. You only had to look at Charlie's face to know what worried him most.'

'Well, I assured him he had nothing to worry about on that score. Not that it would make any difference, 'cos I'm happy as I am.'

Dolly squeezed Lizzy's arm in hers. 'So where're the two of you goin' tomorrer?'

'Seaforth Sands, but only as friends before you go gerrin' any ideas.'

'Does Charlie know that?'

Lizzy nodded.

'He must be keen to hang in there,' said Dolly. 'There's not many who would.'

'Well I'm not interested in a relationship with any man, let alone Charlie, so if he wants to go off with another woman he's more than welcome.'

Dolly looked sidelong at Lizzy. 'No need to jump down me throat.'

Lizzy heaved a sigh. 'Sorry, Doll, I didn't mean to have a go. I suppose I'm just disappointed that we couldn't help Clara.'

Dolly arched a brow. 'Really? Or did I hit a nerve?'

'I like him,' Lizzy confessed, 'a lot, but he reminds me too much of the past, which is summat I'd rather forget.'

'How'd you mean?'

'He's me dad to a T: same sense of humour, same mischievous grin.'

Dolly nodded knowingly. 'I see what you mean, but that's hardly Charlie's fault.'

'I know, but I want to mek sure he's sincere, and not goin' to go off as soon as he gets bored.'

'So keep him at arm's length and see what happens?'

Lizzy nodded. 'Exactly.'

Sally gaped at her employer. 'I swear I never took it, honest, Mr Granger.'

Arthur Granger lowered his gaze. 'Tell me the truth, Sally. These things don't just disappear into thin air.'

'I *am* telling you the truth,' Sally wailed. 'Wharron earth would I do with all that food?'

'Give it to your pals,' said Ivy, clearly delighted at the maid's discomfort.

'What pals?'

Gertrude folded her arms. 'The ones you had in the kitchen last night, or do you deny it?'

Sally's cheeks flushed. 'They weren't pals exactly—' she began, but it was all Gertrude needed.

'So you admit you were lying!'

A tear trickled off the end of Sally's nose. 'Not exactly . . .'

Arthur leaned forward in his seat. 'Who were they, Sally?'

Sally lowered her head. If she told the truth, then she would have blown any chance that Clara had of getting rid of Gertrude and Ivy, and Mr Granger would be angry that she had not told him of the visit; but if she lied, her own job would be in jeopardy. She shrugged. 'I didn't really know them.'

'Yet you let them into the house?' said Gertrude, her voice shrill.

Sally gave a feeble nod.

'Do you think they might've stolen the food, Sally?' said Arthur, who, unlike Gertrude and Ivy, was trying to keep things as pleasant as possible.

Sally shook her head.

Leaning forward, he took her hands in his. 'Sally, I'm trying to help you.'

When she looked up, her eyes shone with tears. 'I know ...' was all she could manage before her emotions got the better of her and tears coursed down her cheeks.

Opening the door to the study, Gertrude stared at her icily. 'Get your things and go.'

Arthur glared at her. 'She goes nowhere until I tell her to, understood?'

Gertrude stared at him in astonishment. 'But she stole ...'

He shook his head. 'I don't believe for one minute that Sally would be capable of such a heinous act. If anything, she made a mistake by letting strangers into the house, probably because they appealed to her better nature, but since when has that been a crime?'

Sally hooked a tissue out from her sleeve and blew her nose. 'Thank you, Mr Granger. I promise I'll not let you down again.'

He smiled kindly at her. 'It could have been worse, Sally; they could have taken a lot more than food. You really have to be careful whom you allow into the house, and that being said I think we've sorted things out here, so off you go and dry your eyes.'

As she left the room Gertrude turned to her employer. 'If I had my way she'd be out of this house, never to return. You don't know who those people were.'

He pulled a face. 'True, but I do know Sally, and I'm sure she wouldn't have let them in had she thought they were up to no good. Besides, we all make mistakes, including me, the biggest one of all being the day I allowed my daughter to leave this house.'

Gertrude fought the urge to roll her eyes. 'You did what you thought best.'

He gave a short, mirthless laugh. 'And lost my daughter in the process. That's why I now think before I act, something you should start putting into practice.'

Gertrude nodded curtly, beckoned Ivy to follow her, and strutted towards the kitchen. 'How dare he lecture me on givin' folk a second chance when he reported our Nathan to the scuffers without askin' where he'd got the stuff from?' she hissed.

Ivy skipped along behind her. 'I told you he was soft on her, but you said Sally was as good as gone.'

Gertrude rounded on her daughter. 'How was I to know she'd lie?'

Ivy gaped at her mother. 'She did?'

'Course she did,' snorted Gertrude. 'A girl like Sally wouldn't allow strangers into the 'ouse, and seein' as 'ow we was the ones who nicked the stuff to get her into trouble, we know she wouldn't steal. Question is, why did she feel the need to lie?'

'Mebbe they were her pals?'

'Mebbe, or mebbe they was pals of Clara's, and if that's the case we've a spy in our midst. How much does she know, d'you suppose?'

'I dunno. I've not been the one on the fiddle— Ow!' Ivy managed to stop herself from barrelling into the back of her mother.

Gertrude gripped Ivy by the elbow and steered her towards the stairs. 'Keep your bloody noise down, you stupid girl. You can bet your boots she's flappin' them big ears of hers just waitin' to hear summat she shouldn't.'

Ivy rubbed her elbow. 'I reckon we cut our losses and go. Surely you've got what you come for?'

Gertrude considered her answer. 'In a manner of speaking, yes, but I'll not be happy till I see Mr High and Mighty beggin' for forgiveness, and if I play me cards right, it might even get our Nathan off the 'ook!'

Ivy rolled her eyes. 'How long's that goin' to take?'

Gertrude pinched Ivy's skinny cheeks and shook them in a jovial manner. 'Not long, my cherub, not long.'

'Gerroff!' squealed Ivy. Rubbing her cheeks, she looked at the glint of malice in her mother's eye. 'What're you up to?'

'I'm goin' to give that 'orrid man a taste of his own medicine. He's got another big auction comin' off in a few months, only this time instead of us takin' our share I'll plant the stuff in his study an' tell 'im you and me've got another placement. When we're out of 'ere I'll give the scuffers a call and give 'em an anon … anonim … a tip-off.' She cackled nastily. 'I'll lead 'em straight to Arthur's study where they'll find the lot.'

A sly grin adorned Ivy's reddened cheeks. 'But what if he points the finger at us?'

Gertrude placed an arm round her daughter's shoulders. 'We shall be long gone. Besides, if we'd nicked the stuff why wouldn't we take it with us? The coppers'll think he's mekkin' it up!'

'Well, all I can say is I'd like to be a fly on the wall the day that fat cow Clara watches her precious father gerrin' banged up for robbin' his pals!'

Chapter Eight

Gazing at the horizon, Lizzy popped another chip into her mouth. 'I wonder what it must be like to live in Ireland. Someone said you'd never know there was a war on.'

Charlie pulled a face. 'Must be pretty strange. It's the only country they've not tried to take over ... yet.'

Lizzy nodded. 'Lucky sods.'

He glanced sideways at her. 'Bet you never thought Cheeky Charlie and Pipsqueak would be sharing a bag of chips one day.'

Lizzy giggled. 'Strange how things turn out, isn't it?'

Charlie slid his arm along the back of the bench. 'If this were a real date, and I know it's not,' he added hastily, 'but if it were, what would you give it out of ten?'

Lizzy wriggled around on the bench as she tried to find a comfortable position. 'I reckon I'd say it were about a six.'

'Six? Is that all?'

She giggled. 'Nothin' to do wi' you, but these chips could've done with an extra five minutes in the fryer, and as for the weather ...'

He wrinkled the side of his nose. 'There's not a lot I can do about the weather, and you saw the look on that woman's face in the chippy. I didn't fancy pickin' an argument with her.'

Lizzy laughed. 'I thought you were meant to be a big strong policeman, not afraid of anyone or anything?'

'Even policemen have their limits!' he chuckled. 'Besides, I didn't hear you complainin'.'

'Too right I didn't. She could turn folk to stone with that glare of hers.'

Charlie cocked a single eyebrow. 'You never mentioned the company.'

'Eh?'

'You gave a low score because of the chips and the weather, so does that mean I pass muster?'

Chuckling, she shook her head. 'Someone's fishin' for compliments.' She glanced shyly at him. 'But if you must know, then yes, you pass muster.'

Fishing around in the wrapping for a more promising chip, he nodded. 'That'll do me.'

Lizzy paused. 'How would you mark it? If it were a proper date, I mean?'

Charlie shrugged. 'A two.'

'Two!'

He laughed. 'Keep your wig on, I was only pullin' your leg.' He cleared his throat. 'I'd score it a ten, because no matter how undercooked the chips or foul the weather, nothin' could spoil me time with you.'

Lizzy rolled her eyes. 'Charmer!'

He smiled, and Lizzy's tummy fluttered as the dimples appeared in his cheeks. 'I hope so. Let me know if it's workin',' he said with a wink, and once again Lizzy's tummy tingled pleasantly.

'A two ...'

Putting his arm round her shoulders, he pulled her close to him. 'You know you're better than a two. You don't need me to tell you that.'

She relaxed into his embrace. 'I should hope so too. I think I'm a pretty good catch!'

'And modest to boot!' Charlie's smile broadened as she dug him in the ribs. 'Soggy chips aside, if this were a date what would you suggest to improve things?'

She folded the paper over the remainder of her chips and stared dreamily out at sea. 'I love swimmin'. Can you swim?'

He nodded. 'Like a fish, or at least that's what me mam used to say. I must admit I've not been for years.' He scratched his chin thoughtfully. 'I think the last time I went for a dip was in the pool at New Brighton.'

Lizzy laughed. 'My dad was suspicious of that pool. He reckoned the kids peed in the water and that's why it was always warm.'

'He was probably right. At least we all knew the Scaldy was warm because it came out of the factory.'

'You used to swim in the Scaldy?'

He nodded. 'When I was much younger, yes. Didn't you?'

Lizzy grinned. 'You didn't go in the nuddy, did you?'

He feigned shock. 'Elizabeth Atherton! What do you take me for?'

She giggled at his expression. 'Me mam used to say I'd go cross-eyed if I looked at the boys in the nuddy.'

Charlie lifted her chin with his forefinger and gazed deep into her eyes. Lizzy felt herself migrate gently towards him. He chuckled. 'They may be a little bit crossed ...'

Coming back to reality, Lizzy punched him playfully on the arm. 'Cheeky beggar. Gettin' back to our date, what would you do?'

'Seein' as how you like swimmin', I reckon I'd take us to one of the baths in the city, probably the one on Allerton Road. I used to like it there. Then when we'd finished I'd take you out for a slap-up meal, 'cos swimmin' always made me extra hungry.'

She smiled. 'Sounds like the perfect date.'

Charlie pointed at the remainder of her chips. 'Shall we see if the birds are hungry?'

She nodded, then laughed as she watched Charlie throwing a handful to the birds before popping a few into his own mouth. 'I thought you agreed they weren't very nice!'

'It's a shame to waste them,' he said with a shrug, then groaned. 'I sound just like me dad.'

Lizzy, who had never met Charlie's father, eyed him curiously. 'Is that a bad thing?'

'It is when it comes to food. He's always saying we shouldn't waste food no matter what, but there are limits!' He read the incomprehension in Lizzy's face and continued. 'We used to have a black lab called Hattie. She was more like a pig than a dog, and if you didn't watch where you put your food she'd swaller it whole. One mornin' me dad come into the kitchen to find her wolfin' down the last slice of bacon. He shouted at her to stop but that just made her eat faster, so he grabbed hold of the end bit that was pokin' out of her mouth and pulled.' He chuckled at the memory. 'Mam shouted at him to let the dog have it, but would he listen? Not a chance! He got the frying pan out of the cupboard and set the bacon on to sizzle. Mam said it was disgustin' but he didn't care, he slapped it on a bit of bread and poured a dollop of Daddie's over the top then bit into it like there was nothin' wrong. Mam said she'd never kiss him again but he finished the lot, sayin' it was wrong to waste food.'

Lizzy giggled. 'Sounds just like my dad. He was allus tellin' us the same thing. He even used to scrape the green off anythin' that'd gone bad and eat what was underneath. We told him and told him he'd mek himself ill one day ...' Her voice trailed off.

Charlie gave her shoulders a comforting squeeze. 'I reckon all those who went through the Great War came out with the same attitude: waste not, want not.' He shook his head. 'Who'd've thought we'd be in the same boat a couple of decades later?' He scattered the chips on the ground a few feet in front of them and they watched as the birds swooped down and picked them up without bothering to land.

Resting her head against Charlie's shoulder, Lizzy wondered how many women would give their right arms to be sitting where she was at that minute and conceded it was probably quite a few. Charlie was very handsome, and even though a lot of women wouldn't pick a scuffer for a partner, they'd probably make an exception in his case. He had made it plain he would like to take her on a real date, and even though she had fished for clues by asking what he would do and where he would take her, she felt she was still none the wiser. What she really wanted to know was what one did on a real date that was different from what they were doing now. She had no idea what was expected of her, or what the rules were. She frowned: were there rules? There must be, but what were they and how could she find out? If only her mother were here.

'Penny for them.'

'What?'

'Penny for your thoughts?'

Lizzy's cheeks flushed pink. 'Nothin' interestin'. Just wonderin' what me mam would say if she could see me now,' she said half truthfully.

He chuckled. 'Gerraway from that awful Charlie Jackson before he does summat daft!'

'Probably, but only because she hasn't seen you for quite a while.'

He raised his brow. 'So you admit I've changed?'

She laughed. 'Proof is in the pudding, Charlie Jackson. It'll take a lot more than today to convince me.'

He rubbed his chin thoughtfully. 'I'm handsome, clever, kind, handsome ...'

Lizzy pointed an accusing finger. 'You said that twice!'

He grinned. 'Did I? What was that then?'

'That you're handsome!'

'Why thank you, Lizzy, that's very kind of you to say so.'

She laughed. 'See? It's goin' to take more than one date.' She clapped a hand to her mouth. 'Not that I'm sayin' that's what this is.'

Laughing, he tousled her hair playfully. 'Would it really be that bad?'

Deep down, Lizzy prayed Charlie would throw caution to the wind, sweep her into his arms and kiss her. If he did she would kiss him back.

Charlie cut across her thoughts. 'Come on, Dilly Daydream.'

'Hmm?' said Lizzy, who had been rather enjoying her little fantasy.

'It's time we were off, especially if you fancy goin' for a stroll around the city.'

'But that's what you do all day every day. Won't you be bored?'

He looked at her in surprise. 'Bored? How could anyone get bored walking round Liverpool? It's gorra be one of the best cities in the world, an' certainly one of the busiest – you've folk from all walks of life, all different countries, rich and poor.' He shook his head. 'How could anyone get bored of Liverpool?'

Lizzy giggled at his enthusiasm. 'But everyone has their routine, and as you do the same beat every day I'd wager you see the same people too?'

'I do night shifts as well as days, and my job takes me all over the city.'

At the station, he handed their tickets to the conductor and led Lizzy to the back of the train. 'Talking of walking round Liverpool, have you ever been for a stroll around the city after midnight?' She shook her head, and Charlie nodded. 'You should try it some time. You've got all your night workers, like the fishermen or the lads from the abattoir – in fact there's all manner of folk, all livin' their lives under the light of the moon.'

Lizzy sank into the seat beside his. 'You make it sound like a different world.'

He shrugged. 'I suppose it is in a way. The whole city looks different under moonlight, smells different too, and it's a lot quieter. There's no birdsong, no buzzin' bees, and the voices ...' he paused as the train lurched into motion, 'you don't get the background chatter like you do durin' the day.'

Lizzy was intrigued. 'It sounds fascinating. I always assumed the only people out at night were burglars and the like.'

He laughed. 'They're around in the daytime too, you know, only they're more easily concealed in the crowds.'

Resting her chin on the heel of her hand she eyed him with admiration. 'I've allus thought scuffers plodded the streets waitin' for a crime to happen, but it's not like that at all, is it?'

He shook his head. 'In this job you get to see the best and worst in people, but if you get to know the streets, who works where and what passes for routine, you can soon tell when summat's amiss.' He smiled. 'When I first joined the force, Jimmy told me that a good copper don't just patrol the city, he *is* the city.'

Lizzy was in awe. 'I'll never look at a policeman in the same way again.'

He chuckled quietly. 'We're nowt special, Liz, we're just regular folk.'

She shook her head. 'You're not, you know, you're much more than that, you're like ...' she tried to think of an appropriate analogy, '... like one of them medieval knights what defended the kingdom ...' She paused for a moment. 'Lancelot! That's who you're like.'

Charlie blushed as some of the other passengers in the train turned to stare at them. 'Blimey! I wouldn't go that far.' He nudged her playfully. 'But if I'm Lancelot does that make you my Guinevere?'

Lizzy burst out laughing. 'Hardly!'

The train drew to a halt and more passengers got on. Lizzy looked out of the window. 'How does your kingdom look from up here?'

Without taking his eyes off her, he smiled. 'Beautiful.'

Blushing, Lizzy shook her head. 'I'm sure you meet your fair share of damsels in distress in your line of work.'

He shrugged. 'Comes with the job. Why?'

'Nothing, 'cept I can't be the only girl in Liverpool who sees you as a bit of a Lancelot.'

He laughed. 'I think you are, or if not you're certainly the first to mention it.'

She cast her eyes over the city. With so many men off to war it would not be long before the women of Liverpool turned their attention towards the handsome policeman, and when they did he would realise that he could do much better than a dowdy seamstress.

As the train reached the Pier Head station, Charlie got to his feet. 'Lewis's?'

She nodded. 'Lewis's it is.'

After their walk around town the pair headed for the Grafton. 'I don't think I've ever seen you dancing,' said Lizzy. 'Who taught you?'

'My sister Phoebe. She used to use me to practise on.'

Lizzy stopped short in her tracks. 'Golly! I've just thought of summat. You're goin' to be the first feller I've ever danced with. Normally me and the girls take turns bein' the man.'

Charlie slicked his hair back with the palm of his hand. 'I hope I live up to their standards.'

Lizzy giggled. 'A blind man with a peg leg could do better'n Clara. No matter what dance you're doin' her feet allus end up on top of yours, even though she allus blames the space around her.'

Handing their coats to the girl behind the counter Charlie slipped his hand into Lizzy's. 'Let's see ...'

As the music started, Lizzy grinned. 'Lindy Hop! C'mon, Charlie!'

To her surprise Charlie knew every move and carried it out with ease and precision. It was several dances later before the pair decided to take a break. Charlie laid a hand across his chest. 'Please tell me I'm better'n Clara!'

Lizzy laughed. 'A lot better. For a start you didn't grunt when you picked me up!'

Charlie laughed until tears formed in his eyes. 'I should hope not!'

Lizzy stared adoringly at him. Whilst she didn't know many men who were as handsome as Charlie, the ones she did know were more concerned with appearances and would never let themselves go the way he did. As he lowered his head she quickly averted her eyes.

'Would you like something to drink?'

She nodded. 'I'd love a glass of lemonade.'

As Charlie left to get the drinks, she cast an eye around the other women in the room and noticed that a few of them were watching Charlie. It's like putting a juicy bit of bait on the end of your hook, she conceded: all the other fish see it and they want to be the ones to snatch it up. Trouble is, some of those fish are just as attractive as the bait, and you're nowt but a sardine, Lizzy Atherton. As she continued to watch, a woman standing next to the bar turned her attention to Charlie. He smiled, nodded politely, then jerked his head in Lizzy's direction. The woman turned to look at Lizzy, shrugged, and walked away.

When Charlie re-joined her she raised a quizzical brow. 'What did that woman want, the one at the bar?'

Charlie placed one of the glasses he was carrying in front of Lizzy before sitting down. 'She asked if I was accompanying anyone, so I said yes.'

Lizzy sniffed. 'I wouldn't mind, you know, if you wanted to dance with someone else,' she lied.

Charlie shook his head. 'Why would I want to dance with anyone else when I'm with you?'

She shrugged. 'I just wouldn't want you to miss out. It's not as if we're on a date ...'

'So you keep reminding me, but that makes no odds, or not to me, at any rate. As far as I'm concerned I'm spending the day with you.'

Lizzy smiled. 'I wish ...'

He cocked his head on one side. 'Carry on.'

'I wish I was a bit braver, and not so worried about things goin' wrong all the time.'

He slid his hand across the table and clasped her fingers in his. 'It's understandable, with everything that's happened.'

She smiled gratefully at him. 'Why are you so nice, Charlie Jackson?'

He chuckled. 'Not a crime, is it?'

She shook her head. 'Not at all. It just makes things harder.'

As the band struck up a slow number he raised his brows. 'May I have the pleasure?'

She nodded. 'You may indeed.'

As they made their way around the floor, Lizzy laid her head on his shoulder and closed her eyes, listening to the rhythmic beat of his heart. If only she could bring herself to take a chance, to lay bare her own heart, but the very thought filled her with fear. She had already lost her father, the only other man she had ever loved; she was not prepared to lose Charlie too.

Charlie spoke quietly. 'Are you doin' anythin' special on Christmas Day? Only I thought it might be nice if I could pop round for a bit.'

Lizzy tightened her grip round his waist. 'Not in particular. We thought it'd be nice to do a cold buffet this year, but you're welcome to join us.'

Charlie entwined his fingers in hers. 'That 'ud be nice. Are you sure Dolly and Clara won't object?'

Lizzy shook her head. 'Not those two. The more the merrier as far as they're concerned. I know that Josh is comin' round before he leaves.'

Charlie shook his head. 'Poor blighter. What a day to go back to camp!'

'He's one of the lucky ones who get to stay in this country. It must be a damned sight worse for those overseas. Clara wants us to see him off on the train, so me and Dolly said we'd take her. You could come too if you like?'

'What time's he off?'

'He's catchin' the ten o'clock train.'

Charlie shook his head. 'I've promised me mam I'd go there for me brekker. She always does a fry up, and she'd be ever so upset if I tried to wriggle out of it.'

'Never mind, you can still have dinner at ours.'

Charlie squeezed her in his arms. 'I wouldn't miss it for the world.'

As the music came to a halt he smiled down at her. 'Come on, Pipsqueak. I'm not sure how much longer I can keep my gentlemanly promise dancin' this close to you!'

Blushing, she tapped him playfully on the arm. 'You'd best be gerrin' our coats then.'

A short while later they stood in the yard below the flat in Pickwick Street. Charlie stamped his feet. 'All that dancin' keeps you warm, but after a while of bein' outside the cold doesn't half start to set in, doesn't it?'

Lizzy nodded. 'I'd invite you in but Dolly and Clara will be waitin', and they won't give you a moment's peace.'

He laughed. 'You mean Dolly'll want the full nine yards.'

Lizzy nodded. 'Not that there's anything to tell.'

He raised his eyebrows suggestively. 'We could always give her summat to talk about.'

Lizzy cast her eyes to the stars. 'Charlie Jackson!'

Stuffing his hands into his pockets, he chuckled beneath his breath. 'Can't blame a feller for tryin'.'

'I've got enough on me plate tryin' to find me mam—'

'I know,' Charlie interrupted. 'I were only teasin'.'

Lizzy relented a little. 'I know you were. If it weren't for me mam things would be very different.'

Charlie arched a single brow. 'You mean I might be in with a chance?'

Lizzy looked around. 'I don't see anyone else, do you?'

Charlie grinned. 'That'll do me.'

Lizzy had opened her mouth to speak when the door to the stairwell burst open behind her, causing them both to jump.

'Lavvy alert!' said Dolly as she shot past Charlie and Lizzy into the yard. 'Wotcher, Charlie boy. You two have a good evenin'?' Before he could answer there came a short sharp squeal from inside the privy. 'Dear God, that seat's cold!'

Chuckling, Charlie raised his voice. 'Lovely, thanks, Doll.' He turned back to Lizzy. 'I'd best be gettin' off. What time do you want me on Christmas Day?'

They heard a chuckle from behind the privy door.

Lizzy rolled her eyes. 'Twelve?'

'Twelve it is. See you then,' said Charlie. 'Ta-ra, Dolly!'

There was a flushing noise followed by a muffled 'Ta-ra, chuck.'

When Dolly emerged from the privy, she looked sombrely at Lizzy and pointed to the flat. 'I'm afraid we've had a bit of trouble.'

'What now?' said Lizzy, following her up the stairs. When they entered the flat the answer to her question was plain: Sally was sitting on the settee beside Clara, her eyes brimming with tears. Lizzy let out a groan of dismay. 'Why don't I get a good feelin' about this?'

Clara, who was holding Sally's hand, smiled grimly. 'She's been threatened with the sack.'

'Why?'

''Cos they want to get rid of her, that's why,' said Dolly.

Sally explained how the Hackneys had seen Lizzy and Dolly leaving the other night. 'They think I'm still in contact with Clara, I know, because Ivy called me a nasty little spy.'

Lizzy scowled. 'If anyone's nasty it's them, not you. Why would they be bothered that you're still seein' Clara if they'd done nothin' wrong?'

Sally shrugged. 'They obviously don't trust me, 'cos they've started lockin' their room.'

Clara frowned. 'What on earth could they be hidin' in their room that they don't want you to know about? Or d'you reckon they're doin' it to prove you can't be trusted?'

'There is summat, but I'm only guessin', mind.'

'Never mind that. Tell us what you know,' said Lizzy.

Sally lowered her voice. 'Well, you know how Gertrude's been helpin' Mr Granger with the auctions?'

They nodded in unison.

'Well, just lately people've started complainin' that stuff's been goin' missin' from their homes.'

'What kind of stuff?' Lizzy asked.

'Jewellery.'

Lizzy folded her arms across her chest. 'It's them, I'd lay my life on it. That's the sort of thing they do!'

'What've people been sayin'?' asked Dolly.

Sally shrugged. 'Not much, just that they've lost the item they'd asked to be valued. At first I thought mebbe they didn't like the valuation and had changed their minds, but now I'm not so sure, 'cos there's quite a few of them what's mentioned it.'

Lizzy bit the inside of her lip. 'You say they keep their room locked. Is there another key?'

Sally nodded. 'I think so. There's a drawer full of spare keys in the kitchen.'

'When are they likely to go out next?'

Sally thought for a moment before answering. 'This time o' year, Mr Granger usually does a charity auction every couple of weeks, and what with everyone wantin' to raise money for the war effort—'

'When was the last one?' interrupted Clara.

'They went to one last night.'

Lizzy nodded thoughtfully. 'You'll be out of plaster in two weeks' time, Clara.'

Clara nodded. 'But what's that got to do with anything?'

'It means you'll be able to join me and Dolly when we find out just what they're hiding in their room.'

Dolly grinned. 'We're breaking in?'

Lizzy smiled mischievously. 'We can't be breakin' in if we've gorra key.'

'Wharrabout me?' said Sally. 'Aren't I allowed to help?'

Lizzy nodded. 'Course you can. We'll need a good lookout!'

Limping through the back door into the kitchen, Ivy threw her hat on to the table. 'Next time you can do your own dirty work. I nigh on broke me bleedin' neck out there.'

Gertrude looked at the hat, which had left a spray of dirty water on the surface of the table. 'Where did she go?'

Ivy glared at her mother. 'I don't know, 'cos I went arse over on a patch of meltin' ice.' She unbuttoned her jacket and swung it round in front of her. 'Look at that! Covered in muck, not that you care.'

Gertrude rolled her eyes. 'Stop whinin'. It'll wash out.'

Ivy slumped into a chair by the stove. 'Well I ain't washin' it, and you can't ask Sally to, 'cos she'll wonder why it got so dirty, so you'll have to do it. And you can forget me doin' any chores until me ankle's better. I twisted it summat awful when I slipped.'

Gertrude picked the jacket up from the floor and pushed it into the sink. 'Which way did she head?'

Ivy shook her head. 'How the hell should I know? I didn't even mek it to the end of the road.'

Gertrude filled the kettle and placed it on the stove. 'Useless, that's what you are. I allus say if you wanna job doin' properly …'

Ivy pouted. 'It's not my fault everywhere's covered in ice; it's like a skatin' rink out there. I'd like to see you tryin' to walk across them pavements in a blackout!'

Gertrude tutted her disapproval. 'I should've known better than to ask you. You're allus gerrin' it wrong.' Ivy gasped indignantly, but Gertrude wasn't interested. 'At least the evenin's not been a complete waste of time.' She took a large bar of yellow soap out from under the sink and placed it on the drainer. 'Whilst you were out there playin' silly beggars, Arthur told me about his pal what's havin' an auction in aid of the war effort. It's goin' to be held at the feller's house in two weeks' time, an' Arthur's goin' to be the auctioneer.'

Ivy rested her cheek against her hand. 'Bully for Arthur.'

Gertrude poured more water into the sink. 'Bully for Arthur indeed. It was plain to see he was pleased as punch they asked him to do the 'onours.' She chuckled nastily. 'It's a pity we won't be 'ere to see his face when the scuffers come knockin'.'

Ivy brightened. 'We're leavin'?'

Gertrude plunged the soap into the water. 'Once we've got all the stuff we need we can hide it until we give in our notice, then move it into his study just before we leave.'

'What if he finds it before we go?'

Gertrude rolled her eyes. 'No fear of that – I'm goin' to stuff it into that bottom drawer in his desk.'

'Ain't that allus gettin' stuck?'

Gertrude grinned. 'Exactly! He never uses it in case it breaks, but when the scuffers come knockin' they ain't goin' to be put off by a dodgy drawer.' She sighed blissfully. 'And when they pull it open it'll be like Aladdin's cave.'

'Blimey, you've really got it in for 'im, 'aven't you?'

Gertrude nodded. 'He got our Nathan banged up. He deserves to be taught a lesson.'

Ivy looked doubtful. 'But Uncle Nathan did mug that old woman, I remember you sayin' as 'ow 'e'd overstepped the mark—'

211

'Whose side are you on?' snapped Gertrude.

'I were only sayin' ...'

'Don't go gettin' a conscience now, Ivy Hackney; you're in this up to your neck, same as me. That git deserves to do time for what he did, an' none of 'is hoity-toity pals will trust him after this. He'll be ruined!'

Ivy frowned as she tried to make sense of her mother's statement. 'But this auction, didn't you say it was in aid of the war effort?'

Gertrude spun round and flung the bar of soap at Ivy. 'Don't you dare question your mother!'

Ivy yelped as the bar connected with her forehead. Small drops of liquid soap entered her eyes, and they began to sting as she flung the bar back. 'Some mother you are! You couldn't care less what 'appens to me as long as you get your stupid revenge. You've allus been the same: the only person you care about is yerself.'

Gertrude clutched a chunk of Ivy's hair between her skinny fingers and yanked it spitefully. 'You ungrateful little bitch! I've put everythin' on the line for you. I've allus put you first. It's not easy bringin' a kid up on your own, you know.'

Ivy cried out as her mother's fingers got entangled in her hair when she tried to pull them free. 'It's not my fault you don't know who me dad is.'

Gertrude took the jacket out of the water and flung it at Ivy. 'Do your own soddin' washin'. And seein' as you seem to think you're some sort of Cinderella, you can sleep in here tonight.'

With tears rolling down her cheeks, Ivy put the jacket back into the sink and stared down at her dress, which was soaked through. 'You'll have to let me up so's I can get changed.'

Gertrude shook her head. 'Not until you realise which side your bread's buttered.' She glanced towards the stove. 'You'll soon dry out in front o' that.' She walked up the stairs to the kitchen door and slid the key out of its lock. 'Good night, Cinders.'

Hearing the key click in the lock, Ivy slid out of her dress, wrung it out over the sink, then draped it in front of the stove to dry. She curled up on one of the benches and watched the steam rise from the sodden material. As the warmth of the stove enveloped her, she felt her eyelids begin to droop. She wouldn't desert her mother, she could never do that, but maybe she could change Gertrude's mind? Make her see that they'd be better off leaving this auction well alone, cutting their losses and leaving. Ivy knew that her mother had a bag full of jewellery which she had taken from Mr Granger's clients; if they sold that they would have enough to tide them over until something came along. She couldn't explain why, but something about this whole auction business gave Ivy a very bad feeling indeed. Putting the matter to the back of her mind, she drifted off to sleep.

It was Christmas morning, and despite Clara's fears it had not snowed during the night.

'I'm glad the streets are clear. I've been lookin' forward to seein' Josh off at the station.' She eyed Dolly with suspicion. 'When you say you've got a proper wheelchair, do you mean you've got a cleaner barrow?'

Dolly turned the bacon in the pan. 'No, I do not! As if I'd try and push you in a wheelbarrow on a crowded platform!'

'Where did you get it from?' Clara said suspiciously.

Dolly began buttering thick slices of bread. 'I borrowed it off me mate's granny.'

Clara looked surprised. 'Won't she be needing it?'

Dolly chewed her lip. 'Not any more.'

Seeing Clara's look of dismay, Lizzy burst into laughter. 'Your face! It's not as if she died in it.' She glanced at Dolly. 'She didn't, did she?'

Dolly transferred the bacon from the pan to the plates. 'No, she did not. If you must know, she died in one of the shelters durin' the bombin' raids. They couldn't fit her wheelchair through the door,' she pulled a face, 'so it's ironic, really: if she'd stayed outside with the chair she'd still be alive today.'

Clara looked uncertainly at Dolly. 'I can't say as I'm too keen to be sitting in a dead woman's wheelchair, but I suppose I've no other option.'

Dolly shrugged. 'We could stick a blanket over the barrow?'

Clara held up a hand. 'I'll use the chair.'

Dolly beamed. 'That's the spirit. Mavis said you could keep it as long as you need.'

'That was nice of her.' Clara glanced at the clock above the door. 'He'll be here in a minute.'

Lizzy rubbed Clara's shoulder reassuringly. 'Look on the bright side. He's only goin' to London, so you could ring him every day if you wanted to.'

'And I will, once I'm a bit more mobile.'

'It's not too far to go for a visit, so you won't have to be apart for too long,' said Dolly.

Clara smiled. 'You two think we're an item, but we're not, you know, we're just very good friends.'

Lizzy's eyebrows rose skywards. 'You do surprise me. I just assumed.'

'I know you did. We can tell by all the exaggerated coughing before you enter the room – either that or you're allergic to him.'

Lizzy giggled. 'It's obvious he thinks the world of you. Why do you think he's not made a move?'

Clara shrugged. 'Maybe he likes me as a friend, but not as a girlfriend.' She glanced down at her ample figure. 'Plump girls aren't every man's cup of tea.'

Dolly shook her head. 'That can't be it, 'cos he goes all gooey-eyed when he sees you.'

There was a brief knock on the door followed by Josh's voice. 'Can I come in?'

Clara's cheeks flushed pink. 'You don't think he heard, do you?' she hissed.

Lizzy shrugged. 'Too late now. Who knows, perhaps it'll give him a push in the right direction.'

Dolly opened the door. 'Merry Christmas, Josh, and don't you look handsome!'

Josh grinned. 'Merry Christmas, Doll, Lizzy.' He turned to Clara. 'Merry Christmas, Clara. You nearly ready for the off?'

Clara nodded. 'I've been lookin' forward to getting out of the flat, but I can't say I'm looking forward to saying goodbye to you, 'cos I don't know when I'll see you again.'

He pulled a face. 'It might be longer than I thought. They're lookin' for someone to go overseas.'

Clara turned pale. 'But surely they can send someone else? Can't you say you're ill?'

He chuckled. 'I don't think they'd fall for that, d'you?'

'You could try?' she said hopefully.

Kneeling down in front of her, Josh took both her hands in his. 'My name's been put forward, but so have a few others.'

'Promise me you'll look after yourself, no heroics?'

He nodded. 'I promise.' He glanced at his wristwatch. 'We'd better get a move on.'

'Wait,' said Clara, 'we've not handed out our pressies yet.' She beckoned Dolly. 'Can you bring me Josh's? I left it in the kitchen drawer.'

Dolly handed her a small neatly wrapped parcel, which she in turn handed to Josh. 'I hope you like it.'

Josh grinned as he opened his gift. 'A penknife! Thanks, Clara. It'll come in handy; you'll see why when you open yours.' He fumbled in the top pocket of his army coat before handing Clara an equally small gift. 'I made it myself.'

Removing the paper, Clara held up a tiny wooden owl. 'Oh, Josh, you are clever. It's beautiful.'

Grabbing a couple of cushions off the kitchen chairs Dolly made her way towards the door. 'I'll get the wheelchair ready.'

Josh frowned. 'I didn't know you had a wheelchair.'

Dolly's whole body sagged. 'Oh, don't tell me some little blighter's nicked it! Didn't you see it on your way up?'

He thought for a moment or two before his eyebrows arched towards his hairline. 'Is that what that was? But isn't that a—'

Dolly interrupted him. 'Come along, you lot. We can't be sittin' round here all day. Lizzy, you get the coats, and Josh, you can help Clara down the stairs.' She disappeared through the door.

Clara eyed Josh sceptically. 'It's not a wheelbarrow, is it?'

Josh shook his head. 'No, not a wheelbarrow ...'

As the others reached the bottom of the stairs they could see Dolly fussing in front of a large black object. Hearing their approaching footsteps, she darted to one side. 'Ta-dah!'

Clara's jaw dropped. 'That's not a wheelchair – it's a bath chair, and as old as the hills, too. No wonder they couldn't fit it through the door to the shelter.'

Dolly smiled encouragingly. 'Wheelchair, bath chair, it's just splittin' hairs. Besides, I couldn't find an actual wheelchair. This was the best I could do, and if you think about it it's a lot better than a wheelchair, 'cos it's got more room and look' – she grasped the hood in her hands and pulled it up – 'it's even got a cover in case it rains— Oh.' She stowed the hood, which had come off in her hands, behind the bins. 'Well who needs a cover anyway? In fact I think it looks better without one.'

Clara started to giggle and held on to Josh for support. 'Dolly Clifton, Langdon's should take you off the machines and put you into sales.'

Dolly grinned. 'I was worried you might not like it,' she said in a relieved tone, then stopped short as the others fell about laughing. 'Oh ...'

Lizzy shook her head. 'Don't worry, Dolly, you did the best you could, and Clara's right, you could sell ice to the Eskimos!'

Josh gingerly lifted Clara into the chair. 'It's not goin' to collapse, is it?' His cheeks flushed crimson. 'Because of the hood, I mean, not any other reason.'

Clara snorted a giggle. 'Don't worry, Josh, this time I knew you were referring to the chair.'

'Solid as a rock, this,' said Dolly, although her tone was edged with uncertainty.

Josh got behind the bath chair, which took up most of the yard, and gave it an experimental push. 'Is it stuck on something? I can't seem to budge it.'

'Ah,' said Dolly, 'it's got a bit of a wonky wheel, from bomb damage, but if you wriggle the bar from left to right like this,' she eased Josh out of the way and started to wriggle the hand bar from side to side, 'and push at the same time ...' The bath chair lurched slowly forward. 'See!' Clapping a hand on Josh's shoulder, she stood to one side and gestured for him to take control.

Not wishing to lose momentum, he called back, 'Can someone carry my kitbag? Only I can't push this thing and carry that at the same time.'

Clara rolled her eyes. 'You can stick it in here with me. It's not as if there isn't enough room.' As the kitbag was stowed between her knees she looked at Josh in astonishment. 'This thing weighs a ton. You make it look like a feather the way you sling it over your shoulder!'

He shrugged. 'You get used to it after a while.'

As they made their way to the station, Clara and the girls filled Josh in on their plan to expose the

Hackneys. He wasn't sure it was a good idea. 'You're takin' one heck of a risk breakin' into their room. What if someone sees you?'

Clara shrugged. 'Who's going to see? There's only Sally and Bert left, and they're not likely to say anything, and the Hackneys will be busy at the auction with my dad.'

'Can't you wait for me to come back on leave?'

Clara shook her head. 'I'd far rather you were with us, Josh, but in all honesty we need to strike sooner rather than later.'

'Is Charlie goin' with you?'

Lizzy and Dolly exchanged glances. 'We don't think it would be a good idea to involve Charlie. He might think we were doin' the wrong thing.'

Josh grunted as he steered the bath chair up the pavement. 'Well he'd be right then, wouldn't he? From what you've said, they're obviously up to no good, but that doesn't mean you can go snoopin' round other people's rooms.'

Clara tutted. 'I thought you of all people would be on our side.'

He pulled the bath chair to a halt at the foot of the steps that led to the station and knelt down in front of it. 'I am on your side, but I don't want to see you gettin' into any trouble. I can't tell the lads my girlfriend's in the nick for breakin' and enterin', can I?'

Clara heaved an exasperated sigh. 'Oh, don't be so silly. I'm not goin' to get arrested.' She frowned. 'What did you just say?'

Josh's cheeks were glowing. 'I've wanted to ask you since I first met you, but I didn't know how to put it,

219

and you come from such a well-to-do family and I – well, I don't, and I didn't want to embarrass you, or make you feel awkw—' His words were lost as Clara's lips met his.

'Ow!' said Lizzy, who was being nudged in the ribs by Dolly. 'Pack it in, I have got eyes.'

As they parted, Clara smiled shyly at Josh. 'Sorry, but sometimes actions speak louder than words, don't you think?'

Josh, his eyes dancing, nodded. 'I reckon talkin's overrated!' The train whistle blew loudly behind him. 'I've got to go.' Swinging the kitbag over his shoulder he turned to leave, changed his mind, and leaned down to give Clara a final kiss goodbye. As he trotted up the steps he called back over his shoulder. 'I promise I'll write every day; we can make arrangements for you to come and visit. Let me know what happens with your father! Ta-ra, girls!'

As he disappeared from view, Dolly grasped the handle of the chair. 'Looks like someone's gorra boyfriend.'

Clara blushed. 'You don't think I was too forward, do you? I wouldn't want Josh to think I was loose.'

'Don't be daft! Besides, you can't afford to sit on yer laurels, not when there's a war on.' Lizzy sighed. 'Only that's not the case with me and Charlie. War or no war, I'm afraid my problems run a lot deeper than that.'

Dolly swore under her breath as the wonky wheel dug into the paving. 'You've got to learn to let go, Lizzy. If you could do that, you and Charlie would be together in no time.'

'How can I learn to let go when I still don't know what's happened to me mam?' Grasping hold of the handle she pushed down hard, freeing the trapped wheel.

'But what difference does it make to you and Charlie whether you find your mam or not?'

Lizzy frowned. 'None, but that's not the issue. Until I know what's happened to her I'm like a cat on a hot tin roof.'

'You've gorra job, and a flat, and a pretty good social life. I don't—' Dolly began, before Lizzy cut her off.

'I have to have a job in order to survive, and I need a place to rest my head. As for the socialising, I don't go out that often and when I do it's a good opportunity to keep an eye out for me mam. If I settled into a relationship with Charlie, I'd feel as though I'd given up the search.'

'Nonsense!'

'It may well be, but Charlie reminds me of me dad, and so far I've lost everyone I love. I don't want Charlie to be next.'

Dolly opened her mouth to reply but Clara interrupted. 'I know what you mean. That's why I left Bellevue, too. I was worried that if I stayed I would say something unforgivable and end up losing my dad as well as Mum.'

Dolly shrugged. 'I never see me dad, not after him and me mam split up, and ever since she married that letch of a husband I don't see her neither, but it wouldn't stop me gerrin' a feller.'

Lizzy shook her head. 'But it's different for you; you don't want to see your parents. Me and Clara do.'

221

Dolly thought about this for a moment before answering. 'So how come Clara's with Josh?'

'Because I know where my father is and I can go and see him any time I like. My problem doesn't lie with him, far from it: it lies with the Hackneys.'

Dolly smiled sympathetically at Lizzy. 'Sorry if I've come across a bit insensitive. I suppose I tend to see things in black and white, but they aren't, are they?'

'I wish they were; life would be an awful lot simpler,' said Lizzy. 'Perhaps time'll help, but at the moment everythin's still quite raw.'

By now they had reached the bottom of the stairwell which led to the flat, and Clara started to wriggle herself towards the edge of her seat. Clasping her outstretched hand in her own, Lizzy began to pull. 'Charlie knows how I feel, and even though he's made it plain he'd like it if we were more than friends he understands my reasons. Besides, you've only said what everyone else was thinkin', includin' me and Charlie, so don't worry that you've upset anyone 'cos you 'aven't.'

There was a wail from Clara. 'Oh heck, I can't get out.' Lizzy held out her other hand but Clara shook her head. 'I'm wedged. It must've been all those bacon sarnies we ate for breakfast!'

Dolly spread her hands on Clara's back and began to shove. 'Blimey, Clara, I'd grease you up only we've not got enough butter.'

Lizzy's shoulders shook as she began to giggle. 'Poor Clara. I'm sure it's not your fault. You can't've gained that much weight, not when the whole country's on rations.'

Moving forwards a little, Dolly slid one arm round Clara's back and signalled Lizzy to do the same on the other side. 'You were right about Josh: he's a lot stronger than he looks.'

Clara, too, broke into a fit of the giggles. 'Well, I know what my New Year's resolution's going to be.'

'Gotcha!' said Dolly as Clara shot forward.

'Never to ride in a bath chair again?' said Lizzy with a chuckle.

Clara aimed a playful swipe at Lizzy's shoulder. 'No! To diet! I've been thinkin' about it for a while, only I didn't want to do it just because I thought Josh wasn't attracted to me. Now that I know he's not bothered about my weight I realise it would be for my own self-respect too, so, I shall start in the new year.'

'Merry Christmas, ladies.'

The girls turned to see Charlie walking towards them.

'You all set for your Christmas dinner?' said Lizzy. 'We've been savin' our coupons for ages and managed to get a good spread as a result.' Holding up a hand, she started ticking the items off on her fingers. 'Cheese, egg, or ham and pickle sarnies, sausage rolls, pork pies and crisps!'

'I'm goin' to need an elasticated waist on me trousers if I eat all that after a full cooked breakfast at me mam's. Not that I'm complainin', mind you.'

By the time they had finished their lunch they were all full to the brim. 'Do you fancy goin' for a walk?' Charlie asked Lizzy as he drained his mug of tea.

'Gosh yes, I think that's a great idea. Anyone else want to come? We could always take you in the bath chair, Clara.'

Clara shook her head. 'It doesn't half wobble when you're sittin' in it, so probably not a good idea on a full stomach.'

Dolly looked up from the Agatha Christie novel Lizzy had given her as a Christmas present. 'I'm halfway through the first chapter so you can count me out too.'

Charlie smiled at Lizzy. 'Just us then.'

'Before we go, I've got you a little summat for Christmas.' She handed him a brown paper package.

Grinning, Charlie fished out a small parcel from his trouser pocket. 'I got this for you.'

Lizzy beamed as she unwrapped her present. 'A tortoiseshell hairclip! It's lovely, Charlie.'

'I know you like to clip your hair back, and I thought this would look nice in your hair.' He held up the bar of Vinolia soap. 'Thanks, Liz. I was runnin' low, so this is just grand.'

As they strolled through the quiet streets, Lizzy pointed at the moonlit sky. 'When I were a kid me dad used to tell me the names of all the different constellations. I used to love gazin' up at the stars with him. It's so beautiful up there, but since war broke out all I see now is a bomber's moon.'

Putting his arm around her shoulders Charlie pulled Lizzy close. 'Don't let 'em spoil it for you, Liz. They're still the same stars you seen with your dad when you were a little girl, and take it from me, they look even better when you're firewatchin'. Talkin' of which, are you still interested?'

She nodded. 'More than ever since they bombed the arches on Bentinck Street. I know we couldn't have stopped them from bombin' but I'd rather be out there doin' summat useful than twiddlin' me thumbs in some shelter waitin' for Jerry to take a pop.'

'That's why I do it. I couldn't bear to think I were doin' nothin' whilst the city went up in flames. Tell you what, I'll have a word with the feller in charge an' see if I can take you with me one night in the new year. Would you like that?'

'Very much. We can look at the stars whilst we're up there. Do you know the names of any of the constellations?'

Charlie nodded. 'That's how I navigate me way around the city at night. Ow!'

Lizzy, who had nudged him in the ribs, shook her head. 'Same old Charlie, allus tekkin' the mick.' She shivered as a gust of icy wind caught the nape of her neck. 'Do you mind if we go back? Only I forgot me scarf.'

Charlie nodded. 'I've really enjoyed myself today, Liz.'

She smiled. 'It certainly beats last Christmas.'

Charlie coughed on a chuckle. 'Aye, it does that.' He glanced up as a flurry of large snowflakes swirled past him.

Lizzy caught a few flakes on her upturned hand. 'If this carries on the roads'll be covered by morning.'

Charlie blinked as the snow began to fall thick and fast. He looked down at Lizzy's shoes before crouching in front of her. 'Come on, Pipsqueak, jump on me back and I'll run you home. Them shoes weren't meant for snow; your toes'll be like icicles.'

Shaking her head, Lizzy jumped on to his back with a giggle. 'I've not had a piggyback since ... well since I were in school with you!' Wrapping her arms around his neck, she buried her cheek next to his as he tucked her legs through his arms.

As Charlie jogged along the pavement towards the flat, Lizzy felt as if she were the happiest girl in the world. How she wished things could be different, and she could stop worrying that everything was going to go wrong. If I could do that, Lizzy thought to herself, I'd marry Charlie tomorrow.

Chapter Nine

February, 1941

Mary trotted up the steps to Admiralty House and showed her pass to the guard at the door. Once inside, she lifted her goggles on to the brow of her leather helmet, removed her gloves and attempted to stamp the life back into her feet, smiling at the woman behind the desk. 'Them goggles aren't bad until you step into a warm building. Then they steam up and you can't see a hand in front of your face.' She rummaged around in the bag that was strapped across her chest and handed an envelope to the Wren. 'I've been told to wait for the reply.'

Nodding, the woman got up from behind her desk and made her way through a closed door, which Mary noticed was also guarded. She raised an eyebrow. She had visited many Navy offices, but there were few that were as heavily guarded as this. She knew James worked here and wondered whether he might be around. Since her last meeting with Jean, this was the first time Mary had come back to Plymouth and she was rather hoping to call in on James before she went on to her next job, wherever that might be.

The Wren guarding the outer door jerked her head towards Mary's bike, which was parked outside the building. 'My mum would have a fit if I said I was goin' to ride one of them. Is it fast?'

Mary grinned. 'Yup, but I wouldn't dream of breakin' the speed limit.'

The Wren laughed. 'I've heard about you lot. You get done for speedin' more than the fellers.'

'We're braver than them, or more stupid, one or the other. It's great in the summer; you get a real sense of freedom ...' She broke off as the first Wren returned with an envelope which she held out to Mary.

'The address is on the front.'

Mary glanced at the envelope, then looked sharply up at the girl. 'Port Edgar? But that's in Scotland! It'll be freezing up there!'

She shrugged her shoulders. 'Don't shoot the messenger.' She smiled slightly at her own joke.

Mary gazed at the envelope again. 'I s'pose I'd best get goin', then.'

The guard smiled reassuringly at her. 'Don't worry; the way you lot ride you'll get there in no time.'

Mary shoved the letter into her satchel and placed the goggles back over her eyes before hastily removing them. 'Still foggy. Well, see you later girls; no doubt they'll send me back with a reply. I feel like a ping-pong ball sometimes.'

She waved a half-hearted goodbye to the two Wrens and trotted down the steps. Straddling her motorcycle, she rubbed the inside of her goggles with her fingers, and slid them over her eyes.

A familiar voice hailed her from behind.

'Mary Tanner! Fancy seeing you here, and what a stroke of luck I caught you before you headed off.'

She lifted the goggles and smiled. 'James!' Glancing at his uniform, she cleared her throat. 'Sorry. I should say Vice Admiral Forbes!' She saluted, and dismounted the motorbike.

James smiled down at her. 'When there's no one around James will do nicely, and may I say you look very fetching in all your gear.'

Remembering she was still wearing the leather helmet, Mary grimaced. 'It's not as nice as what the other girls wear, but I'd look silly riding a bike in a smart uniform, 'specially going up Scotland on those godawful roads they have.'

He raised his brow. 'Is that where you're headed? If so, you must let me buy you lunch before you leave.'

'Are you sure?' She glanced down at the britches, the long leather coat and the large boots she was wearing.

'You look fine to me. Is there anywhere in particular you'd like to go?'

'Lookin' like this, I reckon a back street caff.'

He clicked his fingers. 'I know! How about the Duke of Cornwall? Have you ever been?'

Mary's eyes rounded as an astonished gasp escaped her lips. 'You can't be serious? The most luxurious hotel in Plymouth and you want to take Ragamuffin Mary there for lunch?' She shook her head. 'They'll not let me cross the threshold.'

'Let's see, shall we?' He jerked his head in the direction of a large black saloon car. 'After you.'

Mary stared at the car, then looked back at her motorbike. 'I think it would be better if I went on my bike. It'll save time after they chuck me out.'

He shrugged. 'No one's chucking anyone out of anywhere, but as you wish. Do you know the way?'

Mary laughed. 'I'm a motorcycle messenger; I know my way to most places, probably get there faster too.'

A small smile curved the corners of his lips. 'Is that a challenge?'

In answer to his question Mary pulled the goggles back over her eyes and kicked down on the starting lever. Hearing the bike roar into life, she was pleased to see James jumping into the back of his car as she passed him on her way down the grand drive that led to the house. By the time he reached the Duke, she had stowed her helmet, gloves and goggles into the panniers.

'Well, well, well.' He grinned. 'It's hard to believe you once struggled to stay upright on a bicycle. You're like a bullet!'

Mary smiled. 'Ridin' a motorbike's easy compared to gerrin' that lot' – she jerked a thumb in the direction of the hotel – 'to let me in dressed like this.'

'Follow me!' He strolled towards the main reception and addressed the woman behind the desk. 'A table for two, please, Vera.'

The woman nodded. 'Shall I send your guest through when they arrive?'

Turning, he gestured towards Mary. 'She's already here.'

The woman eyed Mary from head to toe. 'We, er, we …'

'This lady is a very dear friend of mine, and I should like to treat her to a spot of lunch. I think it's the least she deserves before heading off into the wilds of Scotland with a top-secret message, don't you?'

The woman looked from Mary to James and back again. She nodded. 'Follow me.' She stopped and turned to face Mary. 'May I take your ...' frowning, she hazarded a guess, 'coat?'

Suppressing a chuckle, Mary shrugged the long motorbike coat off her shoulders, then looked at her boots. 'Would you like me to take these off? They're a bit dirty, I'm afraid; it's the oil off the engine, everything sticks to it.'

The woman shook her head. 'That won't be necessary. Now if you'd like to follow me.' She led them to a table in the far corner of the room away from all the others, and handed them each a menu as they sat down.

They watched her scurrying towards the kitchen and Mary started to giggle. 'Get the feeling she's briefin' the waitin' staff on my presence?'

He smiled. 'Probably.' He placed his menu on the table and watched with interest as Mary perused hers. 'I take it you've still not heard from Lizzy?'

Mary shook her head. 'Not a whisper. I was rather hoping that my travels might lead me to her, but even though I've asked everywhere I've visited whether they've heard of a Lizzy Atherton I've not had any joy. I don't know whether it's because they're not allowed to say, or whether they really haven't heard of her, but I'm beginnin' to think leavin' Liverpool might've been a mistake. I've only been back there a handful of times, and then only on flying visits.'

He smiled at her. 'I've put feelers out across the entire naval system hoping something would come back, but unless she's bound by the official secrets act I think it's safe to say she's not in the Navy.' He leaned closer. 'If you're serious about moving back to Liverpool, you could come and work in the offices on Rumford Street. That's where I'm going next.'

She frowned. 'You've already done so much for me.'

He shrugged. 'No more than you deserve, and I don't know many Wrens whom I'd recommend for the job.'

Mary looked doubtful. 'It sounds ideal; I'm just worried I might not be clever enough. Ridin' a motorbike is one thing, but workin' in an office?'

He shook his head. 'You need to stop selling yourself short. I've never met a woman who's capable of turnin' her hand to new things the way you do. You learned to swim in one afternoon, and as for the motorbike ...' He smiled. 'You're cleverer than you think.'

'Where would I stay?'

'Ackerleigh House. It's not far from the office, and you'd be close to me – and Jean, as well.'

'I've at least one more trip to make first.' She frowned. 'Are you sure they're going to let me work for you in Liverpool, when they need motorcycle messengers?'

He curled the corner of his moustache between forefinger and thumb. 'I'm not dismissing your job as frivolous, but the need for you in Liverpool is far greater.'

She nodded. 'What shall I say to my superiors, and how long will it be before I start?'

Leaning across the table, he patted her hand. 'Leave that to me. You carry on until you're told differently, although if I have my way I could have you in Liverpool within the next couple of months.'

A waitress appeared beside them. 'Ready to order?'

Mary shook her head. 'I can't decide,' she said, and glanced at James. 'Why don't you order for the two of us?'

'Two lobster salads, please.'

Mary's eyes widened as she hastily reviewed the menu. 'Make that one lobster salad. As a rule I don't eat anything with more than four legs.' Handing her menu back to the waitress, she said, 'I'll have the fillet of cod with new potatoes, thank you.'

A chuckle escaped his lips. 'So no legs, two legs and four legs are fine?'

Mary nodded. 'Yup, but anything that has as many legs as a spider or a beetle is out!'

'Believe me, in some of the countries I've visited those are on the menu.'

Mary grimaced. 'Why would anyone want to eat a beetle? I can't imagine they're very filling.'

He laughed. 'They consider them to be delicacies.'

Her shoulders shuddered. 'Give me fish and chips any day of the week.'

Leaning back in his seat, he smiled to himself. 'I've missed you, Mary Tanner.'

'Why me?' Ivy had whined as her mother handed her the canvas bag.

'Because you're the one who needs trainin' up, so get in there and for goodness' sake stop whingin'!'

As Ivy entered the café behind the railway arches a small bell announced her presence, causing several customers to look up in haste before returning to their illicit dealings.

The owner of the café jerked his head to a nearby table. Nodding her understanding, Ivy made her way to the corner of the room. She apologised to several customers as she squeezed her way between their chairs. It had always been a wonder to Ivy why Mickey – the owner of the café – crammed the dining area with tables and chairs when there were never more than a handful of people, most of whom rarely ate, in there. Taking care to keep her back to the others, Ivy stowed her bag beneath the table. As she waited for Mickey to join her, she ran through her mother's instructions. 'Twenty quid for the lot. He'll try to knock you down to fifteen, Mickey allus tries to gerra quarter off, tell him as he's a valued customer you can go to eighteen and no less, he'll ask to go to sixteen, tell him seventeen tek it or leave it. He'll tek it.'

Mickey addressed Ivy from behind the counter. 'Won't keep you a minute.'

Nodding, Ivy fidgeted with the cutlery on the table. She hated being here – it always made her feel like a rat in a trap. She picked up a rather grubby-looking spoon and polished it absentmindedly on the edge of the table-cloth. After a moment, Mickey sat down heavily on the chair opposite hers and lit a cigarette. 'Lemme see.'

Ivy placed the bag on the table. 'It's what me mam calls the best bits from a house clearance.'

He wheezed on a chuckle. 'Your mam would. 'Ow 'ot is it?'

Ivy shrugged her shoulders. 'It's come from a house in Cheshire, miles away from here, so you won't have a problem sellin' it on.' She pushed the bag towards him. 'Tek a look for yourself.'

Opening the bag, Mickey took one or two of the objects out and examined them carefully under a jeweller's loupe before rooting through the rest of the bag. He glanced up. 'How much?'

Ivy smiled. 'Twenty.'

Mickey took a long drag of his cigarette whilst continuing to eye the goods then shook his head. 'Fifteen.'

Ivy had opened her mouth to make the counter offer when the bell above the shop door rang out. Mickey glanced up as several chairs scraped across the floor, their occupants suddenly eager to leave. Scowling, Mickey shoved the bag back towards Ivy and hissed, 'Gerrit out of sight.'

As Ivy shoved the bag beneath the table she looked nervously over her shoulder at the two policemen who were making their way towards the counter. Desperate to make as much space between her and the bag of stolen goods as possible, she pushed it as far away from her as she could with her feet.

'Evenin', Mickey,' said the older of the two constables. 'Is it just me or are your customers allus in a bit of a hurry to leave?'

Mickey leaned on the counter surface. 'I swear you do it on purpose. You know a lot of my customers suffer from nervous dispositions, made worse by the sight of scuffers.'

The younger constable chuckled. 'Let me guess. They all happened to be in the wrong place at the wrong time?'

Mickey nodded. 'Summat like that. Now do you gentlemen want summat to eat or did you come in just to cause a bit of upset?'

'You've still got one,' said the elder of the two, leaning towards Ivy. 'We 'aven't upset you, 'ave we, miss?'

Ivy, her heart in her mouth, held her scarf up to her cheek as she half turned to face the constable who had addressed her, and shook her head.

He smiled at Mickey. 'There you are, it can't be us!'

Ivy breathed a sigh of relief as their attention returned to Mickey. Had they recognised her to be one of the Hackneys, they might have decided to have a bit of fun at her expense and discovered the bag beneath the table in doing so.

The bell above the door jangled and a female voice hailed the two officers.

'Hello, Charlie, wotcher, Jimmy. I thought it was you. Are you gerrin' a bite to eat?'

'Pipsqueak! What are you doin' in this neck of the woods? It's not' – Charlie glanced through the door to the dingy street outside – 'where I'd expect to find a nice girl like you.'

Lizzy nodded shyly at Mickey. 'Do stop callin' me Pipsqueak, Charlie. And as for what I'm doin' in this neck of the woods, I use it as a cut-through.'

Ivy frowned. She recognised the voice, she was sure she did. Risking a glance over her shoulder she breathed in sharply. Lizzy Atherton! Of all people! If she

236

recognised her … Ivy shuddered. It didn't bear thinking about.

Charlie nodded. 'We're just going to grab a couple of sarnies. D'you want anything?'

She shook her head. 'I'd best gerra move on. The girls know I come through here so they keep an eye on the clock.' She looked apologetically at Mickey. 'I'm sure it's different if you live round 'ere.'

Charlie chuckled. 'You mean birds of a feather?'

'Don't you go puttin' words into my mouth, Charlie Jackson. I was simply sayin' you get used to what you get used to, and we're all used to different things.'

Mickey sighed impatiently. ''Ave you made your minds up as to what you want? I'd've thought you'd got better things to do than give me grief.'

Lizzy gave the café owner an apologetic smile. 'Sorry. I'll be on my way.'

Mickey rolled his eyes. 'Not you, miss; if anythin' a pretty young gel like you would bring the customers in. I was talkin' to these two.'

Lizzy giggled. 'I see.' She nodded at Charlie. 'Mekkin' trouble again, Charlie? Now why doesn't that surprise me?' Before he could reply she was heading towards the door. 'Shall I see you tomorrer?'

'Pick you up at seven?'

She nodded. 'Ta-ra, boys.' The bell jangled as the door closed behind her.

Jimmy grinned at Charlie. 'No kiss goodbye? I see you still 'aven't managed to land her.'

Charlie shook his head. 'When you gerra prize catch on the end of your line you don't just yank it in, Jimmy,

237

you have to tease it gently, else you end up wi' nowt but a pair of fish lips.'

Jimmy chuckled softly. 'Tease the line my arse. You ain't got the nerve to ask the Ice Princess out, 'cos you know what the answer would be.'

'She is not an ice princess. My Lizzy's been through a lot, what with her mam goin' missin'. I'm not some insensitive oaf; she needs time to heal.'

Jimmy grinned as he leaned against the counter. 'I reckon she's stringin' you along. What d'you reckon, Mickey?'

Mickey pulled a face. 'I reckon she can do better than a scuffer. She's more your military type.'

Charlie frowned irritably at Mickey. 'No, she's not.'

Mickey folded his arms across his chest. 'If I were a bettin' man, and these premises were licensed to gamble, which they ain't, I'd lay a quid down that you ain't got the nerve to ask 'er, and even if you 'ad, she'd turn you down anyway.'

Jimmy rubbed his hands together. 'Seein' as there's just the three of us and it's hardly what you'd call gamblin', more a friendly wager, I reckon I'll take you up on that bet. Wharrabout you, Charlie?'

Charlie pushed himself off the counter and held out a hand. 'I reckon you're on. A quid in all round, winner – that'll be me – takes all.'

Mickey flicked the ash off his cigarette on to the floor behind the counter. 'And what do we get when you lose?'

'Your money back plus a quid extra.'

'So what's the terms?'

Jimmy stared thoughtfully at Charlie. 'Bein' as none of us know how long it'll be till this war ends, how about we make it a bit more interestin' by sayin' he has to be officially courtin' our Lizzy before the end of the war, whether that be tomorrer or a year from now?'

Mickey spat on his hand and held it over the counter. 'Deal!'

The constables followed suit, although Ivy noticed that the two policemen wiped their hands against their coats straight after.

Mickey drew a deep breath. 'Now, what sarnies d'you want? I've got cheese 'n' pickle, or plain cheese.'

'One of each please,' said Charlie.

Ivy breathed a sigh of relief as the constables left the café and Mickey sat down opposite her once more. 'I thought they was never goin' to go! Why d'you do business with the likes of them, Mickey?'

Mickey shrugged. 'Their money's as good as any, and a bet's a bet. Everyone knows I like a bit of a flutter on the gee-gees, and when the odds are as good as the ones tonight, I'd've been a fool not to.'

Ivy shook her head. 'You're encouragin' them to come in, and that's not a good idea.' She pulled the bag out from under the table and opened it back up. She glanced at Mickey. 'Eighteen.'

Clara winced as the doctor gently pulled the cast apart. He glanced at her face as he ran a finger up the length of her shin. 'Any pain?'

Clara, who had been staring in horror at the scaly, hairy limb, let out a squeal. 'What's happened to my leg? Why is it so—'

Dolly, standing at her side, broke in. 'Blimey, you're like a gorilla under that cast. Oi, what you doin'?'

Clara was pulling Dolly's scarf from round her neck to drape over the offending limb. 'Sorry, Doll, but my leg's in greater need than your neck!' She pointed at the scarf. 'Why's my leg got such dreadful eczema?'

The doctor chuckled. 'It hasn't. It's just a bit dry because it's been hidden under the plaster all this time.'

'Smells a bit too,' said Dolly, who was peering under the scarf.

Lizzy clapped a hand on Dolly's shoulder. 'Come on, Doll, you can help me look for a taxi.' She addressed the doctor over her shoulder. 'You won't be too much longer, will you?'

'Give me a few minutes to get this off and she's all yours. Just make sure she takes it easy for a few days, and that means no dancing until she's built the strength up in her leg.'

Lizzy turned to Dolly. 'If you get us a taxi, I'll give Clara a hand to the door.'

Clara smiled. 'At least Josh didn't see it.'

'When was the last time you heard from him?'

Clara pulled a face as she tested her foot gingerly on the ground. 'I had a letter yesterday, but the censors have taken most of it out, although they left enough in to let me know that he's all right so far.' She placed a little more weight on her leg. 'It seems okay, no pain or anything, just a bit weak, that's all. It'll be a lot better now that I can get up and go out. That's the trouble with sitting at home all day – you get bored, and in my case that means you eat everything in sight.'

Lizzy smiled reassuringly. 'Don't worry about your weight; you'll find it much easier to diet now you've got the use of your leg back. I'm just glad we can go ahead with tomorrer night as planned.'

Clara's tummy lurched. 'Don't remind me. Every time I think about the Hackneys my belly turns a cartwheel.'

'You've not changed your mind, have you?'

Clara shook her head. 'I'm not bothered about me getting into trouble, it's you, Dolly and Sally I'm worried about.'

Lizzy squeezed her arm. 'Don't worry about us, we'll be fine, and so what if they do come back? It's your house, you've got more right to be there than they have, and you can have friends round if you want, can't you?'

Clara nodded. 'Let's just hope it doesn't come to that.'

Charlie frowned at the three girls who stood looking sheepishly at their feet. 'I know I said there was nothing I could do, but you shouldn't have resorted to self help, and if you want my opinion ...' he frowned at Dolly, who had opened her mouth to speak, 'and I don't care if you don't, Dolly Clifton, you'll go home and pretend none of this ever happened.'

'We're not goin' to steal anythin', just look for clues. You're the one who's allus tellin' us we need proof, and that's what we're after,' said Lizzy levelly.

Charlie shook his head. 'Well, you're not goin' in there on your own.'

Lizzy grinned hopefully. 'Does that mean ... ?'

He nodded reluctantly. 'I'm comin' with you, if only to make sure you don't do anything even more stupid than you're doin' now, not because I condone your actions.'

Clara hugged Charlie. 'I promise we won't do anything unless you say we can – apart from breaking in to Gertrude's room, of course.'

Trotting up the path towards the front door, she rang the bell. A few seconds later they heard the sound of approaching footsteps, the door opened a crack and Sally's face appeared in the gap. Stepping back, she ushered the quartet inside. 'You've got plenty of time; they only left ten minutes ago.' She plunged a hand into the pocket of her apron and withdrew a rather ancient-looking key. 'I found this yesterday. It was in that drawer I told you about, and I've checked and it's definitely the right one.'

Charlie held out a hand. 'Thanks, Sally. I'll take things from here.'

Looking past Charlie to Clara, Sally raised an eyebrow. 'I thought you said you weren't goin' to involve the police.'

Clara nodded. 'Only we bumped into Charlie on the way over, and when he asked where we were off to' – she glared at Dolly – 'someone couldn't contain themselves.'

'I was nervous. Allus am in front of scuffers, an' he caught me off guard!'

Lizzy was already halfway up the stairs. 'Come on! We didn't come here to stand around chin-waggin'; you too, Sally, you've said they won't be back for ages so you can help look.'

With one accord they ascended the stairs. Charlie opened the bedroom door and pointed to the

242

wardrobe. 'Clara, you look in there, check all the pockets. Dolly can go through the drawers whilst Lizzy and I check for loose floorboards.'

After ten minutes of fruitless searching, Clara and Dolly were sitting on Gertrude's bed whilst Sally examined some items she had found in the bottom drawer. 'It's pointless, Charlie, there's nowt here ...' Clara began, before being hushed by Dolly.

'Did you hear that?'

Clara shook her head. 'What?'

Dolly's shoulders sagged in relief. 'I thought I heard ...'

She was interrupted by a shriek of anger. Turning, they saw Gertrude standing in the doorway, her arm shaking as she pointed an accusing finger at them.

'What the hell d'you think you're doing?' she demanded.

Charlie, who had been on his hands and knees, got to his feet, and the colour drained from her face.

Clara groaned as her father appeared beside Gertrude. 'Clara, darling! What's going on? And why are the police here?'

Clara opened her mouth to answer but Charlie interrupted her. 'Hello, Mr Granger, I'm PC Jackson and your daughter and her friends are helping me with my inquiries. I have reason to believe that Gertrude Hackney and her daughter Ivy might be in possession of stolen goods.'

Arthur's brow furrowed into deep lines. 'I don't know what my daughter has told you, constable, but I'm afraid you've made a mistake.'

Charlie shook his head. 'I don't think you fully appreciate just who you've invited into your home.'

Gertrude, who had stepped forward to confront him, folded her arms defensively. 'Never mind that. How about you show Mr Granger the jewellery I'm supposed to've stolen?'

Charlie stared at her. 'Who said anything about jewellery?'

Swallowing hard, Gertrude ignored the question. 'See? You can't, can you? Because there's nothing here.'

Charlie, who was watching her closely, noticed her eyes dart towards the bathroom adjoining the room. He rubbed his chin thoughtfully. 'We've not found anything yet, but whilst I'm here would you mind if I checked the bathroom?'

'Yes, I bloody well would. You can get out, the lot of you,' she glared at Clara, 'and don't think I don't realise who put you up to this.'

Charlie coughed politely. 'I wasn't asking you. After all, this isn't your house.' He looked to Mr Granger, who nodded his permission.

'This is an outrage! An invasion of my privacy.' She glared at Arthur. 'If you allow him to continue, I shall have no choice but to leave your employment immediately.'

Arthur stared at her in astonishment. 'Why on earth would you say such a thing? Unless ...' He returned his attention to Charlie. 'Go ahead, constable.'

Charlie looked around the sparse bathroom. He checked behind the lavatory, under the sink, in the small cupboard and lastly in the ewer, and was shaking his head as he walked back into the bedroom.

'There you are!' said Gertrude, her voice shrill.

Ignoring her, Charlie picked up a chair and headed back to the bathroom.

Gertrude's eyes grew wide. 'What are you intending to do with that?'

'Just checking something.' He called over his shoulder to Sally who was sitting beside Dolly. 'Sally, can you lock the door, please? The one to the hall?'

Sally trotted obediently to the door and turned the key in the lock. Gertrude's attention flitted between her and Charlie, who had placed the chair beside the lavatory and climbed on top of it. He grunted as he began to heave the top off the cistern.

Gertrude glared at Arthur again. 'I don't have to put up with this.' She turned towards the bedroom door and addressed Sally through gritted teeth. 'Get out of my way.'

Charlie's hand clasped something inside the cistern. 'Aha!' Turning his head, he smiled grimly at Gertrude who had whirled back to face him. 'Don't worry. You will be leavin', but you'll be wearin' cuffs when you go.'

Gertrude grabbed Sally viciously by the arm and dug her nails in. 'Open the door!' she screamed in Sally's face.

Clara leapt from the bed and grabbed hold of Gertrude's arm. 'Let go of her, you evil cow.'

Jumping down from the chair, Charlie handed Lizzy a carefully bound parcel before snapping a pair of handcuffs round Gertrude's wrists. 'Odd place to keep stuff, isn't it?'

Gertrude aimed a vicious kick towards his leg, but he managed to dodge out of the way in time. He nodded to Lizzy. 'Do the honours, there's a good girl.'

Lizzy pulled at the packaging until she managed to make a small hole at one end. She peered into the hole and grinned. 'Jewellery. Nice stuff too.'

Thinking on her feet, Gertrude looked up. 'That's nothin' to do wi' me. It must've been here before I arrived.'

As Lizzy started to remove more and more items Mr Granger gave an exclamation. 'That's my chequebook! I've been looking everywhere for that.'

Lizzy handed it to him and he turned it over in his hands. 'They've been practising my signature on the back.'

Gertrude stared icily at him. 'You can't prove anythin'. I know my rights.'

'I expect you do,' Charlie said grimly. 'You've had them read to you often enough.'

Lizzy held up a pair of exquisite diamond drop earrings.

Arthur stared at Gertrude in disgust. 'They were my wedding gift to my wife.'

Gertrude shrugged. 'She don't need 'em now.'

Before anyone could stop her, Clara had crossed the room and slapped Gertrude so hard across one cheek she knocked her off the chair. 'That's for my mum!'

Dolly, who had been sitting quietly on the edge of the bed, held up the items that Sally had been examining when Gertrude had first entered the room. 'Where did you find these, Sally?'

Sally pointed to the bottom drawer. 'Why would anyone keep a wig an' an old shawl in their drawers?' Standing up, Dolly placed the wig on her head, and the shawl around her shoulders.

Clara gave a shriek. 'It's the old woman who came to the house not long after Mum died and said she had a message from her. You remember, Dad?'

Arthur stared at Dolly, then glared at Gertrude. 'It was you! You told me Jessica wanted me to get a new housekeeper to look after me in her place. My God, woman, you even described her!' He turned tear-brimmed eyes towards Clara. 'I know I shouldn't have listened, but she said it would help to ease my pain.'

'Oh, shut up!' snapped Gertrude. 'I only told you what you wanted to 'ear. It's your own fault you're so gullible.'

Clara placed an arm round her father's waist. 'She's evil. She knew you were in no fit state to argue; that's why she did it.'

Charlie glanced at Arthur. 'Can I use your telephone?'

'Of course. It's in the study. Follow me. Sally, if you'd open the door, please?'

Charlie turned to address the girls. 'I'll take Gertie down if you lot can bring the jewellery and clothing? I'll need to take it to the station with me, 'cos it's evidence.'

When everyone had gone, Ivy appeared from behind the door of the room opposite Gertrude's and crept on to the landing to listen to the conversation taking place below.

'Where's your Ivy?' It was Lizzy's voice. 'I'd bet a pound to a penny she had summat to do with all this.'

Ivy held her breath as she heard Mr Granger's voice echo across the hall. 'She came back with us, so she should be here somewhere.'

Charlie shook his head. 'She'll've taken off as soon as she realised summat was up.' He frowned. 'Why *did* you come back so early?'

Mr Granger rubbed the top of his thinning hair. 'I'd forgotten a pair of candlesticks which I was donating to the auction, so we nipped back. The Hackneys wanted to stay, but because some of my clients have had issues with missing items I thought it best if they came with me ...' he chuckled without mirth, 'so they couldn't be falsely accused.'

Hearing that they thought her to be long gone, Ivy breathed a sigh of relief. She could wait until the coast was clear before making her break.

After a brief conversation on the telephone, Charlie came back into the hall. 'They're sendin' a car; it shouldn't be long. I'll take this one outside so you don't have to have her in your house a moment longer.'

Mr Granger smiled gratefully. 'Thank you. I don't know what would have happened had you not uncovered the truth.'

Charlie shook him firmly by the hand. 'Don't mention it, if anything you should be thanking these young women. They're the ones who put two and two together.'

Shamefaced, Mr Granger turned to Clara. 'I've been a very silly old man. Can you ever forgive me?'

Clara, her lip trembling, nodded. 'There's nothing to forgive. I'm just glad to have you back.'

He caught her hand in his and kissed the back of her knuckles. 'Whatever did I do to deserve a daughter as wonderful as you?'

Clara slipped her arms round his waist. 'I should never have left. I knew they were up to no good.'

He shook his head. 'If anyone's to blame it's me. I should've listened to you instead of wallowing in my own grief.'

Charlie poked his head round the corner of the front door. 'They sent a paddy wagon. Does anyone fancy a ride home?'

Dolly's hand shot up. 'Me! I've allus wondered what it'd be like to ride in the back of one of them. C'mon, girls, before they change their minds.'

Mr Granger looked bereft as Clara gently disengaged herself and headed towards the door. 'Aren't you going to stay?'

Clara smiled sympathetically at him. 'I promise I'll come back and see you tomorrow, but I've got a new life now, with responsibilities.'

Crossing the hall, Arthur took his daughter in a firm embrace. 'You're welcome here any time you like.' He glanced at Lizzy and Dolly. 'That goes for all of you.'

Clara kissed his cheek, then trotted towards the wagon, calling over her shoulder as she went, 'Don't worry, this'll be the last time you see me in the back of one of these things.'

'Clara!'

She turned back. 'Yes?'

'I've just remembered. I've got to go back to the auction. I don't suppose you could spare the time to help me out? I'd run you home afterwards, of course.'

'Course I could.' She turned to Lizzy and Dolly. 'Either of you want to come with me?'

Dolly looked from the paddy wagon to Arthur and back again. 'Oh, go on then. I suppose I can allus have a ride another time.'

Charlie raised a surprised brow. 'I jolly well hope not!'

Dolly thought about this for a moment before breaking into a fit of the giggles. 'I meant as a guest, of course!'

The driver of the wagon looked up from putting Gertrude into the van. 'You can drive, Charlie. I'll sit in the back with madam.'

Charlie opened the passenger door for Lizzy. 'C'mon, I'll drop you off on the way.'

Lizzy climbed into the cab, closed the door, and wound down the window to wave a hand. 'Goodbye, Mr Granger. It was nice to finally meet you. Ta-ra, girls – have fun!'

Unseen by any of them, Ivy was making her way across the back garden. She had crammed her pockets with Clara's mother's jewellery and all the money she could lay her hands on, some of which she had found in Sally's bedroom. Serve 'em right for bein' nosy pokes, she thought bitterly. If it weren't for them I'd still 'ave me mam, so I reckon this is the least I deserve.

She climbed over the garden wall and brushed the dirt off her clothes, casting an eye up and down the length of the road. 'Eeny, meeny, miny, moe ...'

As the paddy wagon trundled unsteadily down the dark roads, Lizzy turned to Charlie. 'I must say I was most impressed with the way you found the hidden stuff. How did you know to look in the cistern?'

He grinned. 'First thing the guilty do is look to where they don't want you to search. After that they look anywhere but.'

She shook her head in admiration. 'Poirot! They should promote you.'

Charlie grinned hopefully at her. 'Does that mean you've finally decided to take a chance on me?'

'Take it from me, Charlie, you're better off on your own, else summat dreadful might happen to you.'

'Might I fall in love and live happily ever after?'

She smiled wryly. 'If you're like everyone else I've ever loved, you'll end up leaving me.'

Without thinking, he stepped harder on the brake than he intended. 'Oi, what you playin' at?' shouted the constable in the back of the wagon. 'Keep your eyes on the road, Charlie boy.'

'Sorry!' called Charlie. He eyed Lizzy thoughtfully. 'You don't really think that, do you?'

She shrugged. 'Whether it's true or not, I ain't takin' the risk. I can't afford to lose you, Charlie, I like you too much.'

'I promise you, Liz, I ain't goin' anywhere. You can't seriously think you're cursed or summat, an' even if you do, don't I deserve the chance to prove you're not?'

'But what if I prove to be right? I really, really care for you, Charlie, an' that's why I'm keepin' you at arm's length.'

Charlie rolled his eyes in disbelief. 'Typical! I'm so nice you don't wanna come near me. That could only happen to me.'

She smiled shyly. 'It's a compliment when you think about it.'

He pulled the wagon up alongside the alley that led to the flat. 'You goin' to be all right goin' in there on your own?'

She nodded. 'You fancy comin' for tea this Friday?'

'Aye. I'll bring some of me mam's leftover Christmas cake with me, if you like?'

'That'd be grand.'

Chapter Ten

May, 1941

The warden ushered the girls inside the underground shelter and closed the door firmly behind them.

'D'you suppose it's a false alarm?' said Clara hopefully.

The warden lowered his voice. 'You'd better 'ope so, 'cos rumour 'as it there's more than they can count. They reckon the sky's full of 'em.'

Lizzy looked at Clara, who had turned pale. 'Don't worry, chuck, I'm sure it's nowt but rumours. What is it they call it again?'

'Scaremongering,' said Dolly with ease. 'Only I don't—' She got no further because from outside the shelter came the scream of a falling bomb, followed by a deafening thud. Clara squealed and brought her knees up to her chest. Lizzy and Dolly held her in a snug embrace whilst Lizzy whispered reassuringly, 'We're a lot safer in here than we were in Bentinck Street.'

Clara gave a small nod. 'I wish Josh was here. He'd have us all singing songs.'

The door to the shelter flew open and a boy of no more than nine came clattering down the steps. A young woman hailed him from the back of the shelter. "'Ave you got our Millie's bunny?'

Holding up a rather scruffy-looking toy rabbit, the boy was about to make his way to the back of the shelter when the warden placed a hand on his shoulder. 'D'you mean to tell me this lad's been dillydallyin' out there just to fetch you some stuffed toy?'

All eyes locked on the young mother, who stuck out a defiant chin. 'Not me, our Millie. She can't go to sleep wi'out it.'

Shaking his head with disapproval, the warden turned the boy to face him. 'When you 'ear the air raid warnin' you run for shelter, you do not 'ang around lookin' for stuffed toys, or anythin' else for that matter.'

The boy nodded. 'At least I got to see 'em, though.'

'What did you see?' said the warden, interested despite himself.

'The Luftwaffe. There must be 'undreds of 'em, they's spread right across the city an' they go back as far as you can see.'

Clara's eyes widened. 'Are you sure?'

He nodded again, his eyes sparkling with innocent excitement. 'You know when you go to the seaside and you feed your crusts to the gulls and at first there's two or three, but after a while there's loads of 'em, all fightin' over one crumb? Well, that's what it's like out there.'

All eyes were turned on the boy, who was revelling in the attention. 'Wharrabout the ack-acks? Ain't they shootin' at 'em?' said an older woman who was clutching a flask to her chest.

He nodded enthusiastically. 'Oh, yes, you can 'ear 'em clear as a bell, boom, boom, boom, and as for the bullets, they looks like someone's lerrin' off 'undreds of fireworks.'

'Are any of 'em 'ittin' the planes, lad?' said a man from further down the shelter.

The boy shook his head. 'Not that I seen. It's very dark outside; it'd be hard to hit a plane what's all the way up there.'

The man shook his head and muttered 'Bloody hell' under his breath.

The boy's mother had gone white. 'Come 'ere, Toby. These good folk probably want to get some kip before mornin'.'

Toby obediently trotted towards his mother who enveloped him in her arms. She looked up to where the warden stood, her eyes shining with tears, and shook her head. 'I didn't realise – I thought it was another false alarm. If I'd've known ...'

Another bomb screamed its presence, followed by another deafening thud. A dog cowering against the wall of the shelter let out a string of terrified barks, while the owner gently stroked his head and murmured, 'Don't worry, Buster, it's just those silly Germans.'

The warden arched an eyebrow. 'You know, you really shouldn't have pets in the shelter, miss.'

The woman shot him a warning glance. 'If Buster needs the loo, I shall be sure to come and clean it up in the mornin', but if you think I'm going to leave him out there, alone and frightened …' She shook her head. 'He was my Derek's dog … he's all I've got left.'

The occupants of the shelter stared accusingly at the warden, who fiddled with the brim of his tin hat before placing it back on his balding head. 'Don't worry, miss, I've not gorra dog meself, but I'd not shut one out in this lot.'

Turning her attention away from the warden, Lizzy addressed Dolly over the top of Clara's head. 'I reckon Toby must've exaggerated. I can't see there bein' that many out there, an' you know what kids are like, 'specially boys.'

Dolly nodded at Clara. 'Lizzy's right. There couldn't possibly be that many; he were just showin' off 'cos everyone was lookin' at 'im.'

Clara slid her fingers through her friends'. 'I know you mean well, but I've been concentrating on the noise outside, and ever since that first bomb dropped there's not been one minute when I couldn't hear the sound of those awful planes.'

Closing her eyes, Lizzy blocked out the endless chatter within the shelter and listened to the noise coming from outside. Clara was right – all she could hear was the constant drone of the Luftwaffe engines, whilst endless bombs screamed towards the city followed by explosion after explosion.

Clara gave a small grim smile. 'The way I see it, they have to go back sooner or later. We just have to bide our time until they go.'

After what seemed like an eternity, the all clear sounded. As they emerged from the shelter, Lizzy pulled a face. 'I thought it would look a lot worse than this. It doesn't seem that bad.' She felt hands grip her shoulders as Dolly turned her around, and then she rocked on her heels as she took in the enormity of the sight that met her eyes. In the distance she could see the flames of phosphorus fires as they engulfed the buildings around them, the smoke that filled the air turning the sky red, and the shouts and screams of warning or horror as buildings collapsed.

Still holding Lizzy by the shoulders, Dolly was the first to speak. 'We've got a few hours before we have to be in work. I don't know about you two, but I'd rather be down there helpin' than tryin' to get some shut-eye.'

'I feel so guilty ...' Lizzy began but Dolly cut in before she could say more.

'Why? You never caused this!'

'I know, but I was meant to be on firewatching duty last night, only I've got work this mornin' so they said not to bother.'

Dolly shook her head. 'No one could've known what Jerry were plannin', so there's no sense in blamin' yourself. I'm glad you *weren't* on duty last night, 'cos you might not be here now.'

Clara had already begun to make her way towards the carnage. 'Let's go down and see what we can do.'

That had been the first night of what the Germans called the Blitzkrieg, and despite the girls' hopes that it would also be the last the Luftwaffe had proved relentless. Each night the girls headed for the same shelter; each morning they would head for the worst hit areas to lend a helping hand, whether it be serving refreshments to the workers or helping to find people trapped under bomb debris.

On the third night, Lizzy and Charlie had been fire-watching on top of a large office building in Paradise Street.

'I know you want to do your bit, Liz, but I'd far rather you were in a shelter somewhere deep below the city.'

Lizzy shrugged. 'I joined the fire watch to help keep the city safe. I've already missed two nights; I'll be damned if I miss a third.'

Charlie clasped his chest. 'You wound me, Lizzy Atherton. I thought you joined the fire watch so you could spend time with the most handsome policeman this city has ever seen, yet here you are tellin' me I've got it all wrong.'

Lizzy giggled. 'You ain't 'alf got tickets on yerself, Charlie Jackson!'

He huffed on his fingernails before polishing them on his coat. 'When you're a winner you're a winner …' He broke off as the all too familiar sound of bomber engines came from far in the distance. He nodded at Lizzy. 'Brace yerself, gel. Looks like we've got company.'

Lizzy had stared in horrified awe as the German bombers flew overhead. Crossing her fingers, she prayed for something to happen that would cause them to retreat back to Europe, but there was no such luck. To her left she could see the incendiary bombs as they fell indiscriminately on to shops, warehouses and, worst of all, people's homes. Holding tightly on to her bucket, she stamped her foot in anger. 'The cowards!

They must know they're droppin' them on residential areas. Why aren't they targeting the docks?'

Charlie shook his head. 'Because they're tryin' to break our morale, in the hope that we'll surrender.'

Behind them something crashed on to the flat roof. 'Charlie, a bomb!' squealed Lizzy.

Quick as a flash, Charlie raced over to the bomb, picked it up and plunged it into a bucket of water. He wiped his forehead with the back of his hand. 'Good job we got to it before it had a chance to ignite.'

'Thank goodness it didn't penetrate the roof. It might've been a different story if it had ...' Her voice was drowned out by an almighty explosion. Dropping to the floor, Lizzy covered her ears with her hands, and when she looked up she saw an enormous ball of flame rising from the docks. She pointed with a trembling finger. 'They've hit one of the ships. What shall we do?'

Charlie watched as the ship continued to explode. 'We stay where we are. I don't know which ship that was but I'm guessing it was carrying something highly flammable. They don't normally go up that bad.'

Lizzy stared in anguish as large balls of fire belched from the ship. 'We can't just leave them, Charlie.'

'No one can go near that until it's finished explod-ing, and they're going to need proper hoses, not buckets of water, which is all we have to offer.'

Lizzy hid her face behind her hands. 'Do you think there was anyone on board?'

Charlie turned his attention from the doomed ship and held Lizzy in his arms. 'You mustn't think like that, Liz.' He lifted her chin with the knuckle of his forefinger. 'When the planes turn round we can go down to help, but in the meantime you're more use up here raisin' the alarm if you see a fire.'

When the all clear sounded, Lizzy and Charlie made their way towards the scene of the disaster. As they neared the Huskisson Dock they saw that Dolly and Clara were already serving tea and sandwiches to weary fire fighters.

Dolly called out to them. 'Lizzy, Charlie! Over here.' As they approached, she jerked her head in the direction of the burning ship. 'They hit the *Malakand*. Apparently it was full of explosives and they reckon some of the pieces've been found a whole mile away. Imagine that!'

Taking a mug of tea from Clara, Lizzy nodded. 'We were on top of the roof when it hit; you should've seen the explosion! Charlie said he reckoned it must've been summat bad because it just kept on explodin'.'

Clara nodded. 'I'm just glad Spencer is safely tucked up in his office, although I'm not sure my nerves will take much more of the thought of you standing on some rooftop whilst the Germans throw bombs at you!'

Lizzy grimaced. 'I'd say you had nothing to fear, but we had a close call during the night. Luckily it never penetrated the roof, so Charlie put it out quite easily.'

Clara shook her head. 'I know you want to do your bit, and I admire you, I really do, but couldn't you let someone else do it instead?'

'I feel a darned sight safer on top of a roof with Charlie than I would down in a shelter not knowin' who was on fire watch and wonderin' whether they'd be doin' as good a job as me and Charlie.' She looked at him. 'Do you feel the same?'

He nodded reluctantly. 'I do, only I must admit I'd be a lot happier if you were in a bunker and it was me on the rooftops keepin' you safe.' He held up a hand as Lizzy started to protest. 'We were lucky, Liz. It might've been a different story if that incendiary bomb had gone through the roof on to the floor below.'

She turned to the girls. 'You should've seen him. He ran across the roof, picked the bomb up and stuck it into the water like it was a stick of wood!'

A familiar voice hailed them from the roadside. Lizzy pointed. 'It's Jimmy! Have you come to see Charlie?'

'I came to see if I could be of any help with the ship what caught fire last night, but the fire chief said he'd rather I got a gang of fellers together to start clearin' the wreckage.' He nodded at Charlie. 'You comin'?'

'Be right with you.' He turned to Lizzy. 'We still on for Spam Surprise on Friday?'

Lizzy giggled. 'You are a rotter, Charlie Jackson! See you on Friday.'

As Jimmy and Charlie disappeared into the throng of people, Dolly arched a brow. 'Spam Surprise?'

Lizzy giggled. 'Cheese and pickle sarnies.'

'If it's cheese and pickle, why did he call it Spam Surprise?' said Clara.

''Cos he reckons I always give him Spam when he comes round for his tea. He says the only surprise is whether he's havin' it grilled, fried, or cold. So I thought I'd prove him wrong by doing him something that does not come out of a tin.'

Clara shook her head. 'Bonkers, the pair of you!'

'Two teas, please, when you're ready, luv.'

Apologising, Lizzy stepped to one side. 'I can't stand 'ere gossipin' wi' you two when there's work to be done. What can I do to help?'

Dolly pointed at a cardboard box at the back of the van. 'Get a tin of Spam out of there an' start makin' sarnies. We don't want any surprises, mind; plain Spam sandwiches'll do just fine.'

James Forbes looked up from the piece of paper he was studying and addressed the Wren who had handed it to him. 'This feller here,' he said, pointing at one of the names on the list, 'he's not one of ours. Why is he on here?'

The Wren peered at the name. 'I believe he's a docker. The Navy wanted the names of anyone who'd been affected by the *Malakand* disaster.'

James nodded. 'Do you know which hospital he's in?'

She scanned the clipboard she was holding. 'According to this he's in the Royal.'

He glanced at the clock that hung on the wall of his office. 'Can you go upstairs and tell Mary Tanner to meet me outside in five minutes?'

A few minutes later Mary sank into the back seat next to James. 'What's going on? Is it our Lizzy?' As the car they were sitting in began to move, she added, 'Where are we going?'

He half turned to face her. 'I think I may've found Albert.'

'My Albert?'

He nodded. 'I was looking at the casualty list for the *Malakand* this morning and his name was on it.'

'Albert's in the Navy?' she said in a disbelieving tone.

'No, he's still a docker, but he must've been nearby when it exploded.'

'So why is his name on the list?'

'We have to check everyone who was around at the time, to make sure they weren't up to no good when it happened.'

Mary shook her head. 'Even Albert's not stupid enough to try nickin' off the Navy.' She paused. 'What do you need me for? Is he dead?'

'No, he's still alive, and in truth we don't need you, but I thought it would be a good opportunity for you to speak to him, to find out what happened the night you last saw Lizzy.'

After what seemed like an eternity to Mary, but was in fact only a matter of minutes, their car drew to a halt outside the hospital entrance. Opening his own door before the driver had the chance, James hurried round to Mary's side of the car and helped her out. 'Do you want me to come with you?'

She nodded. 'Please. I know he's no threat, but it would be nice to have you nearby.'

The nurse led them to Albert's bed, saying as she did so that they weren't to get him excited.

Albert wore a large cotton pad over one eye, and his face was a mass of blood and burns. Hearing them approach, he opened the other eye and stared blearily at Mary.

As she came into focus he stared at her open-mouthed. 'It can't be ...'

Mary cocked a brow. 'Why? Did you think I was dead?'

Swallowing hard, Albert turned his attention to James. 'You can't prove nothin'. I didn't do anythin'. It were 'er an' that spoiled brat of 'ers, they're the ones that need arrestin'.' He glared at Mary. 'My life's been 'ell because of you.'

'Me? *Your* life's been 'ell because of *me*?' Her eyes narrowed. 'You threw me into a crate and left me for dead, I haven't seen my daughter since the beginning of the war, and you have the nerve to say *your* life's been hell?'

Albert glanced nervously at James before jutting out a defiant chin, although he was careful not to make eye contact with either James or Mary. 'I wasn't goin' to get done for murder. I never forced you out that winder, and I wasn't about to sit back and wait for the scuffers to arrive and cart me off for summat I hadn't done. I knew that Lizzy would've told 'em it was all my fault.'

Mary shook her head incredulously. 'It was your fault! You were the one who locked the door. You were the one who 'it me. What did you think I was goin' to do? Leave Lizzy to your mercy?'

Albert's brow furrowed. 'I never touched 'er. For your information I 'aven't seen 'er from that day to this, so you can stop pointin' the finger at me! If she 'asn't come lookin' for you that's hardly my fault!'

Mary clenched her fists. 'Yes it is, you stupid man. I went all the way to South Africa after you dumped me in that bloody crate. By the time I got back to Blighty there was a whole new family livin' in Snowdrop Street, and the bakery where I used to work had been sold to different people!'

Albert looked at James. 'I never shoved her in no crate. You shouldn't listen to her; she's makin' the whole thing up. I never even went back to the 'ouse, 'cos I know what a pair of troublemakers 'er and 'er kid can be. If I were you I'd watch me back, pal.'

James shook his head. 'First, I'm not your pal. Second, if you didn't go back to the house how did you know that Mary had tried to escape out of the window?'

Albert drew a deep breath but nothing came out. For a moment or so he looked completely lost, but he soon rallied. ''Ow else was she goin' to gerrout?'

Mary shook her head. 'You're lyin', Albert, an' we all know it, it's written all over your face. Besides, who else would stick me in a crate? Although I s'pose I should be grateful you didn't chuck me in the sea.' Looking at the haunted expression on his face her eyes rounded. 'Oh my God, you were goin' to, weren't you?' She looked at him thoughtfully. 'So why didn't you?'

Standing beside Mary, James placed a supportive hand on her shoulder. 'Did you get disturbed, Albert? Did someone see you?'

'Nurse!'

Bending down so that her nose was inches away from Albert's, Mary stared him straight in the eye. 'Where's my daughter?' she hissed through gritted teeth.

Albert shook his head fervently. 'I already told you, I don't know!'

'You've also told us that you didn't shove me in a crate, and that was a lie, so why should I believe you now?'

His eye darted nervously from her to James and back again. 'I swear I 'aven't seen her from that day to this. I lost 'er in the streets, and that's the truth.'

265

James gently pulled Mary back towards him. 'I think he's tellin' the truth.'

Albert sagged with relief. 'Thanks, mate.'

James shook his head in disgust. 'Don't thank me. I'm not on your side, and I'm definitely not your mate.'

Mary smoothed her hair back with one hand. 'I want a divorce.'

Albert's eyes flickered from Mary to James. 'So you can marry lover boy?'

Mary clasped her hands together in an effort to quell her temper. 'No, Albert, I want a divorce so that I can finally be free from you.'

For the first time since Mary had entered the ward, Albert realised he had the upper hand. He shook his head. 'I meant what I said when I made them vows.'

Mary fixed him with an icy stare. 'Really? Because I seem to remember summat about love, honour, obey, and respect, and you didn't do none of them.'

'That's your opinion, but in the eyes of God we're married and I believe in till death us do part.'

Pulling Mary back, James approached Albert, who instantly changed his demeanour. As James leaned forward, Albert looked as though he was trying to squeeze his body through the mattress in a bid to get away. 'I'll scream ...'

James gave a short, mirthless laugh. 'If you don't give Mary a divorce I swear I will use every possible resource I have at my disposal to prove you tried to murder her that night, and I will send you somewhere where no one can hear you scream.'

Albert's face was a mask of terror. 'You can't – you've got no proof, I – I ...'

James stood back from the bed, a half-smile etched on his lips. 'Watch me!'

Albert looked at Mary. 'You promise you'll leave me alone after?'

Mary nodded.

Albert spoke to James, although he was careful not to look him directly in the eye in case he incurred his wrath. 'She can have a divorce, but she'll have to pay for it 'cos I ain't got no money.'

As Mary and James left the ward, Mary began to giggle. 'I think Albert thought you were goin' to kill him for a minute there!'

James winked. 'That makes two of us,' he said, 'but if truth be known that's why I pulled you back. It was obvious he was deliberately tryin' to antagonise you, just so that you'd hit him. After all, you can just imagine what sort of response you'd get if you hit a badly burned man whilst he lay defenceless in hospital!'

Mary nodded ruefully. 'Thanks for coming with me. It wouldn't have gone at all well had you not been by my side.'

James put his arm round her shoulders. 'My pleasure, and if it's any consolation, I really did believe him when he said he hadn't seen Lizzy since she ran off.'

Mary nodded. 'Me too, but after last night's raids it doesn't make me feel any easier. I wish I knew where she was.'

'We'll find her. We found Albert, didn't we?'

'You were the one who found Albert, not me.' She paused. 'But you're right. Oh, James, do you really think we'll find her?'

James kissed the top of her head. 'Yes!'

Chapter Eleven

November, 1941

Dolly patted Lizzy's knee in an excited fashion. 'I can't wait to meet Clara's brother, can you?'

Lizzy opened her mouth to reply but Dolly was too excited to let anyone else get a word in edgewise. 'D'you reckon he's handsome? Clara's pretty, and her dad's not bad lookin', for someone his age. I hope he's tall. I hate it when a feller's shorter than you, don't you?'

Lizzy hesitated to see if Dolly was going to allow her to reply this time. 'I don't think there's many men much smaller than me! Did you see that picture of Clara's mam hangin' in the' – she put on a posh voice – 'vestibule?'

Nodding, Dolly giggled. 'Vestibule! It was the same size as our flat! I wonder what he'll think of Clara living here with us?'

Hearing the sound of approaching voices, Lizzy widened her eyes fleetingly. 'Looks like we're about to find out.'

The door of the flat opened and Clara beamed at them as she ushered her brother into the room. 'Come in, Spencer, they won't bite.'

Spencer Granger gave the girls a cheery wave. 'Morning, ladies.'

'Hello, Spencer. I'm Lizzy,' Lizzy indicated Dolly, 'and this is Dolly.' Spencer was much taller than Clara and had short, curly, sandy-coloured hair. Dolly was staring at him dreamily.

Spencer approached the sofa with an outstretched hand. 'Pleased to meet you, Lizzy. You too, Dolly.'

'Would you like a tart?' said Dolly, shaking his hand. Hearing the muffled giggles coming from Clara and Lizzy, she hastily added, 'I mean a jam tart.'

Spencer nodded. 'Yes, please. Are they homemade?'

Blushing, Dolly nodded proudly. 'I'm not the best cook in the world but I do mek a good pastry.'

Lizzy got up from her seat and gestured for Spencer to take her place. 'Take a seat, Spencer. I'll mek us a pot of tea.'

As Spencer sat down next to Dolly, Lizzy put the kettle on to boil. Clara joined her by the stove and hissed from the corner of her mouth. 'What's up with Dolly? She's not normally this quiet.'

'Beats me,' Lizzy said. 'She were jabberin' away fit to burst before you and Spencer come back.' She cast an eye over her shoulder to where the two were sitting side by side, Spencer talking whilst Dolly listened. 'If I didn't know better I'd say she was shy.'

Clara snorted on a giggle. 'Dolly's not shy of anyone. She's got more confidence when it comes to men than me and you put together.'

Lizzy nodded. 'That's what I thought, but on the other hand I've never seen her so quiet.'

Clara, who had been watching them keenly, looked at Lizzy. 'You really think she's shy of Spencer?'

Lizzy nodded again. 'It's hard to say, 'cos it's the first time I've ever seen her like this, but lookin' at the way she was before Spencer come in and straight after, I reckon it's the only explanation.' She cocked an eyebrow. 'You must admit, he's incredibly handsome. He looks like one of them movie stars.'

Clara shrugged. 'He's my brother. I've never really stopped to consider whether he's good-looking or not.'

There was a brief knock on the door as Charlie announced his presence. 'Only me. Am I all right to come in?'

Lizzy opened the door. 'Course you are.'

Charlie nodded a greeting to Clara before addressing Lizzy. 'I've not got long,' he began, before noticing Dolly and Spencer. 'Oh, I didn't realise you had company.'

Lizzy nodded. 'Charlie, this is Clara's brother, Spencer. He's come up from Plymouth on a week's leave.'

Charlie smiled fleetingly. 'Hello.'

Spencer smiled back. 'Hello, Charlie.' He looked at Clara. 'Have you told Lizzy about my idea?'

Clara shook her head guiltily. 'It completely slipped my mind!' She turned to Lizzy. 'I hope you don't mind, but I told Spencer about your mum, and he reckons he might know a way to find her.'

Lizzy raised an enquiring brow. 'Really? It would be wonderful if you could.' She took the plate of tarts and two mugs of tea across to the sofa and placed them on the small wooden table, calling over her shoulder, 'Pour yourself a mug from the pot, Charlie.' As she settled herself next to Spencer she looked at him shyly. 'Gosh, you've got the same-coloured eyes as Clara. We've allus said she's so lucky to have such beautiful blue eyes, haven't we, Doll?'

Dolly nodded enthusiastically.

Spencer chuckled. 'Hear that, sis? Lizzy thinks you look like me!'

'Oh ha ha, Spencer. You know full well that's not what Lizzy meant.'

Winking at Lizzy, Spencer patted her knee in a playful manner. 'I'm only teasing.'

A clattering sound from the kitchen area caused Lizzy to jump. 'Sorry,' said Charlie. 'I dropped my spoon.' As he picked the spoon out of the sink he turned his attention to Spencer. 'You were saying about Lizzy's mam?'

'What?' said Spencer. 'Oh, yes.' He turned to Lizzy. 'If you can give me your mother's name and a brief description – height, build, hair and eye colour – I could get the information transmitted to every naval base in Britain.'

Charlie gave a snort of contempt.

'Did you say something?' said Spencer, clearly offended.

Realising he had been rude, Charlie tried to smooth things over. 'Don't get me wrong, I think it's a marvellous idea, or it would be if Lizzy's mam wasn't terrified of water. She wouldn't dream of joining the Wrens.'

Spencer grimaced. 'Oh, I didn't realise.' He smiled apologetically at Lizzy, revealing a set of white and even teeth. 'Sorry.'

Lizzy smiled back. 'You weren't to know, and it was still a very good—' She stopped short in dismay as Spencer began to choke and splutter.

On his other side, Dolly slapped him heartily between his shoulder blades. 'Are you all right?'

His eyes watering, Spencer made his way to the sink and took a swig from a large glass of water. 'That's better. I think I inhaled some pastry crumbs.'

Charlie swiftly sat in the space that he had occupied, much to Dolly's disapproval. 'Charlie! Spencer was sittin' there.'

Spencer shook his head. 'It's all right, Dolly. I only popped in to see the flat and to ask if you and Lizzy would like to join me and Clara for dinner this evening.' He nodded at Charlie. 'You're more than welcome to join us, Charlie. It's my shout.'

'That'd be lovely,' said Dolly, glancing at Lizzy and Charlie. 'Are you two comin'?'

Charlie shook his head. 'I've got to be in work in half an hour, so I'm afraid I'll have to give it a miss.'

'That's a shame,' said Lizzy, clearly disappointed. 'It would've been nice to go out the five of us together.'

'Perhaps another time,' said Charlie, although he suspected that Spencer would far rather have the girls all to himself, especially Lizzy. Draining the tea from his mug, he raised his brows fleetingly. 'That being said, I think I'd better be off.'

'Surely you don't need to go just yet? You've hardly been here two minutes, and you said you still had half an hour,' said Lizzy.

Charlie glanced at Spencer before he replied. 'Can't see much point in hanging around here. I dare say you'll want to get ready, and it won't harm me to get into work a bit early.'

Lizzy started to stand up, but Charlie waved her back down. 'I can see myself to the door.' He glanced around the company. 'Hope you enjoy your meal.'

As the bottom door closed behind him Clara arched an eyebrow at Lizzy. 'Can I have a quick word?' She jerked her head in the direction of the bedroom, and Lizzy followed her through. Clara closed the door softly behind her. 'Looks like Charlie wasn't too happy.'

Lizzy nodded. 'It would have been lovely for us all to go out to dinner. You can't blame him for being disappointed about missing out on all the fun.'

Clara shook her head. 'Do you really believe that's the reason for his bad mood?'

Lizzy looked puzzled. 'Don't you?'

Clara jerked her thumb in the direction of the stairwell. 'That boy is jealous. It was obvious from the moment he walked through the door that he didn't like the idea of Spencer being here, and as for the thought of him taking you out for a meal ...'

Lizzy pulled a face. 'But he's got nothing to be jealous of! It's not as if we're an item.'

'What's that got to do with the price of fish?'

'Well, it's none of his concern, is it? It'd be different if we were a couple, but we're not, so he's nowt to be jealous of,' Lizzy repeated.

'Jealousy's an emotion, not a condition,' said an exasperated Clara. 'The man's besotted with you; it's obvious he's going to get jealous of you spending time with another man!'

'But he shouldn't worry about me goin' off with anyone else. If I were goin' to go with anyone it'd be him,'
said Lizzy as if this were the most obvious thing in the
world.

'Have you told him that?' said Clara.

Lizzy opened her mouth to say yes before realising
that she hadn't. 'I thought it was obvious.'

'Not to Charlie it's not, so it might be an idea to put
him straight next time you see him.'

Outside, Charlie stared up at the flat. Ruddy Spencer,
he thought bitterly. How am I meant to compete with
the likes of him? Staring down at his plain black uniform, Charlie tutted as he took in the unexciting effect.
He didn't like to admit it, but Spencer had looked very
smart in his navy uniform with its gold braid and fancy
buttons. Probably thinks he's much better than me, the
pompous twit, thought Charlie.

He reached the end of the alley and turned in the
direction of the station. Trouble is, it's not my opinion
that counts, it's Lizzy's, and she may think he looks
dashing, he thought as he kicked a small stone with the
toe of his boot. I bet he's got a bob or two an' all, because
I know I couldn't afford to take the three of 'em out for
a fancy meal at the drop of a hat, especially not in war-
time when everything costs double what it used to. He
sighed heavily. Thank goodness Lizzy's mam's scared
of water. I couldn't bear the thought of him finding her
before me. Lizzy would think me a useless lump and
him a bloody hero. He stuffed his hands into his
pockets.

Since returning to his old station, Charlie had spent
as much time as he could with Lizzy. If they weren't

firewatching, he would take her out for a meal, or a trip to the cinema, or to a dance hall. He'd kept his promise to keep his distance, and played everything by Lizzy's rules, and until tonight he had really thought he was making progress. But with Spencer on the scene, who knew? He drew a small paper bag from his pocket and examined the contents, which turned out to be a single Everton mint. He peeled as much paper off as he could and popped it into his mouth. He hated the thought of another man anywhere near Lizzy, always had done. He pondered for a moment or so on that last thought. No, it wasn't entirely true: he didn't mind any of his pals from the station meeting Lizzy, not even the handsome ones, but he hadn't much cared for Josh until he found out he was keen on Clara, and he didn't care for Spencer at all. He frowned. Why had he only had issues with those two? Was it because he didn't know them? He shook his head. Lizzy knew a lot of fellers from Langdon's but Charlie didn't give two hoots about them. He pictured Josh in his army uniform, then Spencer in his. He grimaced. It wasn't them he was jealous of, it was their uniforms. His cheeks reddened as he remembered Mickey from the café commenting how Lizzy was more suited to a military man. She thinks of me as a hero in my uniform, but I'm nothin' compared to the likes of them, he thought miserably. They're the ones layin' their lives down for their country, whereas most folk see scuffers as interferin' busybodies. He shook his head in annoyance. It wasn't Lizzy who saw Charlie as inferior, but Charlie himself. The problem's yours, Charlie boy, not hers, and unless you get your act together and start being polite to the other men in Lizzy's life she'll think you're a miserable jealous sod.

Entering the station, he nodded to the desk sergeant on duty before making his way to the office at the back. Lizzy had never given Charlie reason to suspect that she thought him less of a man for not joining the services, far from it. She had been nothing but complimentary when it came to his work, even comparing him to Poirot and Sir Lancelot. Next time I see Lizzy I shall apologise for my bad manners, and assure her it won't happen again, he thought. Happy in the knowledge that he would be able to move on, Charlie joined his workmates.

Mary jumped aboard the double-decker bus that would take her from her billet in Ackerleigh House to the naval office in Rumford Street.

'Mornin', Sam. Not a bad day for it!'

He nodded. 'Mornin', Mary. Did you hear about the Croxteth Estate?'

Mary grimaced. 'One of the girls told me this mornin'. I must admit I thought we'd seen an end to all that malarkey.' As the bus trundled down the road she looked out of the window. 'It makes no sense. The estate's nowhere near the docks; they're either really bad at aimin' or they're hittin' people's houses on purpose.'

'I dare say they don't care as long as they destroy summat.' Sam paused as he steered his way round a collapsed building. 'I've been thinkin' about your Lizzy. If you had a picture of her I could stick it in me winder. A lot of folk'd get to see it then.'

She shook her head. 'I've already thought of that, but I'm afraid that vile ex-husband of mine destroyed everything.' She heaved a sigh. 'I've told just about everyone I meet what she looks like and where I saw her last, but no joy so far.'

He pulled up alongside the kerb. 'Trouble is, what you tell people she looks like and what they see in their 'eads could be very different.' He turned to face her. 'Wharrabout gerrin' someone to draw a picture of her?'

Mary chuckled. 'How can they when they've never seen her?'

'You describe her to 'em, then when they start drawin' you tell 'em whether they need to change things until they get a good likeness.'

'I wonder if that would work? One of the Wrens in my billet's always doodling in her notepad. I've seen some of the pictures she's drawn of the other girls and they're as good as any photo. I'm sure she'd have a go in a flash if I asked her, and we could keep on it until she got it right. Then all she'd have to do is copy it and I'd have a few to post round and about.'

Sam grinned. 'See? People think us bus drivers is as thick as two short planks, but we're not, we're geniuses.' He chuckled.

Settling into her seat, Mary looked at the passing scenery and imagined the buildings and lampposts covered in images of Lizzy. She said as much to Sam, who pulled a doubtful face. 'I reckern you'd be better off stickin' 'em on trams and buses than buildin's.'

'Why?'

'If a buildin' gets bombed your picture goes down with it. Not only that, you don't know whereabouts

Lizzy's livin' so you'd be tekkin' pot luck, but if you stick it on buses and trams what cover the whole city someone who knows Lizzy is bound to see it – if she don't see it for herself, of course.'

Mary leaned forward in her seat. 'You're right, Sam. You *are* a genius!'

Mary breathed out happily as she looked at the image of Lizzy that Annie had drawn. Considering the other woman had never laid eyes on her daughter, the resemblance was remarkable. Anyone who knew Lizzy would easily recognise her from the picture. Sam, the bus driver, had had a word with a few of his mates and they had agreed to place copies somewhere on their buses where they might easily be seen. She had asked James if she could put one up in the corridor of Admiralty House and he had said yes.

'A lot of people pass through this building. The more eyes that see that picture the more chance you've got of finding her.'

'I'm going to find her, I just know it,' said Mary, and for the first time in a long while she believed her own words.

Chapter Twelve

December, 1941

Ivy ran into the small room she shared with her mother. 'Tek a look at what I've got!'

Gertrude studied the piece of paper that had been thrust into her hands. 'So?'

'Whaddaya mean, "so"? If it weren't for that interferin' bitch Lizzy Atherton and that scuffer mate of hers you wouldn't have spent the best part of a year in jail, not to mention losin' everythin' we'd worked so hard to get. We'd not be livin' in a dump like this if it weren't for her. This,' she snatched the paper from between Gertrude's fingers, 'is the perfect way to take our revenge and fleece 'em of their money.'

She stared at the picture of Lizzy, and the writing underneath.

Ten pound reward offered for anyone with information leading to the whereabouts of Elizabeth Atherton, please contact Mary Tanner at Ackerleigh House.

Ivy carefully tore the bottom half off the picture. 'All I have to do is find out where Lizzy lives, and post the bit with 'er picture on it through her door with a message on the back tellin' 'er I know where 'er mam is and if she wants to know it'll cost 'er.'

Gretrude folded her arms across her chest. 'And that's the only picture? Or are there others scattered all over the city? Didn't think of that, did you?' Her voice trailed off as Ivy drew a further nine pieces of paper out of her pocket.

'I got on every bus I could and took 'em down.'

''Ow much did that cost you?'

Ivy rolled her eyes. 'I didn't pay, I just nipped on and off again. Did the same on the trams too, but I reckern she's only done the buses.'

Gertie nodded her approval. 'I'm proud of you, gel. That's what you call thinkin' on your feet.' Reaching forward, she took the paper from Ivy's hands and examined it with a malevolent grin. 'I reckern you could be on to summat 'ere.'

Ivy, who had been rooting around in one of the kitchen drawers for a pencil, took the picture from her mother. A few seconds later she handed it back.

If you want to know where your mam is it'll cost you a tenner. Meet me by the bandstand in Sefton Park at midday on Saturday. Don't bring the scuffers, or you'll not see me for dust and you'll have lost your mam for ever.

Gertie smiled. 'What'll you do when she turns up?'

'First I shall make her beg, then I shall get her to give me the money, then I'll give 'er this bit.' She flourished the piece of paper which held Mary's message.

Gertie wagged a reproving finger. 'Or you could tek the money and tell 'er to wait there whilst you go and get 'er mam, then when you go to this Ackerleigh House you find this Mary and claim your reward and tell 'er where she can find 'er daughter. That way you'll double your money!'

Ivy nodded slowly. 'I'll find out where she lives, then post it through her door whilst she's at work, that way I don't run the risk of gerrin' caught.'

Entering the flat, Lizzy strode towards the window and peered down at the street below. 'I know you think I'm bein' daft, but I can't help feelin' we're bein' watched.' She took a good look out of the window before drawing the curtains.

'Well?' said Dolly. 'Any sign of the bogeyman?'

Lizzy shot her a withering look. 'No there's not, and a good job too. I don't know about you but it gives me the heebie-jeebies, thinkin' there could be someone out there watchin' our every move.'

Dolly rolled her eyes. 'Well, if they are they must be bored to tears!'

Clara filled the kettle with water. 'It certainly gives me goose bumps. I was quite worried about stayin' in tonight till Dolly said she was stayin' in too.'

'How come you've both decided not to go out?'

Clara took the teapot from the dresser and began spooning tea into it. 'Dancin' always makes me hungry and I think I'm doing rather well on my diet.'

Dolly wrinkled the side of her nose. 'And I'm savin' me pennies for Christmas.' She glanced at Clara. 'Fancy sharin' a tin of soup?'

Clara nodded. 'That's all I eat nowadays, soup, soup and more soup. I'll be lookin' like a can of soup at this rate.'

Lizzy cast an approving eye over Clara's slim figure. 'Credit where it's due, you've done really well. Josh won't recognise you when he gets off that train.'

Clara squealed with delight. 'Do you really think I've changed that much?'

Dolly nodded. 'Your tummy's flat and you've gorra waist.'

Clara danced a little jig. 'I'm sexy!'

'Not to mention modest!' Lizzy laughed.

Clara giggled. 'It's all right for you, Lizzy, you've always been svelte, with handsome men throwin' themselves at your feet.'

'I have? Where are they?' said Lizzy, lifting her feet and looking under her shoes.

'I mean Charlie! Every time you snap your fingers he comes running, but it's not been like that for me.'

Lizzy frowned. 'I'm not sure I like what you said about Charlie. You make it sound as if I'm using him, and I'm not.'

Clara pulled an apologetic face. 'I didn't mean it like that. I just meant you've never had to try to impress a feller, and Charlie doesn't mind waitin' around because he knows he's in with a chance.'

'Mmm,' said Lizzy. 'I sometimes wonder whether I should have told him that.'

Dolly's eyes rounded. 'You don't mean there's someone else?'

'No,' said Lizzy, shaking her head, 'but who knows how I'm goin' to feel in the future. I wish things were different.' Clara and Dolly exchanged glances. 'Why are you looking at each other like that?'

Dolly pressed her lips together. 'It's just ...'

Lizzy folded her arms. 'Just what?'

'Well, different how? The two of you gerron like an 'ouse on fire, you spend all your free time together, you'd 'ave to be tapped in the head not to fancy him, so I don't see what's stopping you from taking the next step.'

Clara nodded. 'Dolly's right, 'cos he won't hang on for ever.'

'I never said he should.'

'We know you didn't,' said Dolly, 'but if you're not careful another girl'll come along and snap 'im up, and what'll you do then?' She looked at Lizzy with kind eyes. 'I suppose what we're tryin' to say is you may as well give things a go, 'cos if you don't you'll end up losin' 'im for certain.'

Lizzy stared at the floor whilst she tried to come up with an answer that would explain her predicament. The trouble was, she couldn't. Everything her friends had said was true. In the past she had blamed the fact that her mother was missing, or that she was frightened that if she and Charlie got together she would lose him just like all the other people she had ever loved. But now she came to think about it, Dolly was right: it didn't make sense. After all, if she persisted in keeping Charlie at arm's length, then one of these days he really would go off with someone else, so either way she ran the risk of losing him. She had also told herself that if she got together with Charlie it would feel like giving up the search for her mother, but deep down she knew this to be untrue. It had just been an excuse. What she was really scared of was starting a relationship with Charlie only to find that they weren't suited. If that were the case, then she would lose not only a possible future lover, but one of her oldest friends. The only reasonable excuse she could come up with now was his immature ways. She turned to Dolly. 'I just hope to goodness that Charlie really has changed and he's not playin' silly games.'

Dolly sighed heavily. 'Has he done anything lately to make you think he's messin' you about?'

Lizzy shook her head.

'Then stop bein' silly and put the poor feller out of his misery,' said Clara. 'Where are you goin' tonight?'

'The Grafton. One of the girls in packin' said they'd put their Christmas decorations up. She reckoned it looked magical.'

Clara smiled wistfully. 'I can't wait for me and Josh to go dancing for the first time.' She paused. 'I've just thought of something. What if Josh can't dance?'

'Then that'll make two of you,' quipped Dolly.

'Oh, ha ha. I only trod on you once ...'

'If you think it were only once, you can't count. Besides, once is more than enough. I still reckon you broke my toe!'

Clara giggled as the image of Dolly hopping around the dance floor on one foot returned to her mind. 'Sorry, Doll. It's not as if I meant to do it.'

'Do you remember that feller what started mimickin' you?' Lizzy giggled. 'He thought it was the latest dance.'

Dolly gave a snort. 'I hope Josh owns a pair of them steel-toecapped boots!'

There was a brief knock before Charlie called from the other side of the door. 'Are you ready?'

'Course. I'll just grab me coat and I'll be right with you.' Lizzy smiled at the other girls. 'Wish me luck!'

On the way to the Grafton, Lizzy asked, 'Do you ever get the feelin' you're bein' watched?'

Charlie chuckled. 'Always! It's part of the job. One of 'em keeps an eye on you whilst their mate's off on the rob. Why?'

'When I was in work earlier I had the strangest feeling, as if someone was starin' at me. I took a good look round but I couldn't see anything, then later on, when we come 'ome, I had the same feelin'.'

'Did you see anyone lurkin' around?'

She shook her head. 'Dolly thinks I'm bein' silly.' She looked shyly at him from underneath her lashes. 'If I'm honest, I've been expectin' some kind of revenge ever since Gertie got sent to prison. I'm damned sure Ivy must remember me, and we all know how intent they were on gerrin' their own back on the Grangers. You saw what the family were like in the courthouse when Gertie were gerrin' sentenced, all shoutin' threats and wavin' their fists in the air.'

Charlie shook his head. 'That was ages ago. If they were intent on gerrin' revenge they'd've done it by now, and I wouldn't take no notice of their behaviour in court 'cos that's what they're allus like, mekkin' threats and shoutin' the odds. They're only doin' it for show, 'cos when push comes to shove they're a bunch of cowards.' Seeing the look of doubt on Lizzy's face, he gave her a brief hug. 'Take it from me, Liz, as far as the Hackneys are concerned, you've got nowt to worry about.'

285

As they entered the Grafton, Lizzy gasped at the beautiful decorations that adorned the whole room. She watched the mirror ball as it rotated, reflecting its light on to the tinsel, which glistened like diamonds. Handing their coats over to the girl, they headed for the dance floor. 'Now this,' Lizzy breathed, 'is what I call Christmas, all these beautiful decorations and a wonderful band playing all our favourite songs. We really are lucky to be living here, aren't we, Charlie?'

'We are indeed, though there is one more thing that would make my Christmas complete.' He cast an eye around the room. 'Only I don't think they've got any mistletoe handy.'

Lizzy giggled. 'That's a shame.'

Unsure whether Lizzy was joking, Charlie eyed her hopefully. 'Are you tellin' me that if I were to find a bit of mistletoe you'd give me a smooch?'

Lizzy shrugged. 'You'll have to find some first.'

Charlie looked her square in the eye. 'You always said you wouldn't kiss a feller unless you were in a relationship ...'

'Quite right too,' said Lizzy.

Charlie slipped his hand into hers. 'Are you tellin' me you've had a change of heart?'

Lizzy took a deep breath. 'Only one way to find out.'

He eyed her cautiously. He felt certain that Lizzy wouldn't be playing games; she wasn't the sort. He took a deep breath. 'Pipsqueak ...'

Lizzy arched a warning eyebrow.

'I'll try again. Lizzy Atherton, will you do me the honour of agreein' to be my girl?'

Lizzy's heart pounded in her chest. It was now or never. 'Course I will.'

With a whoop of joy Charlie picked Lizzy up and swirled her round. 'Finally!'

Lizzy giggled. 'Stop it, Charlie. Everyone's starin'.'

He leaned so close, the tips of their noses touched. 'Let 'em stare. You just made me the happiest man in the world!' He brushed his lips against hers before kissing her, softly at first, then, as the music gathered momentum, more firmly.

Lizzy, who had never been kissed before, felt as though she was about to melt in his arms. As he broke away he kissed the tip of her nose. 'Now that,' he smiled, 'was worth waiting for!'

'Mmmm,' said Lizzy, and laying her cheek against his chest she allowed him to sweep her around the dance floor.

Lizzy had been to many dances with Charlie, but none had been as special as tonight. When Charlie held her close there wasn't a sliver of light between them, and when the slow numbers came on his arms reached further round her waist than they had ever done before. It's almost as if we're the same person, Lizzy mused, and by the end of the evening she felt as though she could burst with happiness.

As she and Charlie walked arm in arm along Pickwick Street, she let out a groan as her eyes flickered up towards the flat. 'I've just thought of summat.'

He kissed the top of her head, making her smile. 'What's up?'

'I'm goin' to have to tell Clara and Dolly, and they're goin' to want to hear every detail twice over at least.'

Charlie leaned his head against hers. 'You sound like you're dreadin' it, whereas I can't wait to tell the fellers down the station tomorrer.'

'I didn't think they'd be interested in that kind of thing.'

'Jimmy is. He's allus teasin' me because you wouldn't be my girlfriend.'

'How horrid. I thought Jimmy was a nice man.'

Charlie chuckled. 'He is, but you know what fellers are like, allus ribbin' each other over summat.' He sighed blissfully. 'Well, not any more. This time I shall be the one who has the last laugh.'

Ivy ducked out of sight as someone pulled the curtains open in the small flat in Pickwick Street. She waited a moment before risking another peek, just in time to see Lizzy disappearing from view. Ivy looked down at the picture in her hand. As soon as that dratted Lizzy and her gormless pals left the flat, she could post it through the letterbox and head back to the room she shared with her mother. Standing on icy cobbled streets in the middle of December was not pleasant and her feet, which were already beginning to go numb, hurt when she stamped up and down in an effort to warm them. After ten minutes had gone by, she was considering giving up when she heard the door in the alley open. Glancing round the corner, she watched as the three girls made their way towards Duke Street, then ran down the alley and with a satisfied smile shoved the picture through the letterbox. Her only regret was that she'd not get to see the look on Lizzy's face when she read her note.

* * *

Picking up the mail, Dolly read the names of the recipients out loud as she entered the kitchen. 'Six from Josh, four of 'em for you, Clara, an' the other two for me and Lizzy, although if I know Josh they'll be identical.'

Lizzy grinned. 'I'm sure he can't realise we read each other's letters. He'd try and mek 'em a bit different if he did.'

'Leave my Josh alone, you two. It can't be easy thinkin' of something entertainin' to say when you know it'll only end up getting cut out.'

Dolly raised her brow as she handed Clara her clutch of envelopes. 'He seems to find somethin' interestin' to say to you.'

A small smile crossed her lips as Clara blushed. 'They're private, Dolly Clifton, not like the ones he sends you two!'

Dolly handed Lizzy her envelope. 'Oh, summat fell …'

Lizzy picked up the piece of paper. 'It's a picture of me! Who on earth would be sending me a picture of myself?' She turned the paper over and, clearing her throat, read out the message on the back. 'If you want to know where your mam is it'll cost you a tenner.' Her voice lowered as she continued reading. 'Meet me by the bandstand in Sefton Park at midday on Saturday. Don't bring the scuffers, or you'll not see me for dust and you'll have lost your mam for ever.' She handed the picture to Dolly and Clara. 'I *told* you someone was watchin' us … or, as it turns out, me. D'you reckon it's some kind of joke?'

Dolly frowned. 'I jolly well hope not, 'cos it's in extremely poor taste if it is.'

289

Clara looked dubiously at the paper. 'I reckon it is, otherwise it'd be a picture of your mum. Question is: what are you going to do about it?'

Lizzy shrugged. 'Meet them?' She saw the look of doubt cross her friends' faces. 'Well, what would you do?'

'I wouldn't give 'em a tenner for a start, and I'd tell Charlie.' As Lizzy opened her mouth to protest, Dolly held up a hand. 'I know what it says, but you can't trust this person. You don't know who it is and they could be dangerous, and after this I reckon you're right, you are bein' watched, which is a pretty creepy thing to do, so if you don't tell Charlie I'm afraid I will.'

Lizzy thought about what Dolly had said before nodding. 'You're right. For all I know it could be that Nathan, Ivy's uncle, gerrin' 'is own back for what we did to his sister. I'll go and see Charlie after I've had me tea.'

'You mean *we'll* go and see Charlie straight after our tea,' said Clara. 'You're not going anywhere on your own until we find out what's going on.'

'Too right,' said Dolly, 'especially if it is one of the Hackneys. I know Charlie said they were cowards, but that Nathan attacked an old woman, which makes him a coward too, so I dare say he wouldn't blink at the idea of attacking a young girl far smaller and weaker than he is.'

A short while later the girls entered the police station. 'Hello, Jimmy. Is Charlie here?'

''Allo, Lizzy. Charlie told us the good news. I must admit I never thought he'd wear you down.' He chuckled. 'I s'pose now you're official we won't be able to keep you two lovebirds apart, eh?'

Lizzy blushed. 'It's not like that. We're here over a criminal matter. Can you fetch him, please? I've got summat I need to show 'im.'

The smile disappeared from Jimmy's face as he headed into the back of the station, and the girls could hear him talking in earnest to Charlie, who quickly appeared.

'I didn't expect to see you so soon. What's up?'

Lizzy showed him the picture.

Charlie read the message and looked at Lizzy with grave concern. 'Looks like you were right about bein' watched. I don't suppose you're any the wiser as to who it could be?'

Lizzy shook her head.

'Well, I don't care what it says, you're not goin' without me. Whoever this is must be a pretty nasty piece of work to try and blackmail you.'

Lizzy chewed her lip thoughtfully, her eyes brimming with anxious tears. 'But if it's true, then this is the closest I've come to findin' me mam. I can't run the risk of them seein' you and runnin' away.'

Charlie held her hand across the counter as he thought it through. 'As it's a Saturday lunchtime the park should be quite busy. I could get there half an hour before you're due to meet and hide well out of sight. That way I'll be close by should you need me.'

Dolly nudged Clara. 'Right little knight in shinin' armour, ain't he?'

Lizzy looked earnestly at Charlie. 'Knights in shinin' armour are all very well, as long as they don't go wadin' in and scarin' off the only person who might know where me mam is.'

He placed a hand across his heart. 'You keep your eyes peeled. If you see me, give me a wave and I promise I'll leave. That do you?'

Lizzy mulled it over. 'So you're goin' to hide, and I'm to try and spot you, and if I can, you'll go?'

He nodded.

'Sounds reasonable.'

He glanced at the picture. 'I know you're desperate to see your mam, but I wouldn't like you to get your hopes up.'

'I know, but the only way to find out is to turn up. The only trouble is I haven't got a tenner.'

Charlie pursed his lips. 'Don't worry about that. If it turns out to be kosher I'll find a way to get the money. In the meantime, just be aware that it's far more likely that someone's heard about your situation and is tryin' to con you, so I wouldn't go worryin' about the money just yet.'

Lizzy, who had been hoping the information was real, looked forlorn. 'What makes you so sure?'

He shrugged. 'They've gone to great lengths to have this image of you drawn up. Not only that, but if someone had been separated from their mother and you knew where they could find her, what would you do?'

She looked up from the picture in surprise. 'I'd tell them ... oh.' Lizzy's voice trailed off, a tear trickling down her cheek. 'You're right. It's a con, isn't it?'

Coming round to the same side of the counter as Lizzy, he placed a comforting arm around her shoulders. 'I hate to say it, especially after the other night when I pooh-poohed your concerns about the Hackneys, but this is the sort of thing they're known for.'

Lizzy had begun to nod when a far more sinister thought occurred to her. 'Albert,' she said, her voice almost a whisper. 'It could be Albert.'

Charlie's eyes widened. 'Your mam's husband?'

She nodded. 'Think about it. He's the only one who knows what's happened to her. I reckon he must've seen me somewhere, followed me 'ome ...' Her eyes rounded in horror. 'I bet it's 'im what's been watchin' me.'

A shiver ran down Dolly's spine. 'And to think I made light of it.'

'But why would he go to such lengths?' said Clara. 'After all, wasn't he the one who wanted you out of his life?'

Lizzy paused before answering. 'Because he wants me to know he's in control, and what better way to do it?'

Charlie looked grave. 'Well, if it is him, he's in for a nasty surprise when I leap out and arrest him!'

Lizzy kissed Charlie's cheek. 'I don't know what I'd do without you, Charlie Jackson.'

He tweaked her nose playfully. 'You'll have me blushin' if you carry on like that.'

Clara hooked her arm through Lizzy's. 'Come on. I don't think it's a good idea for us to stay out too late, and I ain't lettin' you out of my sight until Charlie's arrested someone.'

'But why would people do that?' said Mary in disbelief.

Sam raised a pragmatic brow. 'You offered a tenner reward: people don't want that kind of thing gerrin'

293

about. The more folk who see it, the less chance they've got of bein' the ones who get the reward, so they tek the pictures down.'

'I can't ask Annie to do any more. She's gone to Portsmouth, and I don't know anyone else who can draw like that. Anyway, I don't see the point if people are just going to take them.'

Sam nodded. 'If I'd realised people would go round pulling them down I'd've asked the lads to put 'em somewhere safer, like what I've done,' he nodded to the picture which he'd placed to the left of his steering wheel, 'but look on the bright side, we've still got this one, and no one's goin' to snaffle it wi'out me knowin', so at least there's some hope.'

Mary nodded. 'True, and the one I put up in the office is still there, so it's not as if they've all gone.'

Sam brightened. 'You never know your luck, mebbe the person who took 'em'll find her.'

Mary smiled doubtfully. 'Let's hope so, 'cos it'd be the icing on the cake if I found our Lizzy before Christmas.'

Sam nodded wistfully. 'It's at times like these you realise what's really important. Our Daryl's over in Africa at the minute, and whilst I'd give anythin' to 'ave him 'ome for the holidays, I don't care as long as he's safe and well.'

Mary nodded. 'You never stop worryin' about 'em no matter how old they get.'

Lizzy stood alone beside the bandstand in Sefton Park. She scanned her surroundings for a sign of Charlie but could find none. As he had predicted, the park was

294

packed with people making the most of the last weekend before Christmas. As a couple of children half ran, half skidded past her, she went through the plan once more.

She was to wait no more than fifteen minutes, and if no one turned up she would make her way to where the girls were waiting. They would put it down to a cruel hoax and leave. If, on the other hand, someone did come, she would hear their story before signalling to the others as to whether she thought it was a con or not. If it was Nathan or Albert, rather than alert him to Charlie's presence by shouting for help she would remove her hat, and Charlie would come down and arrest him before he had a chance to work out what was going on.

Her stomach lurched as the church clock began to strike noon. Somebody cleared their throat behind her. Turning, Lizzy saw a woman lurking by the trees. She was wearing a floor-length shabby black coat, a black woollen hat which had been pulled down to hide her face, and a black scarf covering her nose and mouth.

Whoever the mystery person was, it was not Albert. Lizzy folded her arms across her chest. 'Can I help you?'

Nodding, the figure wordlessly handed her a piece of paper.

Lizzy glanced down at an identical picture to the one she had in her pocket. Feeling certain that if the person who had sent the message were Nathan he would have turned up in person so that he could intimidate her, Lizzy glared at the silent figure. 'Albert sent you, didn't he? Well, you can tell that useless coward that he'll have to come and meet me himself if he wants the money.'

The woman appeared bemused. Taking a step forward, she shook her head and pointed at the picture.

Lizzy had had enough. Placing her hands on her hips she glowered at the woman. 'Are you deaf? You heard what I said, so tell him if he wants any money he'll have to come and see me himself.'

Shaking her head in annoyance, the woman leaned closer and prodded the picture with her finger.

But Lizzy, who had spent the last few days in a state of almost unbearable tension, was in no mood for games. In one swift motion, she snatched the hat off the woman's head and pulled her scarf down. 'Ivy!'

Ivy hastily pulled the scarf back over her face. 'So?'

'Where's Albert?'

Ivy frowned. 'Who the bloody hell is Albert?'

Lizzy opened her mouth to speak, but closed it again when she realised that if Ivy was the one behind the picture, she would be doing it for her own benefit and nobody else's.

'Never mind that. Why are you here?'

Rolling her eyes, Ivy glared at the picture in Lizzy's hands. 'Can't you soddin' well read?'

Lizzy nodded. 'Course I can, but ...'

Ivy appeared confused. 'Don't you want to know where your mam is?'

'Course I do.'

Ivy held out her palm. 'Money first.'

Lizzy looked at Ivy's hand, then stared directly into the other girl's eyes. 'I'm not givin' you anythin' until you can prove you know where me mam is.'

Ivy glared at Lizzy. 'How the hell else d'you think I got a picture of you?'

Heavy with sarcasm, Lizzy pretended to mull the matter over. 'Let me see, you come from a family who are well known for thievin' and connivin' and cheatin' folk out of their money, and I seem to remember that you and your mam forged Arthur Granger's signature on his cheques. So when it comes to knockin' up a picture of me I should imagine it was a piece of cake.'

'What? Copyin' someone's handwritin' is a million miles away from doin' a drawin' as good as that. I'd have to hire a professional, an' do you really think I'd go to all that trouble for a tenner?'

'I believe you'd sell your granny for a bag of chips.'

Ivy snatched the picture from Lizzy's fingers. 'You stuck-up bitch! I bet you've not even got the money.'

'Damned right I 'aven't. I knew it were a con from the start. You don't know where my mam is any more than I do!'

Ivy gaped at Lizzy. Out of all the reactions she had been expecting, this was not one of them. She started to laugh. 'D'you know what? I never liked you. You was allus a stuck-up cow, thinkin' you was better than the rest of us. I'm glad your mam's missin', I'm glad you'll never find her, and whether you believe it or not I do know where she is.' She held her hands up. 'I admit, I was plannin' on fleecin' you of a tenner, and then doin' the same to her, but it's a small price to pay for bein' reunited, don't you think?' Before Lizzy had a chance to reply, she continued, 'But you ain't gorra cat in 'ell's chance now, 'cos I've got all the pictures,' she strode forward until her nose was inches away from Lizzy's, 'and I wouldn't tell you where your mam was now if my life depended on it.'

Lizzy swallowed hard. If Ivy was telling the truth then she had just blown her best chance of ever finding her mother. She stared into Ivy's eyes, which were dancing with spiteful glee, and shook her head. This was the Hackneys through and through; they were born liars. 'You're lyin'. That's all you and your rotten family ever do: lie.'

Ivy's eyes narrowed. 'I can't wait to go 'ome and tell me mam. She'll have a good laugh when she hears how stupid you've been.'

Lizzy shook her head in disgust. 'You seem to forget that I was the one who helped put your mam behind bars. If it weren't for me, you and your mam would still be fleecin' poor old Mr Granger, which brings me to another point. Look at the lengths you went to in order to persuade him to take you and your mam in. Dressin' up as beggar women.' She laughed scornfully. 'If it wasn't for me and my Charlie ...'

Ivy spluttered at the mention of Charlie's name. '*Your* Charlie? You mean the Ice Princess actually got off 'er 'igh 'orse long enough to agree to go out wi' 'im?' She shook her head incredulously. 'You mek out like 'e's an 'ero, an 'onest, law-abidin' citizen, but you don't know the 'alf of it.'

Lizzy furrowed her brow. 'What on earth are you goin' on about?'

Ivy's lips curved into a cruel smile. 'You mean you don't know?'

Lizzy threw her hands into the air. 'Why am I wastin' me time standin' 'ere listenin' to the likes of you?' She turned to walk away, but Ivy was having none of it. Gripping Lizzy's elbow, she stared maliciously into her eyes.

'The likes of me? At least I don't pretend to be summat other than what I am, not like your precious Charlie, who acts like a saint when all along he's just as bad as everyone else.' Lizzy tried to break free of Ivy's grasp, but Ivy wasn't letting go until she'd had her say. 'You're a stuck-up bitch, Lizzy Atherton, I know it and so does everyone else, includin' your pals.' She narrowed her eyes. 'Weren't you surprised that someone as good-lookin' as Charlie Jackson wanted to go out with a plain Jane like you, with all your hoity-toity snotty standards, allus turnin' him down, when he's got a line of girls all vyin' for his attention? Well, I'll tell you why. 'E asked you out for a bet!'

Lizzy laughed her contempt. 'You're a fool, Ivy Hackney. Charlie would never do such a thing, and even if he did, do you really think I'd believe he'd confide in someone like you?'

Ivy curled her lip. 'Remember the day you seen 'im and 'is mate in Mickey's caff? Well, I were in there too, and after you'd gone 'im and 'is pals was talkin' about 'ow you were this fancy ice princess. They bet 'e couldn't get you to go out with 'im, an' if 'e lost 'e were to pay them double.' She pushed Lizzy away with a sneer. 'Oh my God, you actually thought he'd asked you out because he liked you!'

Tears pricked Lizzy's eyes. 'It's just another lie. You're nowt but a spiteful bitch!'

'Oh-ho! Liar, am I? Why don't you ask Jimmy? 'E knows the truth, and 'e's not the only one. All your pals've had a right laugh about it.'

Lizzy shook her head. 'Charlie wouldn't talk in front of the likes of you, nor would Jimmy, so that just proves you're lyin'. Besides, I don't remember seein' you.'

Ivy spoke through pursed lips. 'Ask him. Go on, ask Charlie whether he only asked Pipsqueak out for a bet!'

At the mention of her nickname, Lizzy took a step backwards. Ivy nodded. 'That's right, Pipsqueak, you know I'm tellin' the truth now, don't you?' Holding the picture of Lizzy between her hands, Ivy tore it into two halves. 'First you lose your dad, then your mam, and now you've lost your precious Charlie, although I s'pose you never really 'ad 'im in the first place!' Turning on her heel, she threw the two halves of the picture over her shoulder. 'Merry Christmas, Lizzy Atherton!'

As Lizzy bent down to pick up the pieces of paper, Dolly and Clara appeared by her side.

'Who was it?' said Dolly. 'We could see you was arguin' but as you didn't tek your 'at off we thought we'd wait and see what 'appened.'

Lizzy wiped her tears on the back of her sleeve. 'It was Ivy. She said she knew where me mam was but I still reckon she were lyin', 'cos when I reminded her 'ow she'd conned your dad, Clara, she got really nasty.'

Dolly linked arms with Lizzy. 'You know better than to listen to what comes out of her gob. C'mon, let's go and tell Charlie.'

Lizzy shrugged Dolly's arm off. 'Why? So you can all have a laugh? I'm surprised you two can contain yourselves.'

300

Dolly stared at her in disbelief. 'No one's laughin', Lizzy. We wouldn't be so cruel, and I'm surprised you'd think we would.'

Lizzy glared at her. 'Not about me mam. About me and Charlie.'

Clara and Dolly exchanged puzzled glances. 'We don't know what you're talkin' about, but if it's somethin' Ivy's said you'd best remember she's a good liar before you go accusin' us of laughin' at you.'

'She ain't lyin' about this,' sniffed Lizzy. 'I know she ain't, but I hope she was lyin' about you two, 'cos I couldn't bear to think that me two bezzies 'ad been laughin' at me behind me back.'

Dolly stiffened. 'What exactly did she say?'

Relaying the conversation she had had with Ivy, she eyed Dolly and Clara awkwardly. 'Did you know?'

'Of course not!' snapped Dolly. 'I can't believe you'd think we'd keep summat like that to ourselves. As for Charlie, if it is true, and I'd think carefully before you tek Ivy's word for it, I'd string 'im up meself, but I'd certainly not laugh at you!'

'I didn't think you would, but she said all me pals were laughin' at me behind me back.'

'Well they're not,' said Clara in clipped tones. 'What's more, how do you know she's tellin' the truth about Charlie? He'd never do summat like that; he worships the ground you walk on, for goodness' sake.'

Lizzy shook her head. 'There's not many people who know Charlie calls me Pipsqueak, but she did, an' she knows who Jimmy is 'n' all.'

Dolly heaved a sigh. 'The bit about the caff is probably true, so that's how she knows Charlie calls you

Pipsqueak and who Jimmy is, but that's where it ends, trust me. I know Charlie can be a bit of a joker at times, but he's not cruel and I don't believe for a minute he'd speak ill of you.'

Lizzy shrugged. 'If she's tellin' the truth, then the man I thought was 'onest and loyal has proved he hasn't changed one little bit from when we was kids. Let's face it, I allus thought he hadn't changed, which was why I was so reluctant to go out with him. Deep down I allus knew he was still a big kid.'

'What're you goin' to do?' said Clara.

'He's somewhere outside this park waitin' to 'ear 'ow the meetin' went, so I shall tell 'im what she said and see what 'e 'as to say on the matter, although I shall find it very 'ard to believe a word that leaves his lips.'

'D'you want us to come with you?' Dolly asked.

Lizzy shook her head. 'This is summat I've gorra do on me own, but I'd appreciate it if you weren't too far away. I think I'm goin' to be needin' a shoulder or two to cry on when all's said and done, no matter what the outcome.'

'Fair enough, chuck,' said Dolly with a grim smile, 'but if you change your mind just holler.'

Lizzy made her way out of the park. She kept an eye out for Charlie, and as she crossed the road he stepped out from behind her. 'How'd it go? I couldn't see much from here, but you kept your hat on so I assume all's well.'

Lizzy turned to face him. 'You were right, it was a hoax. It was Ivy Hackney.'

Charlie's shoulders sagged. 'I'm sorry, queen. I know you were desperate to hear different, but I did warn you.'

She lowered her head, her heart hammering in her chest. 'Do you really think I'm an ice princess?'

Charlie gaped. 'Who on earth told you about that?'

Lifting her head, Lizzy fought back the tears. 'I believed you when you said you'd never do anything to 'urt me, but it was just another lie.'

His eyes rounded. 'Hold on a minute, why're you havin' a go at me? I never ...'

She stared at him through hollow eyes. 'Why'd you ask me out, Charlie?'

Charlie frowned, thoroughly confused. 'Why d'you think?'

She narrowed her eyes. 'For a bet?' Before he could reply she added, 'If you have any feelings for me at all, then at least do me the courtesy of tellin' me the truth.'

Charlie shook his head. 'It's not how it sounds ...'

Unfolding her arms, Lizzy balled her hands into fists. 'How *could* you?'

'Lizzy, if you'd just listen ...' He reached out to hold her, but she snapped her arm away from him.

'Why would I listen to a liar? Ivy told me everythin'. She even knew you called me Pipsqueak!'

Charlie's mouth gaped like a fish out of water as he sought an appropriate reply, but none came. He was flummoxed as to how Ivy could have known about the bet and was sure Jimmy wouldn't have told her, but someone obviously had. Closing his eyes, he muttered 'Mickey' under his breath.

Hearing the word leave his lips, Lizzy shook her head. Everything that Ivy had said about Charlie had been true. As the tears trickled slowly down her cheeks she stared directly into Charlie's eyes and noted that the mischievous twinkle had been replaced with a look of guilt. 'I can't believe I fell for you, Charlie Jackson, and after everything I've gone through.' She locked eyes with his. 'How could you?' The last three words left her lips in a whisper.

Charlie shook his head. 'You've got the wrong end of the stick.'

She looked at him in disbelief. 'That's what you've been sayin' ever since we ran into each other at Lime Street Station. Tryin' to convince me that I could trust you, that you'd grown up, moved on, weren't that naughty little boy who played tricks on people no more.' She lowered her eyes to hide the tears. 'You lied.' She shrugged him off as he tried to put his hand on her shoulder. 'No matter what I thought about your cheeky ways, I never thought you'd do owt to hurt me on purpose. What a fool I've been.'

As she turned to go back to Clara and Dolly, Charlie called, 'Please, Liz, just give me the chance to explain ...' Hurrying after her, he looked imploringly at Clara and Dolly. 'Tell her ...'

Clara shook her head. 'I think you'd better leave things to cool down for a bit. Maybe call round in a day or two ...'

As the three girls walked away, Lizzy turned to Dolly. 'He admitted the whole thing.'

'No!' said Dolly, clearly floored by the news. 'If it's any consolation, you weren't the only one he fooled, otherwise me and Clara would never have persuaded you to give him a chance.'

'Better I found out now than further down the line when I'd fallen in love with him,' said Lizzy, although in her heart she knew it was too late. If truth be told, she was already deeply in love with him and had been for a long time, which was why her heart ached at the thought of losing him.

'Good riddance to bad rubbish, that's what I say,' said Clara as she kissed the top of Lizzy's head.

When she nodded, the tears dripped off the end of Lizzy's nose. 'Why couldn't he have left me alone? He knew I was going through a bad time. I've allus known he doesn't tek life seriously, but this?' She shook her head. 'This is just cruel.'

'What was his explanation?' Dolly asked.

'Don't know,' said Lizzy simply. 'I didn't want to listen, not after he'd admitted it was true.'

Dolly bit her lip tentatively. 'Don't you think it would have been better to hear his side of the story first?'

Lizzy glared at her. 'Whose side are you on?'

Dolly's cheeks grew crimson. 'Yours, of course, only ...'

Lizzy arched a brow. 'Yes?'

'Mebbe there was a reason for it. I'm not makin' excuses for him, really I'm not, I just don't think he'd have done summat to hurt you on purpose.'

'Well he has, and I can't think of any reason good enough to excuse his actions.'

Charlie watched as her two friends led Lizzy away. He wanted to run after them, to explain that the bet wasn't the reason why he had asked Lizzy out, but it was no use. Lizzy had made her feelings perfectly clear. If only he could get her to listen, she would understand that the bet hadn't even been his idea. The more he thought about it, the more put out he began to feel. Whilst he wasn't completely blameless, Lizzy was being equally unfair by not giving him a chance to put across his side of the story. He thought back to her manner when he first approached her. She hadn't dismissed Ivy's words as untrue; instead, she'd been determined to believe the worst of Charlie, even saying that she knew she couldn't trust him. He shook his head. Lizzy hadn't been interested in hearing his side of things because she had already decided he was guilty. He stared glumly at the path in front of him. She *wanted* to believe Ivy. She never even asked to hear his version of events. If Lizzy would rather believe the likes of Ivy Hackney over him, then more fool her. He shouldn't have to protest his innocence. She was the one who believed a leopard didn't change its spots. Well, she was right about that, only he wasn't the leopard.

What an idiot he'd been, always defending himself, trying to convince her he was a good feller, when she should have been giving him the benefit of the doubt. She never did, though, and now he could see that no matter what he said she would never trust him. He should be pleased it was over – no more trying to prove himself to someone who was never really listening. He set his mouth into a determined grimace. A relationship was no good if there was no trust. He nodded to himself. The trust had gone all right, and this time it was he who didn't trust her.

Chapter Thirteen

Josh stood at the top of the stairs to the girls' flat and rapped sharply on the door.

'Who is it?'

'It's me. Can someone open the door?'

'Blimey, who'd you think you are? The King? Open the door yerself,' said Dolly.

'I can't reach it,' came his muffled response.

Dolly tucked her embroidery under her seat and padded across the wooden floor to the door. 'What's stoppin' you? What ... oh, Josh!'

Josh shuffled the Christmas tree into the small flat. 'Ta-dah!'

Dolly stood gaping. 'What the hell are we goin' to do with that?'

Josh looked the tree up and down. 'Isn't it obvious?'

She shook her head, then nodded. 'I can see it's a Christmas tree, but ...' she looked worried, 'didn't you wonder why we didn't have a tree last year?'

'Yes, but I thought if we got a really good one and covered it in decorations she might realise she's being silly about the whole "Christmas is bad luck" thing.'

Clara walked out of the bedroom mid-conversation. 'Josh! It's not up to us to decide whether she's being silly or not. Lizzy's very superstitious when it comes to Christmas trees in the house. She's fine with everything else, just not trees.'

'Surely you don't encourage her?'

Clara's brow shot towards her hairline. 'I'm not going to take any chances when there's a war on, just for the sake of some silly tree—'

Dolly cut in. 'I know you didn't know, but Lizzy and Charlie split up yesterday. If she sees this it'll only reinforce her conviction that Christmas trees are unlucky.'

Josh's shoulders sank. 'Oh, lor'. I've really messed up, haven't I?'

Clara smiled kindly at him. 'You were only trying to cheer her up, which was a lovely thought, but we'd better get this thing out of here before Lizzy comes home.'

Dolly nodded, then groaned as she looked down at the floor. 'Look at all those bloomin' needles. Tell you what, I'll take the tree downstairs whilst you and lover boy clear up the mess.'

'Are you sure?' Josh began, but Dolly had already grasped the top of the tree and begun to drag it through the open doorway. 'Positive. Make sure you give the stairs a once-over, won't you?'

'But where will you put it?' Clara asked, only to find she was talking to the bottom of the tree trunk. She pulled out a brush and dustpan from underneath the sink and handed them to Josh. 'You can make a start on this lot.'

A short time later Dolly returned to the flat, looking rather pleased with herself.

Clara eyed her suspiciously. 'What have you done with the tree?'

'I gave it away.' Dolly looked at Josh. 'You don't mind, do you?'

He shook his head. ''S my own fault for buyin' it in the first place.'

They jumped as Lizzy entered the room, smiling brightly. 'Anyone fancy a cuppa?'

'I'll make it,' said Dolly hastily. Lizzy followed her to the far side of the room to give a hand.

Clara nudged Josh. 'Is it me, or does Dolly look guilty to you?' she murmured.

Josh glanced fleetingly at Dolly. 'What d'you reckon she's done?'

Clara shrugged. 'I wonder who she gave the tree to? Don't you think it's a bit convenient that she managed to bump into someone who wanted a tree within a minute of leaving the flat?'

He shook his head. 'It's Christmas, and there's norra lorra money about. P'raps she give it to some kid.'

Clara screwed up her lips in thought. 'What kid do you know could carry that tree?'

Josh shrugged. 'Does it matter? As long as Dolly got rid of it before Lizzy saw it, who cares who she gave it to?'

Clara nodded. 'S'pose so.'

Lizzy was sniffing the air. 'Can anyone else smell summat?'

Dolly nodded. 'I've not long had beans on toast.'

Lizzy shook her head. 'It's more like …' She glanced around the room. 'Has someone bought some plants?'

There was a chorus of no's. Lizzy looked around at her friends, who all seemed to be avoiding her gaze.

'They reckon it might snow tonight. Is anyone up for a bit of sledgin' tomorrer if it does?'

Grateful for the change of subject, Josh nodded enthusiastically. 'I dare say you 'aven't gorra sledge, but I'm sure we can find somethin' suitable.'

'I'm sure we can.' She tapped her forefinger against her chin, then added, 'I know, how about we use that soddin' great Christmas tree I found in the lavvy?'

'Dolly!' Josh and Clara chorused.

'How was I supposed to know she'd look in the loo?' said Dolly reproachfully.

'You said you'd given it away,' Clara said accusingly.

'I did, but the kid had to go an' ask his dad, so I said I'd leave it in the lavvy for him to pick up later.'

Lizzy, who was desperately trying not to break into a fit of giggles, eyed her friends with interest. 'What I don't understand is why we had a Christmas tree in the first place. I might add, it is not the sort of thing you expect to find when you're bustin' for the loo! It ain't easy goin' with all them branches pokin' you neither,' she added as an afterthought.

Josh looked embarrassed. 'I'm afraid it's my fault. I thought I could cajole you into liking Christmas again.'

'Oh, Josh, that's very sweet of you, but I'm sure the others explained, it's not that I don't like Christmas, it just brings back bad memories.'

He nodded. 'I know, and I shouldn't have done it without askin' first, although lookin' on the bright side, at least some kid's goin' to have a good Christmas, eh?'

Dolly nodded thoughtfully. 'D'you reckon we could've made it into a sledge? 'Cos if so I could allus tell him the deal's off.'

310

'You can't do that!' said Josh, genuinely shocked. 'Not after tellin' 'im he could have it. He's probably bustin' with excitement!'

Lizzy shook her head. 'Never mind the kid. You couldn't possibly make a sledge out of a Christmas tree.'

'Why don't we get an old car bonnet like the one Charlie had?' Dolly was silenced by Lizzy's steely glare.

'Because they're dangerous, which is why that buffoon was on one in the first place.'

Josh broke the awkward silence. 'D'you reckon they've taken the tree? Only I need to spend a penny.'

Dolly shrugged. 'Chuck it in the yard. I only stuck it in the lavvy so that Lizzy wouldn't see it.'

'Thanks, Dolly,' said Lizzy. She smiled at Clara and Josh. 'Same goes for you two.'

'What for?' said Josh, as he made his way to the door.

'For carin'. I know I'm not easy to live with round Christmas time, and it's not fair on any of you, especially you, Josh. You came home to spend Christmas with Clara and your family, not me and my silly superstitions.'

'Don't worry about me,' Josh called back. 'I love comin' here for Christmas.'

'And they're not silly,' said Dolly. 'You've had a right miserable time of it lately, and when all's said and done it's just a tree. Tell you what, why don't we go to the Grafton and find us some decent men?'

Clara clapped her hands excitedly. 'Spencer is going to the Grafton on New Year's Eve. Do you fancy goin' with him?'

Dolly grinned. 'New Year's kisses!'

Lizzy giggled. 'Spencer won't know what hit him.'

Dolly blushed. 'Don't be silly, Lizzy. I wasn't referring to Spencer; he's bound to have some beautiful Wren on his arm. I meant the other fellers.'

Lizzy shook her head. 'I don't mind goin' to the Grafton, but I'm not interested in findin' a man, decent or otherwise.' She wagged a finger at Dolly, who had opened her mouth to object. 'I'm not stoppin' you, Dolly, I'm just sayin' that when it comes to men I'd rather be on me own!'

'Oh for goodness' sake, will you cheer up?'

Charlie shrugged. 'What's there to be happy about?'

Jimmy rolled his eyes. 'It's Christmas Day for cryin' out loud, not that anyone'd guess that by the look on your mug!'

'Put it this way,' said Charlie, 'I'll cheer up when it's all over.'

Jimmy became serious. 'I know it's not the Christmas you'd imagined, but Lizzy'll come to 'er senses sooner or later.'

'Well, when she does she needn't expect to find me sittin' around waitin' for her, 'cos I shall have found someone better, someone who appreciates a feller like me.'

'Not wi' a face like that you won't,' said Jimmy. 'Tell you what, why don't we pop along to Princes Park, see if my brother and his kids are there with that sledge of theirs? That'd cheer you up.'

Charlie shook his head. 'I'm not in the mood. Besides, Lizzy might be there with her new pal Ivy Hackney.'

Jimmy walked on. 'Now you're actin' like a petulant child.'

Charlie opened his mouth to disagree, but found that anything he had to say would simply prove Jimmy's point. He stuffed his hands deep into his coat pockets and thought about what should have been.

He had planned to turn up just after breakfast on Christmas Day and surprise Lizzy with a romantic stroll around the city. He knew her favourite spot in Sefton Park was by the aviary, and it was here he had intended to give her a Christmas present – an antique ring box in the shape of a heart with forget-me-knots decorating the edges. Inside would be his grandmother's old onyx engagement ring. He would then get down on one knee and ask her to be his wife and when she said yes he would take her back to his lodgings and regale her with stew and dumplings. Once they had eaten their fill, they'd spend the remainder of their evening snuggled up in front of the fire dreaming of their future as husband and wife and enjoying a mug of cocoa.

His bottom lip jutted out. None of that would happen now, of course, and all because of that awful Hackney girl. Jimmy's voice cut across his thoughts.

'Pull that bloody lip in, lad, before you trip o'er it. Tell you what, how about you come wi' me an' my Minnie on New Year's Eve? That'll get you out of the rut you're in.'

Charlie scowled. 'I'm not in a rut. Besides, I can't see how bein' a goosegog at a New Year's Eve dance is goin' to make me feel better.'

Jimmy raised a brow. 'All those wimmin, all lookin' for a New Year's Eve kiss, and you can't see how that'd mek you feel better?'

Charlie shook his head. 'I'd call that linin' meself up for another fall.'

'Blimey, you 'ave got it bad, ain't you?'

Charlie frowned. 'What do you mean?'

'Love!'

Charlie spluttered a protest but Jimmy ignored him. 'It's plain for all to see that youse head over heels, no matter how angry she is with you.'

'Just because I want to stay single doesn't mean to say I'm in love with her.'

Jimmy grinned. 'But you are though, aren't you? That's why youse bellyachin' all the time, and I can't say I blame you, but sittin' round mopin' ain't goin' to mek you feel any better, so why don't you agree to come out with me and the missus? A good-lookin' chap like you won't be stuck on the sidelines for long.'

Charlie rubbed his chin. 'There is one thing I could do ...' He nodded thoughtfully. 'Leave it with me.'

Jimmy clapped him on the back. 'That's the spirit. Now for goodness' sake crack a smile.'

Lizzy admired her reflection in the full-length mirror that hung in the entrance to the Ladies in the Grafton. In a bid to cheer her up, Clara had given her one of her old dresses and Dolly, who was a whizz with a needle, had taken it in.

'Look at you with your hourglass figure!' Dolly had said as she measured her friend for the dress. 'It won't matter whether you want a new feller or not, you're goin' to be beatin' 'em off in the Grafton.'

Now, as Lizzy looked in the mirror, she could see what Dolly meant. The top half of the dress fitted her like a glove whilst the skirt created curves that didn't exist.

Dolly emerged from one of the cubicles and smiled at Lizzy's reflection. 'Done a good job with your hair, didn't I?'

Lizzy patted her hair, which Dolly had painstakingly pinned into place. 'It looks wonderful, Doll,' she said, and Clara, coming out of the cubicle next to Dolly's, agreed.

'You're the belle of the ball. There's not a single feller here that hasn't given you the once-over.' She adjusted the skirt of her dress. 'That Charlie must have rocks in his head to've treated you the way he did. I know you weren't too keen on coming out this evening, but I promise you, you'll enjoy yourself once you let your hair down.' She pointed to the door. 'So let's get out there and get half a mild down your neck. That should help move things along a bit.'

'Oh yes,' said Lizzy sarcastically, 'that's just what I need, to get drunk and mek a fool of meself.'

''S better'n sittin at 'ome mopin',' said Dolly brightly. 'Besides, you're not goin' to mek a fool of yerself just 'cos you've had half a mild.'

'I suppose as long as it's only the one. I want to keep me wits about me in case I bump into Charlie.'

Dolly and Clara exchanged glances.

'What?' said Lizzy.

'Dolly thinks she might have seen him by the bar ...'

'He was with some tart.'

315

Clara rolled her eyes. 'You don't know she's a tart.'

Dolly sniffed contemptuously. 'Bet she is.'

Lizzy shook her head. 'Sorry, girls, but if he's here I'm off home.'

Dolly stood to attention. 'Not on your nellie! We've worked our fingers to the bone to get you lookin' half decent, so the least you can do is get out there and show him what you're made of!'

A giggle escaped Lizzy's lips. 'I didn't realise I was that much hard work.'

Her hands on the back of Lizzy's shoulders, Dolly propelled her friend towards the door. 'You know full well what I meant.' As they left the powder room Lizzy scanned the crowd for any sign of Charlie, and breathed a sigh of relief when she failed to see him.

Spencer, who had bagged a table near the dance floor, stood up to gain their attention.

Clara waved back. 'There's Spencer, and by the looks of things he's already got the drinks.'

Lizzy sat down in the chair opposite Spencer's and rested her elbows on the table. 'Thanks for the drink, Spencer, and I'm sorry if I'm a bit of a party pooper, but I'm worried I'm goin' to bump into Charlie.'

'I've just seen him, although I must say he didn't look too pleased to see me,' said Spencer.

Lizzy gave a small groan of dismay. 'Where? Was he on his own?'

Spencer gestured towards the dance floor. 'He was doin' the rumba with some young ...'

'Tart,' said Dolly stiffly.

'... girl,' Spencer finished.

'Didn't take him long,' muttered Lizzy.

Dolly put her hands on her hips. 'No, it didn't, did it?' She turned to Spencer. 'Two can play at that game. Do us a favour, Spencer, and tek our Lizzy for a spin on the dance floor.'

Spencer frowned. 'I don't think Charlie likes me very much. If I dance with Lizzy it could be like pouring fuel on to the fire.'

Dolly sighed impatiently. 'We don't give two figs what Charlie Jackson thinks, do we, Lizzy? Nor should you, Spencer.' She tugged his arm in an encouraging fashion. 'Come on, where's the harm in takin' a lady for a dance?'

Spencer offered his arm to Lizzy. 'Come on, Lizzy. I can't see us getting any peace otherwise.'

Nodding, she glanced at Dolly. 'Just the one, then do you promise you'll leave us be?'

Dolly nodded. 'One should be enough to show Charlie you're as capable of gettin' a new feller as he is a new girl.'

As they began to glide around the dance floor, Lizzy felt herself begin to relax. She eyed Spencer shyly. 'Sorry about Dolly. She can be a bit ...'

'Bossy? I had noticed, and I must say I'm quite surprised. She's normally quiet, or she is around me at any rate.'

'Her heart's in the right place. If she'd just learn to think before she speaks ...'

He grinned. 'That's part of her attraction, though, don't you think? I like the way you never know what's going to come out of her mouth next.'

'I don't think she does half the time,' Lizzy conceded. She glanced up at him. 'You like her, then?'

He nodded. 'She seems really nice, but painfully shy.'

Lizzy coughed. 'She's not. Well, at least she's not normally. I think she's a bit overwhelmed by you.'

He paused mid-step. 'Really? I can't see why.'

'I can't think of any other reason why she'd be so quiet around you, when she's normally gorra gob like a fog horn.'

He chuckled. 'I've heard her a couple of times when I've knocked on the door to the flat and she hasn't been expecting me. She's got a good set of lungs on her!'

Lizzy smiled. 'Her and Clara have been good pals to me through all this Charlie business. I don't know what I'd have done without them to lean on.'

'Clara told me what happened, and I must say I think it was a rotten thing to do.' He stopped speaking, and jerked his head in the direction of someone behind Lizzy. 'Talkin' of rotten things, he's on the dance floor and he's with some young brunette.'

Lizzy groaned. 'D'you mind if we sit this one out? I really don't want to bump into them.' But the dance floor was too crowded to allow them to walk off it, and as they whirled around Charlie came into view once more. Lizzy stopped dancing for a moment and stood watching as he and the beautiful brunette made their way across the floor.

Spencer pulled her round in a circle. 'Don't stare. He'll know he's got to you if he sees you looking. The best way is to pretend they don't exist.'

But Lizzy wasn't listening. 'Look at them! Laughing and smiling at each other, you'd swear they'd been together for years, not just a few days.' Eyes rounding, she stared up at Spencer. 'You don't suppose he was seeing us both at the same time?'

Spencer glanced in their direction. 'They do seem to be getting on extremely well for a couple who've only just met,' he said reluctantly.

Tears forming in her eyes, she rested her forehead against Spencer's chest, and was comforted when she felt him place his hand on the back of her head.

'I told you not to look. He's probably doing it on purpose to make you jealous.'

Lizzy sniffed. 'As if he hasn't hurt me enough! Why rub salt in the wound?' She blinked the tears away. 'A few days ago we were a blissfully happy couple yet here he is with another woman in his arms, actin' like he hadn't a care in the world.' She watched as Charlie and his partner continued to whirl around the dance floor.

'What you've got to do is show him you don't care,' the unsuspecting Spencer advised, only to be deprived of the power of speech altogether as in one swift movement Lizzy lifted her head and kissed him on the lips.

As they parted she began to apologise at once, but was interrupted by Charlie, who was standing a few feet away, glaring at them. Instead of being jealous, his eyes were filled with anger and disgust. 'The whole time I chased after you, all you ever did was mek excuses as to how you couldn't agree to go out with anyone until you were sure of 'em. Well, you've not known him' – he jerked his head at Spencer – 'more'n five minutes, yet here you are, hands all over each other and kissin' in front of everyone, and you had the gall to call me a liar?'

Lizzy's cheeks flushed hotly as she stared at Charlie and his partner.

'Never mind me, Charlie Jackson. Accordin' to you, I were the only girl in the world ...' her eyes scanned the other woman from head to toe, 'yet 'ere you are dancin' with her as if you'd known each other years.'

Shaking her head, the brunette placed her hand through the crook of Charlie's elbow. 'Come away, Charlie. Don't lower yourself ...'

Lizzy's hands clenched by her sides and she stamped her foot in anger. By now the music had stopped playing and everyone on the dance floor was watching with interest. Lizzy glared at Charlie's partner. 'Lower himself? Lower himself? You wanna check he never asked you out for a bet, luv, 'cos that's the kind of guy your new boyfriend is!'

Charlie was agog. 'Boyfriend?' He pointed a shaking finger at the woman next to him. 'She's my sister, you stupid ...'

'Come on, mate, no need for that,' began Spencer, but Charlie was in full flow.

'I'm not your mate, 'cos no mate of mine would take advantage of a girl—'

Spencer held his hands up. 'Hold on a minute. I haven't taken advantage of anyone. This wasn't my idea, you know.'

Charlie shot Lizzy a withering look. 'You should try gerrin' your facts right before you open that big gob of yours, although I can't say I'm surprised. You never wanted to hear my side of things in the park, and you've jumped to the wrong conclusion yet again.'

Turning on his heel, he called over his shoulder, 'Good-bye and good riddance, Elizabeth Atherton.'

Spencer hooked an arm round Lizzy's shoulders and guided her back to their table. 'I'm so desperately s-sorry, Spencer,' stammered Lizzy as she gulped on her tears, 'I don't know what come over me. I never meant to cause a scene, I – I ...'

He sat her down at the table where Dolly stood, a hand to her mouth. 'Clara's gone to get our coats.'

Nodding, Spencer spoke quietly, 'I'll go and give her a hand.'

Dolly watched Spencer until he was out of earshot before speaking to Lizzy, her voice full of disappointment. 'What on earth made you do that? You know I like him!'

Ashamed of her actions, Lizzy lowered her head. 'I don't know what came over me. I'm so sorry, Dolly, I know I shouldn't have done it. I did it to hurt Charlie; I was so consumed with jealousy it never crossed my mind I might be hurting you too.' She looked at her friend, her eyes shining with tears. 'I hate myself for what I've done. I couldn't bear it if I thought you hated me as well.'

A tear trickled down Dolly's cheek. 'Darling Lizzy, you are one of my oldest, dearest friends. I know you'd never hurt me intentionally, and I could never hate you, especially over summat as silly as this.'

Clara appeared with two coats. 'I got mine and Lizzy's, but I thought Spencer and Dolly could stay and see the New Year in.'

Dolly shook her head. 'I'm not leavin' Lizzy on her own in this state.'

Lizzy buried her face in her hands. 'Please stay with Spencer, Doll. I couldn't bear it if I thought I'd ruined everyone's evening. Besides, I need some time to meself.'

Clara hugged their coats to her chest. 'You heard the lady. You two stay here, an' I'll take Lizzy home.' She wagged a reproving finger at Lizzy, who had opened her mouth to protest. 'I'm comin' whether you like it or not. It's not the same without Josh here.'

As they left the Grafton, Lizzy turned to Clara. 'I'm never goin' to be able to show me face in there or look your poor brother in the eye again, Clara.'

'Oh, I dunno. He got a kiss out of it,' Clara chuckled.

'It's not funny! How could I have been so stupid? I was so jealous, I wanted to show Charlie that I'd moved on.'

Clara grimaced. 'Mission accomplished. He definitely thinks you've moved on.'

'But I haven't, have I? It was all an act. He's right, I am a liar, 'cos I am jealous and I haven't moved on. To mek matters worse, what he said was true: I never give 'im a chance to explain himself in Sefton Park, and I jumped to conclusions again tonight. I've blown it, Clara. He'll never want to speak to me again after this, and what's more I don't blame him.'

Charlie shook his head as his sister tried to make him see sense. 'What's done is done. Don't let her win by leavin', Charlie.'

'If you think I'm goin' to sit by and watch them two fawnin' over each other all night you've gorranother thing comin'. I'm sorry, Phoebe, but this feller's had about as much as he can take for one evenin', and I have no desire to see the woman I wanted to be my wife kissin' another feller at the stroke of midnight.'

Phoebe heaved a sigh. 'I still don't think you should be the one to leave. If anyone was in the wrong it was that dreadful Lizzy.' She rolled her eyes. 'Don't look now, but here comes one of her pals. Shall I tell her to sling her hook?'

Charlie looked up to see Dolly approaching him shyly. He glanced at his sister. 'Can you give us a minute?'

'If you insist, but don't let her mek you out to be the one at fault.'

Blushing, Dolly nodded a greeting to Phoebe, who nodded stiffly back before leaving the two alone.

'I've come over to apologise,' Dolly began without preamble. 'You see, what happened this evening was my fault and not Lizzy's.'

Charlie looked at her in surprise. 'Really? Only I could've sworn it was Lizzy who was kissin' that Spencer feller.'

Dolly grimaced. 'I had to practically force the two of them on to the dance floor. Lizzy didn't want to dance at all. She only did it because I told her you and your sister were an item.'

Charlie stared at her in disbelief. 'Why on earth would you do that?'

Dolly was twisting her fingers round each other. 'Because I put two and two together and come up with five?'

He nodded. 'You did, didn't you!' He sat down at a nearby table and gestured for Dolly to follow suit. 'I shouldn't be angry with you. None of this would've happened in the first place if Lizzy had listened to my side of things.'

'She said you'd admitted everything, from calling her an ice princess to betting she'd go out with you.'

Charlie shook his head. 'I didn't call her an ice princess; that was Jimmy. Ivy must've 'eard him and made out it was me that said it, but she was lying.'

Dolly frowned. 'So she lied about the bet too?'

'No, I admit I made a bet, but that's not why I asked her out. I told the fellers I intended to ask her out in my own good time, and they bet me she'd not want to go out with me because she was more suited to a feller in the services.' He stared sulkily in Spencer's direction. 'Like your pal over there.'

'Oh, dear. I'm afraid Lizzy thinks you only asked her out to prove you could get her to say yes.'

'I'd never do that. If she can't see it then it's just as well we're not together.'

Dolly shook her head. 'Pride comes before a fall, Charlie Jackson.'

He stared at her incredulously. 'Don't tell me that. Tell that pal of yours!'

Dolly looked him directly in the eye. 'The same pal who hasn't got a clue where her mother is? The same pal who goes to bed disappointed every night because she was hoping that that day might've been the one she found out what happened to her mam? The same pal who lost her father, the only man she ever loved, without a chance to say a proper goodbye, and is terrified that history will repeat itself?' She put her hands over his. 'Have you ever seen those people who keep a

324

row of plates spinnin' on top of poles?' He nodded. 'Well, Lizzy's like one of them. She's so busy keepin' them spinnin' she don't allus see what's right in front of her, even if it's obvious to everyone else.'

Someone cleared his throat behind her. 'Are you done, Dolly? Only I feel a bit of a lemon sat there on my own.' Spencer glanced at Charlie. 'If it's any consolation, she was devastated when she saw you and your sister. Love can make people do funny things sometimes.'

Ignoring him, Charlie turned his attention back to Dolly. 'Happy New Year, Doll.'

Her smile faded. 'Oh, righto. Happy New Year to you too. I don't suppose there's any chance of you goin' to see her, is there?'

A muscle in his jaw twitched. 'I doubt it.'

She nodded. 'I know she won't turn you away, if that's what worries you.'

'I dare say, but a lot's happened in the past week and I need to be sure of my feelings.'

As Charlie left the Grafton he spied a group of young boys scrambling over the ruins of a bombed-out building further down the street.

He hailed a warning. 'Oi, you lot! Gerrout of it! You'll not find owt in there save broken limbs!'

'Sod off, copper!' came the united response.

Charlie shook his head. 'Please yourselves. I ain't on duty, so if you wanna break your legs you go ahead.' With so many fathers off to war, gangs of youths roaming the streets were getting to be a common sight, and with no one to keep them in line they had started to become a problem. Putting them from his mind, he

325

mulled over the conversation he had had with Dolly. He knew that Lizzy was constantly occupied with thoughts of her mother's possible whereabouts, but perhaps he hadn't realised how much it consumed her life. He turned his mind back to the moment when Lizzy had confronted him outside Sefton Park. He grimaced. If only he'd had a bit of a heads up he'd have answered differently: not lied, exactly, but got his point across in a manner that would ensure Lizzy knew the truth. He stopped short. He couldn't put all the blame at her door, and even though seeing her in the arms of another man would stay in his memory for some time to come, what he had to do now was figure out what was best for them both. Should he leave things to settle down for a bit, or would that be seen as some kind of punishment? He knew the truth as far as Lizzy was concerned; perhaps it was about time she heard his side? His forehead creased. In an hour or so it would be the start of a new year and with a new year came hope, a fresh beginning. If there was ever a time to make amends and start anew, then this was it. Turning on his heel, he headed in the direction of Pickwick Street.

Clara handed Lizzy a mug of tea. 'There you go. If I'd had a nip of whisky I'd have popped a bit in for good measure.'

Lizzy winced. 'Thank goodness you 'aven't. I've only ever 'ad it once and I thought it tasted like medicine. I can't imagine puttin' it in tea meks it taste any better.'

'When we were little and had a bad cold my dad always used to give us a small nip of whisky mixed in with honey. I don't know whether it had any medicinal value, but it always ensured a good night's sleep.'

'In that case mek mine a double, 'cos I don't think I'll ever sleep again after tonight's farce.'

'Sausage roll?'

Lizzy shook her head. 'Thanks all the same, but I'm not hungry.'

Shrugging, Clara took a large bite, chewed for a moment, then swallowed. 'This has always been my downfall. Whenever I get upset I always turn to food to make me feel better; that's why I got so fat after Mum passed.'

Tears shimmered in Lizzy's eyes. 'I wish eatin' made me feel better, but it don't. Nothin' does.'

Putting the sausage roll back on the plate, Clara sat down beside Lizzy and enveloped her in a warm hug. 'Darling Lizzy, you haven't half been through the mill. I wish I could do or say summat to make you feel better.'

Lizzy sniffed. 'Me too. I had such hopes for the future, and then I met up with that bloomin' Ivy and everythin' went pear-shaped.' She fielded two tears before they landed on her cheeks. 'If I could have that time again I'd've walked away and not repeated her poisonous words to another living soul.'

Clara pressed her lips together. 'But you can't, so you're just going to have to make the best of a bad situation.' She was interrupted by someone knocking on the door at the bottom of the stairwell. 'Who on earth can that be? It can't be Dolly – she's got a key, and besides, I can't see her leaving the Grafton before midnight.'

Lizzy wiped her eyes on the back of her hands. 'Don't answer it. It might be that awful Ivy.'

Clara's brow flew upward. 'Well, if it is, she's going to get a piece of my mind ... a very large piece!'

Before Lizzy could stop her, Clara had trotted down the stairs towards the bottom door. Lizzy held her breath as she heard the door open. There was a moment's silence before she heard Clara say, 'You'd better come up.' Lizzy craned her neck to see who it was. As Clara came in she smiled encouragingly at Lizzy. 'You've got a visitor,' was all she could manage before Charlie's face appeared around the door.

He gestured towards Lizzy. 'I think we need to talk.'

Standing up, Lizzy gave Clara a watery smile. 'Thanks for tonight. Do you mind if me and Charlie leave you for a bit? I promise I'll be back in half an hour or so.'

'Of course not. Take all the time you need; I've got my sausage roll.' Clara frowned as the last words left her lips. 'That is to say, I'll be all right.'

Taking Lizzy's coat from behind the kitchen door, Charlie held it out towards her. 'It's not got any warmer out there, so you'll need to wrap up.'

'Thanks.' She buttoned up her coat and slid her feet into the long woollen socks that she wore in her wellington boots. As she stood up, Clara could see the tears shining in her friend's eyes, so she fished out a handkerchief from the pocket of her skirt and handed it to her. 'Thanks, Clara. I'll see you in a bit.' Shoving her feet into her wellies, Lizzy gestured towards the door. 'I'm ready when you are ...'

As they emerged on to the snow-laden pavement, Charlie held out his arm. 'These pavements can be pretty treacherous. I nearly went a cropper on my way here.'

Lizzy slid her hand through the crook of his elbow. 'I'm so, so dreadfully sorry. I've been such an idiot. I wouldn't have blamed you if you'd never wanted to see me again.'

Charlie set his mouth in a grim line. 'If it hadn't been for Dolly, that might have been the case.'

'Dolly?'

He nodded. 'I was pretty sore after everything that happened and I told Phoebe I was going to go home early. I don't know whether Dolly guessed my intention or not, but either way she came over to explain how she'd been the one who lit the fire in your belly, and how you hadn't wanted to dance with that feller from the Navy until she pushed you into it.'

'She did, but she didn't mek me do anythin' else. That was all my stupid fault.'

Charlie stiffened. 'Best not to split hairs. Point is, if it weren't for Dolly I wouldn't be here, so we should both be grateful she took the time to come over and explain everything.'

Lizzy looked up. 'Everything?'

'She told me how you thought I'd called you an ice princess. I didn't, that was someone else, and the whole bet thing was because the fellers reckoned I didn't stand a chance with a girl like you 'cos you could do so much better than a scuffer.'

Lizzy's eyes rounded. 'What an awful thing to say to someone.' She paused. 'I should've given you a chance to speak instead of jumpin' to conclusions.'

'Yes, you should've, but there's no sense in cryin' over spilt milk. Although there is one thing that's been troublin' me.'

'What's that?'

'Why did you agree to go out wi' me the night we got together in the Grafton?'

Lizzy brightened. 'I'd been mulling things over in my head for quite some time, and Dolly and Clara warned me that if I didn't make my mind up pretty soon I'd run the risk of losing you to someone else. I took some convincin', but—'

His forehead puckered. 'If I were the right feller for you, you'd know it in your heart. It shouldn't take someone else to convince you.'

'But I do know that you're the right feller for me. I allus have. I was just so worried it would all go wrong ...' Her voice trailed off.

'That's one thing you did get right, 'cos it has gone wrong.'

She turned eyes brimming with tears towards him. 'I can't believe you think there's no hope for us. You'd not be here if you did.'

'I came to sort things out, to tell you the truth behind Ivy's lies. As for us ...' he turned his head, 'if there is an us, then it's summat that's goin' to tek time. You may know that I'm the right one for you, but it's goin' to be a while before I can get over seein' you in another man's arms.'

The tears trickled their way down Lizzy's cheeks. 'Your mates got it wrong. It's you who deserve better than me, not the other way round.'

Charlie turned his gaze towards her and drew a handkerchief from his pocket to dry her wet cheeks. 'That's for me to decide.'

'Will I see you again?'

Charlie wrestled with the thoughts in his head, all of which told him to turn her down and find someone else, someone with less baggage, someone less complicated, but one look into those large brown eyes and his heart took charge. 'Of course you'll see me again. I still love you, Liz, it's just goin' to take a bit of time before we can get things back to the way they were.'

Lizzy felt as though her heart could burst with joy. 'Oh, Charlie, you've made me the happiest girl in the world.'

He withdrew his arm from hers and placed it round her shoulders. 'Let's get you back to the flat. Poor old Clara doesn't deserve to be on her own – even with her sausage roll – on New Year's Eve.'

Lizzy slid her arm round his waist. 'I love you, Charlie Jackson.'

'I love you too, Pipsqueak.'

Chapter Fourteen

December, 1943

Mary sank to the floor. Her shift had run over by six hours and she had been advised to 'grab ten minutes somewhere'.

It had been late April the previous year when James and another officer had waylaid her on her way into the building on Rumford Street.

'Here she is!' said James, turning to the other man. 'I've known Mary for a good few years and when it comes to keeping a secret I know we can trust her.'

Mary raised her brow. 'Sounds intriguing.'

James's blue eyes sparkled. 'What would you think if I asked you to sign the Official Secrets Act?'

'That my life was about to get a lot more interesting?'

James laughed. 'I couldn't have put it better myself. Come with us.'

Mary had been taken into a room she had never been in before. It was bare apart from a table and chair, and James pointed to a sheaf of paper on the table. 'Read that, and if you're happy, sign it.'

After signing the Act Mary was led out of the building and round to an entrance she had also never used before. James handed her a pass. 'You'll need this the whole time you're in here: when you go to the lavvy, or to bed, or ...' he waved a vague hand, 'anywhere at all.'

She knitted her brows. 'Bed?'

He nodded. 'There are bunk rooms for the women on shift. Don't worry, I'll show you round.'

Mary stepped back off the pavement and looked at the building's façade. 'I've worked here a long time but I've never seen any bunk rooms before.'

James grinned. 'You've worked above ground. Where I'm taking you is deep below the building you used to work in.'

As they entered the building a sailor briefly examined their passes before allowing them through.

'What is this place?' said Mary. She was looking at the thick walls, which were adorned with various notices advising the reader to adhere to one rule or another.

James put a finger to his lips. 'All will be revealed in good time.' He opened a door and the silence of the corridor was shattered by the sound of lots of people all talking at once, mixed with the clatter of what sounded like an army of typewriters. A stream of telephones rang out and above all that came the raised voices of people giving commands. James placed a hand on Mary's shoulder. 'This is Western Approaches.'

Mary stared in wonder at the rooms below her. 'I can't believe all this was goin' on right beneath my feet and I never even knew about it! What are they all doing?'

James pointed towards a large map that covered one of the walls. 'That map shows the position of every ship and U-boat belonging to both Allied and enemy forces. From here we can see who's where, what's going on, and what needs to be done.'

Mary watched as a Wren climbed a long ladder and fixed something on to the large map. James followed Mary's gaze. 'When the orders come in, the Wrens mark them on the map, and that's why you're here.'

Mary's face fell. 'I – I can't do that,' she stammered. 'I'm terrified of heights. Oh, James, you should've said summat before I signed that paper.'

'Don't worry, I know you're scared of heights – that's how you ended up falling from your bedroom window.' He rubbed a hand over the back of his neck. 'One of the girls fell from the top of the ladder a short while ago, and—'

Mary's eyes rounded. 'Is she all right?'

He grimaced. 'No. We got another girl to step in for her immediately, of course, but that still meant we were one girl down, and that's where you come in.'

Mary cast an eye over the Wrens in the room below. 'They're all a good deal younger than me.'

He laughed. 'I wouldn't recommend you for the job if I didn't think you were capable, would I?'

She shook her head. 'I suppose not. What will I be doing?'

'Taking messages round the bunker.'

'I don't see why I had to sign the Official Secrets Act just to be a messenger girl.'

'This whole place is top secret. No one knows about it, not even you, remember? Even though you worked right above it!'

Since that day Mary's whole life had changed. She no longer lived in Ackerleigh House, but stayed in the bunker during her shifts. The rest of the time she stayed with Jean. Her search for Lizzy had more or less come to a halt as she rarely left the bunker, and when she did the only people she had contact with were other Wrens or the occasional bus driver.

Now, Mary jumped as someone half tripped over her feet. She mumbled an apology and was falling back to sleep when a pair of arms slid behind her shoulders and under her legs.

'C'mon, sleeping beauty, your shift's come to an end. Let's get you to bed.'

'But what about …' Mary insisted before being hushed into silence.

'You're like a dog with a bone.' James chuckled. 'But you've been working twenty-three hours straight and you don't need to worry about the operation. Everything's going according to plan, so you can rest easy.'

Nodding happily, Mary slid into sleep.

'C'mon you lot, turf out your pockets.'

The four boys began emptying the contents of their pockets on to the counter. When they had finished, Charlie glanced at the miscellaneous items. 'Let me see, matches, oily rags and a couple of lighters.' He shook his head. 'One of them goes off and you'll be a human torch! What on earth are you doin' with this lot in your pockets?'

'We gorrem for me mam so she can light the stove.'

Folding his arms across his chest, Charlie eyed them shrewdly. 'So you didn't get them so's you could see your way round deserted buildings in the dark?'

One of the larger boys stuffed his hands into his pockets. 'Why'd we wanna do summat like that?'

Charlie rolled his eyes. ''Cos you're hopin' that them condemned buildings are full of hidden treasures, like jewellery and money and all the other stuff that got abandoned when the folk who lived there weren't allowed back in.'

The young boy tried to keep a straight face. 'We dunno what you're on about, mister.'

Picking up one of the matchboxes, Charlie gave it an experimental shake. 'You do know that if any of this lot went off in your pockets you'd be history?'

The smallest boy shrugged. ''Ow's that goin' to 'appen? Matches don't light 'emselves.'

'It's called an accident, and if your father ever finds out—' Charlie began, only to be rudely interrupted by the boy's older brother.

''Ow's 'e goin' to find out when 'e's in Italy, or wherever the 'ell he is?'

''Cos I shall tell him when he comes home, Harry Pumford, and if I know your father it'll be the belt for the lot of you!'

'What a lovely welcome 'ome that'll be!' said the small boy as he wiped his nose on the back of his sleeve.

Charlie sighed heavily. 'Get in the back.'

'What for? You can't arrest us for 'avin' lighters an' matches, nor rags!' protested Harry.

Charlie ran his fingers through his hair. It had been a long day, and chasing the four boys across broken-down buildings had not been his idea of fun. 'I ain't arrestin' you. It's so's we can keep you safe from yourselves until your mams can come an' get you.'

'Good luck findin' 'er,' Harry muttered.

'Yeah, she'll be at one of 'er boyfriend's 'ouses gerrin' us some money so's we can ... ow, what you kick me for?' The small boy addressed his last comment to his older brother, who was shaking his head, a finger to his lips.

Extending one arm, Charlie pointed to a door beside the counter. 'In there!'

'Can we 'ave us things back?' enquired Billy, Harry's younger brother.

Charlie shook his head. 'No, you ruddy well can't!'

'Can't I even 'ave me picture back?'

'What picture?' said Charlie, beginning to sort through the items on the counter.

'It's a picture of me mam.'

'Where did you get this?' Charlie said, holding up the picture for the boy to see.

He held out a hand. 'Can't remember.'

Charlie shook his head. 'You'd better try. Before you start, I know this ain't your mam. Now where did you get it?'

Harry pushed his brother's arm down. 'Leave him alone. He didn't nick it or owt like that, if that's what you're thinkin'.'

Crouching down, Charlie looked the smaller boy in the eye. 'You ain't in trouble. All I want to know is where you found it.'

The boy glanced at his brother who nodded his permission. 'I gorrit off of one of the buses. Someone'd stuck it on the back winder, by where the conductor stands. No one said I couldn't tek it.'

'So you didn't get it off one of the Hackneys?'

The boy shook his head. 'I already told you, it was stuck on the winder with summat sticky.' He tried to snatch the picture back, but Charlie was too quick for him. Billy glared up at him. 'Do you know where she is? If so, it's my money, 'cos you wouldn't 'ave seen it if it weren't for me, so don't you go tekkin' the money for yerself!'

Charlie ruffled the top of the young boy's hair. 'Don't worry. I know where you live, so if we find the girl I'll make sure you get your reward.'

Harry shook his head. 'An honest scuffer? That'll be a first. You can kiss that reward money goodbye, our Billy.'

Billy scowled and kicked Charlie sharply in the leg. 'Ruddy thief!'

Jimmy, who had been standing behind the counter the whole time, chuckled. 'Teks one to know one, but if it's any consolation I can vouch for Charlie. He won't see you out of pocket.'

Billy frowned at Jimmy. 'What the 'ell's a consolation?' He peered accusingly at his brother. 'Did 'e just say summat rude?'

Rubbing his shin with one hand, Charlie pointed in the direction of the cell door again. 'Get in there and keep quiet.' As the boys trooped into the cell, he clicked the key in the lock behind them.

'You fancy a cuppa?' said Jimmy.

Charlie nodded. 'That bloody Billy's got a sharp kick on 'im. He should try out for Everton.'

Jimmy gestured towards the picture that Charlie held in his hands. 'So what's all the fuss about?'

Charlie turned the picture round for Jimmy to see. Jimmy peered at the image, which was smeared with oil. 'I haven't got me glasses on. What is it?'

'It's a picture of Lizzy, the same one that Ivy Hackney had, only this one's got an address on the bottom.'

Jimmy breathed in a whistle. 'Blimey! So it wasn't a hoax then?'

Charlie shook his head. 'Doesn't look like it. Question is, do I tell Liz, or do I try and find her mam first?'

Jimmy scratched the top of his head. 'You don't want to build her hopes up. That whole thing with Ivy happened a couple of years ago. For all you know, her mam might not be in Liverpool any more.'

Charlie nodded. 'That's what I thought. I'll check things out first, go to the address and see if this Mary ever lived there.'

Jimmy nodded. 'Good idea.' He paused. 'Didn't you say that Spencer feller was in the Navy? Couldn't you ask him?'

Charlie shook his head. 'He works down in Plymouth, so he wouldn't know any of the Wrens up here.'

Since the disastrous New Year's Eve of 1941, he and Lizzy had managed to restore their relationship. It had been hard at first, as Charlie found it difficult to kiss Lizzy without seeing her and Spencer in his mind's eye, but after months of rebuilding their friendship they had each grown to trust and respect the other. Charlie was not about to have all that torn to shreds by giving Lizzy what could turn out to be false information, especially when the picture would bring back such painful memories. His forehead furrowed as he tried to remember where Ackerleigh House was … his eyes shot open. 'Jimmy? Isn't Ackerleigh House on Ullet Road by Sefton Park?'

Jimmy nodded. 'It is. Why d'you ask?'

'Because Clara used to live on Ullet Road … which would mean that Mary's been livin' a stone's throw from where one of Lizzy's best mates grew up.'

'Funny old world, ain't it!'

Charlie shook his head. What were the chances? He breathed out. If it was right … He set his mouth into a firm line. He would go to Ackerleigh House first thing in the morning and ask if anyone knew of a Mary Tanner.

As they entered the Gaiety cinema on the Scotland Road, Lizzy, Clara and Dolly followed the usher's torch. Mumbling apologies for stepping on the toes of those already seated, Lizzy slumped into a chair next to Dolly.

'Can we please not cut it so fine next time?' she hissed from the corner of her mouth. 'I hate bein' rushed. I keep thinkin' I've left the stove on the kettle.'

Dolly giggled. 'Don't you mean the kettle on the stove?'

'See what I mean? I don't know whether I'm comin' or goin', and to top it all I'm on firewatch duty after this, so I shan't even have time for a cuppa – don't blame me if I fall asleep.'

Dolly stared at Lizzy in disbelief. 'But it's Errol Flynn!'

Lizzy shrugged. 'I don't give a monkey's who it is, I'm whacked. Besides, I've told you a hundred times already, Charlie's the only feller for me.'

Clara smiled. 'Have I told you about Josh? He's coming home, 'cos that ingrown toenail of his needs an operation.'

Dolly nudged Lizzy with a giggle. 'How romantic!'

'Can't he have it done where he's based?' said Lizzy.

'Nope, they reckon he'll be more use up here than down there, and he won't have to have as much time off.'

A man behind them leaned forward until his head was between Dolly and Clara. 'Can't you lot give it a rest? I come here for some peace and quiet, not to listen to you three natterin' your way through the film.'

Clara blushed in the darkness. 'Sorry!'

'They reckon the war can't go on for much longer,' hissed Dolly from the corner of her mouth.

The usher shone the light directly into Dolly's face. 'Madam! If you don't stop chattin' I shall have to ask you to leave the cinema!'

Dolly grinned. 'No one's ever called me madam before.' An odd noise penetrated the dark of the cinema, and she looked around to see if she could find the source.

The man behind them pointed an accusing finger at Lizzy. 'Your pal's ruddy well snorin'. Can't you give her a nudge?'

Dolly shook her head. 'I ain't wakin' her up. That poor girl's been workin' days and firewatchin' at night. It's all right for folk like you who gerra good night's sleep.'

'I paid good money to see this film,' the man continued, only to be hushed by two women who flanked him either side.

'Let the poor girl sleep. If you don't like it you can allus move!'

The man got to his feet and edged his way along the row towards the aisle, mumbling his discontent as he went.

Sitting back in her seat, Dolly wore a satisfied smile. 'Some folk've no manners! Ooo look, it's starting!'

Charlie was standing outside the door of Ackerleigh House when a voice from behind made him jump.

'Who's done what?'

Charlie chuckled. 'No one's in any trouble. I'm lookin' for a friend of mine.' He handed the picture of Lizzy to the Wren, who glanced at it and handed it back.

'Sorry luv, I don't recognise her.'

Charlie shook his head. 'The woman in the picture's my pal. It's the woman's details below, Mary Tanner, she's the one I'm lookin' for.'

She pulled a face. 'Don't know her either. Is she new?'

'No, and I'm afraid this poster is a couple of years old.' He paused. 'Do you think one of the other Wrens might know where she is now?'

She pulled a face. 'It's possible; I've only been here since July. I could ask the girls and see if anyone remembers her, if you don't mind waiting, that is?'

He nodded. 'D'you mind if I keep the picture? It's the only one I've got.'

She eyed him curiously. 'Has this girl's mam done summat wrong?'

'No, they got separated before the war. I know where her daughter is – she's my girlfriend – but I only came across this the other day, so I thought I'd better check it out first before she got her hopes up.'

She raised her brow. 'Lucky girl!' The Wren took a step towards the house before pausing. 'You said you only came across this the other day, so how do you know it's two years old?'

Charlie blushed. 'We did see one then, but the person who had it had cut the information we needed off the bottom, then refused to let us know where Mary was, so I'm afraid we thought it was a hoax.'

She nodded. 'Righto. Wait there – I shan't be a mo.'

Ten minutes passed and Charlie was beginning to wonder if the Wren had forgotten him when she emerged through the front door.

'Sorry about that. I've asked around and nobody remembers her, but a couple of the girls think they may've seen a Mary Tanner down at the naval offices on Rumford Street. Do you know where it is?' She giggled. 'Look who I'm askin' – 'course a scuffer knows where it is. Anyway, they suggested you ask there.'

Charlie handed her a slip of paper with his details. 'Just in case anyone should remember anything, this is where you can find me.'

Smiling, she pushed the paper into her pocket. 'I'll make sure I put it on one of the notice boards where everyone can see.'

Thanking her, Charlie slowly walked away. He had a nagging suspicion that although the Wren meant well, his details would probably end up under a table covered in dust. It was a shame that Mary no longer lived in Ackerleigh House, but the news that some of the Wrens thought they may have seen her in the buildings in Rumford Street was encouraging. Just as well you never told Liz, though, he thought to himself. She would've been so disappointed to find her mother wasn't here. He tried to imagine the look on Lizzy's face if he turned up with Mary in tow. He grinned.

'Come on, Lizzy! We're goin' to be late for Josh's train at this rate. Can't you get a move on?' Clara stared anxiously up the stairs that led to the flat.

'On me way,' called Lizzy, her words muffled by the toast she had stuffed into her mouth whilst pushing her arms into the sleeves of her mackintosh. 'It's not like he's goin' anywhere without us.'

'That's hardly the point! I said I'd be there to meet him and I don't want to let him down. He was ever so good to me when I broke my leg.'

Lizzy ran down the stairs and threaded her arm through Clara's. 'Don't you worry. The trains are allus runnin' late; we'll be there in plenty of time.'

Clara gazed doe-eyed at Lizzy. 'I've missed him so much. I'd love it if he got to stay in Liverpool for the rest of the war. You're ever so lucky havin' Charlie just down the road, you know.'

Lizzy nodded. 'I must admit I sometimes feel guilty that I've got Charlie so close when Josh is hundreds of miles away.'

344

A hand landed heavily on Lizzy's shoulder, making her jump. 'Wotcher! I thought I'd tag along 'cos I got out the hairdresser's a bit early. What d'you think?'

Lizzy gaped at her. 'I think you shouldn't go round jumpin' on folk from behind like that. Blow me, Dolly Clifton, I'm surprised I ain't dead of a heart attack!'

Dolly giggled. 'Sorry! Now, what do you think?'

Lizzy smiled admiringly. 'It really suits you.'

Clara nodded. 'It really does. Did you say you were comin' with us to pick Josh up from the station?'

'Course I am. It'll give me a chance to show off me new hairdo. Besides, I'd like to ask your opinions on summat. Do you remember the other day when Spencer come round for his tea, and he mentioned as how I allus mek him laugh?'

Clara nodded. 'What about it?'

'D'you think that's all he sees me as? A good friend who can make him laugh? Only I hoped he might see me as more than a good friend, and I was beginning to think he did when he asked me to the cinema, but then he made that comment, and now I'm not sure.'

'Is that what the new hairdo's in aid of? 'Cos it's not all about looks, you know,' said Lizzy.

Dolly nodded. 'I know, only every woman wants to be physically attractive, don't they? I know I do.'

'I know what you mean,' said Clara reflectively, 'but I think the physical attraction is only the first part of a relationship. Without the rest you've got nothing. Is that what's worrying you? Do you think he doesn't find you attractive?'

'Dunno.' Dolly stared into space and turned the thought over in her head. 'If you put it like that, it never occurred to me for a moment he wouldn't find me attractive. Not that I'm boastin', you understand.'

Clara giggled. 'Then what's the problem?'

'I want to know why he asked me to the cinema. I don't want to get my hopes up or mek a fool of meself by gerrin' dolled up like a dog's dinner, if he just wants to be pals.'

Lizzy shook her head. 'Whether it's a date or not, just be yourself. Spencer wants to go to the cinema with the Dolly Clifton he knows, not some glammed up version. Just go as yourself and see what happens.'

Clara cleared her throat. 'I need to ask you both summat before we get to the station. You know I went to see Dad last night?'

Dolly nodded. 'What of it?'

'Well, we were talkin' about Josh and how he hasn't got anywhere to stay since his parents moved to Abergele. We don't think it's proper he stays at the flat with three women, so Dad suggested he should stay at Bellevue until he's better.'

'That was nice of him,' said Lizzy.

'I know. Only I want to be the one who looks after Josh, so I said I'd move back home, until he's well enough to go back to the army.'

'Oh, so you won't be spending Christmas with us at the flat?' said Dolly dolefully.

'No. That's why I asked Dad if it would be all right if you joined us, only not just for Christmas Day, but as soon as you can pack. I'm going to drop Josh off at Bellevue, introduce him to Dad, then head back to the flat to get my things. I was rather hoping you might do the same.'

Dolly looked startled. 'Move out today?'

'Please say you will. It wouldn't be the same without you.'

Dolly glanced at Lizzy. 'I don't see why not. How about you?'

Furrowing her brow, Lizzy gazed skyward as she pretended to consider the idea. 'Hmm, let me see, spend Christmas in the flat or a bloomin' great mansion?'

Dolly chuckled at her expression. 'I think that's a yes from Lizzy.'

Lizzy grinned. 'Too right it is. It'll be a real treat. I bet Bellevue looks beautiful in all its Christmas decorations.'

Clara nodded wistfully. 'We have a huge Christmas tree by the bottom of the stairs in the vestibule. We cover it in tinsel and baubles, and Dad insists on putting the fairy I made when I was a toddler on top, though it looks more like a scarecrow than a fairy—' She stopped short. 'Oh, heck! I'd forgotten about the tree.'

Lizzy half-smiled. 'I haven't wanted a Christmas tree since me dad died because I thought they brought bad luck, although it was really the star I made to go on top of the tree that I believed to be bad luck rather than the tree itself. But now it makes no odds either way, as I've hardly had good luck wi'out it, have I?'

Dolly coughed. 'I should say not!'

'Exactly. I've been silly all these years – trees can't determine your future any more than a crystal ball.'

Clara beamed. 'So that's that settled: we'll all be staying at Bellevue tonight.'

'It's going to be like a holiday, isn't it?' said Dolly.

'It'll be wonderful having everyone home for Christmas, just like the old days,' Clara breathed.

'Everyone ... does that include Spencer?' Dolly asked.

'Yup! He's only got a forty days, mind you, but it's better than nothing.'

Lizzy's hand flew to her mouth. 'Cripes! I've just remembered. I asked Charlie if he'd like to come to ours for Christmas.'

Clara shrugged. 'More the merrier as far as we're concerned, and he and Spencer made up their differences a long time ago, so there shouldn't be any awkwardness.' She squealed with excitement as the smoke from the train signalled its arrival. 'He's here! C'mon, girls, help me find my Josh.'

They were walking along the line of carriages, looking into each window as they passed, when a voice hailed them from behind.

'Come and give us a hand. It's bloomin' murder tryin' to manage me kitbag as well as crutches!' He struggled down from the carriage they had just passed, dragging his kitbag behind him until it flumped to the ground, narrowly missing his bandaged foot.

Flinging her arms round his neck, Clara planted a kiss on his cheek. 'It's so good to see you! How's the toe?'

Josh looked down at the offending bandaged foot. 'Bloody awful, hurts like billy-o, and I seem to catch it on everything!' He glanced at his kitbag. 'And tryin' to drag that thing round with these crutches isn't exactly a walk in the park.'

Clara pouted sympathetically. 'Don't you worry about your bag. Lizzy and Dolly'll carry that for you.'

Lizzy nodded. 'Course we will. How on earth you managed to get it this far is beyond me.'

Josh shrugged. ''S like a family, bein' in the services. I've had fellers from the RAF, girls from the ATS, you name it they've done it, and I'm jolly grateful 'cos I'd be scuppered if left to me own devices.'

'Well you've got me now, and I intend to get you right as rain in no time. Have you heard any more about stayin' in Liverpool?'

He grinned. 'They've sorted out a desk job for me in Seaforth, so not too far away.'

Clara clapped her hand together. 'That's wonderful news! And whilst we're talking about good news, you know how you said your mam and dad had to go and live with your aunt in Abergele after they got bombed out of their house?'

His forehead furrowed. 'I don't think I'd call that good news, exactly.'

'Well, my dad said we can all go and stay with him until you get better. Isn't that great?'

Josh looked awkward. 'It's grand of your father, but I'm afraid I'll be like a fish out of water. It's very posh where you live, isn't it?'

'Tek it from me, Josh,' Dolly said reassuringly, 'I felt exactly the same, but since I got to know the Grangers properly I realise they're all just like Clara. I feel as comfortable there as I do in me own home.'

Josh hailed one of the taxis. 'In that case, I'd be delighted.'

Dolly slipped her arm through Lizzy's. 'It's not worth me and Lizzy comin' with you. We may as well go straight back to the flat and start packin'. Besides, a good walk'll help calm me nerves before Spencer teks me to the cinema.'

Josh raised his eyebrows. 'Are you two an item now?'

Dolly laughed. 'I'll let you know when I come home!'

* * *

Charlie stood across the road from the entrance to the naval offices in Rumford Street. Several Wrens had entered and exited the building and Charlie had been able to catch a glimpse of a man in naval uniform standing just inside the doorway: probably security, Charlie thought to himself. Not wishing to walk away without any real answers as he had from the Wren-nery, he tried to come up with a plan that would ensure he got a favourable response. He shook his head. No one in their right minds would give away personal information to a stranger – policeman or not – when there was a war on. He would just have to keep his fingers crossed that he got more answers here than he had at Ackerleigh House. This time he would tell the guard that he was looking for Mary Tanner because he had some very important personal information which he had to hand her in person. Taking a deep breath, he crossed the road and opened the door.

The man in naval uniform immediately barred Charlie's entrance. 'Can I help you?'

Charlie nodded briskly. 'I'm looking for a Mary Tanner. Do you know her?'

Much to Charlie's delight the guard nodded. 'Yes.'

'Is she here?'

'No. She's not worked here for quite some time.'

'I don't suppose you know where she's gone?' said Charlie hopefully.

'Sorry, mate.' He turned to a Wren who was sitting behind a desk. 'Have you seen Mary Tanner lately, Sylv?'

Charlie's heart lifted as the Wren nodded. 'Couple of weeks ago, why?'

'This policeman wants a word with her.'

She deflated a little. 'I only saw her to wave to, she was on one of the trams ... can't remember which one.' She glanced in Charlie's direction. 'Sorry.'

Charlie pulled his notebook out of his pocket and wrote on one of the pages before tearing it out and handing it to the guard. 'If either of you should see her, can you tell her to come and see me? I've written down my station address as well as my home one.'

The guard and the Wren exchanged glances. 'Is everything all right?' said the Wren.

Charlie nodded. 'Yes. Please tell her it's nothing to worry about, only I've got something of hers, you see, and I need to identify her before I can hand it over.'

The guard nodded wisely. 'Gotcha. I'll be sure to pass the message on if I should see her, and Sylv'll spread the word, won't you, queen?'

Sylv nodded. 'Good luck.'

Thanking them for their help, Charlie gave himself a congratulatory smile as he opened the door. He felt sure that he had managed to put his case over a lot better this time and that the sailor and the Wren would keep a keen eye out for Mary, especially as they believed he had something of hers in his possession, which, he assured himself, was at least partly true. Lifting his collar, he lowered his head against the sharp wind that was blowing the snow into his face, and headed towards the station at a brisk pace.

Lizzy stood by the window in the bedroom that she shared with Clara and Dolly. The snow had started to fall yesterday afternoon and lay thick on the ground. A snowball thudded against the glass pane, making her jump. She peered accusingly out to the pavement below as she tried to spy the culprit, and was not surprised to see two small schoolboys crouching behind the privet hedge. When they spied her in the window they waddled a hasty retreat, gathering more snow.

'Don't stand there, Lizzy, you'll only encourage 'em, and whilst there's nowt wrong wi' a bit of tomfoolery, some of them balls could have a stone in them.' As the words left Dolly's lips there was a bang at the window. 'See?'

Lizzy climbed back between the sheets of her bed. 'Sorry!'

Rubbing her eyes, Clara turned over to face the other two. 'How thick is the snow? Only Josh is getting his toe done later on this afternoon, and I don't relish the idea of getting him in and out of hospital if it's like a skating rink outside.'

'Will they let him out today?' Lizzy asked as she snuggled down between the thick blankets. 'I'd've thought they'd've kept him in overnight.'

Clara yawned. 'The nurse said it would depend on how the op went, but if all goes to plan he should be home later on today. They'll send a community nurse round to check on him in a day or two so he'll be just as well looked after here as he is in hospital.'

There was another thud at one of the windows. Swinging her legs out of bed Lizzy trotted back towards the sash window, lifted it, and gathered the snow that had landed on the window ledge into a ball before hurling it at the bottom of a schoolboy who was crouching down behind the hedge. As the snowball connected with its intended target, there was a yelp before the bottom in question straightened up and was replaced with the scowling face of a rather elderly lady who was staring wildly around her. 'Who threw that? Come on, you little devils, let's be 'avin' you!'

The schoolboys sniggered and pointed to Lizzy, who ducked out of sight. Holding her breath, she pinched her nose between her fingers and waited to hear the old woman's response.

'Lyin' little bleeders, there's no one there! It was you two. C'mon, admit it, I'll be sure to tell your mams, yer little beggars ...'

Peeping over the windowsill, Lizzy could see the open mouths of the boys as they tried to protest their innocence. One of them pointed a finger at Lizzy, who stuck her tongue out at them.

'It was her, honest to God, missus, go 'n' knock on the door an' ask,' the boy began, but his explanation was falling on deaf ears.

'H'oh yes, I go and knock on the door and mek a complete fool out of meself? I don't think so. Own up. You're the only ones here.'

The boy stood, his finger still pointing towards Lizzy. As their eyes connected, Lizzy winked and the boy's mouth twitched into a smile of admiration. Shrugging, he dropped his arm. 'Sorry, missus,' he said.

'That's better; all I wanted was the truth! Now help me pick up me shoppin' and we'll say no more about it.'

Lizzy gave the boy a silent round of applause as she watched him help the old lady with her bags.

Dolly chuckled. 'There was you complainin' that Charlie allus used to act like a big kid, and there you are throwin' snowballs. Youse like peas in a pod!'

'I must admit, bein' with Charlie has reminded me of what I used to be like before I lost me dad.'

Clara smiled. 'That's nice to hear. Speaking of Charlie, are you going to see him after work, ask him if he wants to spend Christmas here with us?'

'Yes, although I know he will. It was ever so good of your father to say he could stay over for Christmas Eve as well as Christmas Day.'

'Dad just wants an excuse to have a big breakfast. With all our ration books put together, we should have a meal fit for a king!'

Lizzy padded over to the washstand and gasped as the cold water splashed out of the ewer into the basin. 'Cor, I bet the snow's warmer!'

Dolly took her turn at the basin. 'One, two … blimey!'

Lizzy giggled. 'I thought three came next?'

As Dolly rubbed her face with the towel she paused for a moment. 'That's why I never really got your objection to Charlie being a bit of a joker. You and your dad was allus playin' tricks on each other, so why did you come down so hard on Charlie for doin' the same?'

'Have you heard that poem "Stop All The Clocks", by W. H. Auden?'

Dolly nodded. 'Allus meks me cry, that one does.'

'That's exactly how I felt after me dad's passin'. I didn't want to laugh any more, or do any of the things I used to do with Dad; it just didn't feel right to be happy without him around. That's probably why the Christmas tree was such a big deal to me: it wasn't so much a bad omen, more like a nasty reminder. I've been sayin' for years that I don't like Christmas trees, but it's not the tree I don't like, it was the star I was supposed to put on the tree with me dad, the day he died.' She sat down on her bed with a whump. 'I know it's silly, but I blamed meself for him dyin' 'cos he said the star would mek him feel better, and I didn't get it to him in time.' Lizzy pulled a handkerchief from her dressing gown pocket and wiped the tears away before she turned to face Dolly. 'I've been so unhappy all these years, and for what?'

Dolly sank to the floor beside Lizzy's bed and held her in a tight embrace. 'Your father died of appendicitis, not because you didn't get your star home in time.'

Clara sat down beside Lizzy. 'To think you've been carryin' all this blame on your shoulders. Why didn't you say anythin' sooner?'

Lizzy shrugged. 'Because deep down I knew it were a pile of tosh, only death doesn't mek sense to children. I knew summat were at fault and I s'pose I didn't want to blame Dad for his body goin' wrong, so I blamed meself instead.'

'But what had any of that got to do with Charlie?' said Dolly.

'When we were kids, no matter how much he riled me, I was ever so fond of Charlie, and when we met on Lime Street Station he made me feel just the way I did before me dad passed, and those feelin's scared me, made me feel as though everythin' was about to go wrong all over again. And then, of course, I lost me mam.'

Clara smiled grimly. 'Losing your mum brought all those memories flooding back and confirmed your worst fears.'

She nodded. 'Although of course meetin' Charlie had nowt to do wi' me mam's disappearance. Her fate was sealed the moment I left the 'ouse.' Blinking back the tears, she drew in a deep breath before letting it out in one go. 'It's taken all these years to mek me see the truth, but I've got here in the end, and I can finally start being me again with no fear of reprisals.'

Dolly's eyes shone with happy tears. 'Welcome back, Lizzy Atherton.'

Chapter Fifteen

As a flurry of snow entered the door to the station, Charlie pointed towards the newcomer. 'Make sure you shut that behind you. We don't want it lookin' like Santa's grotto in 'ere. It's bad enough we've got his bloomin' elves out and about creatin' havoc.'

The man gave a mirthless chuckle as he shook the snow off his cap. 'I tek it youse on about them little blighters what I've come to complain about?'

Charlie cast his eyes heavenward as he folded his arms on the counter. 'If you're on about Harry Pumford and his little pals, then yes, they've caused me no end of trouble this week. I'll be glad when the war's over if it's just to get their fathers back, 'cos they're running round like a pack of wild dogs without the men 'ere to keep 'em in line. I'm fed up to the back teeth of gerrin' 'em out of other folk's properties.'

The man sighed breathily. 'I reckon it's them I've come to report, then. My old girl reckons she seen a ghostly light movin' round in one of the 'ouses in Lace Street. I went down for a look 'cos she reckons it's the ghosts of German bombers sendin' a signal to the Jerries.' He rolled his eyes. 'I shouted at 'em to put it out before we all got blasted sky high. To be honest, I were surprised when they did as they were told, but as soon as I turned me back the little sods had turned it back on.' He eyed Charlie sympathetically. 'I know you've better things to do than chase round after a bunch of kids, and in truth it's the job of the warden, but they don't respect him. He reckoned the little buggers started throwin' snowballs at him last time he tried to see 'em off.'

Nodding, Charlie fixed his helmet into place. 'Jimmy?'

Jimmy poked his head round the door and brushed a few errant pastry crumbs from his chest. 'What's up?'

Lifting the counter lid, Charlie passed through before closing it behind him. 'It's that bloomin' Harry Pumford and his pals … again,' he added. 'I'm just goin' down to Lace Street to send 'em packin', only this time I'm goin' to call in on Harry's mam on the way, see if I can't persuade 'er to come with me and take the scallywags home for the night.'

'Give 'em a clip round the ear; that'll sort 'em. Don't worry about the desk, I'll keep an eye out whilst you're gone.'

The man who had reported the boys pulled his hat firmly down around his ears. 'It's bleedin' bitter out there. Why on earth anyone would want to be clamberin' round collapsed buildin's when they could be sat at 'ome in front of a warm fire is beyond me.'

'That's kids for you,' said Charlie as he fastened the buttons on his thick woollen police coat. 'Commonsense don't come into it. As long as they're 'avin' fun they don't think of the consequences.'

'The back of my hand would be the consequence if I 'ad my way. Now if you don't mind I'd best be gerrin' back. The missus is probably gerrin' worried, and I don't want 'er goin' down there to look for me.'

Charlie nodded. 'Can't say as I blame you. Given the choice between sittin' in the warm or chasin' kids in the dark I know which I'd choose.'

Mary swilled the tea in the pot before pouring the contents into the china cup in front of her. From the warmth of her seat in the small café, she gazed at the people who scurried along the slushy paving stones, their umbrellas held out in front of them as they tried to shield themselves from the wind and driving sleet.

Earlier in the week she had been approached by one of the girls in the bunker, asking her if she would like to swap shifts as her husband would be coming home on leave the week before Christmas.

'Are you sure?' Mary had said as the girl looked at her hopefully.

'Positive! If I swap shifts with you I can have an early Christmas with my Clive.'

Now, sitting in the café on Peel Road, she smiled as she recalled James's reaction to the news that she was to have Christmas off.

'Excellent! You can come and spend it with me and Jean.'

'Are you sure I wouldn't be imposing?'

'Imposing? How could you be imposing? You live there when you're not on shift, Jean considers it your home, and besides, Jean's new boyfriend's coming for lunch. He drives trains for a living, and whilst he finds the subject fascinating he bores me to tears.' He chuckled. 'I don't know what our Jean sees in him, but that's by the by. I was dreading the idea of spending Christmas Day listening to stories of locomotives, which I have no interest in.'

Now, a young woman in Wren's uniform dashed past the window and waved before bursting through the café door and plonking herself down in the seat opposite Mary's.

'Blimey, there's some brass monkeys lookin' for their watchermacallits out there.'

'Sylvia! Long time no see. Are you meeting someone?'

The Wren nodded. 'I'm meetin' Elsie from the typin' pool, an, we're goin' to the flicks after. You're welcome to join us, if you fancy it, but I dunno what film we're goin' to see yet.'

Mary shook her head. 'I'm afraid some of us have got work to do!'

Sylvia smiled as the waitress approached. 'Hot chocolate, please, and a sticky bun.' As the waitress turned to leave, Sylvia placed a hand on her elbow. 'Make that two hot chocolates and two sticky buns.' The waitress tutted as she made the adjustment on her notepad. Sylvia turned her attention back to Mary, then frowned. 'I'm sure I had summat to tell you ...' She sat back in her seat. 'Where are you workin' now?'

Mary shook a chiding finger. 'Round and about. Are you still in the offices on Rumford Street?'

Sylvia nodded slowly. 'What on earth was it now ...' She clicked her fingers. 'That's it! Some scuffer come to the offices the other day lookin' for you.'

Mary frowned uncertainly. 'You sure he was lookin' for me?'

Sylvia nodded. 'Positive; I was there at the time. He gave his details to Dozy Derek.'

'But why on earth would the police want to speak to me? I've not done anything wrong that I know of.'

Sylvia shook her head. 'He said he'd found summat of yours ...' She cast her eyes to the ceiling as she tried to remember his exact words. 'I can't remember whether it was jewellery, or money, or ...'

'But how would he know it belonged to me?'

Sylvia turned her attention back to Mary. 'Sorry, what?'

'If I had lost jewellery, which I haven't, or money, how would he know it belonged to me?'

Sylvia shrugged. 'Perhaps it was engraved?'

Mary shook her head. 'I've never owned anything that was engraved.' She eyed Sylvia thoughtfully. 'He must've got the wrong Mary. I bet there's hundreds in the Wrens.'

'But he said Tanner, that's how we knew it was you.'

Mary shrugged. 'But I'm not Tanner any more. I got divorced from that pig of a husband of mine, so he's definitely got the wrong person.'

Sylvia waved at Elsie, who was trotting along the pavement with her head bowed to the wind, and as the door opened she turned her attention back to Mary. 'Ask Derek; mebbe he can shed more light on it than me. It was him he was talkin' to, after all.'

Mary got up from her seat. 'Here you go, Elsie, you can sit here if you like. I've gorra go now anyway.' She nodded at Sylvia. 'I'll do that. Mebbe he said summat you didn't hear.'

'Thanks for that, Mary. Your seat's lovely and warm,' said Elsie, who was showering the surrounding diners with drops from her umbrella as she tried to stow it beneath the table.

As the waitress approached the table she said loudly, 'For goodness' sake stop flappin' that thing all over my nice wooden floor and pop it in the stand by the door.'

As Mary left the café, Elsie was garbling an apology to the waitress as the umbrella unfurled itself. Opening her own umbrella, Mary stepped out into the swirling sleet. As she made her way to Rumford Street she tried to dismiss the conversation she had had with Sylvia to the back of her mind, because she needed to concentrate on what she would buy Jean for Christmas. She stopped to look in a shop window and cast her eyes over the various talcum powders, soaps and flannels, but her eyes glazed over as her thoughts returned to the policeman. She knew it was silly to be wondering what he wanted when he had clearly asked for the wrong Mary, especially as she was now Atherton again and not Tanner, but a small glimmer of hope was welling within as she tried to imagine whether it could conceivably have anything to do with Lizzy. She tried to think of what she could possibly have lost that could tie her to her daughter. As she reached the entrance to the underground bunker, she glanced back along Rumford Street. If she really wanted to know what the scuffer wanted there was only one thing for it: she would have to speak to Dozy Derek. She strode towards the door, keeping her fingers crossed in her pocket, she prayed he would remember something.

Lizzy cast a critical eye over her reflection. 'The trouble with curly hair is that it's got a mind of its own!'

'Nonsense!' said Dolly as she attempted to backcomb Lizzy's glossy locks. 'Besides, you want to look your best, don't you?'

'Yes ... ow!' Lizzy rubbed her eyebrow.

'Sorry, I think I must have got a bit too close to the skin,' Clara said apologetically as she eyed the ends of the tweezers.

Dolly pulled another hairclip from between her teeth and drove it into the thick mass of hair that she had created at the back of Lizzy's head.

'Ouch! What did you just stab me with?' said Lizzy accusingly.

'A hair clip. And stop exaggerating, you make it sound as if I skewered you.' She smiled at the effect as she patted the back of Lizzy's hair. 'Do you know, I think I might have missed my calling.'

As Clara turned her attention to the other eyebrow she was gently but firmly pushed away. 'I'd rather keep me eyes, if it's all the same to you. Besides, I don't see why you're mekkin' such a fuss.'

Clara stared in disbelief. 'You can't go out half plucked! You'll look ridiculous!'

Lizzy shrugged. 'At least I'll still have both eyeballs.'

'Oh come on, I'm not that bad, and I promise I'll be more careful on the next one. I always do my own, but it's awkward doin' someone else's, although I think

I've got the hang of it now, and if I say so myself, I've done a decent job.'

Lizzy sat back with a reluctant sigh. 'Go on then, but be careful!'

Clara clapped her hands together. 'You won't regret it.' She turned to Dolly. 'Have you got any Elastoplast?' Dolly snorted with laughter as Clara laid a reassuring hand on Lizzy's shoulder. 'Calm down. I was only pulling your leg.'

Lizzy giggled as an image of meeting Charlie with sticking plasters covering both eyebrows entered her mind. 'I still don't see why all this is necessary.'

Clara stuck her tongue out as she concentrated on the job in hand. 'You've turned a corner, as it were. It's like a fresh start, and for that you need a new look!'

Dolly stood back. 'Finished!'

'Hold on, I'm nearly done here, just one or two ...' Clara straightened up, and grinned. 'You look beautiful!'

Lizzy eyed them with suspicion. 'Mirror?'

Clara twitched the cloth cover which they had placed over her mother's dressing table mirror to one side. 'Ta-dah!'

Lizzy gasped. Leaning closer, she examined her reflection. 'Blimey! Who'd've thought tweezers would mek such a difference?'

Dolly linked her arm through Clara's and the two girls stood behind Lizzy, looking pleased as Punch with their efforts. 'Do you still hate the mascara?'

Lizzy blushed. 'I did mek a bit of a fuss, didn't I? Only it's not nice watchin' someone weavin' their way towards your eye with a black stick.'

'But was it worth it?'

Lizzy nodded. 'I look … pretty.'

Dolly chuckled. 'I think she appreciates our hard work, Clara.'

Lizzy smiled apologetically at them. 'Gosh, I've been so busy admirin' meself I forgot to say thank you!'

Clara dipped a curtsey. 'You're welcome. Now go and ask Charlie whether he'd like to come for Christmas, and don't forget to tell him about the revelation you had before you went to work this morning. After all, that's what all this is in aid of.'

Lizzy nodded. 'Thanks, girls. You've really helped me turn that corner. I can't imagine what my life would've been like without you.' She placed an arm around each of their shoulders. 'We are goin' to stay together after the war, aren't we?'

'You bet we are! And I'll be movin' back to the flat as soon as Josh is better.'

Dolly groaned. 'Can't we stay here?'

'No we can't, Dolly Clifton! I've really enjoyed livin' in the flat. It's made me feel like an independent woman!'

'Me too. It feels like home now,' agreed Lizzy.

Dolly cast her eye around the spacious bedroom. 'But I don't want to be an independent woman; I like livin 'ere.'

Clara giggled. 'You just like it here because of Spencer. Speakin' of which, you still haven't told us how your date went.'

Dolly blushed. 'It's a bit awkward. He is your brother, after all.'

'So it *was* a date!' said Clara with a grin.

Dolly shook her head. 'It was more of a should-we-date? date.'

Lizzy nodded. 'Bit like me and Charlie then.'

'I like him and he likes me, but I was worried that his pals in the Navy might be embarrassed by me, if I said or did the wrong thing at one of their soirées.'

'And what did Spencer say to that?'

'That he'd rather spend the evenin' with me than go to some silly soirée.'

Clara clapped her hands together. 'That's Spencer to a T. He hates pomp and ceremony.' She locked eyes with Dolly. 'So? Are you official or not?'

Dolly blushed. 'We're givin' it a go, whether ...'

The rest of her sentence was lost as Lizzy and Clara erupted into cheers.

Charlie knocked on the door of Harry Pumford's house. Hearing a groan of dismay coming from the upstairs window, he looked up into the downturned face of Mrs Pumford, who did not look pleased to see him.

'What the bloody 'ell's our 'Arry done now?'

'Can I come in, Mrs Pumford?'

She huffed loudly. 'If you must, only go round the back; I don't want word gerrin' round we've 'ad the scuffers in.' She briefly disappeared before reappearing at the back door, where she glared at the house opposite. 'Gorra good eyeful, 'ave ya?' Turning, Charlie saw the curtain drop as someone hastily retreated. Mrs Pumford transferred the glare to Charlie. 'Thanks a lot, copper. Now they'll be spreadin' all sorts about me.' She directed Charlie into the parlour and gestured him to sit in one of the chairs. 'Stay there. I shan't be a mo.'

Charlie picked up an empty mug that was sitting on the arm of his chair and peered inside, wrinkling his nose in disgust at the thick layer of mould growing on the bottom. Beyond the parlour door he could hear Mrs Pumford ushering out a man who was muttering something about being owed half his money back. Charlie tried to ignore his host's indiscretion by taking an interest in his surroundings. The parlour itself was clean enough, but in one corner the ceiling above an old tin bucket showed signs of a leak. He looked around the rest of the sparsely decorated room. There was an ancient clock on the mantel and an empty coal scuttle next to the fireplace. As he peered more carefully, he realised that what at first glance appeared to be patterned wallpaper was in fact mould.

Mrs Pumford entered the room and lit a cigarette. 'So? What's he done so bad you have to come and mither me?'

'He's runnin' round with a bunch of lads robbin' bombed-out houses,' Charlie began before she interrupted without apology.

'And you can't handle that?' she sneered. 'A little kid what's havin' fun wiv his mates, and you come to his mammy for help?'

Charlie drummed his fingers on the arm of his chair. 'Perhaps I might have a word with your husband?' He held her gaze before adding, 'That was your husband I heard just now, wasn't it? Upstairs?'

Her eyes darted towards the back door. 'He were a mate, fixin' ...' her eyes glanced at the ceiling, 'the wonky leg on me bed.'

Charlie fought the urge to burst into laughter. 'I see. Well, if you refuse to discipline the boy, I'll have to wait until his father returns.' He paused. 'Where is he, by the way?'

She shrugged. 'Last I 'eard he were somewhere abroad, so you'll have to ruddy well wait a long time, won't you?' She looked down her nose at Charlie. 'I don't see what the fuss is about. If the 'ouses are empty, who cares?'

'I didn't say they were empty, I said they were bomb-damaged ... doesn't it bother you that your son's runnin' round in buildings that could collapse on him at any second?'

'If he's stupid enough to do it ...'

Charlie tutted. 'He's too young to know any better.'

She folded her arms defensively. 'So what do you want me to do about it?'

'Come with me and have a word with 'im, then take him home.'

Her brow rose sharply. 'You can't be serious? You want me to go through bombed-out buildings in the black of night riskin' me neck ...'

Charlie drew a deep breath. 'If your husband were here I'd ask him, but as he's not I have to ask you, although if you can't control Harry I'll have no choice but to come back and see your husband when he next returns.'

Mrs Pumford clasped the poker from beside the fire-place and jerked her head towards the door. 'Fine. A couple of clacks with this should do the trick.'

Charlie snatched the poker from her hand and waved it under her nose. 'If I hear from anyone, and I mean *anyone*, that you have struck your son with this, I shall be round to see your husband the moment he docks and I will tell him exactly what you've been up to whilst he's been away risking his life for King and country.' Mrs Pumford's eyes focused on the poker. 'What's more, I'll pay a visit to some of your,' he paused for a moment before uttering the next word in disgust, 'guests, and tell their families what they've been up to.'

She turned pale. 'There's no need for threats. I wouldn't really 'ave the little devil with it, just wave it about to frighten him like.'

Charlie thrust the poker back into the stand. 'On second thoughts I don't think it would be a good idea if you came. It might drive them further into the buildings.'

As Charlie left the house he heard Mrs Pumford opening the front door. 'I'll 'ave a word wiv 'im when he comes 'ome an' see what can be done. If I can stop 'im wanderin' round them buildin's, do you promise not to come back?'

Without turning, Charlie nodded.

When she spoke next her voice had taken on a calmer tone. 'Try not to judge me. It's not easy when your 'usband's miles away and you're left alone with no money and 'ungry mouths to feed.'

Without a word Charlie strode off in the direction of Lace Street.

Lizzy struck the bell on the counter of the police station. After a moment or so, Jimmy's face peered round the corner of the office door. 'Lizzy! Blimey, you scrub up well, don't you, gal!'

Lizzy beamed as Jimmy strode towards her, a broad grin etched across his face. 'Hello, Jimmy. Is Charlie about?'

Jimmy shook his head. 'He's gone down to Lace Street to sort some sprogs out.'

'The Pumford boys again?'

Jimmy shrugged. 'Couldn't say. He went about a half-hour ago. Do you want to wait for him? We've got a nice pork pie in the back, goes down lovely with some of my Minnie's homemade chutney.'

'Sounds tempting, but I think I'll go for a stroll down to Lace Street, see if I can find him.'

'Well, mind how you go, and don't go into any of the houses, even if you think you can see him.'

She nodded. 'Don't worry, I'm not that stupid.'

Mary walked along the corridor deep below the building, staring at the piece of paper in her hand. It was obviously a mistake. She didn't know any scuffers, and no one knew where she was; it was just one big coincidence. Yet – she sighed heavily as she shoved the note into the pocket of her jacket – yet there was something niggling away at the back of her mind. According to Derek, the scuffer hadn't said what he had of Mary's, nor where he had found it. The wording was wrong, almost like a mystery. If he'd found something of value, surely he'd have asked her to bring some kind of identification so that he knew he was giving it back to its rightful owner. She shook her head. She was going to be stuck in the bunker for the next forty-eight hours, but as soon as she left she would head straight for the police station and find out just what it was that this PC Charlie Jackson had of hers.

Rounding the corner before the ops room, Mary nearly collided with one of the admiralty. Apologising profusely, she looked up into the downturned face of James.

'Something on your mind?' he said, and when Mary looked more closely she could see the weariness in his face. His eyes were half closed and he looked as though he could drop off to sleep at any moment.

She nodded. 'I see you've done another double shift.'

Removing his cap, he ran his fingers through the tightly curled dark hair, which, Mary noticed, was considerably more streaked with grey than when she had first met him. 'But it's worth it, especially ...' he stifled a yawn behind the back of his hand, 'especially with Christmas just around the corner.'

Mary nodded, and had half pulled the slip of paper out of her pocket when she decided against it. It would be unfair to bother him with such petty details, especially when she was more than capable of solving the mystery by herself. As she pushed the paper back into her pocket, James pointed at it.

'Is that from that copper who came looking for you?'

Mary's jaw dropped. 'How on earth did you find out about that?'

He smiled wearily. 'I wouldn't be doin' my job if I didn't know the ins and outs of everything that goes on in this building, and the one above it.'

Mary pulled the paper back out. 'Do you want to see it?'

He chuckled. 'Already have. Question is, do you have any idea what he wants?'

Mary shook her head. 'I've not lost anything, not that I know of at any rate. If you ask me, it's a mistake.

Either that or he's after the wrong Mary, and considering it says Tanner and not Atherton I should say that's quite likely.'

James raised an eyebrow. 'Is that what you think, that he's got the wrong Mary?'

Mary started to nod, then shrugged. 'I dunno. I did at first; it just seems a bit odd, the way he worded it, don't you think?'

James nodded. 'Very odd indeed.' He checked his watch. 'Are you goin' to the station after your shift?'

She nodded. 'May as well. Strike whilst the iron's hot, as it were.'

'I'll get someone to check this copper out,' said James, 'make sure he's not got any ulterior motives in mind.'

She giggled. 'What ulterior motives could he possibly have? It's not as if I'm anyone important.'

James frowned. 'You work for the Royal Navy in a secret bunker below the city.'

Mary clapped a hand to her mouth. 'Surely you don't think he's a spy?'

James shrugged. 'I hope not, but we'd be fools if we didn't make sure.'

Mary glanced anxiously at the note in her hands. 'I wondered why some scuffer would come looking for me. I mean, no one knows I'm here, and as I said I've not lost anything, so it does seem rather sinister ...'

Stepping forward, James took her hand discreetly in his. 'You know I'd not let anything happen to you. I kept you safe all that time at sea, didn't I?'

Mary smiled as his fingers gently squeezed her own. 'I still can't believe how lucky it was that I ended up on your ship.' Her tummy fluttered as he winked at her.

'Sailors believe in destiny.'

Mary felt the warmth of the blush invade her neckline. 'And what do you believe your destiny to be?'

Clasping her other hand in his, he rubbed his thumbs back and forth along the backs of her wrists. 'To end up with the woman of my dreams, in a cottage down by the sea.'

Mary found herself leaning toward him. 'Sounds idyllic. I must say I rather envy the woman of your dreams.'

Leaning down until his face was inches away from hers, James smiled. 'I don't see why. You—'

A door behind Mary swung open, causing them to jump apart. Her heart racing, Mary shot James a meaningful look as he grinned at her. 'Good work, Atherton. Keep it up!'

Mary nodded curtly before making a hasty departure. Behind her she heard James break into conversation with the newcomers. What on earth was she playing at? She knew she would be in real trouble if they found her flirting with a vice admiral. On the other hand, James wasn't really in the Navy, or at least not by choice, so did that still count? She was pretty sure that when the war was over James would go back to working for the big shipping companies, which would mean he would be free to see anyone he wanted. A cottage down by the sea, with a handsome, kind, and thoughtful man ... Mary smiled.

Hearing what he thought to be a gunshot, Charlie flung himself into the doorway of the nearest house.

After a moment or so, he risked a peep up the deserted street. Deciding he was not in any imminent danger, he ventured out, only to be confronted with a black, hissing, spitting ball of fur, which streaked past him. Charlie looked in the direction from where the cat had come and heard the sound of raised voices. He slowly walked towards them, getting ready to duck out of sight should any of them come his way. A baton was all very well, he thought bitterly, but it was no match for a gun. As he neared one of the jiggers, he heard the sound of a bin lid spinning on the ground whilst a female voice rang shrill in the air.

'Youse a fool, Kelvin Walsh. I told you time and time again you shouldn't keep that thing in the 'ouse, so if you ask my opinion it serves you bleedin' well right.'

There was a wail of pain before a man's voice responded. 'Well I ruddy well didn't, did I? Now shut your trap and give me an 'and.'

'Youse lucky you ain't dead!'

Charlie breathed a sigh of relief. Whatever had happened it appeared to have been by accident. He knocked briskly on the yard door.

'Well done!' said the female voice sarcastically. 'You've only got the neighbours comin' round to gob off!'

As the handle to the yard door jiggled, there was an outraged cry from the man. 'Shut the bleedin' door, you stupid woman!'

The door handle stopped jiggling and Charlie could hear the sound of retreating footsteps followed by the loud slam of a door. '*I'm* stupid? *I'm* not the one who keeps a gun where the kiddies can get at it.'

The handle jiggled briefly before the door opened just enough to reveal the woman's face which, despite the angry exchange of words, was smiling until she saw Charlie. Then her face fell and the door was flung wide open. 'Bleedin' 'ell, word gets out quick, don't it? Our Andy only shot the thing a few seconds ago.'

'I was on my way to Lace Street when I heard the gunshot.' He peered round the deserted yard. 'Did I hear you talkin' to someone?'

She pursed her lips into a malicious smile and strutted towards the privy. 'Kelvin! There's a scuff— policeman 'ere 'oo wants a word with you.'

'Tell 'im I'm busy!' came the panic-stricken reply.

'It's all right, I can wait,' said Charlie. He had no idea what had happened to Kelvin, but his wife appeared to be gaining some enjoyment from his predicament.

''Ear that, Kelvin? The lovely man is kind enough to wait for you.' Leaning against the privy door, she tapped the bottom of it with the toe of her shoe. 'Come on out. You can't hide in there forever.'

'Bugger off!'

She smiled sweetly at Charlie before standing back from the door, raising one leg and booting it sharply. The door swung open and rebounded off the top of Kelvin's head. Kelvin let out a wail of pain. As the door gently drifted back open, Charlie could see an elderly man sitting on the lavatory, his trousers round his ankles.

Charlie frowned. 'What's all the fuss about? He looks all right to me.'

Kelvin's wife smiled serenely. 'He's been shot in the leg.'

'Oh.' Charlie was looking down towards Kelvin's calves when his wife said, 'Higher up.'

Charlie swallowed hard. 'Come along, Kelvin, we can't leave you in there all night. Let's have a look and see how bad the damage is.'

'Go away!' snapped Kelvin. 'I just need a minute or two to get over the shock. If you'd just leave me be I'd be right as rain.'

The woman studied her fingernails. 'You sure he shot you in the thigh? Have you even looked? It could be a lot worse.'

'Sod off! You're evil you are, standin' there gloatin'. I bet you 'aven't even tried to find the cat, 'ave you?'

''E'll be back.' She glanced at her husband through narrowing eyes. 'Lucky for you it weren't 'im what got shot, else ...'

Charlie held up a hand. 'I think your husband's learned his lesson.' He eyed Kelvin curiously. 'How come you've got a gun?'

'Home guard,' Kelvin said proudly.

His wife gave a contemptuous sniff. 'Home guard my eye! Just a bunch of old men blunderin' round the countryside shootin' themselves in the leg. 'Ow's that meant to be of any use to anyone?'

'I did not shoot meself,' said Kelvin through gritted teeth. 'It's your fault, you should've kept a closer eye on 'im.' Forgetting his injury, Kelvin stood up.

Charlie turned his head. 'Would you pull your trousers up, please?'

Snorting with laughter, Kelvin's wife disappeared into the house just as a roll of toilet paper rebounded off the back of her head.

Trying to keep himself together, Charlie turned back to Kelvin who was standing on one leg whilst trying to buckle his belt. 'Once your wife's calmed down, perhaps you could get her to take a look at the wound, make sure the bullet's not still in there.'

Kelvin nodded, and turned to flush the lavatory. To Charlie's horror he gave a cry of triumph and stuck his hand into the bowl. 'No need! Looks like it's only a flesh wound.' Turning back to face Charlie, Kelvin held up a bullet.

Relief swept over Charlie, who had feared to be presented with something a lot worse than a bullet. 'That's good news. Make sure you keep your gun out of reach. On top of the wardrobe, mebbe?'

Kelvin grinned toothily. 'It's a good job I was on the bog when our Sam pointed that gun at me, 'cos I damned near ...'

Charlie held up a hand. 'I can imagine. Now if you'll excuse me.'

Kelvin limped his way back into the house and Charlie could hear the pair squabbling once more. Heading back in the direction of Lace Street, he chuckled to himself. This would give Jimmy and the others a good laugh when he got back to the station.

Walking through the snow-covered streets, Lizzy shook her head as she made her way towards the deserted buildings. As a child she had often walked through here on her way to school, but things had been different back then. The streets had been full of life – everyone knew everyone else and the housewives would stand gossiping on their doorsteps whilst the children played outside. Now, not one of the buildings remained standing and the area was more like a ghost town. She stopped for a moment and peered into the darkness as she tried to get her bearings. In the distance she could just make out the sound of voices. Hoping that one of them might belong to Charlie, she headed towards them. As she drew nearer, she could see that half of one of the houses still stood proud whilst the rest lay in smithereens. The house next to it appeared completely intact apart from the windows, which had been blown in. As she walked past one window her heart leapt as she saw the shape of an individual inside. 'Charlie? Is that you?'

Somewhere in the distance she heard what sounded like a gunshot. Lizzy froze. Who on earth would be firing a gun? Her shoulders relaxed a little as reality caught up with her. It was far more likely to be a car backfiring than someone shooting something. She tutted beneath her breath. That's what happens when you wander round spooky buildings in the dark, Lizzy Atherton: your imagination runs away with you.

She got back to the matter in hand. 'Charlie! It's me, Lizzy. Are you in there?' She squealed as a black cat hurtled past her and dived through another empty window. Holding her hand across her pounding chest, she cursed softly beneath her breath. She gingerly picked her way across the broken garden wall and peered through the window. 'C'mon, puss, you can't hide in here, it's too dangerous.' She heard something fall as the cat moved inside the house. Taking a step back, she surveyed the outside of the building. The front door was hanging by a single hinge and moved easily aside as she pushed it with her fingertips.

Shaking her head in disbelief at her own foolishness, Lizzy entered.

Harry Pumford and his pals crouched in the corner of the ruined parlour next door to the house that Lizzy had entered. Placing his forefinger against his lips, Harry jerked his head, and one by one they all walked crab-like across the broken-down walls into the room next door.

Billy chewed at his fingernails. "Oo is she? And 'oo's that Charlie she's lookin' for?'

Harry frowned angrily. "Ow the 'ell should I know? She's probably some loony 'oo still thinks she lives 'ere.'

'Well, we can't leave her walkin' round on her own in the dark. Summat might 'appen to 'er,' said one of the other boys.

Harry stared at his pal in disbelief. 'Whatchoo want me to do? I ain't takin' her back to the loony bin – it could be miles away for all I know, and I dare say she won't know which one she's escaped from anyhow.'

Another member of the group piped up. 'If she really 'as escaped, then won't someone come lookin' for 'er?'

Harry stared at him whilst he mulled it over. 'I suppose we could come back tomorrer. It's not as if it's goin' anywhere.'

Billy shrugged. 'On the other 'and, the longer we leave it the more likely some other bugger'll come along and 'ave whatever's worth nickin' before we've 'ad a look in.'

Harry slapped his hands down against his legs. 'I wish you'd mek your minds up!'

Billy held up a finger. 'Tek 'er to the scuffers; they'll know what to do. They love pokin' their noses into stuff like this.'

Harry stared at him incredulously. 'Oh yes, and 'ow do we explain that we found her wanderin' round a dangerous buildin' when we're not meant to be in 'ere ourselves?'

Billy shrugged. 'We could say we was walkin' past when we 'eard 'er shouts for 'elp?'

Harry nodded slowly. 'That way we'd be the heroes for a change!'

There was a general murmur of agreement.

Clicking his fingers at one of his pals, Harry held out his hands. 'Chuck us yer lighter and a bit o' rag, so I can mek us a torch.' He rolled his eyes at the look of uncertainty on their faces. 'Only for a minute or two. Besides, them Germans ain't bombed up here for a long time. I reckon they know better than to mess with us Scousers. Once we're outside I'll put it out, but if you think I'm goin' to approach some loony lady in the dark you've gorranother thing comin'. She's probably scared out of her wits as it is.'

He wrapped the rag around a broken piece of window frame and stood up before lighting the end. Holding the torch out in front of him, he moved towards the room where they had heard the woman stumbling in the dark.

''Ello, missus? There's no need to be frightened. We've come to 'elp.'

'Charlie? Is that you?'

Looking at his pals, Harry rotated his forefinger next to his temple and mouthed the word 'Bonkers' before continuing. 'Yes, it's me, Charlie. Let's be gerrin' you out of 'ere and back to safety, shall we?'

As his torch illuminated the room, Harry could see that the woman was far from being old and doddery and appeared to be in good health. She peered at him through the gloom. 'You're not Charlie!'

Shading his eyes from the torch with one hand, Billy piped up. ''Ow do you know he's not Charlie if youse bonkers?'

Lizzy placed her hands on her hips. 'For a start, I'm not bonkers, and Charlie's a policeman. He's come down here lookin' for you lot ...' She stopped speaking as the boys started pushing and shoving each other out of the way in their bid to escape.

Lizzy chuckled as she watched them disappear from view. Turning her attention back to the matter in hand, she called out to the cat and was delighted when she heard a soft mewling sound coming from the direction of the staircase. Wishing she had some kind of light, she peered into the dark. 'There you are, you silly cat. Now just you come down here before you get 'urt. I bet Charlie'll be pleased when I tell 'im I got rid of the boys *and* saved a lost cat into the bargain.' Sitting on her haunches, she tried to persuade the cat to come to her, but instead it retreated further up the staircase. 'For goodness' sake, I said come here, not go up there, you stupid moggy.' Against her better judgement, Lizzy started to ascend the stairs, keeping her eye on the cat in case he ran off, and so failing to notice that one of the steps was partly broken. As that foot took her weight, the step gave way beneath her. Shrieking with alarm, she tried to lift her foot free, but for some reason it seemed to be stuck fast. She rolled her eyes in disbelief at her own stupidity. Thank goodness Charlie was on his way to tell the boys off. She was wondering how long it would take for him to get there when an unwelcome thought occurred to her. Perhaps he'd already searched the buildings; he had set off before her, after all. As doubt started to fill her mind she leapt from one conclusion to the next. There she had been thinking how proud Charlie was going to be when she told him what she'd done, when in reality it was going to be him rescuing her all over again. The cat crept down and began to rub up and down Lizzy's arm. She tickled it under the chin and was rewarded by a loud purr. Pulling her coat around her, she rested her head against the wall. She had no choice but to sit tight and wait for help to arrive.

The torch Harry had made lay abandoned on the parlour floor in the house next to Lizzy's. Its flame had all but died when a small breath of wind caused it to glow, and the curtains that lay in a heap close by began to smoulder.

Hearing the footsteps pounding up the road, Charlie ducked out of sight and waited until the boys were nearly parallel before jumping out in front of them. He grabbed hold of the nearest child and looked into his frightened face.

'And who've we got here? Not Harry Pumford, that's for sure, but I bet you know where he's at!'

The small boy squirmed in Charlie's grip. 'Lemme go. I never done nuffin'.'

Hearing his squeals of protest, a couple of the bigger boys stopped in their tracks and turned back. 'Oi!' shouted the largest boy. 'Lerrim go. He's only a kid.'

Charlie squinted through the dark. The rest of the gang was gathering about their spokesman now. 'I can see that. What I want to know is what you're all runnin' away from.'

The boy's eyes darted between his pals as he tried to think of an excuse. 'We was runnin' 'ome for us teas?' he suggested.

Charlie leaned toward him and laughed without mirth. 'Righto, Harry. Since when's your mam cooked you tea, or any other meal come to that?'

Harry Pumford shrugged his shoulders. 'She says it ain't worth it since there's only the three of us left.' He eyed Charlie curiously. ''Ow d'you know my name?'

In the darkness Charlie smiled. 'All scuffers look alike to you, don't they?'

Harry shrugged. 'Dunno. It's hard to know what any of youse look like as I'm normally runnin' away, on account of you lot allus chasin' me for no reason.'

The small boy stopped wriggling. 'Are you Charlie?'

Frowning, Charlie stared at the boy, but in this light, and with the amount of dirt on the child's face, he was unrecognisable. He tried a different tack. 'Who wants to know?'

The boy shrugged. 'Some loony lady in Lace Street's lookin' for someone called Charlie, and she said he was a scuffer and that he were lookin' for us.'

Charlie glanced at Harry, who was scowling at the smaller boy. 'Don't listen to 'im, he don't know what he's sayin'. We ain't been near Lace Street, 'ave we, lads?'

There was a general shaking of heads and shrugging of shoulders as the boys agreed with their leader.

The small boy shook his head. 'I fought we was goin' to say we 'eard 'er shoutin' for 'elp?'

One of the bigger boys sidestepped so that he was able to place a grubby hand over the small boy's mouth from behind. 'There was some woman shoutin' after a Charlie. We told her not to go in the bombed buildings 'cos they was dangerous, but she wouldn't listen.'

The small boy wriggled out from under the other's hand. 'Then we runned away.'

Shaking his head, Harry levelled with Charlie. 'I know we ain't meant to go in the buildin's and I swear we wasn't on the rob when we 'eard the woman and thought she might be one of the ones out of the asylum. I made a torch so's not to frighten 'er.' He jerked his head towards the small boy in Charlie's grasp. 'What me brother said about 'er lookin' for some feller named Charlie is true, and when she mentioned he was a scuffer we legged it ...' he shrugged his shoulders, 'for obvious reasons.'

'So where is she, and what did she look like?'

'Dunno. Still lookin' for you, I s'pose. It was 'ard to see in the dark even with a torch, but her hair was all piled up fancy like.'

Charlie wagged a stern finger at the boys. 'If I find out you've been tellin' fibs ...'

Billy grinned up at him. 'We ain't, not this time, we's heroes, or at least we would've been if the loony lady would've come with us.'

'So? Can we go?' said Harry.

Charlie nodded. 'Only if you promise to steer clear of the bombed buildings. So far you've been lucky, but I doubt your luck will hold out much longer, and I think you should know I've had a word with your mam.' Seeing the terrified look on Billy's face, Charlie raised a reassuring hand. 'Don't worry, I managed to calm her down before leavin'.' Charlie paused. There was something odd about the young boy's eyes; they appeared to be twinkling, which was odd considering they were in the middle of the blackout.

Billy's eyes grew wide. 'I fink our 'Arry left his torch ...' he said in a scared whisper. ''Arry?' He looked up and down the street, now empty save for himself and Charlie, who was running in the direction of Lace Street.

'Hello? Is there anyone there? I'm stuck, can you help me?' Falling silent, Lizzy listened in vain for a response, but all she could hear was the distant sound of the wind rushing through the house next door. Her eyes fell to the front door, which was gently swaying on its remaining hinge. She watched it for several minutes as she tried to work out what was wrong with what she was seeing. She sighed. Her imagination was getting the better of her. She turned her attention to the cat, which had curled up on her lap and kept tilting its head as though listening to something in the house next door. She was just about to shout out again when the cat stopped staring at the wall and settled down to sleep.

Lizzy concentrated on the door again. Every now and then a flurry of snow would enter through the doorway and settle on the floor. She heard the sound of splintering glass; the cat raised its head and looked intently at the wall before yawning and nuzzling back on her knee. Laying a hand across its ears so as not to frighten it, Lizzy called out, 'Hello? Can you hear me?'

She waited for a response, but the wind was so loud that she very much doubted that anyone could hear her. The sound of breaking glass came again, and this time the noise was a lot closer. The cat jerked its head up then bolted off her knee, down the stairs and through the front door, which was still swinging gently as it ran past. Lizzy called out again, but there was no response.

Her eyebrows knitted into a puzzled frown. The wind should've been blowing that gently swaying door off its single hinge. From what she could hear it was roaring through the house next door …

A loud snapping noise was followed by a whump, startling Lizzy. It sounded as if someone had broken a very large, very heavy piece of wood in two, then dropped the pieces on the floor. A cloud of dust appeared at the bottom of the staircase, and as it hung in the air Lizzy's heart began to pound in her chest.

It couldn't be the wind she could hear because it would have blown the dust away. As realisation dawned, tears welled in her eyes. What she could hear was the roar of a fire taking hold, and the glass was splintering in the heat.

As flames licked the corner of the staircase, Lizzy stood up as best she could and started to pull frantically at her trapped foot, but it was no use. Sobbing, she tried to dig the wooden tread away with her fingernails, screaming for help at the top of her lungs.

The remaining hinge flew across the room as the door slammed open before falling flat on the floor. Lizzy's vision blurred as she tried to see through her tears. Her fingernails were split and bleeding; the smoke was entering her mouth and choking her.

Someone shouted through the doorway. 'Is there anyone there? Shout if you can hear me.'

Lizzy thrust her face into her hands and drew as deep a breath as possible before gurgling out a strangled cry for help. There was a sound of rushing footsteps, and Charlie's face appeared before her.

'Lizzy?' he said, his voice aghast.

She nodded weakly. 'Me foot's trapped. Leave me, Charlie. There's no sense in the fire tekkin' us both.'

Winding his scarf round his mouth, he shook his head. 'Forget it. I'm not goin' anywhere without you.' He removed his jacket and enveloped her in it. Standing up, he ordered her to keep still. He removed the baton from his pocket and pounded at the broken step until it splintered, cracked and finally broke away. Lifting Lizzy into his arms, he carried her down the stairs. The front door had caught fire and was lying across the threshold, the doorway was engulfed in flames, and without allowing himself to think Charlie ran straight through and emerged into the street. Pushing Lizzy into the arms of one of the firemen, he collapsed on the snow-covered ground, he heard a woman screaming, and felt several hands rolling him over and over in the snow, which was blissfully cool against his skin. He heard the small boy who had directed him to the house telling a bystander that he had shown Charlie where to look.

'He's an 'ero, that's what he is! He come straight down 'ere as soon as he knew someone were in trouble and bashed that door in with one kick!'

'I wonder who the woman was?' said a voice not too far away from Charlie.

His mind wrestled with the words. What did they mean 'was'? Surely they meant to say 'is' … you only say 'was' when someone's … He tried to get up, to shout her name, but pain shot through him and smoke filled his lungs so that his voice came out in a whisper. 'She's my Lizzy.'

Charlie blinked at the bright white ceiling above his head, then grimaced as the mixed scents of smoke, disinfectant and burned flesh filled his nostrils. He frowned. Where on earth could he be that would smell that bad, and why did he feel as though he'd been asleep in the sun for far too long? A door opened and Charlie lifted his head.

'Ah, you're awake!'

Charlie focused on the woman who had addressed him. 'You're a nurse!'

She smiled. 'That's right.'

'If I'm in a hospital why does it smell so awful?'

Leaning over him, she adjusted something on his left hand side. 'If you're referring to the smell of smoke and singed flesh, then I'm afraid the awful smell is you.' Seeing the incomprehension on his face, she stepped back. 'Don't you remember anything?'

Closing his eyes, Charlie tried in earnest to remember what had happened. He and Jimmy had been in the station when some feller had come in, the noise of a gunshot sounded in Charlie's memory and he smiled as a picture of Kelvin sitting on the lavvy came into view. Charlie frowned; why had he gone to Kelvin's? He hadn't heard of him before that night, so why … he groaned beneath his breath. Those pesky kids had been causing havoc again. He'd been making his way to Lace Street when … an image of Billy's upturned face, covered in muck, smiled up at him. He was telling people how brave Charlie was, and they'd said … he shot upright. 'Lizzy!'

The startled nurse shook her head. 'If you're referring to the young lady you rescued from the fire, then don't worry, she's in the best possible hands.'

'In the best possible hands? What does that mean? I've got to see her, it's my fault she was in there in the first place!'

The nurse's brow furrowed. 'I think you must be confused. From what we've been told you turned up in the nick of time.'

'Can you tell me where she is? I need to see her.'

The nurse drew a deep breath. 'If I take you to her, do you promise to behave?'

He nodded. 'I promise.'

A tear trickled down Dolly's cheek as she ran a hand over Lizzy's brow. 'How could you 'ave been so silly?'

Lizzy's lip trembled. 'I don't know. I knew it was a stupid thing to do at the time, but I thought I'd only be in there for a second or two.'

Dolly sat on the chair beside Lizzy's hospital bed. 'And all for some silly moggy who had the sense to run off before it all went pear-shaped!'

Lizzy rolled her eyes. 'I know, but it weren't the cat's fault. He didn't know what was goin' to 'appen any more than I did.' She looked at Dolly. 'Do you think he's angry with me?'

Dolly frowned. 'Are we still talkin' about the cat?'

'No! Do you reckon Charlie's goin' to be angry with me?'

'Don't be daft! He knows you've gorra a big 'eart, an' knowin' Charlie 'e'd probably've done the same as you.'

'He probably would,' said Charlie, standing at the entrance to the ward.

'Charlie!' said Lizzy, before breaking off into a bout of coughing.

A stern-faced matron looked up from her desk. 'I 'ope you're not gettin' Miss Atherton overexcited. She needs rest, not stimulation!'

Charlie pulled an apologetic face. 'Sorry. I only popped in to make sure she was all right. I'll leave if you like.'

Lizzy shook her head and pointed at the chair next to Dolly's. Ignoring the matron's glare, he sank down into the chair and took Lizzy's hand in his. 'How's tricks?'

Dolly wrinkled her nose. 'I hope you don't mind me sayin', but you don't half pong. Would you like me to fetch you some clean clothes?'

Charlie chuckled. 'I think it's goin' to take a bit more than a set of clean clothes to get rid of the smell. Maybe a couple of good hot baths might do the trick.'

The sister's chair scraped noisily across the floor as she got to her feet. 'Only one to a bed. You know the rules: one of you will have to leave!'

Dolly rolled her eyes. 'Don't worry, sister. I'll mek meself scarce for a bit.' Leaning forward, she kissed Lizzy's forehead. 'Try to get some rest.' She turned her attention to Charlie. 'They reckon Lizzy should be well enough to go home tomorrer, so I dare say I'll see you then?'

Charlie nodded. 'They've said they'll discharge me after the doc's done his rounds this evening, but I'll meet you back 'ere first thing tomorrer.'

Dolly grinned. 'You won't be allowed in before one o'clock, not with that one in charge.' She jerked her head in the direction of the sister, who was still scowling at them.

Seeing she had their attention, the matron peered at Dolly over the top of her glasses. 'When you said you were leaving, I assumed you meant today.'

Dolly pulled off a mock salute. 'Yes sister, right away sister!' As the door swung closed behind her, Charlie winced as he chuckled. His fingers delicately sought out the sore on the side of his face.

Lizzy grimaced. 'Is that from the fire?'

'The nurse said it'll heal in a couple of weeks or so.'

Lizzy looked at him through eyes brimming with tears before burying her face in her hands. 'I'm so, so sorry, Charlie.'

He gently pulled her hands away from her face. 'What've you got to be sorry for? You didn't start the fire.'

'But it's my fault that you 'ad to rescue me. I should've waited for you at the station like Jimmy suggested.'

Charlie pressed the backs of her knuckles against his lips. 'Why *did* you come lookin' for me?'

'I'd come to ask you whether you wanted to spend the Christmas hols at Bellevue with the rest of us, but also because me, Clara and Dolly had had a bit of a chinwag before brekker and I realised summat I hadn't before, and I wanted to tell you.'

He looked intrigued. 'Oh?'

Lizzy relayed the discussion she had had with the girls earlier that day, finishing with: 'So I've finally accepted that no matter what I do or how hard I try, I can't control the future.'

Still holding her hands, Charlie wiped her tears away with his thumb. 'That's typical of you, always tryin' to keep everyone else safe rather than lookin' after yourself, just like you did tonight with the moggy. Well, all that's goin' to change. Once you're out of here I'm goin' to be the one lookin' after you, whether you like it or not.'

Lizzy grinned. 'Sounds good to me. But what about Christmas? Can you come?'

Charlie nodded. 'I wouldn't miss it for the world.'

Chapter Sixteen

When Mary left the underground bunker she gasped as a flurry of snow whirled around her. Pushing her cap firmly on to her head, she trotted towards the tram stop. It was the morning of Christmas Eve, and for the first time in a long while she found she was looking forward to the holidays. She considered Jean and James to be family, and she was excited at the thought of a traditional Christmas, something she had not had since Eric died. As the tram drew to a halt, she stepped aboard, purchased her ticket, then looked around for a vacant window seat. The carriage itself was half empty, which was surprising seeing that it was still relatively early. Sitting on one of the wooden benches, she used the sleeve of her woollen coat to wipe the condensation off the window, but there was little to see save the odd last-minute shopper hurrying along.

As the tram drew away from the stop Mary groaned inwardly as a rather large man waddled his way along the aisle, his eyes fixed on the seat next to her. Sitting down heavily, he opened a copy of the *Liverpool Echo* and held it so that his right hand was inches away from Mary's face. Fighting the urge to push his hand down, she instead decided to take advantage of the situation by reading the pages she could see. To her disgust, the man wiped his nose on the back of his hand before turning the page. Mary was debating moving seats when she noticed the headline he had just revealed: *Local policeman hailed a hero as he saves woman from burning building.* The report began: *Police Constable Charlie Jackson ...*

Before she could read any further, the tram drew to a halt and the large man closed his paper and got up. Fumbling desperately in her jacket pocket, Mary pulled out the piece of paper the constable had handed the guard and looked at the name written down. *PC Charlie Jackson.* She grasped the man's arm. 'Sorry to bother you, but have you finished with your *Echo*?'

Tucking the newspaper under his arm, he shook his head. 'Sorry, luv. I'd let you 'ave it but the missus'll wanna take a gander when I get in.'

Letting go of his arm, Mary sank back into her seat. 'I don't suppose you read that article about the policeman saving someone from a fire, did you?'

'Nah, but everyone's talkin' about it. They reckon he got there in the nick of time.' He paused. 'Do you know him, then?'

Mary shook her head. 'Just interested to know what happened.'

He shrugged. 'According to them in the know, they're both alive and well. Sorry, luv, but this is my stop. If I don't get off here ...' His voice was lost as he left the tram.

Mary peered anxiously out of the window. She could not explain why, but the knowledge that the policeman was a good man made her heart race. What if he really was looking for her? She bit her lip as an image of Lizzy ran through her mind. If she was right, there was a good chance that the constable had found something that belonged to Lizzy, something with Mary's name on it, but what could it be? Lizzy had run off that night with nothing but an old sock full of pennies. Closing her eyes, she conjured up an image of Lizzy as she was the day she left. Her raven hair lay in loose curls around her shoulders; she wore a white blouse under a navy blue cardigan and a black skirt that fell past her knees. Mary pulled a face. There was nothing to connect Lizzy to anyone or anything. Or was there? Mary concentrated hard, and then her eyes shot open. Lizzy had had a picture of the three of them in her pocket when she left. She had shown her mother the photograph moments before Albert burst into the room. A tear trickled slowly down Mary's cheek. The reverse side of the picture had read: *Mary, Eric and Lizzy Atherton, New Brighton Beach 1928.* She stood up before the tram came to a complete stop and started moving towards the front. She would go to Jean's, tell her everything, then make her way to the police station. Even if the picture had been handed in and the constable in question knew nothing of how it had been found, she would at least have one treasured photograph to remember her family by.

When she knocked on Jean's front door it was James who opened it. 'Have you heard the news?'

She cocked her head to one side. 'About the police constable?'

He nodded.

'I think I might know what he has of mine …' By the time Mary had finished telling him about the photograph James had buttoned up his long coat.

'Come on. I've sent for a car that will take us to the station.' Even before he had finished speaking a large black Daimler came into view.

Sitting in the back seat next to James, Mary threaded her arm through his. 'I know I shouldn't, but I can't help imagining how he came across the photo.' She looked up at him through tear-brimmed eyes. 'What if they … found it on Lizzy? What if …'

James shook his head. 'Best not to play guessing games. Besides, we're here now.'

Mary glanced nervously out of the car window. 'I don't think I can do it, I don't want to know …'

James held out a hand as he stepped out of the car. 'Come on. I'll be with you every step of the way.'

Mary slid along the seat until she could swing her legs out.

As they entered the police station, a skinny constable with a balding head and slightly protruding teeth smiled merrily at them. On seeing Mary's tear-stained cheeks, though, his smile faded. 'Oh, dear! Can I help you?'

Mary nodded, but the words refused to come. She looked helplessly at James, who cleared his throat. 'We're looking for PC Charlie Jackson. Is he here?'

Jimmy shook his head. 'Nah, he's still in the 'ospital. I expect you've heard about 'is 'eroics?'

Mary nodded. 'But that's not why we've come to see him.'

'I'm afraid he won't be back on duty until the new year. Is there anything I can help you with?'

Mary looked hopefully at Jimmy. 'Do you know which ward he's on?'

Jimmy pulled a face as he cast a keen eye over the nautical pair, then shrugged. 'He'll be on Mason Ward.'

'Thank you,' the woman called over her shoulder as they left.

'Welcome, I'm sure,' grumbled Jimmy, who felt he had been cheated out of a chance to relay his pal's heroism. He frowned. Why did he feel so bothered by a Wren looking for Charlie? 'Mary!' Scuttling round the other side of the counter, Jimmy raced towards the door, but he was too late. The couple were nowhere to be seen.

* * *

'You ready for the off?' said Charlie. 'If so, I'll get us a cab.'

'Sounds good to me, although I need to go back to the flat first, to pick up a few bits and bobs, and then I wouldn't mind a quick trip into the city 'cos I want to pick summat up for the nurses, you know, as a thank you for lookin' after me.'

Charlie grinned. 'You've made a remarkable recovery. Doesn't your foot hurt at all?'

Lizzy shrugged. 'I've got a couple of nasty cuts where I tried to free meself, but that's about it. The doctor said I was really lucky because things could've been a lot worse.'

Pulling her close, Charlie kissed her cheek, only to jump when the sister's sharp voice cut through the air like a knife.

'I'll have none of that on my ward, thank you very much!'

397

Lizzy giggled at Charlie's startled expression. 'When you say you're wantin' to buy the nurses a small gift to say thank you, are you includin' the dragon?' he demanded.

'Yes I am! She might be a little short-tempered, but she don't half make sure you're well taken care of. There's no sleepin' whilst she's on the job.'

'I shouldn't imagine there would be with a gob like that. Crikey, I thought some of the sergeants on the force could be bad, but they've got naff all on her!'

'Now what?' said Mary as she sank into the back seat of the Daimler.

'According to the nurse, he left half an hour ago, so he may well be home by now.'

Mary pulled the piece of paper out from her pocket and examined it closely before passing it to James. 'When he gave this to Derek he said he'd written down both addresses where he could be found. The bottom one must be his home address.'

James frowned. 'He's goin' to some lengths just for a photograph. Are you sure you haven't lost anythin' more valuable than that?'

Mary eyed him shrewdly. 'Like what? I haven't got anything worth losin' apart from Lizzy, and that's what worries me.'

James handed the note back. 'Only one way to find out.'

Ten minutes later they were standing on the door-step of Charlie's lodgings.

'I don't think he's home,' said Mary, peering through the bottom window.

'Excuse me! Can I help you?' came the rather indignant voice of a young man who was glaring at Mary.

Blushing, Mary stepped back from the window. 'Sorry, we might have made a mistake. We're looking for a Charlie Jackson. He wrote down this address, so we assumed he lived here?'

The young man relaxed a little. 'He does, but that's my room not his. If you don't mind waitin' here I can see if he's in?'

Mary nodded gratefully. 'Tell him Mary Atherton's come to see him.'

The young man slid a key into the front door lock and disappeared up a flight of stairs. He returned only moments later.

'I've checked his room, but he's not there. You could try the hospital.'

Mary shook her head. 'We've just come from there, and we've tried the police station.'

'If you'd like to leave a message I can pass it over as soon as he comes home.'

'That'd be grand.' She quickly wrote Jean's address on a slip of paper that James handed to her. 'I've written my details on there. Tell him he's welcome to call any time, day or night.'

The young man glanced at the slip of paper before pushing it into his pocket. 'Will do. All the best.'

Mary smiled. 'Merry Christmas.'

* * *

'What took you so long? We thought you'd be home hours ago!' said Clara as Charlie and Lizzy shook the snow from their coats.

Lizzy grimaced. 'Sorry, I wanted to get some cakes from Lyons to give the nurses. Then I had to go back to the flat so I could pick up a few things ...' Her voice trailed off as she took in the large Christmas tree which took pride of place at the bottom of the curved banister. 'It's beautiful. It must've taken hours to do all the decorations.'

'It took me an' Clara the best part of an hour just to get the decorations down from the attic,' said Dolly, who had come to see who was at the door. 'It's worth it, though, especially at night when Mr Granger turns the fairy lights on. I can't wait for you to see it, it's pure magic!'

Lizzy's gaze travelled to the top of the Christmas tree, a frown creasing her brow as she peered at the dishevelled golden object propped on the topmost branch. 'What happened to the ...' she frowned, 'what is that exactly?'

Clara rolled her eyes. 'It's the fairy I made when I was about six. It didn't look too good to start with, but Josh trod on it by accident with his bad foot and, well, she's a lot flatter than she used to be.'

'Got one less leg, too,' said Josh, who was swivelling the amputated limb between his fingers.

Lizzy giggled. 'You can't leave her like that: she looks drunk. Tell you what, if one of the fellers gets her down, I'll see if I can't mend her leg somehow and plump her dress out a bit.'

Clara looked at Lizzy's drooping eyelids. 'Not until you've had a bit of shut-eye. I know what it's like trying to sleep in a hospital ward: nigh on impossible with nurses checkin' on you every five minutes.' She picked up the bags by Lizzy's feet. 'Follow me and we'll run you a nice hot bath, and after that you can either go straight to bed or come down and have summat to eat.'

Lizzy smiled thankfully. 'If it's all the same to you, I'll go straight to bed after me bath. I feel as if I haven't slept for a week!' Leaning over the banister, she pecked Charlie on the cheek. 'Thanks for today. You are staying here tonight, aren't you?'

Nodding, Charlie glanced at the watch on his wrist. 'I'm goin' to go and see Mam and Dad before they go to evening service, and then I'll nip back to me lodgings so I can pick up a couple of things.'

'Are we countin' you in for dinner?' said Dolly.

Charlie grinned. 'You can always count me in for dinner!'

As Charlie stamped the snow off his boots a familiar voice called out to him before he could ascend the stairs.

'That you, Charlie?'

'All right, Alan? How's tricks?'

One of the downstairs doors opened and Alan appeared. 'Not too bad. Have you seen Rick?'

Charlie shook his head. 'Should I have?'

'He said summat about someone leavin' a message for you? Only he's gone out now and I dunno where he put it.'

'Did he mention who it was from?'

'Nah, just that someone was lookin' for you, and I should let you know if I seen you.'

'Fair do's. Can you tell him I'll be stayin' at Bellevue on Ullet Road? He can come there if it's urgent.'

Alan thrust his thumb into the air. 'Will do!'

Charlie ascended the stairs two at a time. 'Ta, Alan. All the best, pal.' He heard Alan return his wishes just before he closed the door to his room. Grabbing his suitcase from the top of the wardrobe, he opened the top drawer of his dresser and pulled out the antique ring box. A slow smile spread across his cheeks as he looked at the ring inside. Snapping the box shut, he placed it inside the suitcase, along with the entire contents of his wardrobe and chest of drawers.

As Charlie entered the hall he heard a chuckle from down the corridor. 'Blimey, you movin' in?' said Josh as he hobbled towards him.

Charlie grinned. 'I know Clara keeps sayin' they don't stand on ceremony here, but it's the poshest place I've ever stayed. I didn't know what would be appropriate attire in a place like this on Christmas Day so I thought I'd play it safe and bring everything!'

'Charlie!' called Lizzy from the balcony above the hall. 'You hopin' they're goin' to adopt you?'

'Very funny, although ...'

Lizzy patted the banister. 'You comin' up? Clara said dinner would be ready for six so I reckon you've got time to unpack.'

Charlie ascended the stairs. 'Do you know which room I'm in?'

Lizzy nodded as she pushed open the door in front of her.

As Charlie entered the room he looked at the three beds, two of which had obviously been slept in, so he pointed to the third. 'I'm takin' it that's mine?'

'Looks like it. Spencer said to hang your stuff in either of the wardrobes,' she giggled, 'only I don't suppose he realised how much stuff you'd be bringin'.'

Heaving his suitcase on to the bed, Charlie clicked it open; glancing at Lizzy he sneaked the ring box out of the case and into his pocket. 'Tell you what, if you pass me the clothes I'll hang 'em up. We'll be quicker that way.'

Lizzy passed him a pair of trousers. 'Clara was sayin' they're holdin' a carol concert in the park tomorrer if you fancy it?'

Charlie nodded. 'I'm game, as long as it's not before breakfast.' He eyed Lizzy quizzically. 'I don't suppose anyone's mentioned what sort of clothes they'll be wearin' tomorrer?'

Lizzy smiled as she passed him a couple of shirts. 'Is that why you've brought so many? So that you'd be covered for all eventualities?'

'Yup. I wouldn't want to look a fool in me mornin' suit, knowin' I'd left me best tux at home!'

Lizzy shook her head with a chuckle. 'Clara told you they weren't doin' owt formal ... oh, Charlie, how sweet. Have you brought this to replace Clara's fairy?'

Charlie's brow furrowed. 'Eh?'

There was no reply, and he turned to see Lizzy holding a star. Her smile had faded, and as he watched her eyes brimmed with tears as she turned it over in her hands. 'I – I don't understand. Where on earth did you get it?'

Taking the star from Lizzy's unresisting fingers, Charlie put it back into the suitcase and was about to shut the lid when Lizzy shook her head. 'No, don't.' She picked the decoration back up. 'I thought it had gone for ever. I don't even remember the last time I saw it.'

Charlie ran nervous fingers through his hair. 'I'm so sorry, Liz; I didn't bring it on purpose. I've had it ever since you left it in the station. I put it in my chest of drawers to keep it safe, and I must have picked it up with my clothes by accident.' He chewed the corner of his lip. 'I'd completely forgotten I had it.'

Sitting down on the bed Lizzy patted the space next to her, indicating that Charlie should do the same. Linking her arm through his, she continued to stare at the star. 'I know you didn't do it on purpose, but I'm glad you did, because it's summat I've been wonderin' about.' She smiled up at him. 'It's all very well for me to say I didn't blame the star for my father's demise, and that I'd grown up a lot, but puttin' this on top of Clara's tree will prove I really have turned a corner.'

Charlie kissed the top of her head. 'Do you think Clara will agree?'

Lizzy sniffed as she chuckled. 'I think Clara would have just about anything up there other than her one-legged fairy, which I was tryin' to mend before you returned, only I'm afraid Josh has rather finished her off!'

Charlie stared adoringly into her eyes. 'Thanks for not bein' mad at me, I really didn't do it on purpose, you know.'

'I know you didn't.' She bit the outside of her lip. 'I'm not sayin' I believe in fate, but don't you think it's a bit coincidental that this star was the only thing Albert left behind? Not only that, but if you hadn't seen it ...' She paused. 'Where did you say you found it?'

'In the station that day you and Fred had words. You'd left it on the counter.'

Lizzy nodded as the memory came back. 'I assumed he'd thrown it away. It's not as if I wanted it any more; I was convinced by then that it brought nothing but bad luck. To think, you've had it all these years and not said a word. What made you keep it?'

'I remember how much it meant to you the day you made it,' he said simply, 'and I thought you might change your mind in the future.'

Leaning up, she kissed his lips. 'You're a wonderful, kind, considerate man, Charlie Jackson.'

Charlie beamed. 'I'm glad it's made you so happy.'

She nodded. 'It's almost like it's follerin' me round. Mebbe ...'

Charlie arched a brow. 'Mebbe what?'

'You'll think I'm bein' silly – even I think it sounds a bit daft – but mebbe it's some kind of sign, like Dad's lettin' me know I shouldn't blame meself?'

Charlie pulled a face. 'Who knows? And as long as you're happy, who cares?'

She smiled. 'Come on, let's go and show the others.'

'Wake up, sleepy head, it's Christmas Day!'

Rubbing her eyes, Lizzy smiled at Dolly. 'Merry Christmas, Doll. What time is it?'

'Just past seven. Me an' Clara thought we'd let you have a bit of a lie-in.'

Lizzy yawned. 'Where's Charlie?'

'He's fryin' sausages. That's why I've woke you up, to tell you that brekker will be ready in ten minutes!'

'Flippin' 'eck, you could've given me more warnin',' said Lizzy, pulling her nightie over the top of her head.

'Like I said, we wanted you to have a bit of a rest.' Dolly jerked her head towards the washstand. 'I've put some warm water in the basin and there's a fresh towel over the rail.'

'Thanks, Doll. Is everyone else downstairs?'

Nodding, Dolly headed for the door. 'I nearly forgot. Merry Christmas!'

'Merry Christmas to you too!' Lizzy yelled through the closed door. A few minutes later she stepped into the hall just in time to hear Charlie shout from the direction of the kitchen, 'Come an' get it!'

Sitting at the table, she stared at the plate of food in front of her. 'You don't expect me to eat all that, do you?' she said, lifting one of the sausages to reveal a fried egg. 'I've got so used to rationing, I don't know whether I could manage it.'

Charlie grinned. 'You need a decent bit o' grub in you after all you've been through. You could march an army on that!'

'I've no doubt you could. Sausage, egg, bread, mush-rooms, tomatoes … good God, the only thing that hasn't been fried is the beans.' She glanced up. 'You didn't fry the beans, did you?'

'Don't be daft! They're what's known as the healthy option!'

Just as they were finishing their breakfast, someone knocked on the front door.

'I bet it's carol singers. Shall we see?' said Dolly.

Spencer frowned. 'I can't hear any singing. Wait here.'

He disappeared through the dining room door before reappearing a few seconds later. 'Charlie, one of your pals has come to see you. He wants to know if you've got a minute?'

Making his apologies, Charlie headed for the front door. 'Rick! I didn't expect to see you. Is everything all right? Alan said you had a message for me but I didn't think it would be important.'

Rick stared round the hallway. 'Crikey, Charlie, no wonder you didn't want to spend Christmas at 'ome.' He handed Charlie the piece of paper with Mary's details. 'She seemed quite eager for you to know she'd called. I hope everything's okay.'

Charlie looked up from the note. 'Thanks for this Rick, much appreciated. Spencer, can you make my excuses? Tell the others I won't be long, only I've been called away on urgent business.'

'Of course. Is there anything I can do to help?'

Charlie shook his head. 'Thanks all the same.'

Charlie checked the slip of paper in his hand before knocking on the front door. The last thing he wanted to do was disturb the wrong house on Christmas Day. When the door opened, a woman of slim build with shoulder-length hair frowned at him before giving a small squeal.

'I know you – you're the copper that rescued that girl from the fire!'

Charlie nodded. 'Are you Mary?'

She shook her head. 'She's gone for a stroll with our James. I think they may've gone to the carol concert in Sefton Park.'

Charlie rolled his eyes in disbelief. 'I've just come from there. Oh, well, never mind. If she should get back before I've had a chance to catch up with her, can you let her know that Charlie Jackson called, and I'm staying at Bellevue in Ullet Road.'

Jean nodded. 'You're the one who's found summat of hers, aren't you?' She paused momentarily. 'If it's that photo, it would be wonderful if she could have it back for Christmas Day, but if you found it in bad circumstances watch how you break the news. She's dreadin' hearin' summat awful.'

'Don't worry, I've only got good news to give her, providin' she's the right Mary, of course.' He paused. 'Do you know if she's got a daughter?'

'Golly, yes. Her name's Lizzy, but she's not seen her in years. That's why she wants the photo back.'

Charlie grinned. 'Thanks. You've been most helpful.'

Lizzy stared up at him. 'Where've you been? And why do you look so flustered?'

Charlie waved a hand. 'Never mind that. Come with me – I've gorra surprise for you.'

'Another one?'

He grinned. 'A better one!'

'Are we going sledgin'? 'Cos if so ...'

Charlie shook his head. 'We're only goin' across the road, to that carol concert in the park.'

'Since I was the one who told you about the concert, I'd hardly call that a surprise.'

Charlie jiggled on the spot. 'Come on, Lizzy. I don't want to miss them.'

'Keep your hair on. They only started ten minutes ago.' She grimaced as she pushed her foot into her wellington boot. 'My ankle's still a bit swollen from that stupid step.'

Charlie rolled his eyes. 'Never mind your ankle. I reckon I've found summat that's goin' to take your mind off everything, includin' your ankle.'

Lizzy racked her brain as she tried to think what she would like so much. 'Have they got real mince pies?'

Charlie guided her arm through his and led her down the garden path. 'This is much better than mince pies, but only if we get there in time.'

She looked up at the sky, which looked full of snow. 'Hang on a mo, I need my hat if it's goin' to start snowin' again, otherwise my hair'll go all frizzy.'

Charlie shook his head. 'Sorry, luv, this is too important. I've been runnin' round like a headless chicken these past few weeks, but not after today, and I ain't goin' halfway across town again!'

As they neared the carol singers, Charlie craned his neck as he searched the crowd. 'Keep your eyes peeled, luv.'

'What for?'

'Not what, who.'

'All right, who for?'

Charlie gripped her hand tightly in his. 'I know I should've said summat sooner, only I needed to be sure. You've had such a bad time of it lately, what with Ivy causin' all that trouble between us, and that picture of you ...' He shook his head. 'If only I could turn back the hands of time.'

She shook his hand reassuringly. 'It doesn't matter, Charlie. All's well that end's well, we've kissed and made up, and if anything it made us stronger. It certainly helped me work out a lot of things.'

'Yes, but we should've listened to her.'

A frown creased Lizzy's brow. 'But that was the problem, we did listen to her, or at least I did. It was you I didn't listen to.' Turning her back to the crowd, Lizzy looked seriously at him. 'Please let's not go over all that again. What's done is done, and I don't want Ivy Hackney to ruin a wonderful Christmas.'

Charlie gazed into Lizzy's eyes. 'I'm not on about Ivy, I'm talkin' about the picture she had of you, the one she said your mam had posted up around the town.'

'I know what she said, Charlie, but she was lyin', same as always.' Lizzy sighed impatiently. 'I don't know why you brought me here, but all we've done is talk about that nasty girl and her vile lies. If it's all the same to you, I'm goin' back to Bellevue.'

Charlie stared at Lizzy. 'But she wasn't lyin', not about the picture. I found one a month or so ago.'

Lizzy pulled her hands free of his. 'It was probably one of her copies, all part of the plan to make me believe her story. Please don't do this to me, Charlie; not on Christmas Day. Let's just go home and forget this ever happened.'

A voice from behind interrupted her. 'Charlie?'

Lizzy froze as she looked at Charlie, who was grinning from ear to ear. He nodded. Kissing Lizzy on the forehead, he murmured the words 'Merry Christmas, Pipsqueak', before turning her round.

Staring into her mother's eyes, a mass of feelings coursed through her body. She stood still for a moment until, overwhelmed by emotion, she burst into tears.

Grasping her daughter in a tight embrace, Mary looked over her shoulder at Charlie. She tried to speak, to say thank you, but the sobs caught the words she wanted to say.

Nodding his understanding, Charlie laid a hand on Mary's shoulder. 'My pleasure.'

Epilogue

December, 1945

Lizzy drew a deep breath as she linked her arm through Mary's. 'I've not felt this nervous or excited since VE Day.'

Mary smiled at her daughter. 'Don't worry luv, you'll be fine. You look beautiful. I wish your father could see you.'

Nodding, Lizzy blinked back a tear. 'He'd have been so proud, and he'd have loved Charlie.' She giggled. 'Like peas in a pod 'im and Dad, don't you reckon?'

Mary nodded. 'I remember your dad chucklin' when he saw what Charlie had done to your pigtails. He reckoned it was boys bein' boys an' that Charlie must really like you!' She shook her head. 'Your father may have been a big softie, but he was a wise man when it came to affairs of the heart. He was certainly right about Charlie.'

Lizzy glanced down at the onyx engagement ring Charlie had given her after she had been reunited with her mother. They had all been gathered at the dining table when Charlie presented her with the ring box.

Lizzy had examined the intricate details of the box with admiration. 'It's beautiful, Charlie, but I'm afraid I haven't got any rings to put in it.'

Putting his hand into his pocket, Charlie had dropped to one knee. Holding out his grandmother's engagement ring, he smiled up at Lizzy. 'If you'll do me the honour of becoming my wife, you'll have more than one ring to put in it.'

Tears of happiness had brimmed in her eyes as Lizzy managed to say the words Charlie was desperate to hear. 'Of course I'll marry you, Charlie Jackson.'

She smiled at the memory as she twiddled the ring on her finger. 'When me and Charlie first started courtin', I used to think you'd be horrified at the thought of us gerrin' together.'

Mary smiled. 'I probably would have, which just goes to show how wrong I would have been.'

'Are you pleased for me, Mam?' said Lizzy hopefully.

Gazing lovingly into her daughter's eyes, a tear trickled down Mary's cheek. 'Pleased? I'm thrilled. You've found a man just like your father, I couldn't have wished for more.'

As Lizzy glanced towards the aisle, a sea of expectant faces turned to face her. 'Thanks, Mam.'

The organist struck up the opening chords of Richard Wagner's 'Wedding March'.

Mary nodded. 'It's time to go, luv.'

'Gotcha!'

Turning, Lizzy was not surprised to see that Dolly was clutching the bouquet of roses as though her life depended upon it.

414

Charlie appeared by Lizzy's side, a glass of wine in one hand and a beer in the other. He nodded towards Dolly, who was beaming with delight. 'Someone'd better warn Spencer.'

Lizzy chuckled as she took the glass of wine. 'Give over, Charlie Jackson, you know how much Spencer cares for our Dolly.' She cast an eye around their guests. 'Have you seen Clara or Josh anywhere?'

'Josh is askin' the landlord if he can bang out a few carols on the piano, and Clara's helpin' your mam with the sarnies.'

Lizzy turned to face him. 'I knew Mam would get on well with the girls. She couldn't believe it when I told her Clara's brother was in the Navy.'

'He was in Plymouth right up until the end of the war,' said Charlie, 'so it's no wonder their paths never crossed, although I do feel a bit of a heel for dismissin' his idea of searching the naval records for her. Imagine if he had.'

Lizzy shrugged. 'I was as much to blame as you, and even though Mam won't tell me what she did when she were in the Wrens, she did say he'd never have found her even if he'd tried.'

He raised a quizzical brow. 'So whatever she was doing must have been top secret.'

'We've missed out on so much of each other's lives. I could swing for that Albert.'

He took a sip of his beer and wiped the froth from his top lip. 'Don't waste your time worryin' over the likes of Albert. The important thing is your mam's well rid, and she got to say her piece. Even if we do find him, there's not a lot we could do about it. I know it's

415

obvious that he was the one who put her in the crate, but with no witnesses we'd be hard pushed to prove it.'

'I know, and I suppose we won in the end, 'cos not only did Mam manage to get shot of him, she got James into the bargain.'

He nodded. 'And she learned to swim, and ride a motorcycle.'

'I can't imagine Mam on a motorbike! I'd never do anything that brave. I'll be proud if I become half the woman she is, but I'm probably destined to remain plain old Elizabeth Jackson, sewing machinist at Langdon's.'

Taking her glass from her hand, he placed their drinks on the table before taking her in his arms. 'You're just as brave as your mam, Lizzy Jackson. You were the one who started a whole new life with no more'n a sockful of pennies to yer name, as well as bringin' the Hackneys to justice, not to mention leapin' into a condemned building to save a moth-eaten moggy …'

'He was not moth-eaten,' Lizzy began before Charlie's lips brushed gently across hers.

'And managed to win the heart of this young scuffer along the way, and all the time never givin' up on your mam.'

Running her fingers through his tight curls, Lizzy gazed into his eyes. 'I couldn't have done any of it without you by my side. You never gave up on me, no matter how many obstacles I threw in your path.'

One of his hands slid up to her shoulders whilst the other tightened around her waist. 'Wild horses wouldn't have dragged me away.' As their lips locked,

Lizzy felt her body relax into his embrace. He continued to gaze into her eyes. 'I love you, Mrs Jackson, allus have, allus will, and I couldn't think of anywhere I'd rather be than by your side.'

'I love you too, Charlie Jackson.' She smiled as Josh struck up a tune on the piano and the guests started to sing 'Good King Wenceslas'. 'Merry Christmas, Charlie.'

'Merry Christmas, Pipsqueak.'

READ IT NOW

Can love see her through the darkness?
Liverpool, 1940

There comes a moment in every child's life when they must learn to stand on their own two feet.

For fifteen-year-old Ellie Lancton, that time has come all too soon. The death of her mother and the increase in air raids leaves Ellie alone and in grave danger. It's not long before she is forced to leave her beloved Liverpool behind and cross the Mersey to seek refuge in the countryside.

But as the war takes comforts away, so too does it bring new opportunities; for work, new friendships, and perhaps a little love…

It will take all of Ellie's courage to find her way without her mother's guidance. But if Ellie can soldier on with grace and dignity, there just might be light at the end of the tunnel.

AVAILABLE IN PAPERBACK AND E-BOOK

arrow books

KATIE FLYNN

Liverpool Daughter

August 1940

As the Luftwaffe turns its attention to Liverpool, Shane Quinn decides to move his family back to the safety of Ireland. But his only child, the beautiful Dana, would rather stay and serve her country than flee to a foreign land.

Determined to make it on her own, she heads to the city, only to have the door slammed in her face over and over again. Lonely and exhausted, she reaches the last lodging house on Staple Row where finally, a young girl named Patty invites her in. They soon become firm friends and together they join the WAAF.

As the two girls journey through the hardships of war, they will find that they need their friendship more than ever. And when Dana discovers a shocking secret about her past, she will realise just how important family is too…

PRE-ORDER NOW

arrow books